Good Night

The Sand Maiden
Book Three

L. R. W. Lee

Paperback ISBN: 979-8-950333-11-8
Woodgate Publishing

Table of Contents

Map of Wake Realm

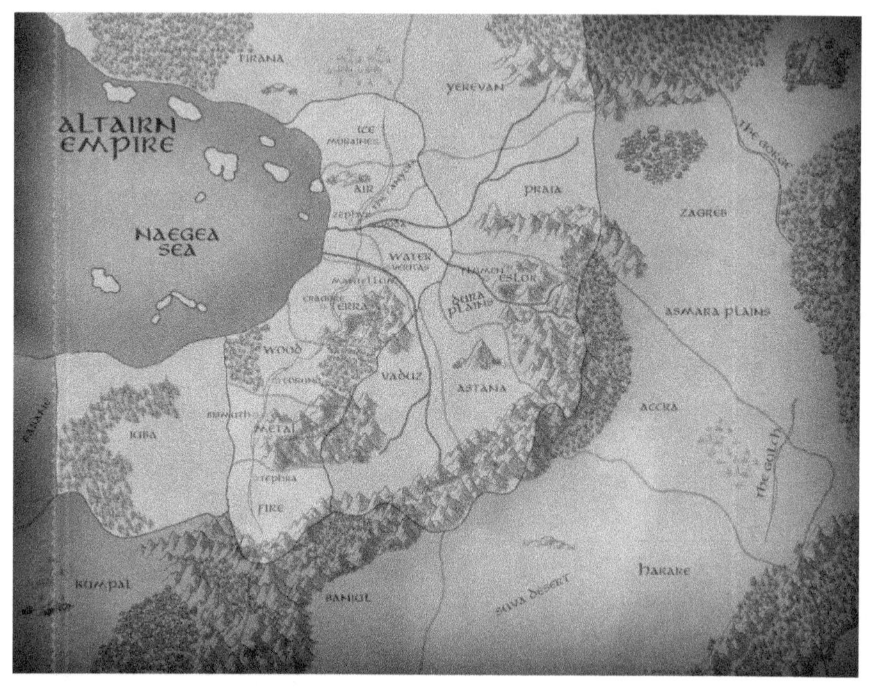

Map of Dream Realm

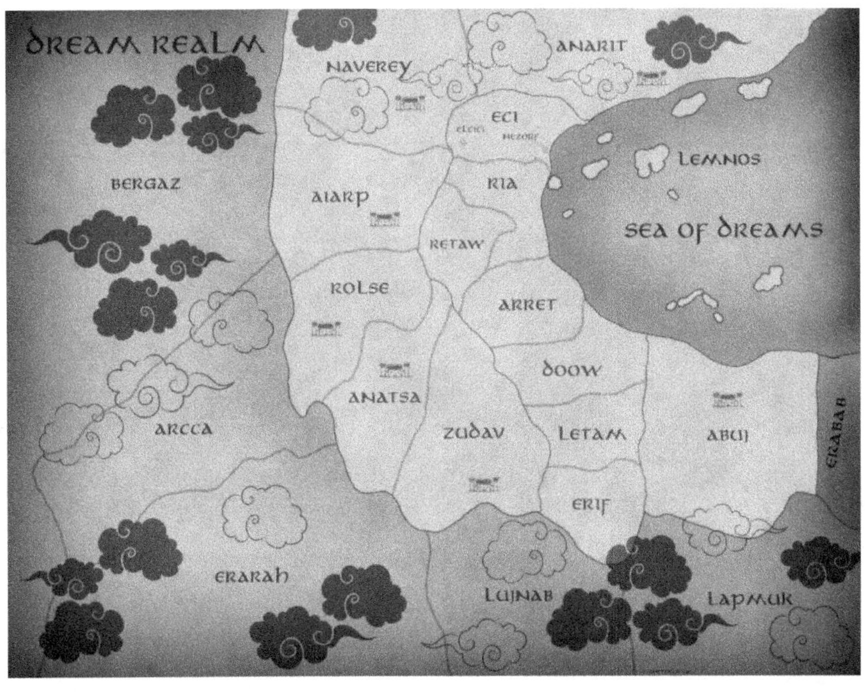

Map of Lemnos Island

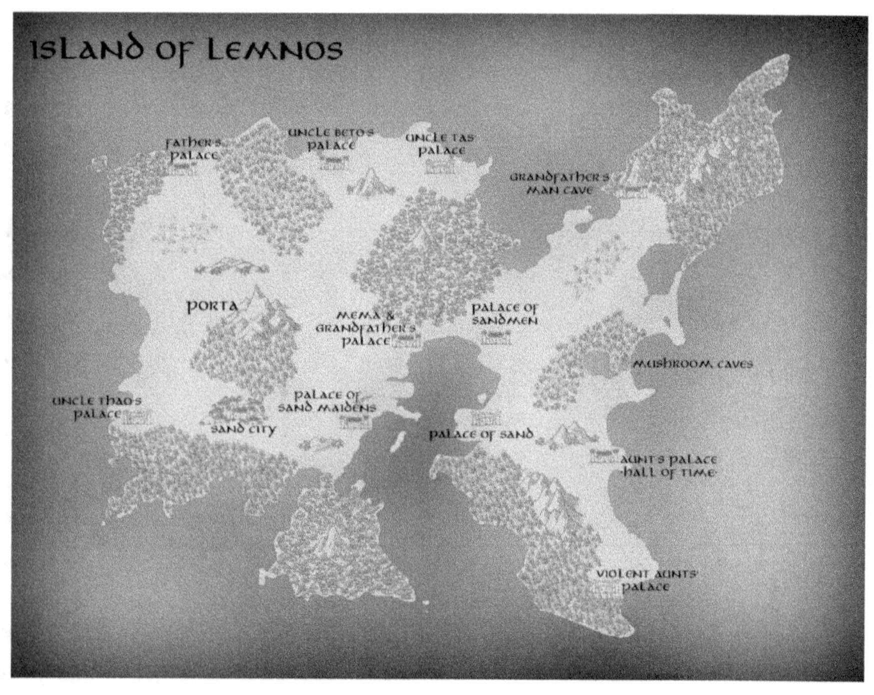

Part I: Nightmare

Lullaby And Good Night

By Johannes Brahms
Deutschland Wake Realm

Lullaby, and good night, in the skies stars are bright.
May the moon's silvery beams bring you sweet dreams.
Close your eyes now and rest, may these hours be blessed.
'Til the sky's bright with dawn, when you wake with a yawn.

Lullaby, and good night, you are mother's delight.
I'll protect you from harm, and you'll wake in my arms.
Sleepyhead, close your eyes, for I'm right beside you.
Guardian angels are near, so sleep without fear.

Lullaby, and good night, with roses bedight.
Lilies o'er head, lay thee down in thy bed.
Lullaby, and good night, you are mother's delight.
I'll protect you from harm, and you'll wake in my arms.

Lullaby, and sleep tight, my darling sleeping.
On sheets white as cream, with a head full of dreams.
Sleepyhead, close your eyes, I'm right beside you.
Lay thee down now and rest, may your slumber be blessed.

Chapter One

"We could both use a bath and our clothes a wash. We stink," I said, wagging my brows as I dropped my saddlebag beside a tall tree. I was betting my suggestion would trigger desire.

We'd *narrowly* escaped Father and his mares grabbing me and dragging me back to Dream this morning—my stomach twisted just thinking about it. Between that and hunting dinner out here in the middle of the wilderness, we both smelled ripe. But more, I was ready to forget the earlier horror as well as the numerous trials that undoubtedly lay before us to rescue Kennan and Alfreda and save Wake realm from Father for just a few heartbeats.

Hunger filled Kovis's beautiful blue and hazel eyes—seemed we shared similar sentiments.

He didn't know he was a fly nearing my web and I wouldn't think much about my plan because he was always listening in through our bond.

I blushed, then grabbed a bar of soap from my bag. I hadn't forgotten what I'd learned from that healer's reference guide, and I was ready to explore "tearing" my maidenhead, something Kovis had resisted last night. I wasn't standing for it. I would make him mine, fully and completely.

Kovis unbuckled my leathers. One. Buckle. At. A. Time. When we reached the bank of the river that burbled not far away. Shivers raced up my back, and he chuckled, mischief dancing in his eyes.

"Getting excited?"

He helped me out of the top, then lifted it over my head, leaving just my underclothes. He steadied me as I climbed out of the legs, then rose and ran a thumb down my jawline. He would follow up with a kiss and who knew what else unless I redirected his efforts. Ardent, that's what he was. He would take the lead, if I didn't. Look at me, sounding so experienced.

"I'd hate to have an imbalance in the number of clothes removed," I said. "Allow me to help you, as well."

"As you wish, Ali dearest."

I took my time unbuckling his leathers. When I attended the fasteners on his back, I pressed kisses to his neck and his heart sped.

"Look who's getting excited now." I teased him.

He tore off the leather-plated top, then the bottoms. They'd ceased to be protection and become obstacles. That done, he stood back and resumed what he'd started before I interrupted. His eyes filled with passion as they roamed over me despite my sweaty underclothes. How unsexy I must be, but he seemed immune. *This* was love.

"I looked up maidenhead in a healer's reference guide. Do you know what it said?"

He chortled. "My Ali." He ran a hand down my cheek. "You truly are amazing."

He hadn't answered my question. The fly was nearly mine. I wouldn't let him escape. "The book said it would tear. Why don't you want to?"

Kovis's cheeks pinked. "Oh, trust me, I do. In fact, it would give me no greater pleasure, but not until I've married you."

I looked around at the barren area. "You're going to wait until some official we don't know announces to the empire that we love each other? It could be a while."

I let my ring glint in the dying sun, its beauty and refinement so at odds with our surroundings. It was a picture of us, against what we faced.

"Kovis, I can't imagine my life without you and unless you can, I'd say we're stuck with each other."

He smiled, but it hid just as quickly.

I cupped his cheek. "Kovis, make me yours. Now."

I was asking him to examine what he believed and again be open to a different way of thinking.

I took his hands in mine and kissed him, then this spider claimed her prize.

When it was over, Kovis still panted, but he beamed, his beautiful face lit up.

"I love seeing you like this," I said.

"I'm happy to be your fly, my spider." He kissed my nose and winked. "By the way, nice work with that funnel, it was quite impressive."

"Funnel?"

He laughed. "You didn't know?"

I cocked my head making him laugh all the harder.

"I felt you pull on my power. You must have combined my Water and your Air, because you made a lovely water spout."

I laughed.

"You definitely make my life... interesting and I love you all the more for it." He kissed my nose as he said it.

"And I love you, Kovis."

Mine. I'd made him mine and he'd made me his.

I held my ring up in the growing darkness. "What would your mother think?"

"I think she'd be very happy for us."

The warm water burbled around and over us and I felt peace and contentment. If only things could stay this way.

* * *

"Well, my dearest, I believe we've quite missed the reason we came down here."

"To bathe?"

He nodded. "And to wash our clothes." He stood and waded to shore to retrieve my soap and our clothes and I ogled every glorious bit of him.

————

Kovis's face still held a satisfied smile as we lay down near the fire after eating the pheasant we'd caught and roasted, our clothes drying not far away, and gathered me against himself.

"How did you know to come, this morning?" I ran my fingers over his arm.

"I felt your panic. You woke me up."

"Father was surprised to see you." I stared into the flames. "He'd put everyone to sleep yet his power didn't affect you."

"Probably because of our bond."

I nodded. I'd reached the same conclusion. "He lied to me, the way he always has. He's changed his name—Morpheus, Somnia, Ambien—upon occasion, but *he's* never changed."

"Wait. What?" Kovis stiffened.

"He lied to me, like he always has."

"No, the other part."

"My father, I don't know why, probably an ego thing, but he's changed his name from time to time. He called himself Morpheus at one point, then changed it to Somnia. He's taken other names over time, but he calls himself Ambien now. But no matter what he calls himself, he always lies to me."

"By the Canyon!"

I clutched the blanket. "Why does my father's name matter?"

"He's a god?" Kovis's breath hitched.

"I thought you knew that."

His breathing labored.

"I thought you only believed in your Canyon."

"The Canyon gifts us with our powers , but I believe the gods created it and Ambien is one of them. Ali, you never said he's—"

"I told you I'm a princess."

"Yes, but—"

"Does it matter? I'm still me." I bit my lip.

"I knew your father was a king and that we'd need to figure out how to fight in Dream Realm, but a god? Anything else you need to tell me that might influence our strategy?"

"I don't think so."

Kovis was stiff, so I took up the lullaby I'd hummed to him from his earliest age and his body slowly relaxed. The fire crackled and insects chirped, chiming in.

We had each other. We'd figure this out, but not tonight.

———

I flailed, fighting the firm, muscled arms that bound me.

"Ali, it's okay. You're okay. It's just a dream, another bad dream."

Kovis's quick words shattered the terror of Father nearly grabbing me and dragging me back to Dream realm—it would have kill me—and I stilled. Various renditions of the same terror had haunted my sleep every night over the last fortnight since Father had found me in Flumen.

Our lone blanket fell down letting in the chill night air as Kovis rose on an elbow and brushed sweat-slicked hair away from my face.

In the flickering light of what remained of the campfire, I saw worry crease his brow. The ink of the tattoo on his sculpted chest shown brown—brown meant heaviness but quietly supportive, if I remembered correctly. Accurate. Too much so.

I hadn't dreamed before coming to Wake. Ever. I'd been fascinated by this new ability when I first arrived, but at this rate, I'd willingly give it up.

Kovis and I had fled the warrior province but we'd had to leave Kennan, Kovis's twin, behind, possessed by Father. What was he enduring as a result? How much did he know of what was happening to him?

My stomach tensed. Kennan had allowed me to be abused when I first arrived in Wake, and while I still hadn't forgiven him for it, no one deserved to be possessed by Father. Would it break him?

Possession would only be possible with help from Alfreda, my older sister and Kennan's sand maiden. I knew my sister. Like all sand beings, she was fiercely protective of her human charges and would never allow anything to happen to him if she had anything to say about it.

My stomach crawled into my throat.

It meant Father had done *something* to her. What torment could my sister possibly be enduring at his hands to allow him such liberties with her charge?

But worse, I couldn't see Father not finding out how I'd escaped. And when he did…Velma would pay. I knew nothing about her situation after she sent me to Wake, but I feared the worst based upon what was happening to Kennan and Alfreda.

Kovis leaned forward and brushed my cheek with soft kisses, bringing me back from the horror.

I rolled over and met his gaze, placing my hands on his muscled chest. I ran them up and down over the smooth muscles and felt their firmness, allowing his strength to ground me. "Thank you."

"A kindness for a kindness," he whispered.

He'd started saying that after the lunch not long ago over which I told him I thought he was a good writer and shared with him all I'd done for him from Dream realm much of which had been the inspiration for his tales. It brought tears to his eyes as it sunk deeply into his soul—he'd thought he'd been utterly and completely alone in his torment.

"You'll never endure anguish alone." He leaned forward and kissed my brow.

The tightness in my chest eased a little. Kovis had experienced untold horrors of his father's making. I was in experienced hands.

As he lay down, I turned back over and pulled the blanket up. He pulled me against himself, wrapping his arms about me. "I love you, Ali. We're going to get them back."

I nodded against his arm that doubled as my pillow. If only I could share his certainty.

I listened to Kovis's breathing as it slowed once more, but the evenness didn't return sleep to me. A few rogue flames from our fire danced in the pit a stride away and brought to mind a lullaby. So I sang myself the soundless tune.

Come and play as the wild fairies play
In a magical circle, a fairy ring
You won't want to leave and forever you'll stay
Where the vision is bright as spring

Come and dance the wild fairy dance
Spin in a circle as fast as light
Once you begin you are caught in a trance
And the world can grow old in a single night

As the tune continued playing in my thoughts, I looked up through the opening in the canopy of leaves that our clearing had created. Stars twinkled in all their glory. The Canyon's lights didn't reach this far, and without that distraction, the stars looked like a blanket of precious gems spread across the night sky—they'd glistened since before time began, so much older than me.

I shifted my bare feet, returning them back under the blanket's warmth.

I'd never paid much attention to the stars in Dream. But I suppose with the length of my days now numbered, I felt a connection with their immortal presence. Sometimes I wondered if they looked down and smiled or frowned at what they saw, grinned at mortals' weak attempts to cope with our fragile lives, or felt pity for our frailties, bad dreams and all.

Stargazing and lullabies must have worked because the sky had pinked when I next saw it. I listened to Kovis's breathing, still slow and deep, his exhales brushing the top of my head.

I lay quietly so as not to wake him, listening to the forest awakening—chittering and chirping, skittering and scampering, animals finding breakfast and doing what animals did all sun. It provided a welcome distraction from the angst that begged to again consume my waking hours.

Not long after, Kovis's nomadic hands stirred. They circled my bare stomach where they'd spent the night. "You seem fascinated by small forest animals."

How long had he been awake? "Listening to my thoughts through our bond again?"

"I can't help it. I like listening in. It helps me understand you."

I stuck a hand out of our blanket and ran my fingers over my pillow, aka Kovis's arm.

He had mentioned trying to better understand our bond so we could use it more. He wanted to understand the entirety of what it might allow us to do since we didn't know what we might face in the wilderness. I didn't disagree. It could prove a valuable tool.

He'd been experimenting on his own, but he needed my cooperation, and therein lay the rub. The idea of entering Kovis's mind again scared me because I didn't know how I'd extricated myself the first time I'd visited—I could have gotten stuck. I knew I was being unreasonable, our bond might be powerful, but when I'd nearly lost myself....

He brushed my golden locks aside and pressed kisses to my ear, then caressed my jaw with his free hand making me forget my worry. Gooseflesh, not from the chill morning air, rose on my arms and I laid onto my back, into his warm chest, and his lips found my mouth. He was so gentle, and a contented sigh escaped me.

"I love to savor every bit of you." His eyes filled with passion.

"And I, you, my Dreambeam." I reached up and ran a hand along his furry jaw. Without a razor, it had become the beginnings of a beard across his strong jawline. I was still getting used to its scratchiness. It was so different than I'd ever seen him.

He caught my hand in his and proceeded to pleasure me time and again until we were both panting, savoring the feeling of oneness, connectedness, belonging to each other. At least that's what fluttered about my brain, which had turned to fluff.

The ring he'd placed on my finger just suns before shone in the light as thinking returned. Every time I thought about the teardrop sapphire surrounded by tiny diamonds, I remembered what he'd said the night he gave it to me: It was my mother's. I always wanted my bride to wear it.

Hulda's father had fashioned the ring for the late empress. And knowing how close a bond Kovis held with his mother, despite never experiencing her love, I could never have felt more cherished.

Bad dreams make lovemaking all the better. I snickered at my rogue thought.

"What's so funny?"

I told him, and he grinned. "I'm open to making love in the middle of the night if it would ease your suffering."

I rolled my eyes. "Such a male."

He feigned offense, drawing a hand to his chest. "What? I'm committed to helping you."

I swatted his arm. "That's very big of you."

But melancholy quickly reasserted itself as I rose. How would we ever overcome all of the challenges we faced?

Chapter Two

So many problems.

I bit my lip as I watched Kovis saddle Alshain and Fiona just after breakfast. "You ready?"

I nodded and he boosted me up, onto my mare.

We'd been hiding, wandering the foothills of the Tuliv Mountains for the past fortnight, continually moving, staying out of sight of all towns and villages. Not once had we chanced word of our presence getting back to Father. Kennan's safety, his very life, hinged on it, because if Father had either of us, he wouldn't need Kennan. I shuddered to think what he might do to either of our siblings if that happened.

Our meager camp hadn't taken long to gather and secure to the horses before we moved out.

As we approached another hulking, ancient tree, Kovis said, "I believe we're still in Eslor province. We'll soon cross into Astana on our way to the hot springs in the foothills there." He wagged his brows.

He'd threatened to do all *manner of things* to me in said hot springs, and my stomach fluttered. I couldn't wait to see what his imagination had dreamed up.

Kovis looked over his shoulder, grinning. "I'm looking forward to it too. And yes, I've been putting considerable thought toward it."

I patted Fiona's neck. Somehow, I had no doubt about that.

We rode in silence, under the forest's towering trees—the same landscape we'd traversed since we'd left the Dura Plains. Sunlight filtered down, illuminating the shrubs, scrub, and ferns lining either side of the narrow animal trail we followed.

My thoughts turned to another of the problems nagging my waking hours—how to stop Father. I'd pondered it over and over and always ended up back at the same place: we were powerless to stop him, let alone rescue Kennan and Alfreda, from here in Wake. As crazy as it sounded, my gut told me we had to return to Dream.

I'd been certain I couldn't return, not without dying, but Kovis had reminded me that I'd thought I'd die coming to Wake. So I'd opened my mind to the possibility and, selfishly, it had grown on me to the point that I was excited at the possibility of seeing my family again. I just had to figure out how to get both Kovis and myself to Dream.

I grabbed hold of the saddle's horn and ducked to avoid a low hanging branch.

Problem was, I'd looked at this challenge from every conceivable angle—upside down, right side up, inside out, outside in—to catch any whisper of a possibility. But so far, I'd drawn a blank.

I huffed. *I* was the problem. I couldn't think outside what I knew. Damn.

My nails bit into the reins making Fiona whinny. "Sorry. Sorry, girl."

Kovis looked back, brow furrowed.

"Just thinking. Don't mind me."

He held my gaze, but finally turned back around.

How pray tell did one discover what wasn't obvious? I'd no idea, but we weren't going anywhere until I figured that out.

I growled.

Velma had envisioned me going to Kovis. She'd closed her eyes, then breathed over me, just as the Ancient One had done to bring the world into existence—he'd gathered sand, dust, and ashes and mixed them together in the caldron of the skies, then envisioned his creation as beautiful and fruitful and everything he loved. His breath over the great cauldron, a breath of wind, had made everything come to be.

A low branch scrapped across my shins and I was again thankful for my leathers as Fiona pushed past it.

But questions plagued me. Did it work if Kovis and I both envisioned or did it have to be someone not going who envisioned? Were we to breathe over each other? Or did we have to breathe out at all since it seemed focusing on what you sought was what held the power?

I'd arrived in Wake unscathed, and it was proof enough that envisioning worked. It shouldn't have been foreign to me. I altered my charges very realities as I wove their dreams. So what was I missing?

I brushed blonde locks behind my ear and set my jaw.

What to try envisioning next?

The image of Kovis and me landing on the hard stone of my bedroom floor at the palace of sand maidens bubbled up. We'd land between Wynnfrith's and my overlarge beds, in front of the floor-to-ceiling window separating them. If she was there, we'd probably scare her half to death.

I didn't wish her ill, but the thought eased a little of the heaviness and I chuckled. I could just see it. She'd shriek. Her dark eyes would bulge, and she'd hug herself. I'd played enough practical jokes on her to know.

Kovis twisted in his seat, tilting his head as he took in my expression.

"I'm just practicing what I want to try tonight to get back to Dream."

"Sounds promising, then I'll leave you to it." He turned back around.

I hadn't considered it before, but would I get my wings back? My breath hitched and my back muscles flexed in anticipation. Wings. My wings. Beautiful with soft, black feathers. Like a bird.

Would Kovis get wings? I threw a hand over my mouth, hardly able to contain my excitement.

Kovis shifted back around and the cutest, quirkiest smirk lit up his face.

I circled my pointer finger, my silent indication that he should return from whence he'd turned. He shook his head and turned back, ever so slowly. Clearly, he'd been listening in through our bond.

Kovis with wings. He'd be so handsome. I let my thoughts run wild for several heartbeats, considering what I would do to the particularly sensitive, erotic innermost feathers at the base of his neck.

While I hated to, I redirected my attention and continued working on a plan for us to try tonight.

I was glad when we stopped for a quick lunch of roasted rabbit left over from the night before. My mind hurt, and the break did it good.

"Ready to practice honing the nuances of your magic?" Kovis asked as we started off again.

I'd practiced fighting and defending myself in preparation for The Ninety-Eight competition. The skills I'd learned were the broad-brush strokes of what I could do with my magic. But I hadn't yet learned the nuances of my powers, at least that's what Kovis said. I didn't disagree. The image of a flower pot slamming into Kennan's head several moons before flew through my mind, and I winced.

Kovis said fine-tuning allowed him to use his powers in more practical ways. For example, his nuanced magic had allowed him to bathe and dry me, unassisted…

Mmm. Mmm. Mmm. My cheeks warmed. I could still feel his hands… enjoying certain of my parts… lingering… I shook my head and smiled.

He'd also blown out candles without damaging anything else around them, warmed the water of the streams we bathed in, used an ice dagger he'd conjured to skin and clean the animals we ate, cooled the horses with his winds when they got overheated, and more. I had no idea what practical things I might do with my gifts, but I was excited to find out.

With me being able to pull threads of other sorcerers' powers and combine them with my Simulus affinity, who knew what I might accomplish—granted I had to be around other sorcerers, not out here in the middle of nowhere but one thing at a time. Between that and Somnus—my sleep-inducing power—it seemed my imagination was my only limitation… *once* I learned how to control it.

Kovis turned around in his saddle. "I want you to use Air to pick up a leaf and draw it to yourself."

"A leaf? While we're riding?"

"Yes, a single leaf, while we're riding." He grinned.

I shook my head. While it sounded like a simple task, I knew it would be anything but based on similar requests he'd made of me. This exercise would definitely refine my winds if I could master it.

Kovis turned back around, and I looked to either side of the path. The horses weren't walking that fast, but their pace still didn't give me time to focus on a single leaf and grab it. This would definitely not be easy.

I held a hand out, palm up, and focused on directing the air between my fingers like I had when I'd learned to fight, then selected a leaf we approached and concentrated on it. My breeze tossed a host of leaves into the air, and Fiona startled, stepping off the path, away from the blast.

"Sorry, girl. It's okay. That was just me." I patted her neck, and she bobbed her head.

● ● ●

Kovis turned in his saddle, a smirk on his face. "Try not to scare our mounts in the process. I don't feel like walking."

I stuck out my tongue and was met with a laugh.

Fiona rejoined the path and continued plodding behind Alshain. Kovis turned back around.

I tried again. I spotted a leaf, held out my hand, and willed my winds to lift it into the air. Fiona whinnied, reprimanding me when a multitude of leaves again took flight.

"Focus on reducing the amount of force you apply first," Kovis called over his shoulder.

I selected another leaf, held out my hand, and imagined myself blowing just hard enough to extinguish a candle. Not one thing moved.

I added a bit more force the next time and made several leaves rustle, but that was it, nothing flew up. Only Fiona seemed to think my effort was acceptable, judging by her lack of response.

Problem was, I could tell I'd never be able to snatch a single leaf this way. If several went airborne, they'd be a clump. I needed just a couple to rise to have any hope of grabbing only one. I felt a trickle of sweat meander down my back and wiped my brow. This would take a while.

———

The forest darkened and Kovis called over his shoulder, "Let's find a place to make camp before the horses stumble."

My head throbbed. I was more than happy to stop.

Not long after, he pointed at an area tucked within a copse of trees. Several large rocks lay scattered around. Fallen and decaying leaves covered the floor. I smiled. They'd cushion the hard ground tonight.

I pulled Fiona to a stop beside Alshain and waited for Kovis to dismount and help me off. I'd just let go of the reins when both horses squealed, then reared, and I flew off Fiona.

I collected my wits in time to slow my landing on a cushion of air that I conjured, a nuance of my magic that I'd worked on just four suns before. My shoulder was still sore from several failed attempts, but it wouldn't take the hit this time.

"Whoa, boy!" Kovis called, struggling to stay on. But spooked as they were, the horses bolted. Alshain darted under a low-hanging branch, and Kovis couldn't duck in time. He thudded to the ground as his destrier galloped on. Fiona stopped not far off and snorted, her lips flapping as she bobbed her head.

"What just happened?" I called.

Kovis rose, dusted off his leathers, and walked toward the rock we'd stopped the horses by. I joined him and gasped when my eyes fell on a large, reddish-brown snake coiled and ready to strike. Its head was darker, and it had a yellow stripe passing through its eye. It had to have been three fingers thick.

Kovis drew an arm against my stomach, blocking my path, never taking his eyes off the snake. "It's a yellow striper. One of the most venomous snakes in these parts. Looks like we disturbed it in its home. How's snake sound for dinner?"

I'd never eaten snake, but how bad could it be? "Works for me."

Kovis froze the thing before I could blink.

Fiona ambled to the edge of the clearing and watched Kovis decapitate the menace with an ice dagger he conjured. Before he moved the body, he directed a spray of ice into the open space beneath the rock in case any other of its relations were at home.

Fiona let out a whinny. I took it to mean she approved.

It was either that or perhaps the "all clear" that convinced Alshain that the threat had been dealt with because he found his way back to us and stopped next to Fiona.

I went over and petted both of them while Kovis blew the dry leaves from the clearing using his Air magic. Both horses whinnied when all the leaves were gone and they could see for themselves that no further enemies lurked.

So much for using leaves to cushion the hard ground. I'd have to learn how to practice creating a soft bed for us to sleep on with my Air magic.

But some of my frustration eased, and I silently applauded myself when I realized I'd had the presence of mind to use my magic in its nuanced form before I slammed into the ground—I'd have catapulted myself into the woods before.

I hadn't figured out how to get us to Dream, but I had learned something.

My stomach twisted.

But what other manner of creatures lurked out here in the wilderness that I wasn't prepared to face?

Chapter Three
Ambien

"*Why* is Alissandra so committed to that pitiful human charge of hers?" I barked the question into the wind and suppressed the urge to growl as I beat my wings.

She'd fled the Ninety-Eight, preferring that human over me. It made no sense. None.

How could she *possibly* care for a frail mortal more than me?

I cursed under my breath.

It had taken my forces four moons to track her down but her indoctrination into Wake and its ways seemed almost complete. Surprise didn't begin to describe my shock. *How* had they done it? And so quickly? I'd never expected humans to possess such capabilities. They were more skilled than my best mare at that rate.

I clenched my jaw. I would find her again. It was only a matter of time, and when I did, I'd drag her back to Dream with me if I had to.

I'd left my palace before sunrise and would soon be at the cave, but as I glided over a patch of forest, my mind continued swirling.

Alissandra had always cared about her charges, but never, ever to the point that she'd allow them to come between us. I'd demanded she show me she loved me more than this human, and what had she done? I growled. She'd said she trusted my crazy, god-of-the-dead brother, Thao, more than me.

I clenched my fists and bellowed my frustration, no doubt sending skittering the forest animals below.

Enough was enough. Disrespectful. Ungrateful. Entitled.

My anger rose. I'd never seen Alissandra act this way. I wouldn't allow it.

I beat my wings staring into the sun's early rays as they peeked over the horizon. They alone lent brightness to this situation.

Alfreda. I barred my teeth.

First Alissandra, and now her. I'd honestly believed I was past this stage of parenting, but clearly not. Alfreda had apparently witnessed Alissandra's behavior and was now mimicking her, despite being older. Damn it.

She should have known better. What could she possibly hope to gain? I'd been right to isolate her from the rest of her sisters. The last thing I'd tolerate was any more of my daughters subscribing to these inane notions.

I didn't want to be forceful with Alfreda like I had with Alissandra, but she'd also pushed me to the end of my patience. She was being completely uncooperative when it came to her charge. I'd made the *simple* request that she control him to help me locate his brother, but for the last sennight, she'd pretended she couldn't, despite explicit instructions that had worked with *every* one of the myriad of other humans my sand citizens controlled.

I clenched my fist. She, like her younger sister, was more loyal to a *mortal* than to me.

She—they all—needed to learn a lesson that thwarting me was shortsighted.

She *would* cooperate and, furthermore, she *would* tell me who had helped her sister reach Wake. This sun.

I clenched my jaw. Mother was too soft on my daughters, coddling them. It was time to restore order and regain my children's respect.

I landed on the sandy beach as the rising sun painted the sky pink. Waves thundered against the sheer, white cliffs in regular rhythm as I strode toward the mouth of the cave. I'd found the narrow-mouthed cavern many annums before, up the coast a ways from the mushroom caves my children loved so much. The hallow had become my retreat when I sought solitude. Judging by the lack of tracks in or out before I'd told my troops about it, no other being knew of its existence.

I kicked the sand from my sandals and pulled my wings close as I squeezed through the narrow entrance. I didn't fit as easily as I once had, but reducing my girth would require work I wasn't interested in pursuing when I had matters far more pressing to address.

"My liege." Zagan, one of my trained mares, genuflected as my eyes adjusted—at least my troops still respected me. Shifted into his sentry form as he was, he didn't illuminate the cave with glowing purple light, but blue crystals lining the wet cave walls did a suitable job, casting a glow that offered dim light.

"Rise." I strode past him and three other guards before taking a hard right and ducking to clear the low archway of the central chamber.

"My liege," Morfran, my mare commander, said as he bowed low.

In the light of several torches that reflected off the white stone of the low ceiling, I could see Alfreda. She'd been lying on a bed of moss with her back toward me, but she turned over at hearing my voice. A scowl marred her beautiful face, her hair was in disarray, and dirt stained her dress in spots.

I returned my focus to Morfran. "Rise and report."

"My liege, she hasn't said a word despite our questioning."

"Has she slept any?"

"No, my liege. You ordered us not to allow it."

"Very good. Please leave us."

Once he left, I stepped toward Alfreda. She sat up, never taking her eyes off me.

"As I've told you, you can go home if you just tell me who helped your sister flee to Wake."

Alfreda pulled her blanket up further, as if it could shield her from my question, but remained silent.

I sat next to her.

She set her jaw and leaned away, clutching her blanket more tightly.

My anger ignited. Such disrespect.

I was her father, but also her *sovereign*. Clearly she'd forgotten. Lashing out wouldn't serve to accomplish my objective, so I took a deep breath and let it out *very* slowly. "I'm afraid silence isn't going to work. You will have to tell me, daughter. I've given you more than enough chances. It's time."

Alfreda didn't move. Under repeated questioning by myself as well as my troops, she'd protected whoever had abetted Alissandra. She was nearly five hundred annums, but she was acting like a child, foolishly defending the weak. I respected her loyalty and perseverance, but she'd taken it too far. If only she'd chosen to use her ideals to a more fitting end.

"Okay, if you won't tell me, you leave me no choice. But remember these are your wishes I'm abiding by."

She tensed.

I latched onto her mind—I would inflict pain but nothing lasting. "Tell me, Alfreda. Who helped Alissandra?"

She shook her head.

I extended my mental claws, and she went rigid.

"Tell me, daughter."

Her knuckles turned white from gripping the blanket, but still she resisted me. Foolish child.

I drew my claws lightly across her mind. She scrunched her face. Under different circumstances, I would have congratulated her. The pain would have been more than a little discomforting. She was tough and rightly so, she was my daughter.

My mental talons made a second pass, a little harder, and she whimpered but still resisted.

"I can do this all sun, Alfreda. You cannot resist me, so don't try to be a hero. You're only hurting yourself."

Alfreda kept her eyes closed, waiting for more pain.

I shook my head, then ran my mental claws across the surface of her mind a third time, deeper. Foolishness.

She moaned and grasped her head.

Four, five, six, seven times, and she collapsed onto her side into a ball and panted.

"You can make the pain stop. It's up to you."

Her lack of response had me dig my claws deeper and go slower on the eighth, ninth, and tenth passes.

That got a bigger reaction. Finally, she screamed. Progress.

"Just tell me. I know you want to."

But still she kept silent. How much would she endure for her ideal? It bordered on the ridiculous.

On the fifteenth pass, she retched all over herself. The smell was more than offensive, but I sensed she was nearly ready to tell me. She couldn't last much longer.

The sixteenth and seventeenth passes had her completely emptying her stomach's contents, and she'd already screamed her voice nearly into exhaustion. We were almost there.

The breakthrough came when my claws were halfway across her mind on the nineteenth pass.

She whispered, and I couldn't make out what she said, so I leaned over her balled-up form. The stench of her retching nearly made me add the contents of my stomach to the mess, but I swallowed hard and put my ear near her mouth.

"Tell me again, daughter. I couldn't hear you."

"V... Vel..."

"Velma helped Alissandra escape?"

She barely moved her head, but it was enough to acknowledge.

My eldest had been the instigator. I growled. Velma and I hadn't seen eye to eye for quite some time, but she'd never blatantly encouraged her siblings to go against me. There was a first for everything. She'd become a bad influence.

I would have to deal with her.

"Very good, Alfreda. See, that wasn't so hard to tell me, was it? You could have saved yourself suffering. You knew you couldn't outlast me. But I am impressed by your determination. I didn't figure you would last as long as you did." I patted her thigh, then rose.

"Morfran," I called.

"Yes, my liege."

"Let her sleep a bit, but then its right back at it with her charge. He needs to find Alissandra and that human. They'll be awake for a while and no doubt traveling if their recent activities are any indication. He needs to make better progress, or we'll never find them."

"Yes, my liege."

"Use whatever force is required."

"I understand."

I ducked as I strode out of the central chamber. "Zagan, take another troop and retrieve my daughter Velma. You'll find her at the palace of sand maidens. Bring her here in secret, then send word."

Chapter Four
Kennan

would befall Kovis and Ali if I didn't reach and protect them before they left Flumen to return home from The Ninety-Eight. Terror had overwhelmed me, and I'd rushed out of Veritas in a daze, not even taking time to inform my guards of my intentions or destination.

But the haze of my dream had continued on and on, over so many sunrises and sunsets that I lost count how long it had been.

I'd sighed with relief when I imagined I reached the competition. It was the only place I could have been with crowds that size. While I'd known Ali would have to fight, what I saw seemed crazy. Her competitors forfeited in the final round. Forfeited. Competitors in The Ninety-Eight would never forfeit. I sighed with relief because only dreams thrived on the absurd.

But before Ali cleared the arena, a blade had hurled at her, struck her back, and she fainted. My heart had climbed into my throat. It quickly become a night terror.

The next thing I knew, another sunrise came and I talked to Ali. She'd been healthy, and I'd exhaled for the first time in a long time. What I'd said to her, I couldn't remember. Kovis had bounded to her side, his leathers not even done up properly, and interrupted us. He begged her not to come to me. Like the rest of it, it made no sense. My brother wouldn't have done that, but such was the way of dreams.

My dream shifted, and when I next opened my eyes, Ali and Kovis were nowhere to be found. I was hungry, but that urgent, ominous feeling that they were still in danger again overrode my hunger, and I rode after them, to the point of exhaustion. My welfare didn't matter. I needed to find them again before something happened.

At points, my mind sensed that this nightmare had persisted for too long, nearly an eternity. I couldn't ever remember a dream like it. It had become a haze of sorts, outside of time. But try as I may, I couldn't wake. I wasn't sure whether to be alarmed or not. But that sense of urgency only intensified. I had to track them, find them.

It almost seemed as if they were trying to hide from me, and I again reminded myself that dreams didn't have to make sense. It didn't matter.

I knew Kovis as well as I knew myself, and I knew all his little tricks to hide their path. Only someone who knew my twin like I did and could anticipate his moves would ever be able to track him; he was that good. I'd picked up his trail, so it would only be a matter of time before I found them and they'd be safe. I just knew it. At least I told myself that.

I felt completely parched, and I panted, dreaming I trotted Onyx, my raven stallion, up a steep hill.

I'd thought I'd been close, but in my haste, it seemed I'd somehow missed one of Kovis's telltale signs—the virtually invisible swish markings he left behind as he tried to erase their tracks with his water magic. I knew because I hadn't seen any of Alshain's or

Fiona's footprints in quite some time. Despite my prowess, he'd outfoxed me again and I'd need to backtrack.

I turned Onyx around, patting his sweaty neck, before urgency reasserted itself and compelled me onward.

———

The sun beat down on me from its peak, and I wiped my arm across my brow. I was so thirsty. Onyx was no better, lethargic as he was. I needed to find water.

"Let them stop and rest." I'd begun hearing voices—a woman's and a man's to be exact. The woman always pleaded my case, but the man she beseeched either ignored or snarled. The woman wasn't Rasa, couldn't be because no man in his right mind would say the things this one did to my sister and expect to live. It wasn't Ali either. I knew the voice of my love. I couldn't place it.

In my haze, thoughts flitted about my mind. Was this really a dream or had I suddenly, inexplicably, gone mad? Was this how people who could no longer reason experienced the world? Would I ever stop dreaming and return to myself? Or was this to be the way of things until I perished? If it was, I'd sooner leave this life—I couldn't dream endlessly, thinking I wandered the world, Kovis and Ali forever in peril. I couldn't.

Ali had said she was Kovis's sand maiden and that her sister, Alfreda, was mine. So, *why* didn't her sister awaken me? I huffed. Wouldn't that be part of her responsibilities? How could she have abandoned her responsibilities when I *really* needed her? Just my luck. I'd been assigned the black sheep of the family.

Or had Ali been jesting, her whole story a farce?

I frowned. But she'd been so insistent.

I shook my head.

I loved Ali. Could I focus on that notion and have it be my guide back to sanity? If I could just see her again, talk to her, surely I'd wake from this nightmare.

Ali was incredible. After what I'd allowed, she'd still kissed me. Yes, that kiss... she'd been just as passionate as me. What kind of woman was so kind, so loving, so compassionate that she could look past what I'd allowed and kiss me so thoroughly? I felt unworthy of her. We shared... feelings. It was clear.

Ali. Just her name sent a calm through me. I'd never felt about anyone what I did her. I could be completely open, and she wouldn't judge me. We could bare our very souls to each other.

Wait. Wait.

I slowed Onyx as I sucked in a breath.

Was this whole nightmare the gods punishing me for what I'd allowed to happen to her? My conscience again burned as it had ever since. It was my penance. I deserved to feel this way.

My heart sped. But had the gods decided it wasn't enough?

I'd only been following the Council's intake manual—the excuse, my old friend, tempted me once more. I again beat back that ugly, nagging truth that no manual for prisoner treatment, even authored by the Council, would ever condone what I'd allowed.

Kovis covered in blood, howling, and convulsing, a naked stranger in his room—the horrific images again terrorized my thoughts.

All reason had fled. She'd gotten into his bedroom while he was asleep. Panic and rage had filled me.

Onyx snorted and pinned his ears back, clearly unhappy that I'd pulled the reins sharply as my panic reasserted itself.

"Sorry. Sorry, boy." I patted his neck.

She hadn't succeeded in harming him, but she could have.

I'd acted on pure instinct—no one would harm my family. After what we'd endured, I wasn't about to be gentle. I'd needed answers that very heartbeat, and I'd used whatever means necessary to get them.

I'd been out of control... and I was ashamed.

I exhaled heavily.

Onyx nickered, seemingly commiserating.

. . .

The gods knew what I'd done, and this daze seemed of their making—it forbid thinking or reasoning or relying on myself. I was completely vulnerable and at their mercy. I had no doubt it's how they would want a subject needing correction.

What punishment would they be satisfied with? I shuddered. I deserved everything they threw at me, but would I be strong enough to withstand it?

If I endured, my conscience would finally be clean before them—the rogue thought broke through the malaise. I needed to apologize to the gods. Not some quick, cheap attempt to appease— no, that would only anger them more. I needed to be honest, to lay myself bare at their mercy.

I cried out with every ounce of earnestness I possessed. "I'm sorry. I couldn't bear the thought of Kovis coming to harm. I panicked. I needed answers and would have permitted *any* punishment to get them. So I ignored when my men..." I stopped myself.

I wasn't taking ownership by blaming my men. I had been responsible for their actions. I should have stopped them, but I hadn't. I'd actually looked away, as if it would keep me unsullied.

I shook my head. I was a miserable wretch, I couldn't even honestly apologize to the gods.

I owed Ali an apology, a truthful one this time.

My conscience again seared like a hot iron. My first had been a joke. I'd blamed the rule book. She didn't know what it said, and it had been an easy scapegoat in the face of me lacking the balls to admit why I'd allowed what I had. I'd buried my guilt as the lie slipped from my lips.

When she'd bought it, my very soul had burned with shame. Enduring the gods' punishment might be easy compared to her reaction when I confessed. I grimaced.

She deserved the truth; I only prayed she'd take me back. No, she would. Our love would overcome even this. I refused to acknowledge any other outcome.

• • •

I felt utterly exhausted, Onyx, too, judging by his slowed pace, but we continued on.

I had to find Kovis and Ali before something happened to them. I loved them both too much to have them come to ruin because of me. Would the gods cause them pain and make me watch as part of my punishment? My stomach rolled at the thought. Too much had happened to Rasa. If harm came to anyone else I loved because of me…

———

I dreamed that I pulled back on Onyx's reins as we crested a hill, my heart pounding. I had to reach them. Only thoughts of Ali and the life I hoped we might build together eased my panic and kept me going as weariness, hunger, and thirst consumed me. I feared I might faint.

"Please, let them stop." That woman's voice had turned pleading.

Hope rose in me. Exhaustion would win if no one showed mercy. But nothing happened. No food or water appeared after what felt like an eternity, and my spirits plummeted.

The gods had chosen to ignore my need, as was right. They pressed my punishment. I hadn't yet sufficiently paid for my transgressions, not to their satisfaction. Keeping Ali and Kovis under constant threat, just out of reach, only added to it, and the gods knew it. This was a test of endurance, and I would never give up, not when their lives were on the line.

I clicked, urging Onyx back into a cantor.

I forced my thoughts to stray from the frustration of the situation and again found my only solace in Ali. She was forgiving and optimistic, and she cherished my art, my expression of me. We were so much alike, and my heart overflowed with love for her. This and similar thoughts eased the trial for some time.

My heart lightened as I picked up on Kovis and Ali's trail again.

I clenched my jaw. They would not come to harm because of me. I didn't care how hard the gods made it.

————

The sun set in this unending dream, the haze clouding all but my immediate surroundings. Sunrises, sunsets, light, dark—time had become meaningless. Everything seemed meaningless, except for the continual press of needing to find them.

The gods must have decided I hadn't yet turned from my wicked ways, or they believed I'd return to them if they released me and let me find my loved ones. What more would they put me through? If only they'd have told me what to do to atone, I would have done it in a heartbeat.

In my haze, I collapsed under a tree near a riverbank. I drank my fill of water, which had never tasted so sweet. Onyx waded in the shallows, enjoying the refreshing coolness as well.

An inquisitive pheasant strutted near to see what manner of beasts we were. My stomach rumbled, and I conjured a dagger. My aim would have to be true, I didn't have energy to magic another.

I sighed, relieved, when the fowl dropped to the ground, its demise in the blink of an eye. No suffering. Too quick for pain. If only the same would happen to me, but it couldn't. If I perished, Ali and Kovis would be lost.

I'd thought confessing to Ali would be far worse, but the gods' punishment was too much. I was at the end of what I could endure.

————

"Please, you *must* allow him to rest. You'll kill him before he finds the pair!" The woman again pleaded on my behalf.

I wondered if the gods had her there to tempt me to hope that someone cared about my plight, only to crush me when the authority ignored her. It worked. Every damn time as my dream went on and on and on. I'd walked and ridden and eaten and drank and slept and pissed and still the nightmare, the haze, hadn't ended.

The woman howled, then barked in pain.

The gods had caught on to my game and had made it increasingly difficult for me to ignore her because she now yipped or screeched or howled courtesy of the man, if she pleaded my case too forcefully, which she was wont to do.

Her agonized sounds were the same as when I interrogated uncooperative female prisoners. But this woman's pain made those pale in comparison. It nearly sent me over the edge—she endured pain, not caused by me, but on my behalf, and that made it so much worse.

I wanted to pummel the man, but I couldn't. I couldn't see him, much less grab him in dreams. The gods had to know it cut me to the core—it brought back the horrors of my past. They were accomplishing their ends all right. I thought they'd already broken me, but clearly not enough because this nightmare persisted.

When would it end? How much more penance would they require of me? I couldn't endure more.

Perhaps that was the point. Perhaps they sought to push me over the edge of what I could bear. Somehow, they'd decided I hadn't yet reached that point. But I had to endure no matter what. I couldn't go through this ever again. I forced my thoughts to something pleasant, how Ali and I would paint and read and make music together.

———

Onyx plodded under the setting sun. He'd always been a good mount, and despite our trial, he was bearing up well, or so I dreamed despite both of us being spent. Only the fact that I'd found fresh tracks buoyed me. We were getting close to them.

I furrowed my brow as I gazed into the distance and my heart picked up pace as I realized I could see farther and more clearly than I'd been able the entire dream.

I took in my surroundings as we trod in a forest. The leaves and branches and shrubs came into sharp focus. Mud splattered the legs of my leathers. Except for birds and small ground animals, we were completely alone. The panic that had been my constant companion eased and my chest felt lighter than it had since this whole ordeal began. Was I finally waking from this nightmare?

Onyx stopped, turned his head, and eyed me, as if unsure what I'd do next, despite he and I having developed a trusting relationship over nearly twenty annums.

Where were we? Nothing was familiar. Not one thing. A new wave of panic surged through my gut. How had we gotten here? How long had we been riding? What had happened to me?

Onyx whinnied, then bobbed his head, his way of telling me to follow his lead when I felt lost. How he always knew, I'd never deduced, but he'd never failed me. At times, I thought I was just his puppet and he humored me.

"Okay, boy, lead us."

Onyx meandered around and through the gaps in the undergrowth and through the dense foliage as the light faded. I prayed that, once we emerged, I'd recognize something. Never in my life had I felt so lost and alone in the world. What awaited us? No, I couldn't think about that. I'd face it when it came.

To beat back fear, I focused on the fact that I *had* finally awoken. It could only mean one thing—I'd done sufficient penance to satisfy the gods. And my conscience was now clean before them.

Never, ever would I test them again.

If only my conscience was clean before Ali too. I'd apologize, I would, because it was obvious that she and I were meant to be together. The gods wouldn't have put me through all that otherwise.

Now, Kovis just needed to understand.

● ● ●

Chapter Five

My teeth chattered. I was frozen. Again. I couldn't handle much more.

The quiet was loud. Creatures of the light still slumbered, making the night and cold seem that much more fierce. Only the hot springs burbling not far off tempered it—if only we could sleep in them.

We'd been on the run for nearly two moons because I hadn't yet figured out a way back to Dream. I wanted to scream. The temperatures had started to cool, and the leaves on the trees would soon turn a myriad of colors, at least that's what Kovis had said.

Dream realm didn't have any seasonal changes, *let alone this abominable cold*, and while I'm sure my many charges had experienced this, I'd never paid any attention since I'd never expected to live here. That and my focus was on helping my charges by organizing their thoughts, not noticing their surroundings.

I wasn't a wimp. I wasn't. I'd proven to myself that I was tough, that I could fight against cutthroat competitors and win. But cold... it was an adversary of a wholly different nature, and equally fierce, equally indifferent.

We'd raced off without so much as a copper between us. At this point, I'd do whatever it took to be warm. I couldn't live like this. What could we do to get more blankets and warmer clothes… *this* sun? But my mind was as frozen as the rest of me and as useful as a wooden pot over a cook fire to procure a solution.

I clenched my jaw.

Kovis rose onto an elbow, disturbing what little of a cocoon of warmth our blanket provided. I screeched as a rush of cold air breezed between us.

"Autumn is my favorite season because of the magic of the leaves." He leaned forward and nuzzled my numb ear. "Most think leaves are green. But cooler temperatures make their green covering fade and reveal their true colors."

I frowned as I shivered.

His exhaled chuckle warmed my aching ear. "I believe it's one of nature's metaphors, revealing their inner beauty."

"Well I could stand a little less inner beauty and a lot more warmth." The crisp morning air nipped my nose.

Kovis snickered, then kissed my ear thoroughly. "Better?"

"If only you would do that to all of me as we sleep." I clutched the blanket at my chin.

He tweaked my nose.

Our fire had burned itself out. The few faint orange embers were the only sign that it had ever given off heat.

I pulled my nearly numb toes back inside our blanket—no matter what I did, they always found a hole. "I'm beginning to think your Ice magic makes you impervious to the cold."

"Are you?"

"Yes. I think it neutralizes it."

He grinned. "Then I invite you to pull some of my Ice and see if it cures your chill tonight."

I breathed on my fingers. "I may just do that. But if it works, you may not like the amount of your magic I draw to stay warm."

His blue and hazel eyes danced.

The first pink rays of sunshine *finally* showed through the canopy of leaves and I prepared myself to give up the blanket and face the cold.

But Kovis tapped a finger against his lips and he eased me forward, eyes scanning the surrounding trees.

My breathing labored as I matched his study.

Not again.

Since we'd been on the run, other than that snake, we'd had to fend off a silver vebros, a miniature dragon the size of a large dog, as well as a fanged chutnook, but it seemed the gods had thus far spared us confrontations with some of the viler creatures that roamed the wilds.

According to Kovis, during his military service while his father's campaigns persisted, they'd had to cut down a horned thorg—apparently the quick, waist-high creature had a whip tail that was highly venomous. I'd shuddered at his telling and prayed we didn't encounter any.

Gooseflesh pebbled my arms.

Kovis used his Air magic to set sensors of some sort around the clearing we selected each sunset, to warn us of large animals approaching. If such a creature disturbed the invisible barrier, Kovis would be alerted. Small mercy.

I quickly spotted something moving in the trees, lurking, stalking near the edge of the clearing, and my heart sped. I couldn't yet see the creature's piercing eyes, or smell its stench, but I knew of only one beast who wore a violet coat that would glow eerily in the dim light.

"Mares," I whispered. My whole body stiffened from the cold as I rose, but I never took my gaze off the enemy.

It was a creature of the night. And where there was one, there were more. They traveled in packs. Kovis must have sensed them breech the magic wards he'd set.

I'd had too many encounters with the beasts as I shepherded the dreams of various charges over the eons. Inducers of nightmares, they preyed on human fears, changing from their usual large wolflike form into whatever most terrified my charge. For better or worse, humans couldn't see or smell them, only experience the terror they brought. But once a mare had control, I was powerless to help until my charge woke. Mares were menaces, pure and simple. They'd rip you to shreds as soon as look at you.

Kovis nodded then slowly stood, taking position on bare feet between me and the sleepy fire. Muscled arms extended in front of him, palms out, tattoo blazing red, he was the picture of readiness.

Had there not been a threat, I would have savored the sight of his lithe and naked body, his round but firm and dimpled butt, and… other parts. But this was not the time.

He didn't question my assessment despite not being able to see the creatures. He'd heard me tell tales of the brutes. Only I had visibility of them with senses that had somehow followed me through my transformation from immortal to mortal human body.

We'd tied Alshain and Fiona to trees not far off. They didn't startle much less bob their heads in alarm, so clearly they didn't sense the threat. The menaces ignored them, focusing only on us, thank the gods.

A twig cracked behind us, and I pivoted. Another mare, still behind the tree line but creeping closer.

Panic welled in me. They could wound us, fell us with the swipe of a mighty paw, but a quick death would be a mercy, which was why they wouldn't kill us that way. They would do far worse. They didn't feed off the physical, they fed off fear; they thrived on it. They'd dredge up memories of what we most feared then feed and nurture that fear until it became paralyzing.

I'd have rather had my soul sucked from me than that.

But still they wouldn't end us, not when prolonging our terror would make their feast that much more delectable. The only thing that would end us would be our hearts nearly beating out of our chests. We would die of heart attacks—literally. We'd battled terrifying creatures since we'd been out here, but nothing compared to mares and what they would do to us.

We had to win. It wasn't a choice.

• • •

I tried to calm my raging thoughts, but they refused. Were these wild mares or Father's trained abominations? Had he found us despite our best efforts? If so, how?

Kovis and I shared dream sand, and its scent should have made us invisible to them. I prayed these were wild and not Father's.

My theory was quickly tested as a hare hopped between us and our pursuers. It didn't see us, unmoving as we were, nor our foe, and was easy prey. But the mares didn't fall on it. Wild mares would have gone after it, wouldn't they?

Dread pooled in my stomach.

Another violet beast—this one to our right—returned my stare. These monsters were huge. This one came up to my chest, perhaps even to my shoulders.

The cold no longer bothered me despite being naked.

I counted as I scanned the perimeter. Nine. Nine mares, maybe more, had us surrounded. A chorus of growls began as their circle grew smaller, their noose tightening.

Even combining Kovis's Water and Ice powers with mine, there were too many of them, and they were too large to freeze like we did the small animals that sustained us. We'd have to engage the fight with them one at a time.

I took a ready position, matching Kovis at my back. Blood raced through my veins. Kovis was equally alert, his heart rate loud through our bond.

Our enemies continued closing in, and wisps of their stench hit me, making my stomach sour. I swallowed hard, forcing down bile, then opened my mouth and took calming breaths in and out.

The first mare pounced from the tree line in the blink of an eye. I inhaled sharply as I saw its true size, even bigger in the open. It was a marvel of strength and grace and force. Its enormous, muscled body was elegant as it stretched for us.

I clenched my fists. We had no less than nine of these to defend against.

Alshain let out a whinny, no doubt sensing Kovis's distress as together he and I raised a wall of impenetrable air that swirled around us, cocooning and protecting. Small mercy, it blocked much of their stench.

The first mare's muzzle slammed into our barrier and crumpled to the ground, dazed. Other brutes followed on its heels but averted the barrier as they landed. Saliva dripped from bared canines as they prowled around the perimeter, searching for weaknesses.

Kovis was the most powerful sorcerer the Altairn Empire had ever known—tri-affinitied in Air, Water, and Ice magic—but blind as he was, his effectiveness rivaled a mule deer crossing ice. He tried nonetheless, drawing water from the air then freezing it into a multitude of needle-thin icicles. These he sprayed through the wind wall, hoping to hit something, anything.

A mare stopped dead in its tracks, eyes and nose suddenly leeching blood. Another, its ear and side spouting red through violet fur, halted. Both slumped to the ground. Kovis swore as they materialized, the hulking, lifeless bodies giving up their shields of invisibility.

The horses whinnied and stomped their hooves.

Holding my winds steady, I borrowed a thread of Kovis's Water magic and drew liquid from the air. I pried the muzzle of another beast open with a strand of my winds and forced the water down its throat until it overflowed. It's what I'd done with my final competitor during The Ninety-Eight, and the move produced the same result. A third body turned visible.

Fiona whinnied, her tone becoming panicked.

I added sand from the clearing to my winds and blasted another mare. Blood sprayed as the abrasive struck its nose, then eyes, then ears before it succumbed. Red flowed from the nearly headless corpse as it showed itself, adding to the carnage littering the clearing.

Kovis threw an ice mist that would freeze anything it touched, but it hit only the hind quarters of another attacker. The beast's back legs collapsed, but it fought its infirmity and struggled forward, teeth snapping. I ended it, blasting it with sandy air.

I downed two more mares, drowning one and shredding the head of the other, but as I eyed the next adversary, my bond with Kovis went silent. I pivoted and screamed.

Both horses reared, fighting their teethers.

Not more than a stride away, a beast had Kovis's leg clamped in its maw. It tossed him like a rag doll, side to side. Kovis yelped. With him blind, his wind wall must have separated from mine and a mare found a way between.

Oh no you don't! The thing had made it past our defenses, but I would never let it keep him. Not without a fight.

I wrenched Ice magic from Kovis at the same time I realized his eyes had closed and the mare was shifting, changing into what Kovis most feared. The thing had put him fast asleep quicker than I could blink.

Kovis's protective winds about us ceased, leaving only mine, as he thudded to the ground and the form of a powerful, robed, black-winged god emerged. Father, or Kovis's interpretation of him, bent over and grabbed his neck in a death grip. I blasted the impersonator with ice until I'd encased all but where it held Kovis's neck, then turned my winds on it. It shattered into a million pieces inside my protective winds.

Kovis didn't move.

But something in my periphery did, and I shot up to find two more monstrous mares lunging for us. In rescuing Kovis, I'd taken my focus off the last of our opponents.

Perhaps it was the direness of the situation, but panic didn't raise its head. Rather, an icy calm suffused me.

I'd been frustrated, increasingly so these past sennights. My frustration had turned to anger then morphed into rage as a solution back to Dream continued to hide itself while Kennan and Alfreda's lives lay on the line. Between the biting cold, our primitive conditions, battling for our lives in this gods forsaken wilderness, and now these mares, I was done.

My calm was that of all my wild emotions, no longer roiling, but solidified into hardness, into resolve. I clenched my jaw as I lowered the protective barrier, then thrust my arms out wide. Eyes closed, I let my winds fly, holding nothing back.

I heard my name as moisture pelted my face. I didn't stop.

Ice flowed through my veins. These mares would pay for all they and their kind had done to my charges over the annums, pay for Father's scheming. I'd make them suffer like I had, like Kennan and Alfreda no doubt were, at his hands. I would show no mercy. I would utterly destroy them.

Insistence filled the voice, but still I ignored it as I let my winds obliterate the foe. I was done freezing outdoors, done running, done feeling helpless.

"Ali! Stop." Strong hands gripped my shoulders, forcing me from my fury.

I opened my eyes to find Kovis staring into them, panting.

Chapter Six

"I've said it before, but it's true. You're fierce when you're angry, Ali." Kovis grinned, but I wasn't in the mood.

He drew two fingers to my cheek and brushed them across. The tips came away red.

I jerked back, returned to reality in a heartbeat. He motioned with a finger, tracing the outline of the clearing. My eyes followed.

Six bloodied and mutilated corpses littered the clearing, but their stench lived on. The devastation I'd wrought was total, complete. I almost wished I felt remorse. Almost, but no, they were our ancient foe, and I would spare no pity for them.

"You completely obliterated the last two," Kovis said, reading my unspoken question.

"The blood is from them?"

Kovis nodded. "And bits of hair and bone and… You may not have learned the nuances of your magic, but I'll have you fight on my side every time." He swatted the air and grimaced. "They reek." He coughed, trying to control his stomach.

"Yes, they do."

Adrenaline forbid the chilly air from bothering me as I looked about. My gaze hadn't gone far before Kovis grimaced and I glanced down to see blood gushing from his right leg where the creature had grabbed him. "You're bleeding."

"Yes." His face contorted as he shifted making my stomach clench. It had to be deep. And we were in the middle of nowhere, no healing supplies to be found.

"Come, we need to stop the bleeding and clean it out before it gets infected." I couldn't keep a tremor from lacing my words.

I helped Kovis over to a log near the fire and had him lay on the ground, propping his leg on the stump to slow the flow.

I shuddered to think what diseases that beast had carried. If we didn't get the wound thoroughly cleaned out… I didn't want to think about what would happen.

My body shook, but I forced myself to hold it together. If only I possessed the Wood and Terra affinities that healers did, but I didn't. My Simulus affinity might be powerful, but it required that I leverage the powers of others and there was no sorcerer with those affinities around. It would keep me humble, that was for sure.

Kovis lay with his hands locked beneath his head. While he tried to force a smile, I knew he knew how serious this was. My eyes swept his form. Blood colored his hair, face, and arms and covered his tattooed chest.

The wound was too deep for bandages, and I had nothing to stitch it shut with. He would keep losing blood unless I could find something to clot it with.

I scanned the clearing. Red coated every surface, thick close to us, misted further away. Alshain and Fiona had calmed and gone back to foraging on low-hanging tree leaves, still tethered. But their coats had taken on reddish casts.

What could I use to staunch the bleeding? I looked further, into the woods, and sighed with relief when I spotted several pine trees. "We're in luck."

Kovis furrowed his brow.

"Pine sap will make it clot, and it's a disinfectant that will keep it clean."

"You're sure?"

"I learned it from Master Lorica. But first we need to clean your wound out." I gritted my teeth knowing what I was about to suggest would hurt considerably. "Can you flush it thoroughly with your Water magic?"

Kovis met my gaze and held it before slowly nodding. He grimaced as he lowered his leg and sat up. The blood flow had lessened with it elevated, but it resumed to nearly its earlier pace. I positioned his leg so he could get to the whole wound.

My stomach tensed. "Do you want something to bite on while you do it?"

"No."

I scrunched my face. "Use some force so it gets as much of the bacteria out as possible."

He took a deep breath and closed his eyes, then held up a hand. I adjusted it so his magic would strike the laceration.

"Here goes." He bellowed as a stream of water blasted it. My stomach clenched, but there was no other way.

"Just a little more." I bit my lip then repositioned his hand to get what he'd missed.

His face writhed in anguish.

"Okay, stop! Stop."

His shoulders slumped back onto the ground, and he threw an arm over his eyes, panting.

I didn't allow myself to relax. I moved his leg back onto the stump then examined the bite, moving it this way and that to get a good look, but never touching it so as not to contaminate it again. A trickle of blood quickly reappeared.

I leapt up. I needed sap ASAP.

"Wait right there," I told him, pausing to remove my ring and set it by his head to keep it from getting sticky. "Don't lose it. It's very important to me."

He forced a corner of his mouth up despite his exhaustion. "Glad to hear it, and I wouldn't dream of it. I'll fight off all the rogue animals who come to claim it for themselves."

I sprinted for the pine trees I'd spotted and picked one. It wasn't as large as some, but it would do. I found lumps resembling acne on its trunk and popped one. Like draining a boil, the sap ran out like honey, and I caught it in my hand. I did the same to several more lumps, stopping only when the sticky stuff overran my cupped palm.

"My healer returns," Kovis joked, waving a hand.

I knelt and began filling the wound. "Glad you missed me."

"And how." His body tensed, his face contorting, as the sap hit raw flesh.

"That's its antiseptic properties killing any bacteria you missed. It'll also reduce the swelling with its anti-inflammatory properties and pull the wound closed as it dries. Almost done."

He fisted his hands at his sides, clenched his jaw, and gritted out, "Me thinks the cure may be worse than the problem."

I sat back on my heels and gave him my best frown. "There, all done, but don't move until the sap sets."

"Far be it from me to disobey my healer."

With the crisis averted, I looked down at myself. My hand was so sticky I had trouble opening it. Dried blood caked the rest of my body, too. I was a mess, but I'd wait to clean up until Kovis was able to as well.

I shuddered as a chill slithered up my back. No doubt the adrenaline would soon wear off, and not only would I be exhausted, but my nemesis, the cold, would assert itself again.

I ran my sticky hand across the ground, trying to remove some of the sap or at least coat it so it was less tacky. I'd be wearing it for a long while, especially since it was waterproof, but I didn't regret it. I'd do the same thing again in a heartbeat.

Kovis returned my ring to my nonsticky hand and sealed it with a kiss. "Since it seems we'll be here for a bit, I think its time you practiced accessing my mind through our bond."

I met his eyes as my heart rate increased.

He held a hand up. "I know it scared you ending up in my head, not knowing how to get free again. I'm not making light of that. But I really do think we need to understand more what our bond enables us to do."

I knew I'd been silly about refusing to try to access his mind again. We'd chatted countless times, mind to mind through our bond, and he'd ventured into my head more than a few times without any complications, but still….

Kovis continued, "You asked me to open my thinking about the source of your affinities, and I did. I see this as the same thing."

I inhaled. He'd used the one argument he knew I couldn't refuse. At length, I nodded. "You're right. I need to do this."

"Ali, I don't want you to do this because you feel obligated. I want you to want to join my mind"—he looked away—"because it's mine. It's me."

In the blink of an eye, the situation shown in a whole new light. "Oh, Kovis, I'm so sorry. I never…."

I'd been looking at this as a practical matter that had scared me to death to repeat. I hadn't understood he'd wanted to share himself with me in this way. There couldn't be any deeper way of knowing each other. He was opening more of himself up to me, and I'd declined him. Again and again.

His eyes were full of understanding. "I know. You had access to my mind as my sand maiden. It's what allowed you to know me so thoroughly. I want to share that connection… that intimacy… with you again."

My heart brimmed with love for this man. "I had no idea that's how you saw this. I don't know what to say. I'm honored you want this." I swallowed hard. "There's nothing I'd like more, my Dreambeam. Thank you for putting up with me and helping me see things from your perspective." I leaned forward and pressed a kiss to his lips.

"Too bad I have to keep my leg elevated." An amused expression erupted across his furry face.

"You're insatiable." I grinned.

"For you, Ali. Always. But seeing as I have no ability to make good on my desires for the time being, let's have you try accessing my mind again."

My stomach quivered, but I tamped it down.

"I'm still discovering new things about our bond," he said. "But I've frequented your mind enough that I feel confident guiding you through this. Hopefully, once you know how to do it yourself, you'll feel better about it. Much of it involves… desire." The last word came out as a purr.

I felt my cheeks warm, as he'd intended. I bit my lip then nodded.

"I'll speak sweet nothings when you reach me."

I snickered. He was doing a good job of loosening me up. *You need to tell me "dirty somethings."*

Kovis chortled, obviously listening in. "So be it, if that's what the maiden wishes."

I fanned myself.

"Okay then, you need to desperately want to join my mind." He winked.

I'd told him that's how I'd ended up there the first time, and he'd never let me forget. *Arrogant royal.*

"Focus."

I closed my eyes and let my thoughts about him roam. It wasn't hard. Physically, Kovis was hot, mmmm, but adding to his seduction, he'd opened up, making himself utterly vulnerable to me, allowing me to help thaw his bruised and tender heart. I longed to be one with him, to—

In a heartbeat, my view to the world shifted and I looked up to see a blood-covered female kneeling beside me. Wait.

I looked down then yipped. I was in two bodies, seeing as both him and myself at the same time, just like before. To say this was an out-of-body experience was putting it mildly. This was downright mind bending.

• • •

Welcome to my head and well done, Ali dearest. It'll take a bit to get used to it. Being in two places at once is…

Crazy. Disorientating. My heart beat faster. I'd done it, but would I be stuck here?

Ali, calm yourself. You won't be stuck here. I promise.

I took deep breaths, nearly choking on the stench of dead mares, and willed my heart to slow.

It's alright, my love, you're okay. Try to acclimate.

I, rather Kovis, looked up at the treetops. The gentle breeze made the branches sway back and forth.

I, in my own body, tried to relax too. I decided I'd be better off lying down.

He turned his head, and through his eyes, I watched myself lie down beside him and turn on my side, drawing an arm to cradle my head. I closed my sappy hand in a fist to try and protect my hair.

At the same time, as myself, I watched Kovis lying there, watching me.

I could move, and I had awareness in two places at the same time. Short of the one time I'd visited his head while he was recovering from my arrival, it was the strangest thing I'd ever experienced. Every once in a while, I'd wished I could be in two places at once—well, I was getting my wish, and I wasn't sure I liked it.

Beside Kovis, I moved my free hand over, found his red-splattered nose, and pushed it. I watched me through both of our eyes and chuckled at how odd it all was. *I love your nose. It's very cute.*

Is it now? You've never told me that before.

It is. I ran my hand over his red-tinged, scruffy chin. Would he let me do whatever I wanted to him? It seemed so since he hadn't moved to stop me. *Such liberties you're allowing.*

I promised you dirty somethings. I'd love you to take these kinds of liberties with me all the time.

My eyes grew large, while Kovis beamed.

Is that so? Well then… I watched my hand as I eased it down his hairy chin, then down his neck, beyond where his facial hair ended, stopping at his collarbone. No matter that the blood of our enemies covered him, he was still the sexiest man I'd ever seen in the flesh. I chuckled to myself.

Mmm, where should my hand explore next?

He swallowed hard, and I saw the bump in his neck rise and fall quickly. *Anywhere you choose.* He turned his head, and we locked eyes, but I had no doubt not every part of him was near this picture of calm.

I think I'll... My finger wandered downward, making him tense. He was ticklish where I was heading.

Play nice.

I am, but you've given me free reign.

We grinned.

My fingertip meandered across his blood-splattered chest, across his tattoo that I couldn't tell the color of under the gore, brushed his nearly nonexistent chest hair, approaching my intended destination. I made sweeping circles about his breast.

You're having way too much fun.

Amazing how attuned he was when my body wasn't distracting him.

He sucked in air as my finger continued teasing. He held his breath. A heartbeat later, he closed his eyes, and with it, his view to the world, but I didn't stop.

A groan escaped him. *I can't keep my leg elevated with you doing this to me.*

I stroked once more before replying, *Fair enough.*

I pulled my hand away and he exhaled loudly, his whole body going slack again. He opened his eyes. *Ready to return?*

I'd gotten caught up in the fun, no doubt as he'd planned—anything to help me forget my fear and I smiled. *Yes.*

As I said before, it's a matter of desire. It again came out as a purr. *Long to return to your own body, your own mind. Will it to be so.*

I focused. *I want to be back in my own head.*

Nothing happened. I still saw the world through both of our eyes and my heart picked up its pace.

Calm, Ali. Think back to how desperately you wanted to know how I fared when you first came.

I tamped down on my rising panic and forced myself to remember back. It wasn't hard. I'd been desperate to know I hadn't harmed him or his magic permanently. I tried again, with more force of will. *I need to return to my own body, my own head.*

My perspective shifted. Kovis lay on his back beside me, one hand beneath his head, the other by his side.

I rose on an elbow and leaned over, planting a kiss on his lips. "Thank you for getting me there and back again."

"I've found that it's a matter of willing something. Our bond somehow understands our desires."

"If they're strong enough," I cautioned.

"Yes, but now that you've done it again, I want to experiment more with our connection and see what else we can do with it."

"Bend the cold to our will?" I laughed.

"Don't laugh, you may not be far off. It could just be a question of our imaginations and what we need."

"But how? This isn't our magical affinities, is it?"

"I think we can leverage them, but no. I believe it's far more. We have something very special. Jathan mentioned reading about couples who were paired. I haven't investigated all he'd learned about them though."

"Why us?" I asked.

"Who knows. Maybe we were joined because you were my sand maiden, maybe the gods knew we'd need it to face whatever is in store, I've no idea. But we have it, so let's figure out what we can do with it."

'*... whatever is in store...*' The thought made my stomach tense.

● ● ●

Chapter Seven

We'd escaped a dire situation with those mares. Somehow the thought did little to ease my mind. It could have easily gone the other way. What would we have done then? The pesky notion just wouldn't leave me alone.

"It's dry," I said of Kovis's sap "bandage."

I'd practiced joining and returning from Kovis's mind several more times as the sun rose more than halfway to its peak. It got easier, although I doubted I'd ever get over the disorientation of being in two heads at once.

Thankfully the air had warmed with the sun's climb, but a chill still beset me in the shade of the dense woods. My sappy hand was still sticky although some of that sap had hardened too. It would definitely be a while before it wore off. I rubbed it in the dirt again to coat the worst of it.

"We need to clean up," Kovis said as I helped him up. He wobbled as blood rushed to his head but he declared himself fit before putting weight on his leg. While tender, he took a tentative step, then another.

I took his arm with my sapless hand and helped him hobble through the carnage, steadying him at points. The further we got from camp, the cleaner the air, and I breathed in deeply. I'd gotten accustomed to the stench, but fresh air cleansed my nose.

We walked the distance to a trio of hot spring pools that ran above and below ground throughout the woods. They were the sole source of water for the area.

Steam rising off the surface of one beckoned to me and I padded across the flat, wet stones, waded into the largest of the three, and sat.

Oh, blessed heat. A moan escaped as warmth surrounded me.

Kovis paused on shore. "Will the sap wash out?"

"No, it's waterproof."

He hissed as he eased into the pool beside me a heartbeat later.

The water turned crimson, cleansing us of the gore of battle and I sucked in a deep breath then dipped under.

I'd been focused on other things and hadn't had time to contemplate the source of the blood that covered every bit of me. But as I did, revulsion filled me, and I scrubbed harder, the task made more difficult with the use of just one hand. It took three dunks before I felt clean, well, all but my hand. It would definitely be a while.

Kovis had cleaned himself up too and again looked the part of my handsome, dashing prince. "Better?"

"Much." I'd finally stopped shivering and my body went slack from exhaustion, along with my mind. Kovis seemed to sense my condition because he laid back in the bubbling water, not saying a word.

We lounged, enjoying the quiet, and I picked at hardened sap. I let the smell of fallen leaves soothe my soul as I laid my head against the side of the pool and watched birds dart past and the occasional butterfly flutter by. A gentle breeze rustled colored leaves. *This* was the image I'd painted of what I'd thought this adventure would be like. If only.

My toes had shriveled by the time Kovis broke the quiet. "I'm impressed with your healing abilities. To think what could have happened if those mares—"

"Thank you. But let's not talk about what could have happened. It didn't. But I would like to talk about what *is* happening. I wake before the sun every morning because I'm freezing, and it's only going to get colder. We need supplies—blankets, warmer clothes, bandages perhaps"—I raised an eyebrow—"maybe a pan. And what I'd give for coffee."

"Have I ever told you how seductive you are when you talk like that?" He wagged his brows.

"Kovis, I'm serious."

"And where do you propose we procure such items?"

"There has to be a village around somewhere."

"You'd risk it?" Worry clouded his beautiful blue and hazel eyes.

"It's not even close to winter, and I'm already a shivering mess every morning."

"Looks like you've made up your mind."

I tilted my head and gave him a pointed look.

"Well, at least we have something to trade for what we need. Those pelts should fetch a pretty sum once we clean them up."

"You did notice their stench, yes?"

"If they're like kelpies, they'll have stink glands. Once we find them, we can get rid of the smell."

My eyes went wide. "Kelpies? You've dealt with the beasts?"

"I've heard." He laughed.

I exhaled sharply. "I hope you're right, because you won't be able to give them away at this rate. But even if we can, they're purple. Won't people wonder what happened or where we got them?"

He wrinkled his brow. "I'll tell whoever we trade with that... my wife... loves the color purple so we dyed them. Happy wife, happy life and all."

I splashed him. "You think they'll believe it?"

"I don't think we have a choice."

• • •

"Fair enough."

Kovis rolled toward me with a hungry look in his eyes. "Enough about those beasts. You seem to have warmed up."

I nodded and bit my lip. I knew that look.

He brushed my wet locks aside and pressed a kiss to my nose, then moved on to my ears and downward. He had definitely recovered.

My core was toasty by the time we climbed out of the hot spring. Kovis took my nonsticky hand in his, and we ambled back to camp to find our clothes. The stench lingered but seemed to be dissipating, or perhaps my nose was adjusting to it.

———

It took the rest of the sun to properly clean and prepare the enormous pelts. Kovis had been right about the stench. It died as he carefully removed the scent organs and buried them. And despite the risk, the possibility of supplies—coffee even—lightened Kovis's spirits too, and he joked as we worked. Amazingly enough, I dripped sweat before we finished.

The sun had set by the time we'd cleansed camp and the horses of that layer of dried blood and laid out the pelts to dry.

"We might as well eat the meat rather than have it go to waste," Kovis said.

I wrinkled my nose. "I've never tasted mare, never had the desire to, never had the opportunity, and I'm okay with that."

"Think of it as sustenance." He grinned.

I rolled my eyes making him laugh. "Fine."

Kovis grabbed a chunk of what we'd discarded, cut a couple thick steaks, and rigged up a makeshift spit for over our fire.

"Amazing. They don't smell half bad," I said not long after, as they roasted.

Despite what he'd mentioned earlier, I'd still imagined their stench oozing out of the meat. Those beasts were evil through and through in life; surely they wouldn't give up their noxious ways in death. But they were proving me wrong. Small mercy.

As we were about to dive into our dinner, Kovis tapped a finger against his lips, silencing what I was about to say.

What now? I asked down our bond.

I don't know. I was afraid predators might smell our kills, and it seems they have.

My stomach tensed as we set our steaks aside and rose, taking ready positions, searching the edge of the clearing, bracing.

I spotted our "foe" in a heartbeat and yipped as Kennan, atop Onyx, emerged grinning from the trees.

Chapter Eight

Kennan spread his arms wide as he said, "Brother! Ali! I *finally* found you. You made it nearly impossible, but I know your tricks."

Kovis and my heads jerked back. My face was no doubt a mirror of Kovis's. I reflexively drew a hand to my chest.

"Ken… Kennan you're here." I exhaled a shaky breath but didn't move. My thoughts raced. *He's okay. He's okay… How did he find us? Is he still possessed? If he touches us, will he drag us to Dream? Will it kill us going that way?*

The last time we'd seen Kovis's twin, Father possessed him—his brown eyes had been cloudy and his voice that of my father. Neither seemed to be true now, but still…

My stomach clenched when Kennan slid off his horse and raced for us, throwing his arms around his brother. "I wondered if I'd ever find you. It's so good to see you."

I tensed.

"I was worried for you too, brother." Kovis hugged him tight.

When nothing nefarious happened, I exhaled.

"You'd never believe what I've been through."

Kovis pulled back and grinned. "On the contrary, I'll believe about anything considering Ali's father possessed you the last time we saw you."

Kennan's eyes bulged as he looked between Kovis and me. "What?" Disbelief filled the one syllable.

I laughed, and Kennan turned and wrapped his arms around me in a hug.

"I missed you too," I said.

Kennan didn't reply but buried his face deeper in my shoulder as he tightened his embrace. It felt as though he saw me as some long-lost treasure he was afraid of losing again. His hug lingered and bordered on uncomfortable before I pushed back.

Kovis tilted his head and furrowed his brow, questioning his sibling's behavior. I responded with a raised eyebrow of my own.

He's been through a lot, I told Kovis.

I can only imagine.

"Come sit. Let's hear your tale." I took Kennan's hand and lead him to a log near the crackling fire.

"Say, that smells good. I haven't eaten in…" He shook his head.

"Roast mare," Kovis informed.

"Mare? Wait. You don't mean those creatures that caused Rasa all those nightmares a few moons ago?"

"He does, and they are." I smiled. "Normally they're invisible, but they materialized when we killed them. Nice pelts, don't you think?" I pointed at the six skins laid out fur-side down opposite the fire.

"What? How? Wait, is it the firelight or… is that fur purple?" His mouth fell open.

"Yes they're purple, but that's another story. Let's eat before our dinner overcooks." Kovis bent over the fire and freed the two steaks from the spit, then replaced them with one from our stores. There was no shortage of the meat. I only hoped it was savory, unlike those creatures when alive. I could imagine it giving me indigestion or worse.

• • •

Once we'd all dug in, Kennan asked, "What did you mean by, 'I was possessed by your father'?"

"Just that. My father spoke through you. I don't know how, but he controlled your body."

Kennan stared at me, mouth gaping. "He... he..."

"Yes. You sounded exactly like him when you spoke. He's done something to my sister, Alfreda. It's the only way."

"My sand maiden." Kennan's voice was a whisper as he tried to digest it all. He set his steak back down on his makeshift plate, a flat rock. "But I thought...."

Kovis rubbed his jaw, and I leaned in.

"I thought I'd been dreaming, that it had all been one horrendous nightmare. I had a sense of time passing, and I vaguely remember seeing you at The Ninety-Eight, but it was a blur...." His voice trailed off.

I reached over and placed a hand on his.

He looked up, into my eyes with a pleading look. "I thought it was the gods punishing me for what I'd allowed to happen to you in prison, that or I'd lost my sanity."

I inhaled sharply as thoughts of all I'd endured at his hands again flooded my mind.

Kovis put a hand on my arm, his gaze darting between us.

I was thankful for the anchor. Moons before when Kennan apologized for not believing me and torturing me on that chair, I'd forgiven him. His acknowledgement had been enough to repay the torture, but I hadn't forgiven him for the sexual abuse.

I honestly didn't know if I could—I'd been violated. It had been so personal, so invasive, so inhumane. I'd committed to not expending energy nursing ill feelings because I refused to let it control me, and it hadn't. But I hadn't forgotten. I'd vowed to take action to change things myself if Kennan didn't, but even that I wasn't sure would be the balm I needed to put it behind me.

Kennan continued, "I know I apologized before, but..." His chin began to tremble. "Ali, I lied to you. We weren't following that intake manual."

I jerked my head back, and my thoughts stumbled. He'd lied?

Kennan held up a hand. "Please hear me out."

He'd lied? About why he'd abused me? He'd seemed so sincere, and I'd bought it. I'd been contemplating ways to reform that manual as a way to fix the situation so it never happened to anyone else. It had helped me begin to heal. But he'd lied about it? Disbelief flooded my mind. I couldn't rein in my anger, and I shouted, "You lied to me?"

"Ali, please. Listen to me."

Kovis squeezed my arm and shook his head as he glanced up at his twin.

Kennan barreled on before I could stop him. "Kovis was in agony and bleeding when they found you in his bedroom. *He'd been asleep.*" Even now his words oozed with terror. "After all that's happened to my siblings—" He sucked in a breath. "—I panicked. I needed answers, and I was committed to getting them by whatever means, especially when...." He let the words fall.

I finished his sentence, "Especially when the story I told you wasn't believable." My shoulders curled in, and Kennan looked at the ground. It felt like he punched me in the emotional gut.

I'd taken responsibility for that part. I hadn't expected my arrival to create the stir it had, and I hadn't invented a credible story. He'd seen my tale as stalling and gotten completely fed up. It was hard to breathe as my thoughts whirled. Groping had been him lashing out when he'd reached his wits end and still hadn't gotten answers out of me.

"It doesn't explain why you lied." I tensed my jaw, and my voice came out cold. "Why did you blame your treatment on the manual?"

Kennan closed his eyes. Then in not more than a whisper, he confessed, "Because I'm weak. What I allowed was despicable. Terror clouded my judgment. It wasn't until this nightmare, or whatever this was, that I could even admit to myself that I was capable of... of that. It was too awful."

He opened his eyes, turned, and looked into mine. "It's why I'm confessing all of this to you, the first chance I've had. Because you need to know the truth. So you can heal."

Words abandoned me. So I could heal? He'd lied about why he'd treated me as he had. I thought I'd begun healing, but it had been a rouse.

Kennan grew anxious with my silence and began, "I'll resign my position." His pace picked up. "I don't deserve to hold that role after what I allowed. I'll personally see that those guards are punished. I'll—"

I put my hand over his mouth as I barely leashed my anger. I didn't want to hear any more from him. I shuddered to think what Father had put him through to produce this, but he'd lied. I'd believed Kennan's first apology, and the truth stung.

My stomach churned as I let the silence drag on. I counted to ten, then to fifty before rational thoughts surfaced. His first apology hadn't borne introspection and self-loathing, not like this. Evil in me longed to prolong his discomfort. He'd wronged me, and I wanted my pound of flesh. But that wasn't me. I wasn't vengeful. If I succumbed to that darkness, I'd never find my way out. That path was only death.

I considered his words again, forcing myself to remain calm. I knew he'd spoken truth—he was earnest. He'd been brought low by the horror of his actions.

It took me several breaths to compose myself enough to speak. "Kennan, thank you for admitting that. I suppose it makes more sense, but it doesn't erase the emotional scars you caused me. It's hard to think about, let alone try to get past." I shook my head. "How I wish I could just let go of it, but I can't. It's not that simple. I can't erase the memory of how it made me feel."

Kennan nodded.

Kovis studied the ground, taking it all in. He looked conflicted. Kennan was stepping up and becoming responsible—his lack of leadership had caused Kovis no little angst—but lying about the manual didn't sit right with him either. I could see it in his eyes. No doubt it's why he hadn't reacted more forcefully early on—he hadn't known the extent of my abuse.

Kennan looked to Kovis. "Brother, I'm sorry I made this so difficult for you. I knew you didn't approve of those guards, but I now understand why you demand better from anyone you allow to protect you and Rasa."

Kovis nodded. "I'd hoped you'd eventually come around."

Kennan looked back to me.

"I need time." I fisted a hand.

Kovis gently squeezed my arm, letting me know he'd be there to help in whatever way I needed.

Kennan bobbed his head, and silence again reined across our campsite.

The fire crackled and waved. A pair of owls chatted.

Kennan finally broke the quiet. "It seems I'm wrongly giving the gods credit for my lesson. So if it truly is your father who did this to me, what happened to your sister? Is she okay?"

My stomach tensed. "I don't know. It's why Kovis and I are trying to find a safe way to go to Dream. We have to save Alfreda."

Kennan's eyes bulged at hearing that, or I thought it had been because of that. But he took on a conflicted look, and his breathing grew ragged. "No! You can't! I won't let you!" His dinner fell to the ground as he leapt up and held his head.

"Kennan! What's wrong?" Kovis and I yelled.

"Don't come close! Don't touch me!" He waved his arms.

The night had grown dark, but in the firelight it looked like milk had been added to his tea-brown eyes.

And then Father spoke through Kennan once more. "Alissandra, you've been a hard one to find. Your human has made it difficult to say the least, but no matter. Now come to me."

My breathing grew ragged.

Father had found us. It felt like someone wrung my stomach out like a wet rag.

Kennan had gone still beside the fire where he'd fled. My heart ached for him. No matter what he'd done, no one deserved to be a puppet. What horrific things was Father doing to Alfreda in this heartbeat? She'd never willingly allow this.

Despite my inner turmoil, I replied, "I can't do that, Father."

"You anger me, daughter. The longer you resist, the longer this one will experience my displeasure."

My breath quickened, but Kovis put a reassuring arm around me.

Father chuckled. "You do realize that Alfreda's human's romantic feelings for you, confirmed by that secret, but oh-so-passionate kiss you two shared is the only thing that has kept him sane as he traipsed about the wilderness in search of you? If he didn't believe you love him more than his brother and would eventually marry him, he'd have no hope to cling to."

I froze. Father would spare no weapon in this fight. He'd rummaged through Kennan's mind and found everything he could to control me, then carefully calculated the deployment. The fact that it had been Kennan's mouth delivering the confession made it all the worse, and he knew it. He'd planned it that way.

Kennan let out a howl and waved his arms. "No! I won't let you have me again… or them! I won't!" His body squirmed and danced erratically, clearly trying to expel Father but to no avail.

Kennan stumbled over to where Onyx had been grazing on low-hanging leaves beside Alshain and Fiona. He crawled up into the saddle and, with great difficulty, compelled the stallion forward into the trees.

"Kennan! Kovis, stop him!" I ran after him. He was crazy to try to navigate through the woods at this time of night.

The darkness quickly swallowed him up, and it wasn't long before the sound of hoofbeats faded. He was saving us from Father. I held myself, staring after him.

At length, I turned around and my heart climbed into my throat. Kovis stood with his head down, arms at his sides, shoulders slumped.

In the blink of an eye, I knew. I'd never told him about that kiss.

Chapter Nine
Kovis

"Is it true?"

The words felt like sand on my tongue. I didn't look up. I couldn't. I longed for it to be a lie, but my gut told me otherwise.

She hadn't protested his words.

Ali's father was a god and a brilliant strategist. He would never invent a weapon like that, not when the truth would be that much more damaging. And Kennan had given him an arsenal, it seemed.

Ali grabbed my arm. "Kovis… let me explain."

It was happening again. Dierna had hidden the truth too. The noise of blood rushing through my veins drowned out all sound even as Ali tugged me back to the log. I didn't want to listen to her pleas to understand.

My whole body felt numb as I collapsed to sitting. The night was dark, so, so dark. They'd kissed. My twin and Ali had kissed… passionately. And Kennan… his betrayal was even worse. He had romantic feelings for Ali. They had to be strong if they were what gave him hope through his ordeal. He wanted me out of the picture. My twin. How could he do that to me?

It had to have been some kiss. Kennan believed Ali loved him more than me. What else had they done together? I was the idiot once more. Why did I let myself trust again? Why?

I covered my face in my hands.

Ali tried to pull them away. "Kovis, you *have* to listen."

All those promises that we'd never hide anything from each other, they were platitudes. What a farce. I'd believed I could bare my very soul to her, and I had. This was what I got for it. Who could I ever trust?

"Kovis, please. It was an accident."

I pulled my arm from her clutches. I needed space. Passionate kisses weren't accidents.

Ali finally composed herself, placing her hands in her lap and sat staring at me, no doubt collecting her thoughts. Mother's ring glinted on her finger in the firelight. It seemed a dozen annums since I'd given it to her after professing my love. Now it mocked me, shouting what a fool I'd been.

"Kovis, I love you and only you with my whole heart. Not Kennan, but you. My father knows that, and he's jealous. I'm not the naïve little girl I once was, and he wants to destroy us. He thinks he can have my affections all to himself again."

I met her gaze. "Your father is a brilliant strategist. With all due respect, I understand why he said what he did. That doesn't excuse what happened. I thought we had an understanding that we would always be completely honest with each other, but apparently I was mistaken." I shook my head. "If you'll excuse me, I've lost my appetite. I'm going to turn in."

"Kovis...." Her voice fell silent.

I couldn't make sense of that kiss. Treachery from my own twin. My heart felt like it was shrinking.

I blew out a long breath and refocused on our situation, right here, right now. It was the only way I could cope.

Ambien knew where we were.

Regardless of what had happened, Kennan was still my brother and had protected us. He was again possessed, but the fact that he'd run despite Ambien's will told me he still had some control. He wouldn't come back, not this night.

So unless the god had another means of attack at hand, there was no point in risking our, or our mounts, necks moving camp in the middle of the dark. My wards would alert us to any surprises.

I just prayed kinder gods protected Kennan. My chest tightened.

Ali hadn't moved from near the fire and it highlighted the tears that streaked her cheeks but I refused to be moved. She well and truly had betrayed me and it seared my very soul.

She looked on silently as I checked the dryness of the pelts and, finding the moisture nearly gone, used my Air magic to finish the process on two of them.

I flipped one over and set the other atop to form a fur-lined bed. I didn't care that we wouldn't touch tonight, damn the consequences. I wouldn't sleep anyway, not at all, my stomach was in knots, but at least I'd be comfortable.

I hadn't said anything more, and I wondered what Ali would decide to do when she retired. But I wasn't surprised when she followed my example with two pelts of her own a while later. Wise decision.

I lay on my back and feigned sleep while she dried her bedding. I didn't want to interact with her. None of the reasons we'd originally taken to sleeping together mattered anymore. This would be the first time in moons we wouldn't share intimacy, and I was okay with that.

I huffed, had we ever?

My stomach remained cramped even after Ali's breathing slowed a long while later. *Glad one of us could sleep*, the mocking thought drifted across my consciousness.

My thoughts still raced and twisted with all that had happened. Funny, I'd thought my life was improving. My heart had begun to thaw as I let her in to see the real me, and then this happened. What an idiot I was. Bile rose in my gut.

My mind tormented me, rehashing so many moments with her that I'd taken comfort in. Had they all been lies?

How could she have kissed Kennan passionately? How?

I couldn't wrap my head around it. How could he have romantic feelings for her? I was his brother. How could he do that to me? How long had it been going on between them? And under my nose.

I needed to think on something else or I'd make myself sick. Despite what had happened, we still needed to work together to stop her father from conquering Wake. Tonight's events would add an extra measure of challenge, but it wasn't a question, god or not, Ambien couldn't control Wake's citizens. And clearly Ali's sister needed rescuing.

Then there was the question of survival. I knew from the annums I'd been at the front in the wars that, if we split up, we'd never make it on our own out in this inhospitable wilderness—some beast was always looking for an easy dinner. No, we would need to somehow come to an understanding and work together. Too much was riding on us.

Regardless of my thoughts about Ali, she had been right about needing supplies. Autumn was lengthening, and winter might well arrive before she figured out how to get to Dream. We'd need blankets and warmer clothes at a minimum. And I wouldn't complain if we managed to get coffee in the process.

But as of tonight, we had another problem. Kennan had run off to protect us, but her father now knew where we were. We'd need to get a long way away from here before more of his mares arrived, because I knew he would send them, if he hadn't already given the order.

My thoughts shifted to what we'd need to do to stop Ali's father once we reached Dream. It was a subject I'd mulled countless times while Ali practiced her magic as we rode, but I hadn't yet settled on a plan. I knew next to nothing about Dream, nothing but what Ali had told me, and I hadn't yet gotten creative enough to form a coherent strategy.

● ● ●

We'd be fighting at least one god, Ambien. Who knew if other gods supported him. Or, even if they didn't support him outright, would a family member or relation be rankled if we tried to stop him? I'd been thinking through the legends of the gods I'd been told countless times as bedtime stories by a nanny or two. They weren't beings to take lightly. I shuddered to think what we'd face.

Even if we had just one god to fight, Ambien was powerful. How exactly did one stop a god? The only thing I'd come up with so far was to ask Dyeus to intervene. He was king of the gods. Surely Ambien would have to obey him, right? It didn't escape my notice that Dyeus had killed his own father to gain his position, and I held *great* respect for him as a result.

Hopefully, Ali or one of her relatives would have enough influence to make a request for his help, because I wasn't naïve enough to believe one could just waltz into his throne room and ask.

The sky lightened to gray. My mind was still a swirl of unanswered questions, but some of my initial anger was subsiding. I still didn't care to hear Ali's weak excuses, but I was resolved to work with her, although I'd learned my lesson. I would guard my heart while we did—guard my heart and block my mind from her.

I was done opening myself up. It only led to pain.

Chapter Ten

I woke with the light, for the first time in moons, not shivering. But in the blink of an eye, the situation came front and center as I found myself alone between the two layers of skins—the skins of my mortal enemies, not Kovis, had kept me warm through the night. How ironic.

I pushed back the wave of sadness that threatened to crash over me. It would do no good. Kovis had taken the news as I'd feared he would, which was why I'd never brought it up. I'd been a wimp, too scared of his reaction.

A groan escaped me. My lack of courage had cost both of us. He was right to be upset. If he'd done the same with another lady, I would have felt betrayed too. But I wasn't Dierna. I was in the wrong and would make it up to him—if he'd let me.

I glanced over to see that Kovis had risen, dressed, and had much of our camp packed on Alshain and Fiona, including four of the pelts that we'd use to pay for supplies. I only hoped a night of rest had opened him to hearing the truth of what had happened between his brother and me.

"We need to move out quickly," Kovis informed me a heartbeat later. "No doubt your father has already dispatched troops to capture us. We need to get as far away from here as possible. Breakfast is on the fire. Eat while I pack up the last of camp."

No humor. As serious as a dragon on the hunt. My hope of talking it out this sun evaporated. I prayed the situation wouldn't last as long as before. I didn't know if I could endure that, especially out in the middle of nowhere with no one else to talk to.

Kovis seemed to be walking fine, not favoring his right leg, as he finished packing up. That seemed the only positive, although he'd have a scar.

He took to petting the horses whose back sides were mounded high with the bulky pelts. Despite being rolled up, the purple-furred skins would come to at least the middle of my back when I sat in the saddle, if not higher. Thankfully, the horses didn't seem to mind. They continued munching leaves from the trees they were tethered to.

I finished breakfast and spread out the coals to extinguish our fire. My sticky, sap-coated hand made it harder, but I managed. Kovis's body was loose as he talked to and stroked Alshain, but in the blink of an eye, as I approached, he tensed.

I stopped beside Fiona. "Would you please help me up?" I reached up, ready to grab the horn when it came level.

He came around behind me and, without a word, placed his hands on my waist. There was none of his usual playfulness or taking liberties with a few of my other parts—he used my vulnerability to tickle me, and I usually ended up shrieking, amusing him greatly, before I sat atop my mount. A heartbeat later, I perched in the saddle and he turned back to untie our horses.

Kovis handed me my reins, mounted his stallion, and with a clicking sound, moved Alshain into the dense forest. Fiona followed without protest.

We needed to trade these pelts for supplies, but with things as they were, I wondered if he'd decided not to. Who knew what this sun would bring… other than an overabundance of silence. That seemed assured.

Kovis had mentioned several suns before that he believed we'd reached Astana province. The territory had been the second to fall in his father's conquest of the seven territories surrounding the magical Elementis empire. Its people, insorcelled, or nonmagical, lived by a proud warrior code that I'd first learned about during The Ninety-Eight. Nomarch Norman presided over this region from its capital, Rothan, in the north, on behalf of the empire.

Unlike Elsor, which had grown strong by building infrastructure with the infusion of money from the empire, Astana hadn't seemed to fare as well. Whether it had been squandered or the nomarch had grown rich at the expense of his people, I didn't know. It just seemed primitive. At least that was my impression from the areas we'd skirted so far. Kovis had said its capital was much nicer and that he'd purposely kept us away from civilization.

I sure hoped so because my heart went out to anyone who had to live this way. Perhaps I was just done with the whole outdoor life, but to have to do this annum round… definitely not for me.

Kovis sat up straight in the saddle ahead of me. Normally, such a posture set me on edge because it's what he did when he sensed danger, but I doubted that to be the case this morning.

I checked our bond, but it felt cold and lifeless. He'd blocked it somehow. I'd have to ask him how sometime. Probably something to do with desire, or in this case desiring not to have anything to do with me.

I sighed then continued picking at the dried sap still coating much of my hand as Fiona moved us forward along the forest path. It was becoming a habit, but I was making some progress. I turned my focus to the woods. All was peaceful. I wished I could say the same of myself and my thoughts.

The longer the silence between Kovis and I stretched, the more antsy I grew. I needed to distract myself. I decided to practice nuancing my Air affinity. It would consume my attention, I had no doubt.

Leaves had turned colors and dropped with the changing of the seasons, and there was no shortage of them scattered along either side of the path. I closed my eyes and pictured lifting just one leaf and drawing it to myself, like I'd attempted countless times before.

I *would* figure this out. I put the reins in my sappy hand and held the other out, palm up, feeling the air as it flowed between my fingers. I'd usually send it crashing into my target at this point, but I waited and let the air continue flowing across my hand.

I concentrated until a picture filled my mind: it felt like threads of air cocooned it like a living glove. If I could send just one finger's worth of air at the pile, surely it wouldn't scatter all the leaves about. Then I could work on grabbing just one. But first things first. I imagined redirecting the air flowing around my pointer finger toward the leaves littering the right side of the path.

The puff of air stirred up a handful of red, orange, and gold leaves. Fiona didn't complain about the disturbance. "I did it! Kovis, I did it!"

Kovis remained a statue atop Alshain. I stuck out my tongue. It didn't matter. It was the first step, and I'd finally done it. I'd celebrate my success.

Now, to grab just one leaf and float it to me. I continued practicing until we emerged from the forest into a sloped glade and I had nothing more to practice with.

Waist-high grasses grew sparsely, like the hair atop a balding man's head. It looked like giants had played a game of catch, because boulders were randomly scattered across the undulating hillside.

The sun had just passed its peak when Kovis pulled Alshain to a halt. I drew even.

"I believe the village of Sanis is just over that ridge," he informed.

I wouldn't ask how he'd deduced that; it was the first thing he'd said since sun up, and I wouldn't risk silencing him. I was just glad to hear he still planned to attempt to trade for supplies.

"If any citizens attended The Ninety-Eight, they will have returned a moon or two ago, and the village may not take kindly to us if they know we're sorcerers."

I slapped the leathers covering my thigh. Of course, how could I not have realized? Rasa's declaration about ending The Ninety-Eight, an event that celebrated the proud traditions of the insorcelled provinces, hadn't gone over well. It had never occurred to me that we'd be attempting a trade with these same folks who had felt shunned.

My conversation with Nomarch Kett during the championship dinner had opened my eyes to seeing more than one view of their traditions, most of which at first glance seemed barbaric, and I'd purposed to learn more, but this didn't seem the time.

"Our dress will give us away. We'll need to borrow a few clothes."

I'd grown accustomed to our leathers despite their inadequacies with the cooling temperatures. Mine were certainly well worn by now—they'd abandoned their creaking ages ago.

"How do we do that?" I kept my tone even.

"They hang wash out to dry."

I gave Kovis a long look, but he made a clicking sound and eased Alshain into a trot. Fiona followed. He had a plan. It was more than I'd known of his thoughts all sun.

We'd need two blankets at this rate. I frowned then stopped myself. No, I deserved this. Kovis's hurt and silence were my fault. I should expect nothing less.

Warmer clothes. Maybe coffee. I forced myself to think on these little luxuries. I just hoped the pelts fetched a good sum despite their color.

I saw the first humble homestead as we crested the hilltop. The dirty gray house, which I guessed had originally been white, looked as old as time itself. It leaned toward one side, like someone resting against a wall, except there was no wall to support it. Its roof dipped in the middle. Chickens pecked about the yard. The skeleton of a barn, which hadn't been so fortunate, had collapsed and its bones jutted up at odd angles not far away.

A ways on, we approached another sorry farm, nearly identical to its neighbor. The scene repeated itself multiple times. But I knew that we'd nearly reached the village when houses began to be situated closer together and were in better repair.

Kovis stopped his stallion behind a pair of ancient shade trees and dismounted. Such towering giants were scarce in these parts, and he must have figured they would be about the only cover for the horses. At least that was my theory. I checked our bond to see if I was right, but he continued to block me. The ache in my heart grew.

He helped me down from Fiona without a word then tied the pair to a low branch. I crouched beside them, mirroring him as he scanned the area.

Several hundred yards away, the road passed by a shortish stone wall. On the far side of the wall stood a one-story wattle and daub home. Sticks, twigs, and grasses had been woven together to form its walls, then covered with mud.

Two clotheslines stretched across much of the ample yard— they were what had prompted our stop. It must have been wash day for the lines sagged under the weight of a plethora of men's, ladies', and children's clothes.

I felt guilty. Nearly all of the garments bore patches. These people needed what few clothes they possessed.

"We'll return them, don't worry," Kovis whispered. "We're only borrowing them."

He'd listened in to my thoughts. Maybe there was hope for us yet.

He scanned both directions up and down the road then focused his attention on the line. Dust stirred in the yard. He was using his winds. I prayed the homeowners didn't notice. A heartbeat later a clothespin leapt from the line, then another, freeing a girl's lavender print dress that shot across the road, right to me and I caught it.

"See if it's the right size."

I held it up. "I may be small, but I'm not this small." The dress looked to be for a child with its narrow waist and bust.

Kovis motioned to give it back to him, which I did, and he whisked it back across the wall and replaced it on the line. It wasn't quite how we'd found it, but it would do.

He retrieved a woman's sky-blue dress next. It would be a bit long on me, but it would work.

He floated a pair of brown trousers and a coordinating long-sleeved, collarless shirt over for himself. Our boots would have to do because we had no other footwear options. Good thing the skirt was long.

While it seemed we had no company, I moved Fiona away from Alshain to give us room between them to change. I had become comfortable naked with Kovis in the wilderness but had no desire to expose myself to strangers, and the pair provided adequate covering.

I stripped off my leathers, down to my braies, then hoisted the overlarge woolen dress over my head and let it fall. Roomy would be an understatement as I attempted to adjust the bust to cover my breasts and not my midriff. Thankfully work dresses were usually loose and this one had a sash. I'd stuff the excess fabric into the skirt, then tie it. Hopefully I wouldn't need to move much, or it would come out.

Kovis watched but said nothing as I removed my ring. It would look out of place, but it pained me all the same as I put it in the bottom of my saddle bag so nothing would happen to it. My finger felt naked.

I rewove my braid. No sense in looking like we'd been living in the wilderness. My hair had grown out again, and I'd taken to wearing it that way.

Kovis preferred my hair down and loose. He said its unusual light blonde color made him want to run his hands through it. And he had. Frequently. Not that he'd be looking to do so this sun. My sadness grew heavier as I finished my braid. At least it was functional and kept my hair out of the way. It would make me fit the role of the impoverished citizens we needed it to.

Kovis had fared better it seemed as I looked him up and down. At least the shirt fit him, although the trousers were overlarge in the waist. Holding his pants up with one hand, he wandered into the grass, bent down, cut a few stalks, then tied the ends together to form a length that would reach around his waist and secured it in front. Who needed a leather belt? It was probably closer to what folks in these parts did to hold their pants in place anyway.

"How do I look?" I asked.

He looked me over, but no passion sparked in his eyes. "It'll pass. Me?"

"Good. You look good," I replied in an even tone. He looked amazing. Not even these poor clothes could rob him of his good looks. But he probably wouldn't appreciate hearing me say that with him shutting me out.

The horses were overburdened already with the pelts, so after I pulled my dress up and Kovis hoisted me into the saddle, he handed me my leathers—we'd stash them close by, not weigh down our mounts more than necessary. We'd return for them, but they would betray us if anyone saw us with them.

I adjusted my skirt as much as possible to cover my boots. Kovis grabbed his leathers and mounted Alshain, then eased his stallion forward at a walk.

We ambled down the dusty road until another road, running perpendicular, appeared on our left, the only one that ran through town. Kovis directed us to the right to the nearest copse where we dropped our leathers and he stashed them out of sight.

Load lightened, Kovis had me ride even with him to create the impression that we were husband and wife. If only. I shoved the thought aside as we continued down the main street.

One and two-story wattle and daub buildings stood on either side with signs out front announcing the nature of business conducted inside: cobbler, tanner, smithy, farrier, tavern, and more.

Townspeople stopped and stared as we passed. Despite our change of appearance, we were strangers and stood out.

Kovis ignored how out of place we looked. I found it hard to.

They're staring at the pelts, not us. Relax, Ali.

I chanced a look around. He was right. Their eyes lit on our furry cargo before curiosity drove their sight to us. But would they stay that way?

• • •

Chapter Eleven

My heart ached as Kovis schooled his features, *pretending* he loved
me as we stopped the horses before a building with a weathered
sign that read Ulster's Mercantile.

It had a wooden porch that wrapped around its front, and its
white paint was peeling. Playing the part of dutiful husband, he
dismounted and tied Alshain to the hitching post next to three other
mounts, then came around and helped me down.

Kovis extended his elbow, and I took hold, trying to keep the
stickiest part of my hand clear. I hitched up the overlong skirt and
prayed I wouldn't trip and draw more attention.

It felt like everyone nearby stared as we ascended the four steps
and strode inside, although my mind was probably exaggerating. I
was glad when the door closed behind us.

A man and a woman, who I presumed to be his wife, perused a
shelf of candles to our left. Another man whose muscles bulged
beneath his shirt looked over an assortment of axes. A woman with
two small children clinging to her skirts examined a metal washtub.

Pelts from a variety of animals hung from the rafters in the far
corner of the shop. We were in the right place. A handful of other

townsfolk milled about; I speculated they waited on a spouse and whiled away the time dreaming of owning a curiosity or two. The hum of chatter from neighbors exchanging news filled the place, and I relaxed.

The shopkeeper, Ulster, I presumed from the sign out front, emerged from the back.

Kovis stopped at the counter. "We were just passing through and would like to sell several pelts. Would you be the one to speak with?"

I stopped by his side.

Ulster furrowed his brow and looked first Kovis and then me up and down. "That all depends. You ain't from around these parts," he drawled. "Where you from?"

"Does it matter, sir?" Kovis asked, trying to steer the conversation back to safer territory. "We aren't looking for trouble. If we can just sell our pelts, we'll be on our way. They're burdening our mounts overly. And we need supplies."

Ulster's eyes roamed between Kovis and me, lips in a thin line. I couldn't begin to guess what he looked for—some invisible sign that told him he could trust us? Or was he trying to intimidate, he was insorcelled after all. Such behavior would probably be consistent with the picture originally painted for me that warriors sought to gain advantage over another in any way possible off the battlefield.

I resisted fidgeting and prayed our disguises made us look insorcelled, not that I had any clue what "looking insorcelled" meant. If he was sharp enough to know we bore magic, after Rasa's edict, we might be in trouble.

Too many politics to consider, I shut the thoughts out. I'd begun to question the whole narrative about warriors being barbarians after my conversation with Nomarch Kett at The Ninety-Eight championship dinner. I wouldn't indulge in speculation when Ulster hadn't done anything but scrutinize us.

Neither Kovis nor I flinched. Perhaps our calm or determination was what swayed him, but he finally said, "Fine, show me what you got."

Ali, gather the supplies we need while I negotiate a trade. I'll be right back.

I gave a small nod as he turned, then headed to the section where I'd seen blankets stacked. I bit my lip but grabbed two. A pot was next on the list, and I'd just located a modest selection of copper vessels with lids when I overheard Ulster.

"What in tarnation? These pelts is purple! What kind of beast is this? How'd you—" The shopkeeper's voice carried, and several patrons turned their heads.

I couldn't hear Kovis's reply. I guessed he intentionally spoke softly. He'd told me he used the tactic when people were upset because it nearly always calmed them down—they had to quiet down to hear him.

I waited to hear Ulster again. Would we need to make a hasty exit? I hoped not.

I waited, but not hearing any further exclamations from the shopkeeper, I went back to pan selection, deciding on a medium-size pot that would serve the purpose but not be too large to stow as we traveled.

Next up, rope, a metal poker that would double as a spit for roasting meat, salve and fabric to bandage wounds—gods forbid we needed it—woolen braies, and two fur-lined cloaks. I saved coffee for last as it was our one luxury. I hoped Ulster gave Kovis a good price for the furs.

Arms overflowing with my selections, I wove my way between the shelves and patrons, back to the front, laying everything down on the counter near Kovis.

Two women were chattering while running their hands through the purple fur of one pelt that was spread across the counter—if they only knew what manner of beast they fondled. I held back a snort.

Ulster was frowning, Kovis grinned. It seemed the pelts had just increased in value.

The shopkeeper said, "I'll give you a groat and peran for the lot of 'em."

Kovis frowned. "They're worth a crown and you know it."

"You said you needed to unburden your horses; I'm just trying to help," Ulster replied, as another shopper joined the first two.

I rolled my eyes. Perhaps the reputation of insorcelled people was more on point than I'd thought.

"Throw in these supplies, and you can have the pelts for a groat and peran," Kovis said.

Ulster's nod was begrudging at best, but he accepted.

I let out a breath. We'd both been worried about coming into town, being recognized, and having Father find us. It was looking like we'd get in and out without any problems.

"Hal!" A woman appeared from the back room. "I need—" She cut herself off, stopping behind the counter beside Ulster, who appeared to be her husband. "Oh, pardon me. Say, that's a pretty color on you, what with your golden hair."

I shifted nervously, hating the attention. "Thank you."

Time to go. Kovis picked up our provisions and nudged me.

"I have a dress the same color. It's my favorite," the woman continued, smiling.

"Thank you, but we best be on our way." I waved.

"Hey, wait..." The woman's mouth moved like a fish beneath her furrowed brow.

"What is it, Krea?" Ulster grumped. "Spit it out, woman."

"She's... That's my dress she's wearing!" The woman pointed and waved.

"Now, dear—" her husband objected.

Customers, disturbed by the outburst, started moving toward us.

Run! It took no convincing. Kovis grabbed all but the blankets, which I managed, and we raced for the door.

"And look! Hal! He's wearing your shirt! I'd recognize that stain. There, right by the collar! You got who knows what on it when you were putting stock away. I've never been able to get it out."

The burly man who'd been perusing axes stepped into our path. We couldn't both evade him with his arms stretched wide as they were. He grabbed me and held on tight despite my kicking. The blankets fell to the floor before me.

Another shopper grabbed Kovis from behind, forcing him to drop the rest of our supplies. Kovis was strong, but his captor had clearly spent time in the fields and had plenty of muscle of his own.

Don't use your magic, Kovis warned through the bond.

I nodded.

"You stole our clothes! Hal, they stole our clothes!" Krea ranted.

"Hush, woman," Ulster commanded, then scowled. "I thought something was familiar about you, but I couldn't place it. Now that she says it, I agree, you're wearing our clothes. Explain yourselves."

Every shopper in the store had been drawn by the commotion and surrounded us.

The man holding Kovis jerked his arms further back, forcing a grimace from my Dreambeam.

I gave my shoulder a strong jerk, even though I knew it was futile with this man's arms wrapped around me. He tightened his squeeze.

Don't fight him, Ali. Pretend you're just an average woman.

An average woman?

Don't let them know you have any idea how to fight. They could recognize you from The Ninety-Eight.

I stilled. *What are they going to do to us?* The question poured from me, despite knowing he knew no more than I did.

We need to wait and see; only then will we know how to fight.

Kovis had more experience dealing with conflict than me. I just hoped he could figure a way out of this.

Kovis met Ulster's eyes. "You are perceptive. Ma'am, I apologize. We meant only to borrow your clothes." Krea harrumphed. "You were correct, we aren't from these parts. We ran into a bit of foul luck and had nothing to wear into town that wouldn't offend your sensibilities."

Stretching the truth a bit, but it wasn't a lie.

"I want our clothes back! That's my favorite dress!" She glowered at us.

"You heard my wife." Hal nodded, and our captors released us.

I took a step away from Long-Arms. Kovis stretched his arms.

"Well…" Krea grew impatient and thrust her hands on her hips.

I caught her eyes. "What? Strip here?"

She crossed her arms and gave a single nod.

My mouth dropped open, and I glanced over at Kovis.

Do it.

"Shoulda thought about this before ya decided to steal from us," Krea griped as I reached to undo a bust button.

Kovis had the shirt and britches off in no time and handed them back to Hal. Krea swiped them away.

I felt every eye on me as I undid the final button, took a deep breath, and pulled the dress over my head. The woman grabbed it before I'd brought my arms fully down again. She turned with a huff, clutching the garments to her chest, and marched into the back.

I drew my arms close, covering my chest. Onlookers ran their eyes up and down my unmentionables.

"Hey, he's got a tattoo. See there." The observation came from a tall, skinny man standing at the back of gawkers. He pointed at the part of Kovis's tattoo that peeked above the neckline of his braies— the funnel cloud that depicted his Air magic. The ink changed from violet to bright red.

"It just changed colors!" a woman screeched.

"He's a sorcerer!"

I didn't know who shouted the last comment, but firm arms again captured Kovis. Grumbling and murmuring and all manner of complaining about Rasa's edict emanated from the crowd. Kovis had been right. Her declaration had not been well received among these people.

Hal stepped forward, drew his hand to the top of Kovis's braies and yanked, leaving everyone to ogle the design on Kovis's muscled chest.

"Hey, she's that girl who won The Ninety-Eight!" another onlooker announced. "I'd recognize that blonde hair anywhere!"

It didn't take them long to deduce the rest. If I'd won, Kovis had to be the crown prince, for he'd made no secret of his feelings for me at the tournament. A heartbeat later, arms again constricted me, and I felt a blade at my throat.

Really? I resisted rolling my eyes. Now that they knew our secret, this brute couldn't possibly believe he could hold me. And surely he didn't believe Kovis, the most powerful sorcerer the Altairn Empire had ever known, wouldn't fight back. He was crazy if he did. Who knew what they might do to us to voice their dissatisfaction to the empress.

This changes things, Kovis said.

I pulled my shoulders back despite strong arms. We would not be intimidated. I scanned those gathered and caught a man's gaze. He wouldn't be cowed—he stared right back. The woman beside him mimicked, fixing a piercing gaze on me.

But the next man's eyes were cloudy and I gasped.

What now? Kovis asked.

Cloudy eyes.

Kovis found the man I stared at. *Shit!*

I continued around to find another three with eyes bearing the same whitish cast. We'd evaded Father after Kennan found us, but he would again know our whereabouts.

Time to go before things get out of hand, Kovis declared, and with that he drew his foot back between his captor's legs, hooked one, and quickly straightened. The man wobbled, trying to regain his balance, but wasn't in time. Kovis pushed him down with his winds.

With the distraction, I brought my heel down hard on my captor's instep. He groaned as his grip on my arms slacked, and I slipped out, then used my own magic to force him to the floor.

Shall we? Kovis asked, stooping to pick up our supplies while I held the lot of them back with my Air magic.

Don't worry about nuancing your power, he added, to which I chuckled.

I caught movement in the crowd and grabbed a thread of Kovis's magic, conjuring an ice dagger, which I sent soaring at a hand that held a knife above the heads of onlookers. A yelp erupted from the back, and the weapon dropped from sight.

Nicely done. I thought I detected the hint of a smile, but he schooled his features once more.

Arms bulging, he nodded toward the door. I scooped the blankets up from the floor, and we beat a hasty, half dressed retreat.

Shouts, obscenities, and complaints about ungrateful sorcerers chased us, but my winds blocked anyone from leaving the store while Kovis strapped our purchases to the horses. He threw me up in my saddle, and we headed out of town at a gallop.

Shoppers spilled out into the street waving fists. A few raced after us. I turned around, and with a thought, our pursuers as well as the lot of gawkers collapsed into the dirt, fast asleep.

"Yes!" I celebrated, throwing a fist above my head, but Kovis didn't react. I sighed.

We stopped by the copse of trees just outside of town and retrieved our leathers. Despite Kovis's coldness, I released my pent-up energy by babbling about what we'd done to the horses who proved an attentive audience.

It felt good to have my leathers on again. I'd felt unprotected without them. I dug out my ring from the bottom of my saddle bag.

Kovis watched out of the corner of his eye. I knew he did. But he refrained from comment as I put it back on.

He could continue sulking all he wanted. Forget that I was responsible... I stopped the thought. No, I wasn't responsible for his moodiness. This was his choice. He wouldn't even listen to my explanation. I wouldn't allow his melancholy to squelch my joy.

I'd allowed his emotions to control me the last time, and it just made me miserable. It's what had spawned that forbidden kiss. And then I'd gone and ignored Kennan's council to not get wrapped up in Kovis's moods. Never again. Not if I could help it.

I forced a smile as I surveyed the blankets and cloaks strapped to the horses. With these and the abundance of other supplies, including coffee, no matter how long it took me to figure out how to return to Dream, I wouldn't wake up frozen anymore… whether Kovis and I shared intimacy or not.

The thought brought a fresh wave of hurt.

• • •

Chapter Twelve
Ambien

The rhythmic sounds of dripping water greeted me as I stopped just inside the entrance to the cave as the sun sank below the horizon. I forced my inhales to match the slow drip. Only after I'd calmed myself, did I stride forward.

Zagan, one of my mares, saluted. "My liege."

I returned his gesture then continued past. My objective lay in the heart of this cave. I took a hard right and ducked to avoid the low archway.

"Report."

Morfran, one of my commanders, bowed low before me. "It wasn't easy finding her, my liege. They tried to hide her, moving her between palaces. It took patience, but we finally secured her when she emerged from your sons' residence."

No surprise. They'd done the same trying to hide Alissandra. I met Velma's gaze. Even in the dim light of the cave, it was easy to see her wings tucked tightly, but she'd thrown back her shoulders.

Clenched fists rested on her hips as she tried to stare me down. There was no repentance, let alone fear in her. Silly child.

"Good work, Morfran. Dismissed." I nodded at Bate, the other guard, to leave us as well. This was a family matter that demanded discretion.

Alfreda sat rigid on the moss-covered bed, face drawn. My men had followed orders, that much was clear judging by the dark circles under her eyes. The bruise on her cheek disturbed me though. What measures had they been forced to go to to withhold sleep? And did she bear any other marks? I pushed the thought away. I'd address her treachery after.

I refocused on my eldest. "Your sister told me you were the one who facilitated Alissandra's… exodus to Wake."

"Escape, you mean?" Velma corrected, clenching a fist.

Was she trying to infuriate me? Surely, she didn't expect me to dismiss her behavior and let it go unpunished, but to anger me further was unwise, even for her.

"Semantics. So you admit it?" I continued.

"It was the best option in my judgment," Velma replied.

Matter of fact. No cowering despite what she surely had to know would happen. I respected that.

Alfreda whimpered behind her. "I didn't want to, Velma. He forced it out of me."

Her whimpering got under my skin, and I couldn't crush a growl. She'd been so strong under my questioning. Now she just sounded pitiful.

Velma didn't break eye contact with me. "I'm sure he did, sister. I hold no ill against you. No doubt you held out as long as you could."

"I must say I am impressed that you discovered a way to send your sister to Wake. It's not common knowledge that it's possible. There have been a few others who have made the journey, but never in such a fashion."

. . .

Velma's eyes grew large before she could school her expression again. Alfreda sucked in a breath and drew a hand to her mouth.

"Why are you telling me this, Father?" my eldest asked.

"Can't I praise my daughter?"

She didn't speak or break her stare.

"By doing what you did, I'm sure you realize you've created a problem for me. Yes, others of the gods have heard about it. Temis, Thena, they're just the ones I know of, but I'm sure there will be more."

Velma's expression didn't change, but Alfreda's eyes grew large. At least one of them was sharp enough to understand... or care.

Alfreda's look told me she remembered my reaction when the regents I'd appointed to oversee the provinces challenged my authority and forced us all into a war—several goaded me over it for eons, calling me weak. I'd vowed never to allow it to happen again.

Why oh why did it have to be my own daughter who'd challenged me?

"I am your Father, but perhaps you've forgotten I am also your sovereign. Velma, you have been disloyal, treasonous even. Do you know what the punishment for treason is?"

Velma clenched her jaw but made no reply.

How I respected her. If only every member of my family were as strong.

"Before I pronounce sentence, I want you to understand the full depth of what you did in convincing your sister to become mortal, because I'm not sure you do. If you did, I doubt you would have encouraged her." I took a deep breath. "Velma, to be mortal is to become less. You've sentenced your sister to death, but worse, you've condemned her to grieve the passing of those she loves."

Velma shifted her wings.

Yes, she should be uncomfortable.

I continued, pressing my point. She needed to understand. "As gods, the only time we are touched by tragedy is when we care for a mortal beyond helping them dream. When we become attached, we expend our energies doing what we must to care for them. It's our own choice to make, but if we do, it means we are no longer free. And worse than being a parent caring for the welfare of our immortal children, we are brought low and suffer because of *their* frailty. I should not have to remind you of Dyeus's grief and lamenting over his son Sarpedon's death. Or Thetis's knowledge that her son Chilles's life would be short and full of grief. She was reduced to groveling and making bargains with others of us gods in desperate attempts to save him. It was hard to watch. What she endured, I would not wish upon anyone, despite her bringing it on herself. She was shortsighted."

Velma tucked her wings tighter. "With all due respect, Father, I believe that loving has made Ali stronger and more courageous. Before her current charge, she was naïve and easily swayed."—she gave me a long look—"But as she has come to understand how she truly, deeply feels about him, she has taken a stand and will defend him, no matter what."

I barely hid a huff.

She continued, "Ali has grown in ways I never would have imagined. Yes, she will necessarily endure grief, but she can live fully, completely. Mortals, through their very mortality, have the potential for great nobility. Our lives seem trivial in comparison."

"You speak so highly of their lesser state, daughter. Do you wish me to send you to Wake? To make you human? Is that what you're saying?"

Velma's gaze held for several heartbeats before she looked away.

"I thought as much. Yours are the ideals of a spoiled child who has never experienced any degree of adversity."

Alfreda shot up, wings flaring. "Velma is not a spoiled child! No doubt she feels she needs to stay to protect us. You act like all you sought was Ali's good. You tortured her just like you're torturing me!"

"That's enough, Alfreda. I will deal with you shortly. Trust me when I tell you, you do not want me addressing your conduct until your sister and I have resolved this issue. Sit down and wait your turn quietly."

Alfreda glared for several heartbeats but at length she furled her wings once more and reseated herself on the mattress.

"That's a good girl. At least one of you obeys."

I returned my focus to Velma. "So now that you understand my perspective, perhaps you can understand the error of your ways."

Velma clenched her jaw. "We shall have to agree to disagree, Father."

I nodded. "I see. Very well, then I shall have to effect a punishment that may assist you in reaching my conclusion."

Alfreda sucked in a breath. I ignored her.

"As your sovereign, I would be well within my rights to have you executed for treason."

I watched for Velma to react. She did not. She must have steeled herself for this outcome. My pride in how I'd raised her grew.

"But as your father, that would cause me to grieve, exactly what I wish to avoid for it would make me appear even weaker. So, I believe I have a fitting punishment that will also help instruct." I turned toward the archway. "Morfran!" My bellow echoed through the cave.

"Yes, my liege." My soldier strode forward and bowed low.

"Have Zagan and Bate join us as well."

Alfreda tensed visibly. I doubted she could gather her wings any tighter. Velma's eyes darted between me and the three guards as they appeared.

"Velma, it is up to you how you endure your punishment. You may do it with dignity or without, but my men will ensure it is carried out."

I turned to Morfran. "Cleave her wings."

"No! You're a beast!" Alfreda shouted, rising. "Velma!"

I nodded for Bate to restrain Alfreda, which he did, despite her kicking and flapping.

She was trying my patience. I boomed, "Alfreda, if you cannot control yourself, you will force me to have him shackle you."

"Sister, don't resist for my sake. He's already hurt you enough. He can do whatever he wants to my body, but he will never break me. Never again," Velma ground out. Alfreda stilled, but tears flowed freely down her cheeks.

With order again restored, I nodded to Morfran.

"Kneel," he commanded. Then turning to the other guard, he said, "Zagan, hold her down."

Velma complied without coaxing, kneeling three strides from me. She would take her punishment with dignity. Wise. I expected nothing less.

Zagan forced her forehead to the ground, fully exposing her wings. She didn't even try to tuck them.

Alfreda whimpered but didn't fight Bate.

Morfran removed his sword from its sheath. "Extend your wings fully or I won't be responsible for cutting your back too."

Velma's wings trembled as she stretched them wide, their full span. The shaking grew the longer she held them open. They weren't the largest among my children, but they were certainly noteworthy. I just hoped she learned the lesson I hoped to teach her through this, that becoming less would never make her noble. That notion needed to stop before she led more of my children astray.

I watched her. I didn't need to see her face to know she hadn't yet learned the lesson. The vein bulging in her neck told me as much.

Morfran held the blade up and, with one swift motion, brought it down and across the stem of one wing.

Velma let out a muffled cry. Zagan held her head firmly in place.

Alfreda wailed and became a crumpled mess on the mattress behind Bate. She writhed and thrashed as tears streamed freely. I'd lost all respect for her.

• • •

Blood flowed as the wing went limp, then fell free.

Morfran brought his sword up again and a heartbeat later an agonized cry was wrenched from Velma. She'd never want to give me the satisfaction of hearing her, but she'd had no choice. She moaned as blood coursed from the other stump and the other wing dropped to the floor.

Zagan stood, and Velma slumped onto her side, onto the severed member that no longer possessed life but remained extended. Bate moved to restrain Alfreda again as she rushed him.

"Let her comfort her sister," I said, waving him away.

I dismissed my men and watched my children. Alfreda's tears continued unabated, but she composed herself enough to examine Velma's stumps. She swiped an arm across her face and, without a word, took to tearing the bottom of her dirty dress into strips.

Velma's sides heaved, and her face grew wet with tears as her body reacted to the loss. I wouldn't kid myself that she'd yet learned the lesson. That would only come in time as she had to cope with being less.

"This may hurt a little," Alfreda whispered to Velma as she began wiping the blood on her skirt. Velma tensed but did not reply—she trembled, from shock probably, but otherwise remained still and balled up as her stumps were wrapped.

I waited patiently. I still needed to address Alfreda's behavior.

Chapter Thirteen
Ambien

Velma slept on the moss mattress, Alfreda stroking her side when I reasserted myself. I'd been more than patient waiting for the drama to end. It was time to address her behavior.

"Alfreda, come here."

She scowled, but rose at a slug's pace and approached me, tucking her wings tightly. With a closer view of her face, the circles under her eyes seemed darker. It was hard to say how long she'd been denied sleep, but the shadows would soon be the color of her raven hair. My troops had certainly followed orders. I'd trained them well.

She stopped within arm's reach, and I grabbed her chin. I wanted a better view of that bruise on her cheek.

She tried twisting her head out of my grasp, but when that didn't work, she grabbed my arm and tried to pull away.

"Calm yourself, daughter. I merely want to examine your bruise."

She stopped struggling but held my arm. Her wings twitched.

I turned her head this way and that. I could guess what had caused it, but I wanted to get her talking. We'd start with something neutral and go from there. "How did this happen?"

"They hit me. I couldn't stay awake, but they wouldn't let me rest. My jaw throbbed for a very long time."

I released her face. "Did they do anything else to you to keep you awake?"

She nodded. "They plucked some of my feathers."

I looked her wings over. My troops had thinned them but not so much as to cause notice unless one looked for it. And they'd left her flight feathers untouched.

"Anything else?"

She shook her head.

So they hadn't resorted to stroking her wings… or more. We still had room to go with her.

"You managed to get your charge to locate Ali. Well done."

Alfreda sighed.

"Unfortunately, as you know, he's run off. What do you have to say?"

"I don't control him. He has free will. He means to protect Ali and his brother from you. I won't interfere with that. I won't."

She was weak and deluded, pure and simple. Her charge was nothing but a sniveling mortal, and he needed to assist me in my cause, desire or not. She'd spent too much time with Velma.

"Oh, but you must, daughter." I raised my brows to press my point. "You don't have a choice."

Alfreda frowned and crossed her arms.

Like her sister, she'd chosen the difficult path. I crossed my arms and drummed my fingers.

I'd located Alissandra in an Astanian border town but lost her again. And now that Alissandra knew I had eyes nearly everywhere, she and that mortal wouldn't surface again anytime soon—her charge was too smart for that. Mortal he may be, but he had a head for strategy.

* * *

"You don't seem to understand, you *will* help me. I intend to make an example of Alissandra, so it is imperative I find her. If you force me to, I will be happy to make an example of you first, but I'd like to avoid that if possible. Unless you want me to."

She glanced at Velma's sleeping form. "No." It came out clear and without hesitation.

"I thought you'd see reason. So then, connect me with your charge. You indulge him in his fantasies of free will. I shall help him see reality."

She gave me a long look before her shoulders slumped and she moved to sit.

"I think not, daughter. There will be no sitting. You need to remain awake."

She sagged but managed to remain upright as she closed her eyes to envision the dream canopy and connect with her charge. She knew where he was, and I latched on to her mind. She would connect me to him.

In her sleep-deprived state, it took her eons to finally reach her charge, but when she did, I grabbed his thread before she could. I needed to reset his reality. It would no doubt require force, and she would fight me unless I found something to occupy her.

"Alfreda, put your hands above your head and hold them there."

"But I'm tired," she whined, rustling her wings.

"I don't care. Arms up. Now."

She whimpered but slowly raised her hands.

"No, do not rest them on your head. Up. All the way."

That would keep her occupied. I could now accomplish what I needed to.

I turned my focus to her human, following his thread into his mind. Darkness held sway all around him except for the light from a small fire, next to which lay a blanket. He licked his fingers as he perched on a log beside the fire. It looked like he dined on pheasant.

His thoughts oozed of sentimental drivel, and I couldn't help but shake my head—love for his brother and Alissandra, nonsense about protecting both of them, and a charming stretch of romantic pining for her despite feeling unworthy of her love. It was no wonder Alfreda's thinking was so weak. Between Velma and Alfreda's charge…

The connection faltered, and I eased back. "Alfreda, put your arms all the way up. Do not make me tell you again." Her lips trembled. She approached tears, I just hoped she could endure until I reset the man.

I refocused. I couldn't stand hearing any more of his sentimentality. It was making me sick.

Quiet! You will listen and do as you are told.

The human had the good sense to be still. Progress.

You have run off in an attempt to thwart me. I will not tolerate insubordination. You are my tool, and you will do as I say.

I am no one's property!

The gall of this human, my anger rose. *You do not want to experience my wrath. It is unpleasant, as your sand maiden can attest.*

I will not do your bidding.

Correcting this mortal would necessitate more pain than I'd planned, so be it. I had no problem doing what he requested. Too bad Alfreda would experience it too, but he left me no choice. I needed his assistance, and I would not be denied.

I stretched my mental claws into his mind. This was only the second time I'd had to do this with a particularly difficult mortal. I needed to be gentler than with immortals or I'd destroy his mind, fragile as it was—I couldn't risk thwarting my own designs. I stroked lightly. He screamed in unison with Alfreda's moan. Bless her heart, she kept her hands raised. She was mentally weak, but she would obey with enough persuasion.

Are you now prepared to do as I request? I asked.

Never!

I shook my head. Honestly, this was monotonous. What was it with these notions of resistance, mortal and immortal alike? I was a god. Idealistic fools. They couldn't win. Why did they even try?

Four light brushes later and Alfreda collapsed. I'd pushed her to her limit. She was unresponsive, probably for the best, because I still held her charge's thread. I *would* teach him obedience.

I stroked his mind with a bit more force, and he again cried out but still fought me. Damn human. Another brush of my mental claws had him falling off his log perch, clutching his head.

More force, more screaming as my claws caressed his mind a seventh, then eighth time. He'd lose his voice completely at this rate, but he still refused my commands. Arrogant, willful mortal. I found it harder and harder to hold my anger in check.

By the tenth brush, the human writhed on the ground. He so infuriated me with his hubris—he actually thought he could resist me. *Crush him like a gnat.* The thought flitted about my head, but I resisted, instead taking several deep breaths. I needed him.

Anger turned to amazement as he fought me, despite the agony he endured on the next three passes. He'd been abused, no doubt about it, and he'd learned how to cope with pain.

By the fifteenth brush, his face was wet with tears and he'd pissed himself.

Stop, I beg of you. I'll do whatever you require, just stop.

I smiled. He'd shown mental toughness, holding out longer than I'd expected. Alfreda could take a lesson from him. He would come in handy.

He was barely conscious—optimal conditions to plant a thought in the deepest recesses of his mind, a thought that even Alfreda would be unaware existed. It would make him useful and guide his actions to the end of his suns, which depending upon how vigilant he became on my behalf, might be sooner than later. No matter, he was mortal and expendable.

Repeat after me: I swear my allegiance to Ambien for all my suns. I will do all in my power to further his ambitions and expand his kingdom. I will allow nothing to thwart me in this pursuit. This is my solemn vow.

Like the puppet he was, he repeated it word for word, sealing it into the core of his thoughts, then lost consciousness. Alfreda hadn't put him to sleep nor would she weave any dreams for him this night, but he would rest. He'd need it, for he would not be permitted more rest until he tracked down that sibling of his. Again.

I wouldn't tell Alfreda what I'd done, lest she search for the seed in hopes of ferreting it out, but I'd won his allegiance and he was mine to command with or without her. I grinned at the perfectness of it. A prince of Wake realm itself, assisting me.

I stooped and lifted Alfreda, laying her beside her sister on the moss. I allowed myself a moment of peace as I stroked her raven hair. Both of them were precious and beautiful to me. They were my offspring after all. I sought a good future for them, though they could not yet see it. I only hoped they would support my cause in the end.

On my way out, I stopped by Morfran. "Alfreda knew where her charge was. See that she gets him to Sanis, the last village Alissandra was spotted in, post haste. Then ensure he tracks his sibling."

"Yes, my liege. It shall be done. What would you like us to do with your other daughter?"

"Hold her. I don't want her telling everyone where we are. Shackles are unnecessary unless she becomes unruly, which I do not expect. Procure clean bandages, but if she needs more attention from a healer, notify me immediately."

"It shall be done."

Chapter Fourteen

"No!" I shouted, waking myself.

Kovis stirred on his blanket. While we held hands, he lay four handbreadths away. It might as well have been the next village. "You okay?"

What was I supposed to tell him? No. My nightmares are worse without your arms around me making me feel like nothing could ever hurt me? Or, you've no idea how much I miss your flirting, tickling, and teasing. Or, I long for the intimacy we shared. They were all true. But if I told him any of those things, I knew what would happen. Kovis would freeze up. He'd at least taken to talking again, but every time I hinted at closeness, he distanced himself.

The only hope I had for restoring our physical closeness was that we still held hands all night. It was the only way we could dream. He hadn't wanted to at the start, but he found that not dreaming left his mind restless. He'd relented after that.

His dreams were not peaceful judging by his thrashing, but he reported that if he dreamed, his mind was clear while awake. Our bond, however, was silent, even as we slept. For better or worse, I had no visibility to what he dreamed. As his former sand maiden, it was the toughest potion to take.

"I'm fine. Just another bad dream," I assured him.

Kovis nodded and rolled back over, still holding my hand.

My nightmare had been of Father torturing and controlling the sand people who stewarded my healer friends'—Haylan's, Hulda's, and Jathan's—dreams. My mind had no trouble imagining appalling scenarios.

My stomach twisted. We'd rushed off from The Ninety-Eight with them sound asleep and we'd had no news on whether Father had left them alone. But at the rate folks were being possessed, I shuddered to think what they might be going through, no different than Kennan.

I wasn't going back to sleep anytime soon, so I forced my mind back to the problem of returning to Dream. I'd tried to will us back to Dream like I thought Velma had in order to send me, but nothing happened no matter how many times I'd tried. Somehow, I had missed some critical step, but I had no idea what. So I'd abandoned it in the end.

I exhaled heavily.

Of late, I'd been replaying my dance with Father during the winter solstice ball. I well remembered soaring higher than I'd ever danced, so high that the citizens below looked like gnats. Father had grinned as we approached the dream canopy.

Excitement had welled up in me knowing it was what I reached my thoughts out to every night. But as we soared into the cloudy layer, dizziness had assaulted my head. I couldn't tell which way was up or down. Father had steadied me, but my vertigo hadn't relented until we'd descended to just below the canopy.

Dream and Wake were reciprocal in their territories, and I'd reasoned out that the dizziness had to have been the result of being stuck in the space between Dream and Wake where things were right side up or upside down depending on where you approached from.

I'd never experienced that disorientation as I reached out to my charges because I wasn't physically there, only my thoughts. And it made sense that things might be awry. I wished I'd held on a bit longer during that dance just to see if we emerged into the skies above Wake. I theorized we'd have to have.

My theory was all well and good, but I'd hit a snag. If we somehow used our Air magic to soar that high, what would happen when we emerged into Dream. Dream didn't have magic, and I speculated we'd lose ours in the process if we experienced the reverse of what I had when I came to Wake. And who knew what would happen to our bodies—being mortal, I wasn't sure we'd sprout wings. We'd plummet to our deaths. I couldn't risk it on a hope that we'd be able to fly.

All that work and reasoning and I'd resisted throwing it away and starting over. But in this heartbeat as I refocused on what was most important, I finally let it go. We had to get back to Dream and soon.

I saw my breath in the firelight as I pulled my heavy cape tighter, then tucked my head under my blanket, warming my ear.

I had no idea where to even begin finding yet another way back, so I let my mind wander. Velma had worked through the creation myth to find a way. What other stories touched on going to Dream or Wake? There were fairy tales I'd heard as a child. Most were based in facts of some sort.

I furrowed my brow. Fairy tales… Fairy tales… My mind took off at a trot. There was a story about the rise of Porta, the tallest peak in Dream realm. Dream had been perfect before that, but evil by its very nature wanted to destroy what was good.

After it's rise, or so the tale said, all manner of grotesque monsters had entered Dream. Those who believed the story to be true maintained the peak was a connection with Hades itself, allowing all that was bad to enter. I'd hated listening to this tale. It always set goose pimples on my arms, but desperate as I was, I forced myself to review the parts of the story I could remember.

Once upon a time… my mind replayed the tale. There were two brothers, one rich, the other poor. The rich brother had more than he or his family could ever want or desire. Despite his overabundance, the rich brother would not share with the poor brother who eked out a subsistence living—many sunsets his family had naught to eat, so poor was he, despite working diligently.

Then one sunrise, as the poor brother was soaring over the path he always flew, he noticed an unfamiliar sight ahead. A slender mountain had risen up, and great was the height thereof. So strange was the sight that he could only land, stop, and stare.

While he was thus gazing, he heard others approaching. Not knowing the nature of these beings, he hid in the trees, but gained a vantage point so he could see what happened. Three burly beings with large, raven wings swooped and landed on the path and soon stopped before the mountain.

"Mighty mountain, mighty mountain, open up!" the three cried in unison.

In a heartbeat, a crack of light appeared top to bottom from within the mountain as it opened wide, and the three men went inside.

The poor brother barely stifled a gasp as the mountain closed again. Curiosity held him in place atop his perch, and a short while later, he heard the mountain rumble again. It opened, and the three beings strode out with sacks upon their backs.

Once outside, they turned and cried, "Mighty mountain, mighty mountain, shut thyself!"

The mountain closed and there was no longer an entrance to be seen. The trio took flight, vanishing against the clear sky.

When the poor brother could no longer see or hear them, he shimmied down from the tree and approached the mountain to see if he could ascertain where the opening in this new mountain was and what it had given them.

After careful search, he could find no entrance, so he stepped back and cried, "Mighty mountain, mighty mountain, open up!"

As it had before, the ground trembled as the mountain opened. He cautiously stepped inside, and after going a short way, he found himself in a room with gold, silver, and great piles of pearls and precious stones heaped like grain. It sparkled in the light.

The poor brother hardly knew what to do so excited was he, and debated whether he might take some to ease his situation—food so his children's bellies were full, a repaired roof, grain in the barn. He was not greedy. At length he pocketed some gold and silver but left the pearls and precious stones, which were far more valuable.

He walked back outside and turned. "Mighty mountain, mighty mountain, shut thyself!" And it did.

His heart was light as he took flight toward home, feeling some measure of the burden that had been weighing heavily, lighten. His wife would rejoice with him.

In time, despite hard work and toil, the money ran out. Hoping the mysterious but miraculous mountain remained, he borrowed a bucket from his rich brother and went in search of it again. He joyed when it came into view and again filled his container but did not touch the most valuable treasures. Returning home, he celebrated with a glad heart.

When the not-quite-as-poor brother again needed money, he went to his rich brother to make a request to borrow his bucket once more. The rich man, having noticed the inexplicable change in his brother's situation, had grown curious, if not envious. He decided to find out what his brother had done to improve his lot, so he put a spot of pitch on the bottom of the bucket before handing it over.

When the not-as-poor brother returned the container, his rich brother saw a silver coin stuck on the bottom and asked, "What have you been using my bucket for?"

"What does it matter?"

The rich brother pulled the coin from the bottom and demanded he tell him or threatened to turn him over to the magistrate if he refused. So the poorer brother told him everything, just how it had happened.

Once his brother left, the rich brother journeyed to where his brother had said and also found the mysterious but miraculous mountain.

But he'd been too caught up in the possibilities of treasure and hadn't listened well. "Miraculous mountain, miraculous mountain, open up!" he called, but nothing happened. "Mysterious mountain, mysterious mountain, open up!" he tried, but alas the mountain did not move.

He stood staring at the mammoth mountain, racking his thoughts for the proper command. Magnificent, majestic, melodious, and more he tried to no avail. In desperation, he yelled, "Mighty mountain, mighty mountain, open up!" He nearly fainted when the ground began trembling and the face split open.

He hurried inside, and it shut behind him but he cared not, for the sight before him made all thoughts flee. He marveled for some time, not knowing which treasure to take first. In the end, he loaded up some of each—pearls, precious stones, gold, and silver—until his pockets and arms brimmed over. When he could carry no more, he turned and tried to remember the command to open the mountain once more, but try as he might, his memory failed him. He sat down dejectedly, for he realized his treasure was worthless if he could not leave.

That sunset, the mountain opened and the three beings his poor brother had first seen entered. "Little bird, you have become trapped by your greed," they admonished. "This mountain was set here to care for the needy, and we with it, but you have stolen for your benefit alone, with malice in your heart. You are greedy and wicked, and because you came with treachery in your heart, you shall lose it. But more, you have desecrated the purity of this mountain. So from this sun on, evil shall come forth into your land."

Despite the rich brother's supplications, the three beings grabbed him and cut out his heart, and to this sun, malevolent, vile, and destructive beings find their way into the world, treading the path of evil this brother sowed.

I shivered as I always did at the tale's conclusion, and it wasn't from the frigid air. If the story was to be believed, mares were definitely part of the creatures that had found their way into Dream thanks to this greedy bastard.

Rather than focusing on the end as I usually did, I took a deep breath and stepped back, at least in my mind.

I'd flown over Porta not long ago on my way to Father's. Could it really be an entrance to Dream? I wouldn't dwell on the creatures, but might it be the possibility we sought?

My stomach fluttered as I considered.

Dream and Wake were reciprocal. Porta had to have an opposite in Wake, right?

Part II: Wake

Twinkle, Twinkle, Little Star

By Jane Taylor
Essex Wake Realm

Twinkle, twinkle, little star,
How I wonder what you are.
Up above the world so high,
Like a diamond in the sky.
Twinkle, twinkle, little star,
How I wonder what you are!

When the blazing sun is gone,
When he nothing shines upon,
Then you show your little light,
Twinkle, twinkle, all the night.
Twinkle, twinkle, little star,
How I wonder what you are!

Then the traveler in the dark,
Thanks you for your tiny spark;
He could not see which way to go,
If you did not twinkle so.
Twinkle, twinkle, little star,
How I wonder what you are!

Chapter Fifteen
Kovis

Worries that snow would fly and we'd still not have a breakthrough concerning how to get to Dream realm, had become my constant companion.

If that possibility materialized, I wasn't sure how we would cope—we'd have to hold up somewhere or risk exposure. Our purchases in Sanis had prolonged the possibility, but every sun we remained in Wake made the need to shelter in one place all the greater as winter closed in. And we both knew the risk—it was a recipe for discovery.

The other worry dogging me was that Kennan would come to harm the longer we delayed. I had no doubt Ambien was forcing Ali's sister to make him search for us. And he would continue to do so despite inhospitable weather. He'd be out in the freezing cold and snow. My brother's life was in our hands, and I would not fail him.

"Kovis, I think I know how to get to Dream." Ali practically bounced the heartbeat she rose and her new theory for getting there bubbled out.

Squatting, I stopped tending the fire and listened, allowing her words to replace the ever present hurt that hearing she and my twin had shared a passionate kiss had created; it had turned my world upside down and I couldn't get past it.

I rubbed my blackened hands together as she continued.

There was certainty in her voice as she spoke. It was the first time concerning going to Dream realm and I couldn't help but allow a corner of my mouth to hitch.

"You mentioned Wake and Dream are reciprocal," I said.

Ali nodded as she continued pacing, no doubt too excited to sit.

"So we need to figure out where this Porta mountain is in Wake."

Another nod. "I hope your tutors drilled you in geography."

I shook my head. "You've no idea. But you're correct, I know the territories of Wake." I reversed the letters of Porta—Atrop, or what I presumed was the peak's equivalent here—and furrowed my brow. "I don't know of a mountain by that name."

Ali gave me a hard look. "But there has to be."

"I'm not saying there isn't. I just don't know where it is." I sighed.

"Well, where is Lemnos's reciprocal in Wake? It's got to be there."

Lemnos, Ali's home. I reversed the letters. "Wait, *Sonmel Island*?"

"What?"

I rose and put a hand to my head. "There are stories about that place. Some say it's haunted."

"Are they true?"

"No idea, I've never been."

"You know where it is?"

"It's out in the Naegea Sea." My mind buzzed. "Do you suppose the stories might be a means of concealing a door to Dream?"

Ali met my gaze. "It makes sense. And gives my theory all the more credibility." She beamed.

"Yes... it does." I exhaled loudly. "We'll need to cross The Canyon to get there."

• • •

"Will that be a problem? Nomarch Kett said they crossed it on the way to Flumen."

"For insorcelled, its nothing. For sorcerers, it might be a different story because it's the source of our power."

Ali raised an eyebrow. She still hadn't granted me that her power stemmed from that canyon, though she couldn't disprove it either.

I held up a hand. "Fine, it is the source of *my* power at least. I've never been that close to it, but I can only imagine that I'll feel something because of it."

"Hulda and Haylan told me about winter solstice. They said The Canyon belches out its overflow of energy in a lightning storm and every sorcerer feels like they're on a high." Her eyes sparkled.

I nodded. "Yes, I'm guessing it's a similar feeling. I just hope it isn't so strong that it overloads me."

"Too much of a good thing?"

"Something like that, yes."

"The trek to The Canyon and across it will probably take a good four or five moons from here, if all goes well." I exhaled heavily, chafing at my helplessness to save those in need sooner.

Ali ran a hand through her blonde locks. "That long?"

I frowned, not at her, but at the situation. "We'll travel out of Astana, dip south to skirt the mountains, then cut across parts of Wood and Terra, finally reaching the sea. From there we'll need to hire a boatman, if we can find one who'll risk a haunted island as a destination."

Ali resumed pacing, but with slower steps.

Four maybe five moons. It would take too long. Who knew what might have happened to Kennan and Alfreda by then. I drew a hand to my brow and circled my fingers.

Was there a way to speed our journey? What I'd give to be a bird about now.

Like a small bird, the notion flitted about my mind.

"You used to fly, right?" She'd told me stories but I still couldn't picture her with wings.

Ali stopped on the other side of the dead fire. "That's right. Why?"

I stilled my fingers, but my mind took off and started to soar.

"What are you thinking?" Ali smiled at me when I finally refocused.

"We won't be birds, but might we use our Air magic unlike ever before?" My eyes danced.

Ali drew a hand to her chest. "We can fly? I could fly again?" Tears welled up in her eyes.

My breathing hitched. She'd endured the loss of her wings to come to me. The traitorous thought romped about my head, and taunted me. No, I insisted, actions spoke louder than words. That kiss had certainly been action. Ali's actions were inexplicable, pure and simple.

"You know how?" Her violet eyes filled with hope.

I beat down my conflicted feelings. "No, but I believe that our abilities are limited only by our imaginations."

Ali swiped at a tear.

My gaze fell on Alshain and Fiona, tethered to nearby trees and my heart sank.

"What is it?" Ali strode to me and bit her lip as she waited. "Tell me."

I exhaled heavily. "If we succeed in flying, I'll have to give up Alshain." Why was he even a consideration? What was Kennan's life worth? Surely my sibling came before my horse.

Ali glanced at our mounts and her hands went limp at her sides. "Oh, Kovis."

She knew. I'd had Alshain since I was seven. He'd been with me through every trial since. He'd listened as I poured out my angst over Rasa, knickered in understanding as I told him about Father's berating me when my powers dallied to manifest, and lent an ear when Dierna did what she'd done. He'd carried me into battle and back. He was even the inspiration for some of my writing. He'd been a rock in my often tumultuous world.

Beside my brother, he was the only one I trusted with my life. Kennan had his books, paints, and music to work out the overflow of angst we'd endured. I had Alshain and my writing.

"I remember when you named him," Ali said.

I bobbed my head. "I hadn't fully understood the power in a name—Alshain, the second brightest star in the Aquilla constellation, it's brilliance behind only that of Altair, after which our family took its name—but he's become that and more, to me."

"We don't have to fly." She ran the toe of her boot across the dirt.

I closed my eyes. "Anything else will take too long."

"You're sure?" She closed the gap between us and placed a hand on my chest.

I swallowed hard and nodded.

As soon as we finished breakfast, we cleared a large patch of ground, away from the fire. As we worked, I buried my angst about Alshain and focused on the task ahead. It would take my full concentration as we made our first attempt at flight.

"Good thing I've been practicing nuancing my power," Ali said, smiling, as we finished.

"True enough. Did you fly like a bird, belly down?" I asked. I wouldn't assume.

"How else would one fly with wings the size I had?" Her smile faded.

"Then move a step further away so we don't touch. We'll probably need to stretch our arms wide to stabilize us."

Ali did so, and we extended our arms.

"We'll need to conjure a cloud of air to float on. It shouldn't be much different than when you buffered your fall from Fiona. Can you do that?" I asked as I gathered a cushion of air before me.

"I'll try." Ali furrowed her brow in concentration then opened a palm to the clearing. "Nuance it," she mumbled to herself.

Leaves swirled before her. She waved her arm about as if building a large pillow. "Okay, I think I have it," she reported several heartbeats later.

I couldn't tell; I couldn't see it. It was air. I hoped she was right.

"Lay forward." I was guessing, but it seemed the next logical step. I leaned and felt my winds catch me.

"Ow!" Ali cried out, tumbling. She nearly planted her face in the ground and came up sputtering.

I suppressed a laugh as I looked on. Sprawled face down across my cushion as I was, there was nothing I could have done to save her. "Try it again," I encouraged, brushing a hint of power over my cushion to keep myself afloat.

Ali frowned at me before picking herself up, dusting off her leathers, and returning from whence she'd fallen.

I kept our bond closed. I didn't need to hear her thoughts. I could guess her sentiments.

Ali made a second attempt. At least she rolled before hitting the ground this time, but her reaction was much the same. It was clear she longed to return to the skies. I hoped she didn't defeat herself with frustration.

Standing again, she huffed, "It's like I can't hold my winds stiff. They collapse just as I need them." Determination shone in her eyes.

Several heartbeats later, she sighed, then shook her head as if considering. A mumble followed, but I couldn't make out what. She finally turned and in a pleading voice asked, "Would you let me see through your eyes and experience how you're doing it?"

I gave her a long look. She wanted me to open my side of our bond. While I'd mastered a full block of our connection, I hadn't yet figured out how to open just a portion.

How quickly did I want to rescue Kennan?

Chapter Sixteen

Still bolstered by his wind cushion, Kovis took a deep breath, as if worried about all I might see, then nodded.

I wanted to celebrate. He was willing to make it easier and faster for me to learn, but his hesitancy…. A collage of curiosity along with angst flooded my mind, making it hard to concentrate.

But at length, I took a deep breath and focused, desiring with every fiber of my being to join Kovis's mind. I longed to see and feel what he was doing to make his winds obey. A heartbeat later, I felt the usual disorientation as I viewed the world through two sets of eyes.

I felt him shift, no doubt wanting to restore the block to our connection. He was like a scared creature longing to hide. He moved again, and I decided I'd better hurry.

I tried to focus on his thoughts as he maintained his wind cushion, but I couldn't help seeing more. Images flew by as his imagination dredged up Kennan leaning down, meeting my lips, then pressing the kiss further, taking my mouth with his tongue while I leaned in, an eager participant. I winced. Is this what he saw every time he looked at me?

I half expected to see snippets of Dierna in bed with his guard next, but memories of his father molesting Rasa stampeded after. In the blink of an eye, his father transformed into my likeness and Rasa into Kovis. I nearly gasped. In his mind, I'd raped him.

The images dissolved as quickly as they'd come. It seemed Kovis was figuring out how to shield them even with me in his head. He replaced them with benign images of our travels. But I couldn't unsee. A queasy feeling beset my stomach. Clearly, he hadn't wanted me to view them, but I now understood.

I attempted to refocus on what I'd come to learn. *Kovis, can you start over so I can hear everything you think about to make it work?*

He stood up and dismissed his air cushion, then began again. He envisioned a navy, cloth pillow, a ball of sorts, with the empire's eagle insignia—I smiled, of course it would have that on it—that rose to his waist. It became invisible as he directed air magic to replace the cloth, then leaned forward. Unsurprisingly, it held him.

You picture a solid object first, I observed.

Of course, how else would you get it to support you? His tone came out clipped, and he shifted again.

I felt like a fool. Of course. I knew I had to envision what I wanted. I hadn't started with imagining something firm, but rather a cloud of sorts. I'd gotten exactly what I'd pictured.

He released a heavy breath that lingered in the crisp air.

I wouldn't dally. Kovis clearly didn't want me here so I willed my mind to return to my own body. Then I put into practice what I'd discovered. When I succeeded, I didn't pat myself on the back. Not after what I'd seen.

Neither of us were in a mood to practice more after that, so we packed up camp and headed out. We exchanged hardly a word. Not surprisingly, our bond was again deathly silent.

The next morning we agreed to practice again. I'd been anxious to, Kovis not so much despite knowing it would get us to Dream that much faster. I longed to feel the breeze in my hair as I soared over the land again. Nothing else compared. I'd missed that freedom more than I'd realized, and now that the possibility stared me in the face, I couldn't master flight fast enough.

We separated, and I succeeded in constructing a pillow of Air magic that supported me, the first time. Kovis withheld comment. His mood hadn't improved since last sun, and I wondered if he knew what I'd seen and it was making him more distant.

I listed left and thrust my arms wide to steady myself—it felt so natural—then flattened out. Perhaps my former skill would come in handy despite not having wings to buoy me on the breeze.

"We need to imagine our cushion expanding, having it raise us higher," Kovis said a while later, his voice was flat.

And so began the next series of trials and errors.

I pictured the ball of air expanding as my magic infused it with more and more power. I concentrated so hard that I'd lifted myself to my height above the ground before I realized it.

My shock burst my control of the magic and I plummeted. Unfortunately, I didn't have the quickness of mind to cushion my fall, and I met the unforgiving ground with a thud. I'd have a nasty bruise down my side, I could already feel it.

Concern laced Kovis's face, but he didn't say anything. I took a deep breath, buried my upset, and stood. I'd endured worse while training and competing in The Ninety-Eight. He hadn't yet fallen. He soon floated twice his height above the clearing, bobbing and shifting, then stabilized himself with outstretched arms.

Our winds whipped about the campsite, stoking the fire. The flames grew higher and higher the longer we practiced. They nearly licked the trees when Kovis landed and doused it with his Water magic.

By the time the sun had climbed to half its peak, I could reliably hover twice my height. I thrilled. I was ready to go higher, but Kovis called a halt.

"We've done well, but we need to keep moving. Let's pack up." His words held no emotion, no celebration, nothing.

I sighed. Was this all my doing? Had breaching his barrier caused this? He'd taken to talking to and spending more time with

Alshain. It seemed he was retreating into himself, and I had no idea what to do. He didn't want to talk, he'd made that abundantly clear.

————

A sennight later, as had become our custom we again practiced as soon as we'd finished breakfast. A light dusting of fluffy snow covered the ground as the sun rose. It filled the air as our winds stirred it and became nearly blinding until we rose above the trees, which I could now do.

I'd taken to layering both my linen and woolen braises under my leathers to keep warm as I rose ever higher, and they made it difficult to bend, but I persevered. The cold reminded me of flying back home—the heights we flew at made my nose and fingers numb.

Kovis was double the height I flew at, and he'd taken to maneuvering about, turning and diving, rising and spinning. He was doing it; he was flying. I could only hover, but I would master this. I was so very close. I could taste it.

"Ali, rise higher and start directing yourself." It came out gruff and a command. I gave him a long look. Could he not see how hard I tried? I huffed. He was in no mood to argue with, so I bit my tongue and did as he bid.

————

I could reliably steer myself and dive six suns later but Kovis was growing increasingly antsy at the length of our journey. We still rode in Vaduz province, and while we'd avoided all towns and villages so our chance of discovery was minimal, he worried about Kennan and exposure in the cold temperatures. We needed to move faster.

"We find the nearest village, release the horses, and fly from there," he declared after breakfast.

I gave him a long look. "Are you sure?"

"We're ready." There was no joy in his voice.

"I'll put the fire out," I offered.

He nodded, then turned and took a long look at his mount.

Alshain and Fiona were focused on the ground, brushing snow aside with their lips to nibble what little scrub they could find.

With a heavy sigh, he trudged over to them and began talking quietly to Alshain while stroking his onyx neck. The horse brought his head up. Several heartbeats later, Kovis rested his brow against the stallion's neck and his open palm stilled. Kovis's body trembled.

Was he crying? My heart ached for him. They'd been together for most of his life. I busied myself with packing up. I'd give him as much time as he needed.

At length, Kovis inhaled deeply and swiped his arm across his eyes. He patted his stallion's neck once more, then moved on to brush snow off the blanket covering Alshain's back and saddled him. He repeated the process with Fiona, but there was no emotion.

Kovis's eyes were red as he helped me up into my saddle.

I wanted to tell him I was here if he wanted to talk, but I held back. I wished he'd open our bond.

We moved out into the woods. The tops of the trees were pretty with snow coating their branches. It looked like a baker had frosted them all with white icing. Not much snow had made it to the forest floor, but it seemed all life had gone into hiding.

Over the past couple moons, we'd noticed that there were fewer and fewer animals about, and hunting had become more of a challenge. Of late, spotting an Axis, a quick, four-hoofed animal, had become rare. Even the birds had left. Only the sounds of our mounts negotiating the path met my ears.

"If I've judged correctly, we're not far from the town of Croft," Kovis said over his shoulder a while later. It was the first thing he'd said since we broke camp. "We'll approach, find a suitable stable, and...." He let the words hang.

As the sun reached its peak, the forest thinned, and a smattering of wattle and daub structures appeared, nestled amongst the trees. Unlike Sanis, these looked in fair repair. Relief should have filled me because we'd no doubt find a farm that would care well for the horses, but with Kovis already feeling the loss of his stallion it didn't ease the ache in my heart for him.

I moved forward and rode beside Kovis as we passed several homesteads. I watched as he scanned each one we approached. What he looked for, I couldn't tell, but it was clear he had some criteria in mind for he dismissed the fifth, then sixth, then the seventh, before pulling Alshain to a halt at the tree line near the eighth.

The barn stood tall and proud beside a modest home. Unlike most of its neighbors, the daub was fully covered by white-painted wattle. No cracks or defects marred the outside of either structure between the dark timbers of the latticework. It had to be the home of a wealthier farmer.

Kovis patted Alshain's neck before dismounting and helping me off Fiona. He removed Fiona's saddle then set it near the foot of the tree I stood by.

"These saddles are too fine a quality to be from these parts. We'll leave them here," he explained.

I rummaged through my saddlebag, pulled out what I could carry, and put it in the large pockets of my cloak. It wasn't much. Our blankets wouldn't make the trip, not with their weight. If it got too cold, Kovis would have to give up his distance from me and share my body heat—I certainly wouldn't complain. Perhaps it would get him past our breakdown. But even as I thought it, my gut told me no. I stared at the sapphire on my finger. One could always hope.

I looked up to see that Kovis had leaned Alshain's saddle against another tree and was removing a medallion, of the altairn, from the back of the seat. There were two pendants, one on either side, that adorned only the saddles of the royal family. Good idea. Father didn't need to know we'd been here.

Kovis moved on to do the same with Alshain's bridle. Medallions in hand, he studied them briefly, then closed his hand around them. He closed his eyes. Three, four, five heartbeats expired before he slipped them into a pocket of his leathers.

"Nothing I can do about your shoes, boy," Kovis said. He peered into one of his stallion's big, brown eyes. "We'll just hope they don't look, at least not right away. So don't get a pebble stuck in your hoof anytime soon, okay?"

"What's on his shoes?" I asked.

Kovis startled, clearly lost in the moment. "Alshain's shoes have an altairn engraved on them. They'll know who he belongs to. With dissent brewing, I just hope...." He shook his head but didn't turn.

I took a step closer. "Kovis, I'm here if you want to talk about… him, this, anything." I added an unspoken "us."

He bobbed his head but didn't reply.

"Are you ready to check out your new home, old friend?" Kovis's voice cracked on the last words.

"Bring Fiona," he called over his shoulder as he grabbed his stallion's reins. Alshain plodded along beside Kovis.

Fiona followed meekly behind me.

While Kovis had been tending to Alshain, I'd surveyed the homestead. It appeared no one was at home, so I wasn't surprised when Kovis stepped boldly up to the barn door and opened it, then led us in.

The farmer would certainly have a surprise.

The inside of the barn was orderly. Hand tools hung from wooden pegs, larger farming implements had been arranged in some fashion that made sense to the owner. Six stalls, only two of which had occupants—a donkey and a goat—lined either side of the space. Both animals seemed well cared for judging by the abundant food in the feedboxes and clean stalls.

Kovis led Alshain into the stall next to the donkey. Fiona followed me into the space next to Alshain.

I heard him unbuckle Alshain's bridle and knew he'd hung it up when the metal ring brushed against the wall separating the stalls.

I did the same for Fiona.

Kovis lingered, so I found some hay and oats and filled both their feedboxes. The water looked fresh. I hated to interrupt him, but I didn't know how much time we had.

I peeked out the barn door and scanned the area. Still clear. I returned to Fiona and scratched behind her ear. She liked that.

I'd repeated the process no less than five times when my nerves got the better of me and I said, "Kovis, we need to go."

"You're right." It sounded muffled.

I patted Fiona's soft nose then shut her stall. When I reached the neighboring door, Kovis had his arms wrapped around Alshain's neck. His face was buried in the thick winter fur just above the horse's muscled shoulder. Alshain's head nuzzled Kovis's back as if the stallion understood this was goodbye.

Kovis had told me that once he decided to love someone, he held nothing back. While our current situation tested that notion, he hadn't lied when it came to his horse. I feared how he'd bear up.

Kovis pulled back and inhaled sharply, then turned and breezed past me without looking back. But not before I saw that his face was wet. I closed Alshain's stall door and joined Kovis, who surveyed the coast. He didn't look my way, only nodded for me to follow.

We crept out the door, and he latched it behind us. After one more scan of the area, he burst into a run and stopped only when he reached the safety of tree cover.

I inhaled, slowing my breathing as I stopped beside him. He knelt, rummaged in his saddlebag, and withdrew a few small items then stowed them in his cloak, all the while taking calming breaths.

His beautiful blue and hazel eyes were red but fierce as he looked up at me. My heart ached for him, and I only barely swallowed a sob. I'd suffered the loss of my family in silence, and it seemed he was choosing to suffer similarly.

He schooled his features, although his quivering lips told me emotion threatened to overwhelm the façade, and clenched his jaw. "Let's fly to Atrop."

I bit my lip as my heart broke for him. It was all too much.

How would he endure?

Chapter Seventeen

We walked until we couldn't see the farm or any part of the modest settlement through the trees. I swallowed hard. I couldn't cry, or I'd probably draw out the tears Kovis struggled to stifle.

"Ready?" I asked, pushing emotions down as I buttoned the top button of my cloak. I was glad these capes had abundant fabric. It allowed me to stabilize myself while keeping my hands inside during flight and kept me from becoming a projectile icicle.

He nodded.

I conjured my pillow of air, leaned forward, then expanded it to push myself up into the sunshine, above the tree tops. Kovis rose and floated even with me to my left, never looking back.

The air was crisp and there were no clouds, so we could see a long way in the distance. The landscape ahead was populated with rolling hills, with a thin layering of trees much as we had enjoyed since setting out this sun.

I glanced back and saw the white tipped peaks of the Tuliv mountains off in the distance—how I missed the warmth of their hot springs… as well as a few activities we'd engaged in. They were towering to be sure, and we hadn't even ventured past their base. I understood why the former emperor hadn't bothered expanding the empire past them. No enemy would ever make it over, not without significant effort.

My thoughts roamed as we flew. I'd fled Dream to save Kovis as well as Wake from Father and his schemes. I'd sacrificed my family, my future as a dream weaver, and become mortal, but despite all that, it hadn't changed anything. Father still threatened Wake. And worse, I began to wonder if Kovis and I would ever have the happily ever after I longed for.

I forced my thoughts to happier things, namely imagining what it would be like returning to Dream and seeing my family again. The wind wiped the moisture that welled up from my eyes. How I missed them.

We flew over several towns and villages. I wasn't worried about being spotted. No one ever looked up, and even if they did, who would believe? We soared over a river some time later. Despite the cold, it continued flowing with ferocity.

The sparse tree covering eventually surrendered to plains that looked like an artist, perhaps Kennan, had gone crazy painting with white, flaxen-yellow, and brown.

My ears and nose had started aching ages before, but by the time the sun was halfway to the horizon, I could tolerate the cold no longer. I couldn't stop my teeth from chattering. With the wind whipping past, it was impossible to talk to Kovis—how I wished he would open our bond—so I motioned, pointing down.

We landed, and the first ray of sunshine I'd seen from him in ages shone when he smiled. "We're making good progress. At this pace, we should reach the coast within a sennight."

"That is good news. When we reach the sea, do you suppose we'll be able to fly over water?" I hopped up and down and blew on my frozen fingers, trying to work some warmth into them.

Kovis furrowed his brow, then shook his head. He didn't comment on my calisthenics. "I've no idea. It's not solid like land. Our cushions of air might sink. I guess we'll find out. But it we can, it would beat finding a ship to take us to Sonmel Island."

I pushed my cloak behind my shoulders and tried jumping jacks, but with all the layers I wore under my leathers, I nearly cried out in pain the first time I threw my arms above my head.

Kovis took to running in place. While he looked funny, like a tent bobbing up and down with his cloak, he looked more dignified than I did, so I mimicked. My ears and nose stopped aching soon after. My core finally warmed, and I even broke a sweat.

"I'm ready to keep going," I declared.

He caught my gaze and then looked to the ground. In a hushed tone he said, "Thank you. For giving me space to grieve. It was nice not going through it alone." Unbidden, my brain added "like usual," but I kept quiet.

"Any time, Kovis. I'm here for you. And if you ever want to talk more about it, I'm happy to listen. No doubt it'll take a while to work through."

He pressed his lips in a line.

I wasn't sure how to interpret the gesture. I hoped it was just his way of acknowledging my words, not a decline. He was still hurting, and it was probably just too hard to talk about.

I buttoned my cape, and we returned to the skies. Kovis still held his side of our bond closed, but he'd loosened up. Or maybe I was just hoping. But he seemed to look around and appreciate the scenery more.

Kovis pointed at a city we approached off to our right a short while later. He'd mentioned that we would pass Vaduz's capital, Colmar, so I assumed that's what it was. Similar to Flumen, several large structures dotted the landscape. One of note was a large oval that I speculated served much the same purpose as Flumen's arena. It seemed the former emperor's resources had been put to good use and Rasa would have a stiff battle if she was to ever eliminate The Ninety-Eight.

We landed as the sun kissed the horizon. I was again chilled to the bone and my ears ached, but we'd made significant progress. A lightness we hadn't known in ages infused both of us, which was a good thing because it promised to be a very cold night out in the open without blankets and no fire since there was nothing with which to build one.

Only the thought that we'd hopefully be in Dream with warm temperatures within a fortnight, or sooner, buoyed my resolve to hold my tongue and not complain. I just hoped it didn't snow despite the sky looking pregnant with it.

I stooped and gathered a handful of snow, packed it and popped the ball into my mouth. At least water wasn't scarce.

Kovis scanned the area. "I see no sustenance. We'll have to ration what little we brought and hope we can find more to eat when we get to Wood." Translated, we'd be cold *and* hungry tonight.

After we'd both had our fill of melt, I blew what snow remained from a circle of barren ground with my Air magic. If we had to sleep in the open, we didn't have to endure wet clothes. Kovis still set his wards, even though I couldn't imagine any predator being crazy enough to be out in these parts. I couldn't even imagine mares way out here. No, only we were this insane.

I wrapped my cloak more tightly, then sat down. Kovis followed.

"How will we stay warm without blankets or a fire?" It wasn't an innocent question. I wanted to get a read on "us."

Kovis gave me a long look but finally said, "Body heat."

While his words were what I'd hoped for, my chest felt heavy seeing his reluctant posture. It told me everything. He'd appreciated me being there for him earlier, but it hadn't swayed him otherwise.

An overwhelming feeling of loneliness came over me. I longed for someone to talk to. I'd come from Dream with Kovis as my hope and I'd focused on him—I'd have shattered if I hadn't—losing my family and everything I knew for him and for Wake.

Along the way, I'd convinced myself only he could understand who I really was. I hadn't told anyone about my past other than Kennan. Not Haylan, much less Hulda. But in this heartbeat, I realized that Kovis couldn't be my focus. He was too prone to upset, and when he was, my whole world was upside down.

My actions had been the cause this time as well as last, but it seemed unhealthy. He hadn't even let me explain about that kiss. I loved him wholly, but he couldn't be my focus, not to the exclusion of everyone else. I needed balance.

Dusk fell then morphed into darkness. It was just as well since there was nothing to do but try to sleep. I felt emotionally numb, which made me more tired, so I lay down. I chided myself when I thought back to my hopes from early this morn of the cold forcing intimacy whether he liked it or not. I'd been a fool.

I didn't plan to remove a single layer of clothing. I would need every stitch on me to stay lukewarm, forget about hot. I curled into a ball, arranged my cloak tightly around me, then popped my head inside my cocoon.

Not long after, Kovis spoke through my cape. "We won't be able to exchange body heat if you keep your leathers on, Ali, and you'll freeze to death."

I pushed my head through the top of my cape. He just looked at me. I knew he was right, but it was *freezing*. "Fine, but I'm keeping my braises on."

"As I would encourage," he agreed.

I climbed out of the beginnings of warmth and shed my leathers faster than ever before, then scrambled back into the sandwich of my cloak. Kovis climbed in behind me then threw his cape over us, and we tucked it in around.

While it was stuffy under two capes, in not too long, I began to feel his heat—through a double layer of braises—but heat, nonetheless. Blessed warmth. Kovis was an engine, and with his arms wrapped around me, I began to relax. Unlike before, his hands remained still, but weariness overwhelmed me before I could mourn them. I let sleep claim me.

Nature had laid another blanket over top us during the night, a good two-finger thick blanket of snow. And she'd done it without a sound. Our leathers beside us were piled with the white stuff.

Only the thought that in just a few more suns we'd be in Dream, made the sudden frigid cold and stiffness bearable as we shed our cocoon, brushed precipitation off our leathers, and dressed. I couldn't imagine how miserable our night might have been without the cloaks and Kovis's warmth. Even though he hadn't warmed to me, he'd still warmed me.

I nibbled a few remaining seeds that I'd stowed in my cloak pocket, but with nothing more to eat and no fire to tend, we were back in the skies in no time.

I ignored my stomach's rumblings as we flew over more desolate land. A cluster of homesteads popped up every now and again but not much else. With the monotony, my thoughts returned to last night. It seemed rest had done me good for I warmed to the realization I'd had—no matter what happened between Kovis and me, I would always love him, but I couldn't let him be my sole focus.

This thought would have sent tremors through me when I'd first arrived. Now, it felt… right. I'd endured much, and my trials had changed me. They'd given me a different perspective.

I thought about Haylan and Hulda, Myla and Arabella, and all the other apprentices and master healers. I couldn't wait to see them again, and when I did, I wouldn't be closed to telling them about my past, as unbelievable as it might seem to them. They were my friends… my Wake family… and I needed to treat them as such. No more holding back.

I just hoped they didn't react the way Kennan had.

• • •

Chapter Eighteen

I squinted and shivered, drawing my cape tighter as I flew beside
Kovis, trying but failing to focus on anything but my frozen nose
and my ears that ached.

The sun had crested and nearly blinded me as it reflected off the
snow-covered ground. Making matters worse were the frigid
temperatures up high and the tedious, utterly boring,
unremarkable, mind-numbing plains we'd been flying over nearly
the whole sun.

It had become routine—we flew for a while, landed to thaw,
then it was back at it. The terrain held no trees and only the wind
forced any signs of life as it played with the dead grasses, making
them bow and sway.

I exhaled, the strain on my eyes easing as hills with evergreens
that cast shadows replaced the blinding snow not long after. Kovis's
determined expression never changed.

I'd been focused on the land, but my skin started tingling as we
flew on, this time not from the cold. I furrowed my brow and
glanced over to catch Kovis smile. Was he feeling it too?

The tingling increased, spreading from my hands, up my arms, then across my middle and down my legs. It wasn't unpleasant. In fact, it felt good... really, really good.

"Magic," Kovis shouted above the wind. "We've just entered Wood province."

The heartbeat he said it, it felt like a wave of the stuff crashed over me, wrapping itself around me like the arms of an old friend— it felt like coming home.

I took a deep breath. Considering I hadn't had magic for even an annum, the strength of the feeling surprised me, but there was no mistaking it. My body suddenly felt... right again.

We'd been outside Elementis for five, nearly six, moons counting The Ninety-Eight competition. Apparently I'd acclimated to the feel of thin magic. Only now that we'd plunged into the flood of it did I realize magic must have been thickening as we approached, but it hadn't yet been dense enough for me to notice.

Kovis was grinning, no doubt enjoying the feeling much the same as me.

The size of the trees increased as we continued on, but as I studied them as we glided over, I realized they weren't just trees. Had it been summer and they flush with foliage, I probably wouldn't have spotted the suspended walkways linking them together into a huge hive. We approached a city, and not a small one either. I could make out people walking about, lots of them.

I nearly squealed with delight when I picked up on the first wisps of Wood magic living within the sorcerers below. I hadn't gotten to use my Simulous affinity in too long, and I itched to do something with it. Just for fun.

Making sure my Air magic kept me aloft, I scanned the area and pulled just a thread of power from several sorcerers, as I'd done so many times before. They would never miss it, but the rush of accumulating it was indescribable. I wondered if this was how sorcerers felt on winter solstice.

What to do with it. I grinned as I carefully balanced on my winds, then directed power at a particularly large tree we approached. In the blink of an eye, tiny green buds materialized and grew into mature leaves, decorating the monolith as if spring had arrived early.

Kovis glanced over with raised brow. I gave him a playful shrug.

We'd barely cleared the city when my stomach grumbled and I motioned to land. I was cold, yes, but more, we hadn't eaten much for several suns and I was starving. With the Wood magic I'd lifted, I was ready to grow something tasty and gorge myself.

How I loved Elementis as well as my simulous affinity.

———

Bellies full of tomatoes, beans, and apples—the seeds and tree I'd most easily located and forced to bear fruit—I scanned the skies and my chest tightened. I wasn't alone. Kovis's shoulders were tense right along with mine because the sky had turned more somber and threatening while we ate.

"I hope the snows hold off," I said, watching a particularly dark cloud race by.

Kovis didn't comment, just gave me a long look as he formed his Air pillow beside mine and we launched. But as the afternoon wore on the clouds grew even more ominous, as if frustrated that they couldn't send their bounty down on Wake.

Kovis motioned to land not long before the sun ducked behind a hill and we held up in a copse of trees and erected a primitive lean-to of branches and twigs that I magicked together using a vine I found—I grew a tendril and bound the branches together. It wasn't perfect, but if precipitation found us, we would have some covering. It was more protection than we'd had in ages, and despite still being outside, it also kept the wind at bay and I quickly fell asleep in Kovis's arms.

But as I discovered when I woke, the clouds hadn't slept. They were dark gray and hid the sun, making it look as if it were dusk.

Kovis wore a furrowed brow and kept scanning the skies as we gulped down apple leftovers for breakfast. He didn't have to open our bond nor speak for me to understand his concerns.

"See those mountains? Those are the Lapides," he said after swallowing. "We'll reach Terra in not too long and head toward Cochem Pass. Crystal and gemstone caves populate much of those mountains." He traced the hills with a finger. "If snows catch us, we can shelter in one of the caves."

While I didn't have a clue about the locations he mentioned, I was glad to hear he had a plan.

"Are we going near the largest gemstone mine in the empire that rebels destroyed?" I hadn't forgotten that Father was the reason we were out in the wilderness, freezing our behinds off in the middle of the cold and snow.

Kovis sighed. "No, that's near the center of Terra. We'll be navigating the northwest part of the province."

I bobbed my head, swallowing my last bite of apple.

We launched in record time.

I turned whiny when the first flakes appeared not long after and my heart sped up. The mountains were still a good way off in the distance. We hadn't made it into Terra yet, and there would be no good place to shelter until we did.

Flakes fell faster and faster, then the wind picked up, driving them at us. It was becoming impossible to see. I squinted, keeping one eye on Kovis, who flew to my right, and the other eye focused ahead.

The mountains soon disappeared in the blizzard, and I prayed Kovis knew how to keep us on course, but his stiff posture didn't allay my fears. Harder and harder and harder the snow pelted us, and I lost sight of him.

"Kovis! I can't see you! Don't leave me!" I called out in panic.

His hand appeared a heartbeat later, clutching the fabric of my cape at the shoulder.

His beard and eyebrows were caked in snow. His face was red, and I spotted a blister forming on his brow—the first sign of frostbite. From the numbness in my face, I wasn't any better off. We needed to find shelter fast.

Despite the fact that he still kept his side of our bond closed to me, he must have been listening to my thoughts because he gave a nod then let go of my shoulder.

He stretched out his hand and directed power at the storm. Whether it was his Ice or Water magic that helped, I didn't care. What I knew was that he diverted the snow away so we could again see at least a short ways in front of us. I nearly cried for joy when ice crystals stopped pummeling my face—those things stung when hurled at that speed.

I moved closer to Kovis and grabbed his cape, even though my hand quickly froze. I wasn't taking any chances of getting separated.

On and on we flew, the blizzard not letting up, intensifying, if anything. How long could we endure? My nose lost all feeling, as did my ears. I scanned the area for sorcerers from whom I might draw power but sensed none.

Perhaps I could use my winds to propel us faster. The idea burst forth, and I acted on it in a heartbeat. Keeping one hand on Kovis, I moved the other over just a bit so my magic would propel us forward and not put us in a spin, then let it flow. Surging forward nearly ripped my grip from Kovis's cape, but I held firm.

Kovis's alarmed gaze shot my direction but when I nodded, he gave me a slow smile. We still couldn't see where we were going, but we were getting somewhere faster. I studied the white field in front of us, willing it away, but it stubbornly remained. My stomach roiled with anxiety that we wouldn't see a mountain in time and we'd smash into one.

"Stop! Brace!" Kovis's bellow pierced even the storm's fury, and I killed my winds.

Kovis threw both hands forward and drew a cushion of Air as gray and white rock filled my vision. It no doubt lessened the crunch, but the jolt of impact still rattled every bone in my body, and I dropped, then tumbled, head over heels.

Rocks, pebbles, snow—it all swept along with me as I cascaded down a steep incline. I couldn't cushion my fall with my winds fast enough, and my elbow found a rock that refused to give way.

I ducked and tried to cover my head as my shoulder hit another large stone. How much further? My knee hit something on the next revolution. Finally, I forced a cushion of air around me and began to slow.

I stayed tucked until I came to rest… somewhere. I infused more magic into my cocoon to deflect the storm's winds as the blizzard raged on around me, but I had no idea where Kovis was, or if he was alive, let alone conscious.

"Kovis!" The wind and snow swallowed my cry.

Ali? Are you okay? Where are you?

They were the seven sweetest words I'd ever heard, and through our bond.

Are you? I don't know where I am, I replied.

I think we made it to Terra.

But how would we ever find each other?

Do you have any seeds left? Kovis asked.

Seeds?

I opened my cloak just enough to find the pocket and sift through it. *Six,* I replied.

Grow the seeds into vines and I'll follow it to you.

But where are you?

Near the base of the mountain.

I swallowed down fear of not finding him and with frozen hands, I set the six seeds on the white ground then willed them to grow, three in either direction because I had no idea which way he was from me. I prayed the freezing temperatures didn't kill them before they found him.

Anything? I asked several heartbeats later.

No. Keep trying.

The first tendril turned brown at the source not long after, reinforcing my angst. I infused the tendril with more of the Wood magic I'd stored and it turned green again, then continued growing. Small mercy.

Anything yet?

I'll let you know.

I was infusing life back into four of the plants by the time Kovis said, *Got one! I'm coming. Don't move.*

I wouldn't dream of it. I exhaled heavily.

I'd been so focused on finding Kovis that I hadn't taken stock of my injuries. But with relief at locating him, my elbow, shoulder, and knee shouted, and I moaned. I couldn't keep tears at bay, and I felt their warmth on my cheeks until they froze.

Oh gods, it hurt.

Wind and snow raged outside my wind cocoon as I waited, panting from the pain. What was taking him so long? *Are you okay?*

I'm coming as fast as I can. Just a bit of loose rock to crawl over, snow drifts to wade through, boulders to skirt around, ice to keep my footing on—

Sorry. Got it. Take as long as you need. I bit my lip. I had to get a grip. I'd been hurt in training plenty of times, and this was no worse.

Thank you for your kind indulgence. I believe I will. Humor laced his words.

At least the ordeal hadn't spoiled his mood. Either that or he joked to ease his angst.

I expanded my cocoon a ways, and my heart leapt as Kovis, in his black leathers, came into view. Head down, he focused on his next step in the knee-high drifts.

"Kovis," I called.

He stopped and looked up. His shoulders drooped, and he held up the brown tendril he'd been following.

He slid on the loose rocks as he took another step. No wonder it had taken him so long. *Yes, it isn't exactly easy going.*

He collapsed next to me in the snow, rolled his head back, and exhaled. The gesture told me everything. He'd been scared shitless.

"What do we do from here?"

Kovis looked over at me, and the corner of his mouth rose. "Well, fair maiden, I suggest we find shelter."

I rolled my eyes. I'd asked for that response.

His expression turned serious. "You look pretty beat up."

"Yeah, I couldn't conjure a cushion until the mountain had had its way with me."

Kovis raised a brow. "Can you still fly?"

"I think so. But I don't think I can walk." My knee complained as I shifted.

"Then what say we venture forth, but a bit slower and lower perhaps?"

"*A lot* slower."

A corner of his mouth hitched. "We'll fix you up once we find shelter."

"Sounds good." I winced as I stood, my shoulder not letting me forget its infirmity.

We rose on Air cushions and followed the foot of the mountain, scanning the rock face for any openings. We found one, but it proved not to be a cave, just a recess and would not provide adequate shelter from a storm this ferocious. Two more we passed on for similar reasons.

The blizzard seemed to grow yet more fierce, and anxiety gripped me.

What would we do if we couldn't find a place to shelter?

Chapter Nineteen
Ambien

"But, Father, Kennan tracked them diligently. He did," Alfreda groveled before me. She was a pathetic mess from lack of sleep. Tears stained her face as seemed to be the norm these suns. I pushed down my disgust.

"Be strong, sister," Velma ground out from the next room.

I'd had my troops separate the sisters. Despite her own injuries, Velma intervened when they attempted to keep Alfreda awake with force, even inserting herself between her sibling and my guards. I wouldn't stand for that.

I'd told my troops not to physically restrain my eldest. Alfreda had gotten much too much sleep in the last sennight because of it. Only now was she reaching the previous levels of sleep deprivation, where I needed her.

So a rock wall separated my daughters, and I forbid them communication. Enough juvenile, idealistic narratives—they weren't just sickening, they could be dangerous when used in the manner she had. I would break Velma of them if it was the last thing I did.

"Silence!" Morfran commanded from the archway between. He wouldn't strike Velma unless I gave the order, which I didn't. Not yet.

"Kennan picked up Ali and Kovis's trail in Sanis," Alfreda whimpered, swiping a grimy sleeve across her eyes. "They wandered around for a while, but he tracked them."

I'd known her charge would find their trail, he couldn't go against my wishes now that I controlled him, but I had to keep up pretenses or Alfreda—or more probably Velma—would know something had changed.

"So where are they?" I added an impatient tone.

"That's just it, Father."

I growled.

Alfreda cowered.

Zagan forced her to stand up straight with a prod, then made her hold her arms at her sides once more, with only a look. Such compliance didn't come without training, but he'd accomplished it. He'd grow toughness in her whether she liked it or not and make her into a daughter I could respect. Clearly, he hadn't finished his task, but he'd made progress.

"Continue," I commanded.

Alfreda swallowed hard. "He followed them to Croft, but their trail disappeared."

I frowned. "You expect me to believe that?"

Alfreda raised her hands in supplication. "It's true. You have to believe me, Father."

"People don't just disappear, daughter."

"But they did. Kennan found their saddles stashed behind trees near a farm. He found their horses stabled there too. He searched until they ran him off."

I could always tell from their eyes if someone lied to me—if they met my gaze, they told the truth. If they looked away, they lied. I gripped Alfreda's chin and brought it up. She narrowed her eyes and didn't break my gaze. She told the truth.

Unease clouded my mind as possibilities raced past. They'd left their mounts. How was that possible? What were they doing?

"Was he searching for them in the nearest town?" Humans were notorious for being too fragile for the cold their land suffered several moons out of each annum. They had to be holding up there, perhaps waiting for milder weather. I despised guessing, which is what I was doing.

"I don't know, Father."

"Then I suggest you find out." I raised my brow.

"Yes... yes, Father. I will." Alfreda's shoulders slumped, and she loosed her wings a measure.

This was not good. If Alissandra wasn't there, where could she have gotten to? And how? I would force Alfreda's human to discover them no matter if I had to kill him in the process. I'd had greater plans for him, but I needed Alissandra back if I were to ever prove my strength to my peers. I would sacrifice him if I had to. Her leaving Dream was becoming too big a blow to my reputation.

I left Alfreda in Zagan's capable hands and ducked under the archway to check on Velma. She rose in a heartbeat, fire in her eyes, and planted her feet. Despite her show, she couldn't hide the dark that marred under her eyes.

I chuckled then chose my words purposefully. "All this anger and energy you expend. It's not aiding your cause, only making you tired. No doubt your... stumps... are sapping considerable strength in their healing."

Velma redoubled her show, clenching her jaw.

I shook my head. "You should rest, regain your strength. Have you let my troops change your bandages?"

"I wouldn't let them touch me if it was—"

I held up a hand. "Then at least allow me, before they become infected. You may be immortal, but if you get sick, that would slow your learning the lesson I wish to teach."

The fire in her eyes quieted a bit. Yes, she was very tired.

"I'd prefer Alfreda do it."

"I'm sure you would, but that won't be happening. You see this is not just about healing, it's part of learning that when you are less, you don't get what you wish."

Velma looked into my eyes, but the fight had left her. "Fine."

I nodded then called Bate to bring clean water and the salve and bandages they'd brought way out here. "Lie down."

Velma complied without a word, collapsing onto the moss bed and turning her back toward me, exposing her bandaged stumps. I stifled my inhale. The makeshift bandages Alfreda had bound them with—lengths of her dirty dress—barely clung to them. They were brown and stank. In her stubbornness she had refused treatment and so was learning more of the lesson of being less. She couldn't reach them much less tend them herself.

Velma's back arched as I pulled off the soiled bandages despite being gentle. The skin around both stumps was red and swollen, and greenish pus oozed from both. I'd seen worse, but not much.

She shuddered, and I realized she was trembling. I reached over and felt her brow. She didn't resist. She was burning up.

Bate handed me the supplies. I hated that my voice rose, but it couldn't be helped. "Go get something to reduce her fever. Quickly."

"Yes, my liege." He turned and was gone in a heartbeat.

I turned my attention to cleaning out the infection. It would hurt, but this again was more of the lesson. I wasted no time, dipping the cloth in water and bringing it to her skin.

Velma arched again and moaned as she fisted her hands.

Despite her pain, I continued working.

By the time I finished cleaning it out, she'd yelled herself hoarse and Zagan had needed to restrain Alfreda in the other room. I applied salve to another round of cursing—from both of them—then wrapped Velma's stumps in the clean dressing. It wasn't pretty, but it would do.

Velma sighed, clearly relieved when I finished.

I put a hand on her shoulder. She shirked it off. Very good. It seemed the lesson was being learned. She didn't care for being less. Not like this. And the thing about being less, you didn't get to choose when or where it happened. You were at its mercy. As she was finding out.

"It's okay if you hate me, daughter. I'm pleased that you are learning." I brushed a black lock from her cheek.

She turned her head away.

"I suggest you take what medicine Bate brings, but it's your choice, of course. And one of my guards *will* be the one to change your dressing when it needs it going forward. You see, you don't get to decide, when you're less."

Velma moved her shoulder forward, away from me.

"That's fine. All I care is that you learn, as it seems you are. Now get some sleep."

I rose.

On my way out, I stopped before Morfran. "How hard is it becoming to procure Alfreda's compliance?"

"Increasingly, my liege."

As I had anticipated. And it would become ever more difficult the more tired she became, but pretenses were critical. "If you need to stroke her wings or rub certain titillating spots—"

"Don't you dare!" Velma snarled, shaking a fist at me though her back was still turned my way. Hardly intimidating. "If you so much as touch my sister in any inappropriate manner, I will tear you limb from limb."

I shook my head. Her bluster was just wearing her out further.

Morfran didn't react, exactly as I would have expected of my commander. "If it becomes necessary, I will see to it personally, my liege."

"Just remain in this form when you do."

"Of course, my liege. I understand."

"Walk me out," I commanded.

When we got out of Velma's hearing, I stopped. "That last bit was for Velma's benefit only. Do no such thing to Alfreda."

He turned a questioning look at me.

"Pretenses only."

He bobbed his head. "Yes, my liege."

Chapter Twenty

The elements continued pummeling us, showing no mercy as we struggled to find shelter. The wind blew so strong that flying became nearly impossible, but hurt as I was, I couldn't walk. We moved forward at a slug's pace, neither of us talking, even through the bond.

All hope of finding shelter fled at some point. I was frozen like an icicle, and my nose, fingers, ears, and toes had gone numb. No one would rescue us. We would die out here. They'd find our corpses in the spring when the snow finally melted.

The thoughts had just crossed the void of my mind when there, on the mountainside, up a ways, I thought I saw a dark spot. It seemed different than the numerous rocks jutting from the mountain.

I squinted, not trusting my eyes, and struggled to see through the driven flakes. Could it be? I looked hard, and my heart leapt when the dark spot persisted.

Kovis!

He looked up, and I pointed.

Let's go see. He'd been searching at ground level, I'd been looking higher.

The storm's winds made us wobble as we rose to the level of the opening, which was circular, no more than to my thigh if I'd been standing. Regardless of its size, I wasted no time debating its merits and plunged in. Kovis followed immediately.

"We made it." I didn't care that my voice quaked. I collapsed onto the stone floor and savored the peace and calm. We'd made it out of that monster. I'd stopped believing we ever would.

Kovis found the floor beside me a heartbeat later. He collapsed on his back and drew an arm over his eyes, chest heaving.

I listened to the wind howling past the opening, and a feeling of thankfulness I'd never known before welled up in me. We could have died.

My wounds reminded me of their presence, and I rubbed my shoulder as I looked around in the dim light. The cave was taller than the opening but not by much. I was short; I'd be able to stand up straight. Kovis, never. Curved walls that looked like some animal had hollowed them out surrounded us. It had to be quite the animal to drill through this rock.

Dried grass and twigs littered the floor, and more had been piled up around the perimeter. With all this material available, we'd even be able to build a fire. I might actually be warm for the first time in ages.

Kovis sat up and followed my gaze. "Shit!" He leapt to his feet, slammed his head on the ceiling, then drew his hand up as he ducked again. He peered into the darkness that filled the back of the space then removed his cape with quick movements and tossed it against the wall.

What is it? I didn't dare speak aloud. I stood with difficulty and removed my cape too.

Big bug. They've been known to kill people with their pincers.

Kill? The voice in my mind raised an octave, and my heart rate accelerated. It had to be some bug.

Kovis bent forward and took a ready position. With my knee banged up as it was, pain surged through me, and I wasn't exactly steady when I attempted a ready position of my own beside him. I rested my weight on my left leg, trying to compensate. My elbow and shoulder screamed as I raised my arm, but I ignored it. I joined Kovis in his staring contest with the dark.

It wasn't long before I heard scratching along the rock floor, and my stomach clenched. Closer and closer it came. But the harder I listened, the more I realized there were more than one.

A low hum filled my ears. *What is that?*

Their wings.

Wings? These things have wings?

And an armor-hard shell. Aim to strike between the plates.

What? Was he kidding?

It was dim in the cave, but not so dark that I couldn't see a pair of long, narrow, plated pincers a heartbeat later. They appeared iridescent, their color shifting with their movement. The thing came to halfway up my thigh and was a fighting machine. It continued toward us, pinchers flexing, and I saw its full armor—plates covered every part of it, except its wings, which stood tall to create the impression of even greater size.

"Shit!" I echoed Kovis's earlier assessment. Out of the storm and into this thing's lair. And I'd thought mares were bad.

Kovis wasted no time. He conjured ice darts and let them fly at the creature's joints. I followed suit after grabbing a thread of his power as a second bug appeared and skittered around the first, toward me.

I became a cannon, pummeling it with wave after wave of ice. But my ice darts had no impact, bouncing off the plates. I changed tactic and aimed at the wings, shredding the thin membranes. While that slowed mine down, its pincers flexed faster as it continued toward me.

Kovis wasn't having much success either.

I hadn't practiced much with Ice magic, but I'd seen Kovis conjure a dagger multiple times as we skinned our kills. I focused on the result I sought and stifled a yelp when a crude knife appeared in my right hand, the hand attached to the shoulder and elbow I'd dashed against the rocks in my fall. I pushed aside the pain and examined the blade. It wouldn't win any prizes, but it had a sharp edge with a point, and that's all I needed.

If I could just get behind them… I yelled as I pushed off the rock floor, pain exploding through my body, but my winds caught me and wafted me over the thing. I screamed again as I landed and fought to regain my balance, but I'd gotten behind it. And with its wings shredded, it exposed its body that didn't have the thick plating.

The creature tried to turn around, but with its partner filling much of the space, it couldn't.

I hobbled forward, spotting the junction of the wings and the back. I moved the blade to my left hand and took aim—it felt clumsy, but I brought it down as hard as I could.

Black liquid began oozing from the wound, and I thought I might be sick. What foul fluid ran in their veins? Black seemed the antithesis of life. I pulled the blade out and struck again. And again. And again. Until the blade broke off, impaled in the thing. The bug's movements slowed, and its pincers stopped flexing.

I'd been focused on the conflict with my bug and had lost track of Kovis and the other one. But when I looked up, he held it at bay, pummeling it with a host of pin-sharp icicles. He'd destroyed its wings, but despite his focus on the thing's joints, it continued forward, albeit slower than it had been.

Each step was agony as I hobbled over behind it. I conjured another ice dagger, but my left hand was frozen from holding the first one for so long and I dropped it. "Damn!"

You won The Ninety-Eight. You can beat this thing, Ali. I know you can. His tone wasn't panicked, but calm and confident, as if he spoke the obvious. As if he was just keeping the creature occupied until I could spare the time to do it in.

He continued pummeling the bug but locked eyes with me. Despite everything we'd been through, were going through, I let his words wash over and buoy me.

I bent and swiped the dagger up, begging another jolt of pain to ravage me. It didn't hold back. Regaining my balance sent another zap of pain through me for good measure. I gritted my teeth, wobbled forward, then raised my arm and took aim.

I put every measure of strength into my downswing and was rewarded with a spray of black blood. I'd hit a major vessel. The black coated my leathers. I was going to be sick. Black didn't belong in veins. I swallowed hard and forced myself to keep striking it, to do it in.

A handful of blows and this bug ceased movement, but more black leeched from its wounds.

I collapsed to the floor and retched.

Chapter Twenty-One

Kovis

I rushed forward, skirting the beetle, wrapped my arms around Ali, then buried my face in her neck. I didn't care that she'd thrown up, or that black beetle blood coated her leathers.

We'd survived, just barely. Twice. And she'd been the reason.

My mind swirled like the tempest outside. Perhaps it was that we'd cheated death from the storm as well as these beetles, or perhaps it was the last vestiges of adrenaline raging through my veins, but I felt lighter than I had in ages. We'd been given a second chance.

She sat up, turned and threw her arms around me, hugging me for several heartbeats before pushing back. Her brow was furrowed, and I could only imagine what she was thinking, to cling to her like this after how I'd behaved over the last several sennights.

I opened my mouth, but she held up a hand. "It seems we have much to discuss, but I need you to get those things out of here first." She shivered with revulsion.

"After that performance, it's the least I can do." I was giddy. I'd have done anything for her.

Ali looked away as I stood and levitated the first rock beetle's corpse toward the entrance.

Before Ali had spotted the cave, I'd despaired that we'd make it. That blizzard had risen quickly, and we'd had no choice, die of exposure or continue on. She'd saved us.

And she'd been amazing in this fight, despite her injuries. Rock beetles weren't the smallest of creatures, and they'd been known to amputate limbs or worse with those pincers they used to tunnel through rock.

Ali had handily defeated them. It had been pure instinct to leap over them and attack from behind. She was small enough. I would have hit the ceiling. Ali was powerful as well as smart. I only wished I could find more soldiers like her to fill the ranks of our military.

Ali hobbled as far away from the beetles as she could and sat on a stack of twigs against the wall, watching with disgust as I reached the entrance with the first carcass. She shuddered as I tossed it and the wind snatched it away.

I'd never seen her so repulsed, not even when she'd sanded the heads off a few of those mares and red had splattered everywhere— it had coated both of us and she'd never shuddered. But now, she swiped at the black on her leathers and a chill rocked her body. I doubted it was from the cold.

Careful that my head didn't hit the low ceiling, I turned and retreated for the other body. As I did, my mind returned to the conundrum I'd been wrestling with since I'd had to leave Alshain behind.

I believed actions revealed the heart. I'd found it to be true and it had become a guiding principle in my life. It was why I'd been unable to reconcile Ali sharing what had been described as a passionate kiss with Kennan, with her being such an emotional support as I'd given up Alshain. I just couldn't make the two actions work together.

I'd experienced my share of heart-wrenching situations, but nothing close to how I'd suffered giving up my horse in annums. The scene had haunted my dreams, playing itself over and over again. And every time, Ali had been there for me. She'd rightly sensed that words were not what I needed, had stayed her tongue, and let me grieve in peace. But she'd been there in the way I'd needed her to be. For the first time, I hadn't had to endure sorrow alone.

Trouble was, I'd had plenty of scenarios running through my mind concerning that kiss too.

She'd said the kiss had been a mistake. A mistake. I'd been so wounded, I'd dismissed her claim out of hand. And I'd refused to hear her story—I couldn't suffer the details. I'd closed up and withdrawn from her since. It was the only way I knew to deal with something this hurtful. But a "mistake."

My body squirmed as I approached the entrance with the second beetle body. "Mistake" implied a *temporary* lack of judgment. I sucked in a breath.

We'd been given a second chance, I reminded myself. I didn't know why, but how could I not give Ali a second chance too?

I'd only known one other truly intimate relationship, and right or wrong, it was the only filter I had for whatever it was I had with Ali. Dierna had not just flirted with betrayal, she'd danced in its arms, knowing full well what she was doing. But had Ali? Was she different even in this?

Damn her. She'd woken me up from the self-imposed prison my heart had become and made me want to truly live. But I hadn't been this whole time I'd shut her out. I'd fled to safety. But I was dead here.

My stomach clenched. What would happen if I listened to her story?

My limbs turned shaky and my magic wavered—it made me almost drop the beetle as I neared the entrance.

Listen to her story. I felt my heart accelerate as the thought again swirled through my mind.

I forced myself to concentrate as I finally tossed the other foe into the elements.

• • •

Relief flitted across Ali's face as I turned, but it quickly morphed into a furrowed brow. "Kovis, what's wrong? You look... scared shitless. Is there another—"

I felt like a baby bunyip tentatively peeking out of its mother's pouch. She had no idea just how scared I was to initiate this conversation, but I waved my hands. "No. Nothing like that."

"Then what?" She ran a hand across the straw beside her.

I sat down on the pile of twigs, turned toward her, and looked into her eyes. My heart nearly pounded out of my chest, and I took a deep breath. I could do this. I rubbed my hands on my legs. "Would you tell me about that kiss?"

She didn't flinch. She didn't move at all for several heartbeats, just held my gaze as if looking into my soul. I couldn't imagine what was going through her mind. "Are you sure?"

"I am." I compelled my voice to remain steady; it took every ounce of effort I possessed.

She continued staring into my eyes, as if giving me time to change my mind. But I wouldn't, now that the question was out. It felt as if Alshain had taken off, galloping out of control, and I held on for dear life.

When I didn't flinch, she finally began. "It happened when..." She looked at her hands, at the ring I'd given her, then clenched her jaw and looked up again. "It happened when you were behaving much the same as you've been these suns."

Her words stung, but I deserved them. So I nodded.

"I was lonely. I didn't have anyone, not even my sisters, to talk to."

An arrow piercing my heart would have seared less. She'd chosen me over her sisters when she'd come... She was close to them, much as me and my siblings, yet she'd done it, and why? To tell me of her father's plans. To save Wake. She hadn't had to. But she did. I swallowed hard, struggling to remain still.

"Kennan was the only one who knew me, almost as well as you."

"Not your friends?" I choked out the words.

She closed her eyes and shook her head. Clearly there was a bigger story, but I didn't probe.

"I felt unloved and worthless. I just wanted you to love me again. Kennan encouraged me not to let your moodiness and insecurities make me question myself, my worth."

I blew out a breath. My moodiness and insecurities… She gave me far too much influence if that was true. But from the look in her eye, I didn't doubt it.

"I hadn't realized how starved I was for your affections. It was a quick kiss, but yes, there was passion. But it was never about Kennan. Not to me. Only after we kissed did I realize I'd substituted your brother for you. I only ever wanted you back, Kovis." She sniffed.

The twigs sighed as I shifted and squeezed my eyes shut. I believed her. Every word.

I hadn't trusted her. After all she'd done and endured for me, *how* could I have thought she'd betray me? Breathing became hard. I hadn't even been willing to listen to her. It felt like my throat constricted. I was a complete and utter ass.

Ali continued. "I'm so sorry I didn't tell you, Kovis. I was afraid you'd react, well, the way you did. I didn't want to lose you. It was wrong of me. I was stupid to think it would stay hidden forever, and it only made things worse when it did finally come out."

I opened my eyes to see her bite her lip.

"Kovis… can… can you forgive me?"

Guilt seared my heart. She blamed herself when it was my cowardice that had caused this. I shook my head. "Can I forgive you? Ali,"—I threw my hand against my chest—"I'm such an idiot. I've behaved horribly because I'm so damn insecure." I looked to the ceiling and huffed.

She leaned in and choked out words I didn't deserve. "I promise to always be open with you, Kovis." Tears leached down her cheeks as she looked at her ring and ran a finger around it, composing herself. She took a deep breath, then said, "The night you proposed was magical. Do you remember?"

I nodded. "Like last sun."

She set her jaw. "We bared our very souls to each other, hiding nothing. It was a picture of the future I hoped to share with you. That I still do."

"Ali, I've made a huge mess of… of us. I can't tell you how truly sorry I am."

She pulled her shoulders back. "I helped."

I forced a smile and looked down. I didn't deserve her.

She opened her mouth to say more, but I stopped her. "Let me finish. What I promised you that night, I meant. Every word of it." I closed my eyes again. "Ali, you tore down that fortress I'd built around my heart and helped me love again, feel again, but despite your love, it seems I've rebuilt those walls." I shook my head, angry at myself. "It took you nearly dying at the hands of the rebels the first time and almost dying at nature's hands this time to knock sense back into me." I huffed. "It's a bit extreme."

A corner of Ali's mouth hitched up for a heartbeat, but determination lit her eyes. "You can't do it on your own, Kovis. You've been hurt too much, too many times. Our leathers and our magic protect us from physical harm. Let me help do that for you against the darkness of your heart. I did it as your sand maiden when the night begged to overwhelm you. I wove your dreams and beat it back. Had I not intervened, I fear it would have swallowed you whole with you taking your life. Thank the gods you didn't, but I couldn't eliminate it all, and what remains has done damage. It makes it impossible for you to fully trust another, even me."

Of course she knew about me wanting to end my pain. She'd known but hadn't condemned me.

The darkness shrieked inside me, then lashed out at the light, the hope she held out to me. It knew if I chose her light, it could not survive.

She drew a hand to her heart. "Between the two of us, we couldn't defeat it before, so you can't expect to do it on your own now. Let me help you, Kovis. Let me be your defense, your protection, an affinity of light. This is more than just about us. It's about you. I love you far too much for you to fight this on your own."

My heart raced; I could feel it thumping wildly in my chest. I opened my mouth, but no words would come. I'd been serious about overcoming my darkness. I had. But it didn't matter. It had still won, again. She was right, I couldn't defeat it on my own.

My limbs trembled. It gripped me, shut me off. Like an enormous snake, it had wrapped its coils about me and had been slowly squeezing for annums. It now crushed me, strangling the very life from me. I had no power against it, none, and if I did nothing different, I would die, perhaps not physically, but emotionally. I'd be reduced to the mere husk of a man. I panted.

I wanted to look away, but I forced my eyes to meet hers. "I'm undone. Ali, you know my darkness. You alone know it completely." I hugged myself, trying to make my body still. It didn't. "Take it, Ali. It's got me, and I thought I could… but I can't break free."

She grimaced as she rose to meet my lips and she laid on a crushing kiss. It was wild and abandoned and full of passion. She grabbed my cheeks between her hands and deepened it still more.

I held the kiss as I jerked her onto my lap, wrapped my arms around her, and held on for dear life. It would take both of us. But she was committed to not just pushing back my darkness but beating it senseless, kicking the stuffing out of it once and for all. With me. Always with me. So I could truly live. She would be fierce and relentless, I knew she would. Every step of the way.

My heart overflowed with love for this amazing woman. Despite how I'd acted toward her, she still loved me. A sense of gratitude, deeper than I'd ever known, filled my heart. And for the first time in forever, I felt a glimmer of hope rise in me. I truly wasn't alone anymore.

It was a good thing, because only the gods knew what perils still awaited us.

Chapter Twenty-Two

It would scare Kovis shitless to face the whole of his darkness.
Would he?

On Kovis's lap, I held his scruffy face and moved my lips against his, my heart overflowing with love for this man. I'd hoped for this opportunity for so long. In Dream, I couldn't be as effective as I'd needed when I only had the time in which Kovis slept to shift his darkness, and it hadn't been enough.

I pressed more kisses to his lips and he reciprocated.

I'd now have the whole of every sun, that, combined with his courage, I felt confident it would be enough. I sensed his commitment, and he'd allowed me the honor of helping him. If he could get truly healthy, we could have the future I dared to believe we both hoped for.

I traced his lips with my tongue, savoring him.

I had work to do too. We were both flawed. He had been my world, my whole focus since I'd come to Wake. He was the only one who really knew me, and it was unhealthy. It was time for me to open myself up and share my true self with others, because if I didn't, I was just as dead inside as he was.

He opened his mouth to me and our tongues found each other.

In isolating myself, I'd insulated myself from scrutiny, critical looks, and scathing assessments—that incident in the dining hall when fellow apprentices had ostracized me still haunted my thoughts. Yes, I had trust issues just like Kovis. Not as dark, but I hadn't believed that even Haylan and Hulda would understand and accept me. I hadn't trusted them. My best friends. What kind of a friend was I?

I moaned. Even if I wasn't suffocating and withering in the tumult of Kovis's erratic moods, I needed to trust others.

I pulled back and Kovis furrowed his brow. Being vulnerable would be uncomfortable, maybe even… excruciating but I needed to do this. *We* were worth it.

"What's wrong?" His beautiful blue and hazel eyes held worry.

"Nothing. Absolutely nothing." I pressed another kiss to his lips.

The storm continued raging, snow swirling past the entrance, and we held each other. It was a perfect picture of how I saw our inner storms warring against us. We would hold on to each other no matter how hard they raged or what they threw at us. We would not let go of each other.

———

Sometime later when resolve had firmed itself in both of us, we pulled apart. I think we both sensed that we had changed and would never be the same. But the storm hadn't changed. It still raged.

I nodded to the blackness at the back of the cave. "Since it seems we'll be staying a while, we need to make sure there aren't more of those things back there."

"Good idea, but let's tend your wounds first."

"No, I won't rest if I'm worried there's more back there. I'll tend my wounds after."

"Suit yourself." Kovis retrieved his cape, rummaged through the pocket, and pulled out his flints. "I think a torch might be in order, first."

I couldn't agree more. I floated two of the thickest branches over to him. Fire caught on the first and then the second. Kovis handed one to me.

"Ready?"

I took a deep breath and nodded. I couldn't stand these beetles. They disgusted me to my core. They had black blood. Black. What good creature had black blood?

I stretched out, belly down, torch out front on a cushion of my winds. "After you."

The ceiling sloped lower and the sides narrowed as we made our way back. These beetles had done an amazing amount of work. The rock was hard and not easy to tunnel through, but they'd done it. We progressed single-file, Kovis hunched over at the waist.

The walls held a bluish cast, but the further we ventured, pink and raspberry and purple and white and lime green added to the mixture.

They're sapphires, Kovis said through the bond.

He'd used our bond and it warmed me.

Vulnerability was scary as Hades, but it had left me feeling clean and renewed. It seemed it had left him similarly if he'd opened his side of our bond.

Would you mind me joining your mind so I can see what you're seeing? I asked.

There was no hesitation. *Please do.*

Holding my air pocket took effort and the usual disorientation beset me as I joined Kovis's mind, but soon I saw the tunnel through two sets of eyes—one the cave before him, the other... his cute butt.

He chuckled.

"Just appreciating the view." I snickered.

I refocused as we moved forward, the only sound Kovis's boots echoing on the stone. How far had these bugs tunneled?

Not long after, the sides and ceiling started widening again and my stomach clenched. I had a feeling we were about to find their home. I prayed we didn't find more rock beetles.

Kovis's torch illuminated the new cavity, similar in size to the one at the front of this cave. Kovis took several steps, and an enormous stash of acorns came into focus.

Seemed we wouldn't be starving. Turning to his right, the torch illuminated what looked like a bowl filled with large-ish round balls. Like the walls, they shimmered iridescent pink and blue and green as they shifted.

I screamed. "Eggs! Kill them!" I was back in my own head without realizing I'd ended our connection. I hit the ground as I lost concentration on my winds. Despite my wounds, I scrambled back. I couldn't get away fast enough. I skittered back toward the dark tunnel.

A bright flame shattered the darkness. Then Kovis yelled, "Ali! Stop! They're dead."

I collapsed, panting. My heart raced.

Kovis stooped over me, then smiled. "Not a fan of rock beetles I see."

"Anything with black blood filling its veins cannot be of this world." A shiver ran up my spine. "They're evil."

He snickered; it was the first time in ages.

"So glad I amuse you."

His eyes danced as he grinned. "I've never seen you move so fast." He couldn't hold in a snort, and it grew.

I burst out laughing.

He fell to the ground beside me chortling. "You... you...," he wheezed. He drew his hands to his stomach, unable to stem the tide.

A cackle erupted from me. I sounded like a wounded chicken.

It only made him laugh harder.

My sides and stomach hurt, but I couldn't stop.

"You should have seen yourself…" He finally got the words out but burst out laughing again as his mind replayed my desperate actions.

My stomach ached, but it felt good.

The next heartbeat, an explosion rumbled from the back of the cave, and the floor trembled. Dust rained down, squelching our revelry. Confusion marred his face, no doubt mine too, as we looked at each other. Listening.

"What?" I whispered.

The mountain stilled, and Kovis bolted up, torch in hand. I eased up to sitting, stretched and snatched my torch from the floor, and floated after, on his heels. I ignored the stench and sight of the burnt eggs as we rushed past, plunging further into the belly of the mountain.

The tunnel narrowed again. Had these disgusting creatures carved out an inn and tavern that bug villagers frequented. I prayed not. But even if they had, it wouldn't explain the explosion.

Kovis stopped and threw out a hand. *I thought I heard voices.*

He crept forward. I followed, nearly on top of him.

He stopped when a waist-high barricade laced with a tangle of magic from several affinities blocked the end of our shaft—I sensed Water, Terra, Wood, and Metal.

To keep the rock beetles from going forward? I questioned.

Not sure.

We looked past the barrier to find a large cavity that had been hewn in the middle of the mountain that stretched into the blackness above. Torches, spaced a man's height apart, rimmed the perimeter at floor level. Several other openings, no doubt the work of more rock beetles, dumped into the space at irregular heights and intervals.

I did a quick count and got to twenty-six men, miners I guessed. There were probably more inside a two-story structure that stood in the middle of the cavern.

It was hard to see much, dim as it was, but we ducked back into the shadows as a beefy man strode past. A shout and a good ten men, each with a palm-size, silver ball in one hand traipsed past in the other direction. Some of them were sorcerers from the magic I sensed coming off them, but not all. A man at the front of the pack and another halfway back carried lanterns.

I sucked in a breath. They'd passed close enough for me to see their eyes. Every eye had been cloudy. I'd bet my life they all were.

We'd stumbled on a rebel hideout. It had to be.

The group returned for more of whatever it was they were moving. Back and forth, back and forth.

Explosives. Kovis said on their next trip past.

Shit! Rebels had attacked the largest gemstone mine in Terra just moons before. People had died. One of Hulda's brothers had been injured. It was all part of what we'd surmised to be Father's plan to crush the economy of the Altairn Empire and bring it to its knees in order to conquer it. And it looked like these rebels were gearing up to do it again.

I glanced over. Kovis watched, a conflicted look marring his face. I tunneled through our bond and listened in.

If we don't stop them, another mine will be destroyed, but more importantly, citizens will die. But stopping them won't be easy. There's only two of us. And the longer we spend here, the longer Ali's father will have free reign. Who knows what else he's got those he controls doing? If we stay, would we be… maybe… hopefully… winning a battle, but losing the war? And Kennan… no, this can't come down to rescuing him.

Kovis blew out a breath.

My heart hurt for him. I agreed, there was no easy answer. But when family was affected, it made any choice all the harder.

We watched for a while longer, but clarity remained elusive.

They can't do anything while this storm rages. It's been a while since we've eaten. Let's build a fire and roast some of those acorns, and you can continue pondering, I suggested.

Kovis closed his eyes and nodded, then reached his hand over to me. *We need to take a look at your injuries too.*

My injuries… I hated to contemplate their severity out here in the middle of nowhere with a storm raging.

Chapter Twenty-Three

The storm had raged for five suns. I was beginning to wonder if it would ever stop.

The only positives, it gave me time to heal. It also provided us the opportunity to observe the rebel outpost and become familiar with their activities. Well, that and Kovis took advantage of our confinement in… other, more intimate ways. I smiled.

Gods it felt good to have him back. I'd missed that intimacy. I had my own work to do to grow stronger, healthier, but that in no way diminished my love for him. I loved him completely and to linger in his arms after he'd given me pleasure… He was home.

We'd made the cave a little homier. I'd borrowed a thread of Kovis's Ice to erect a wall to block the winds coming in the entrance. Kovis had started a fire. Between that, our capes, our bodies, and his arms surrounding me, I was happier than a bug in a rug—not a rock beetle mind you, a normal bug. I didn't mind those.

I'd untangled threads of Wood and Terra magic the rebels had used on the barricade and leveraged them to accelerate my healing. In fact, my body felt whole again.

Kovis had conjured water and blasted the beetles' black blood off my leathers then warmed more up and hosed both of us down to remove our stench. Despite not having soap, my nose appreciated the improvement.

Kovis had me give him a shave with an ice blade he conjured. To say "doing the honors" made me nervous would be an understatement. I'd never shaved a man, not even one of my brothers. As it was, I nicked him twice, but healed him right away.

What a difference. He'd gotten so scruffy—hair on his upper lip had grown over his mouth and he'd had to part it in order to eat, as well as kiss me. It had also grown over his ears and hung unkempt from his chin. I hated it. Having his clean-shaven face to again appreciate gave me a few "ideas" to try on him. He loved them.

But all the while, the storm raged on and on and on, a constant whistling and rumbling filling our ears. So when I woke in Kovis's arms this sun and all was deathly quiet, not one thing stirring, I soaked in the stillness, starring at the ceiling in awe. That mighty tempest had at last blown itself out. In its fury, it could not withstand the full force of its own power. Dared I hope this foreshadowed what would happen with Father?

Cheery sunlight filtered through the ice barrier at the mouth of the cave. Curiosity coaxed me from our warm cocoon, and I dressed quickly. Winter and snow were a whole new thing for me, not having seasons in Dream. Thus far, I hadn't exactly appreciated the experience, so I wanted to see what all that bluster had left behind. I'd decide then if winter had any redeeming qualities. I wasn't optimistic.

What are you doing? Kovis's voice was clogged with sleep. *Come back to bed. You've left me defenseless against the cold.*

I snorted. *Poor Dreambeam.* "If you must know, the storm stopped. I want to see what it left."

Lots of snow, satisfied? Now come back to bed.

"No, come join me." I moved toward the ice barrier and flicked my brows.

You wouldn't.

"Hehe, I would."

Kovis groaned.

A smile climbed across my face as I watched him toss aside our capes, all warmth left behind. But before he could even get to the first stitch of clothing, I blasted Air at the wall of ice.

"No!" His eyes were wide as he rushed for his braises.

I don't think I've ever seen you move so fast. I couldn't stop laughing as the ice wall fell away.

He finished buckling his leathers and barreled toward me, a grin on his face.

I squealed as he wrapped his arms around me, pinning my arms to my sides and smothering the back of my neck and the sides of my face in kisses.

That was mean, but I suppose I deserved it. I'm still as hot for you as ever though. It came out a purr.

I twisted in his arms, then looked up into his eyes, those blue and hazel pools that I'd first fallen in love with. "I love you, Kovis." I ran a hand over his smooth skin, still adjusting to his lack of facial hair. He had to stoop with the short ceiling so, for the first time, I had no trouble planting a kiss on his lips. I made a mental note: order the ceilings be lowered for his rooms back at the palace.

"I love you." What had been playful turned passionate as he picked me up and hugged me tight to himself, then claimed my mouth with his.

While we'd had our share of problems and we had a ways to go to being completely healthy with our relationship, I knew that if we could keep the love we had for each other alive, we could overcome anything. The truth of the thought sent a tear trickling down my cheek. Aside from my siblings and grandparents, I'd never known such love and acceptance.

Sensing my roiling emotions, Kovis pulled back. "Hey, what's this?" He put me down then traced the path of the rogue tear with his thumb.

"I'm just happy."

"Me too." He held my gaze for several heartbeats before planting a kiss on the tip of my nose. A nod had me turning to see the view.

I sucked in a breath at the sight. Everything. Every single thing was covered in a thick, white blanket that sparkled in the sun. Its beauty left me speechless.

"Careful," Kovis warned.

I'd walked to the edge of the cave opening. More snow covered the floor of the valley and opposing side of the pass we'd been following, so much that not one patch of rock had managed to escape. Only the tops of the tallest trees stood taller. Perhaps I'd been hasty in my judgment about winter.

"I've decided what we need to do." His words lingered on the chilly air. He didn't have to say about what. He'd been wrestling with the rebel situation since we'd found them and had been observing, sometimes with me, sometimes alone. I'd never had to weigh lives in any decision, and I knew he needed time by himself to sort through it all.

I waited as his mind organized his thoughts.

"There is no right answer. People will die no matter what we do, citizens or those your father has control of. In a perfect world I'd save both."

"You'd save the rebels?"

"They are not acting of their own accord. I do not believe anyone would willingly fight against their empire. Perhaps there are a few dissenters, but I believe their actions are your father's doing, not their own, and I will not punish anyone without first understanding what or who drives them."

He had a point.

"I want to disrupt their operation, leave them something to remember us by, before we leave this sun."

"Disrupt? You plan to leave?"

"I want to stymie their progress without harming the rebels themselves, and yes, I plan to leave. Wiping out this base will take planning and time that we don't have and give your father opportunity to instigate more trouble in the meantime. We're on defense. We need to be on offense if we are to stop him."

"So stymie rather than wipe out? How do you propose we do that? It's just us."

"They gave us a gift when they set up that barricade. As you know, its Water, Terra, Wood, and Metal magic are what kept the beetles back. Well, it seems to me that we might just leverage those same affinities, throw in a little Air and Ice, and we could have quite a lot of fun. All while ensuring none of the rebels are harmed."

I gave him a long look. "But there's only two of us."

"Fear not. Those explosives have Wood and Metal magic woven around a metal casing. But at the core of each"—he looked into my eyes before continuing—"there's a rock beetle egg."

My mouth dropped open and my eyes grew wide.

Kovis held up a hand. "When it's deployed, the Wood magic grows the beetle and it tunnels a path into wherever it lands. The Metal magic follows that path, reshaping the casing and bringing it with it. A strong sorcerer makes the metal explode with just a thought. When the beetle's blood mixes with the shrapnel, it burns, starting fires everywhere."

"I knew those things were evil! At least the beetle's destroyed."

"Most definitely." The side of his mouth hitched.

"Okay, so knowing that, what's your plan to stymie them?"

"We need to destroy the stockpile of explosives as well as the rock beetle eggs. We destroy the eggs, and it'll take them a while before more become available. I know where the various nests are that they've been collecting eggs from."

"The nest in our cave—"

"I erected an Air barrier the first time someone attempted to come in."

"You didn't tell me—"

"I didn't want to worry you. It wasn't important."

I opened my mouth to protest, but he waved it off.

"It's an insorcelled man they've got collecting eggs. He was confused when he couldn't get in, but he eventually gave up."

"An insorcelled man? What, by himself? But what if the beetles…" I didn't finish the thought.

My stomach twisted. Humans were expendable to Father.

"So what do we do?" I asked.

"I know where they're assembling the explosives as well as where they're stockpiling them. We destroy the nests first."

I drew back. I wasn't going anywhere near rock beetles unless Kovis begged me to.

"And you won't have to." Clearly Kovis had been listening to my tumultuous thoughts. "Everything we do will be from the protection of this cave."

I raised a brow.

"They're collecting eggs from ten caves. I'll point out each one, then using the Terra magic that the rebels so kindly gifted us, you can sense the position of the nest within. You tell me where the nest is, and I'll freeze the eggs."

"I've never used Terra like that before."

"I have every confidence you can do it, Ali."

"Won't the rebels see ice soaring overhead?"

"I'll send my Ice magic on my Air. I'll manifest the ice only after it's inside the cave. No one will see anything."

I put a hand on his arm. "You can do that?"

Kovis chuckled. "I didn't say I'd done it before, but I don't see why not. I *am* the most powerful sorcerer this empire has ever known."

I rolled my eyes. "Braggart. So how do we knock out the stockpile?"

Kovis wagged his brows. "I believe it's a simple matter of you melting the metal casings down."

"Like what, in a puddle?"

"Exactly, using the barrier's Metal magic. A quick freeze will kill the eggs inside. I'll also freeze the eggs in their assembly area while I'm at it."

"And they're just going to let us do this?"

● ● ●

"Oh, that's where we have a little fun. We're going to drench them with water from every direction. You use the Water magic from the barricade, I'll use my own. You've gotten a whiff of them. They could all stand baths."

"So we're doing them a favor." I grinned and shook my head.

Kovis turned his hands palms up. "What? That's how I see it."

I snickered. "Somehow I doubt they'll agree."

"Which is exactly why I shall redouble my Air barrier and we'll beat a hasty retreat."

It was a plan, imaginative as well as daring. I just hoped nothing went wrong. Too much rode on our reaching Dream.

Chapter Twenty-Four

We gazed out over the rebel outpost. We'd readied our capes at the entrance. We'd don them then float out on pillows of Air, *if* all went well. Yes, if...

I'd battled in The Ninety-Eight, so this exercise shouldn't have been any big deal. But I'd relied on skills I'd practiced time and again for that. I would have to figure out how to use Terra to sense the location of those nests, which I'd never done before. I'd also never melted metal down. And Kovis... I had to stop, or I'd be a complete mess with no hope of success. And we had to succeed, or citizens would die in the next rebel attack on a Terra mine they seemed to be readying for.

Just do your best, Ali. It's all we can ever do. Best for best.

Kovis hadn't used that phrase in ages, but it certainly applied.

Ready?

As I'll ever be.

Kovis pointed at the first beetle cave. It was situated about two men's height above floor level. A crude set of steps had been carved from the rock, and that poor insorcelled man had undoubtedly been forced to climb them to harvest the eggs. I hoped he had no awareness of what he was being made to do.

I halted my thoughts and focused. I needed to locate the nest. I grabbed a thread of Terra from the barricade before us. How to sense? I imagined becoming part of the floor just inside that cave. As I did, I started to perceive the difference in density between the walls and the open space. Score one for Ali. I moved out across the floor, but nothing weighed on me. Was I doing this correctly?

Where would the nest be? Wait, how was *our* cave organized? Surely these creatures built them similarly.

Ours had a long tunnel connecting the back entrance and the nursery. I refocused and felt my way along the shaft until the density of my surroundings again told me I had reached another open area. Score two. But was the nest here? Or the beetles themselves. I shuddered. Fanning out around the space, I felt a largish something above me, but it moved. I nearly shrieked.

Kovis put a reassuring hand on my shoulder. *You can do this, Ali.*

I continued feeling my way across the space until I located something with weight… in a circular shape. This had to be the nest. It didn't weigh as much as that creature had. And it didn't move.

I think I found it.

Kovis joined my mind through our bond. It still felt odd having him in my head, but I was getting more used to it. With each time he'd done it, it had grown more intimate and less foreign. I'd done it to him, but it was a different sensation when he joined me.

He homed in on the location I'd identified. Then on his Air he sent a rush of Ice magic. A heartbeat later he exclaimed, *Yes! Well done! There were a dozen eggs, but they're frozen now.*

How can you be sure they were the eggs?

My Ice felt them. They were spheres.

I wished we could just freeze the beetles, but they were too large. I returned my presence to the cave and listened. No noises sounded that would indicate anyone was the wiser. I'd have been surprised if there had, but you never knew.

Let's do it again, Kovis said.

He was right, time was moving.

I reached out again and again, to each of the ten nests, and together we destroyed those eggs. I shed no tears.

Task one complete, we turned our attention to the stockpile. Destroying this and the eggs in the assembly area would attract attention, so we had to be quick. At least we knew exactly where everything was located.

I grabbed a thread of Metal magic from the barrier and looked to the stockpile of explosives. The rebels had placed them in several straw-lined wooden boxes, wood dividers separating each. The crates had been stacked on top of each other to a man's height. I'd start on the ones at the back and move forward.

Melting metal couldn't be that hard. The metal casings attracted my Metal affinity, and I located the first sphere. I imagined it melting, turning into liquid that flowed from the crate onto the ground below. I gave Kovis a thumbs up when I sensed the sphere lose it shape.

You're doing great, Ali.

I'd made it through half the cache when three rebels ambled toward the supply, more explosives in hand. Despite starting at the back, with metal oozing down the crates and pooling on the floor, it was impossible to hide the mess.

The rebels cried for help then launched into the pile, furiously moving the crates to get to the cause.

Keep going, Ali. I think it's time for their showers.

I focused and redoubled my efforts. Sweat started trickling down my back as a torrent of water began spraying the rebels, driving them off.

But more rebels joined in the fight. Kovis expanded the field of spray, pummeling them so they couldn't stand.

I kept melting spheres. More and more and more of them.

I had ten explosives left when I heard the shout, "Over there!"

Not to rush you, Ali, but…

Kovis iced the eggs I'd uncovered, and I melted the metal on the seventh remaining sphere. I worked quickly—six, then five, then four left.

We need to go.

Just three left. I can do it.

I focused and melted another.

Ali, no time. Kovis grabbed my arm.

Metal flowed off another sphere, exposing the egg.

Kovis dragged me away and threw up an Air barrier.

You didn't freeze the eggs in the assembly area, I protested.

I did.

When?

Talk later. Run!

I heard shouts behind us, but they weren't growing closer. Not yet. It seemed they hadn't broken through, but it wouldn't be long.

Kovis threw up another barrier behind us as we reached the open area at the front of the cave. We grabbed our capes and buttoned them as shouts sounded directly behind us.

"Here we go!" Kovis said as he raced out the entrance, with me on his heels. I caught myself on a pocket of Air, but a heartbeat later I plunged down, down into the snow. It surrounded me, and I panicked. I needed a hard surface against which to cast my winds in order to fly. The snow was light and powdery, and I sank down until I'd hit a solid layer. *Which way? Which way?*

Calm down, Ali! Move toward the light.

I expanded my Air and burst through the snow into the crisp air. But a shout overhead had me flying toward Kovis in the blink of an eye.

The rebels peered out of the cave, mouths gaping, no doubt because they'd never seen anything so strange as a person flying. By

• • • •

the time their minds caught up with their eyes, we had made it a good way up the pass. Anyone wanting to follow would have no trouble tracking us with the trail we left in the powdery snow, but I doubted anyone would be able to navigate the white stuff anytime soon.

That had been close, and my heart still beat faster than usual. Kovis's heart thumping wildly through our bond told me he fared similarly.

You said we'd beat a hasty retreat, I said some time later.

Kovis let out a full-bodied laugh. *Indeed I did. That'll teach me.*

We stymied them, Kovis. I smiled. *And not one rebel was hurt.*

Of course your Father will know where we are.

My mouth fell open. *You had to go and spoil my celebration.* Of course Father would know. I hadn't expected to be seen, so I hadn't even considered it.

It's fine. Do you suppose he knows about the connection between Wake and Dream on Sonmel Island?

I don't see how he could. No one knew it was possible to go to Wake from Dream and live.

I hope you're right. If he does, he'll know that's where we're headed and be expecting us.

My stomach lurched at the notion, but no, Father couldn't possibly know. Velma had figured it out, but it had never been done before. I refused to think differently.

• • •

Chapter Twenty-Five

The landscape of Cochem Pass had all been similarly decorated, like white icing on a chocolate cake, but as we drew closer to The Canyon, I could feel its immense energy intensify. My skin prickled much like waking an appendage that had lost feeling after sleeping on it. How would this go?

Sunlight muted the nighttime brilliance of the rift's colors, but like after a rainstorm, greens and purples and reds and turquoise and yellows and blues still danced in the sky. It seemed as if we flew in a rippling rainbow.

Gods, this is amazing! Kovis enthused. *Almost better than sex!*

I snorted. *Must everything be compared to sex?*

I thought you would have figured this out by now, Ali dearest. We men measure nearly everything in terms of food and sex. The only question is, which one is winning at any given time.

My laugh broke free of all restraint, and I cackled until my stomach ached.

Not long after, we reached the yawning gorge. Sparks of energy made me squirm, and I couldn't stop the tremors. It was exciting but also a bit scary to have so much energy pulsing through me. It wasn't like when I'd overloaded myself with another sorcerer's power at The Ninety-Eight. No, this was an exciting, pleasurable scary, like I might enjoy it so much that I'd never want to leave. If winter solstice was even remotely close to this, I understood why my friends had reacted as they had, blushing and gushing about it.

Kovis held up a hand, and we stopped, floating above one of the canyon's craggy brown walls. His body trembled with power too. He couldn't hold himself still.

"Still enjoying it?" I asked.

"And how. I could stay here forever." His voice came back dreamy sounding.

"Kovis, we can't. How do we get across?"

"Why cross? Mmm." Kovis's arm jerked randomly, then one of his legs lurched. He bobbled on his air cushion. "Whoa…"

Based upon how buzzed I felt, I had to accept that perhaps my Air magic stemmed from here, but not all of my powers did, because I wasn't overcome. But it was clear that wasn't the case with him. I needed to act, and fast.

"Because we have to save Kennan from my father, for starters."

"Kennan. Mmm. Yeah, Kennan. Save him." Kovis giggled. "From your mean old daddy."

I rolled my eyes.

I peered over the edge and couldn't see a bottom. It went down, down, down into the abyss. While I could see the other side, it was a long way off. How had Nomarch Kett and his insorcelled warriors crossed this? How would we cross when we needed something stiff on which to buoy our air cushions? I pushed down rising panic. I had to think straight, I was the only one who could keep us moving.

We floated in a field of turquoise. It was Ice magic, definitely. I knew the feel of it. Was this why Kovis was so blitzed? I shook the thought away. It didn't matter.

"Kovis!"

"Mmm?" A grin lit up his face.

"Kovis look at me."

His eyes were only half open when he glanced over. He'd be of no help.

What to do? My mind swirled as I looked over at the opposing side of The Canyon, so far away. Wait… it might just work. Kovis was always saying we needed to innovate and try new things. No time like the present. I'd build an ice bridge.

Kovis rolled onto his back beside me, and then over again and again, rolling right into me with a mischievous grin. "What's say we take a tumble on our clouds." He guffawed.

Kovis, get a grip.

Nothing I'd like more. He laughed.

I tried to ignore him as I unbuttoned my cape and pushed it back over my shoulder so I could use my hands. Careful to maintain the cushion of Air beneath me, I held out a hand and felt the magic flowing past. It felt dense. I'd never felt magic so thick before. I'd always leveraged magic from a sorcerer, never in its raw state. Could I harness it? I had to try.

My muscles quivered with nervous anticipation, as well as the glut of magic, as I envisioned shooting a stream of ice clear across the chasm on the back of my Air, much as Kovis had done to kill the rock beetle eggs. I held out my hands and Ice magic surged at my bidding. I blew me back, away from the edge on my air cushion.

Whoa… Kovis murmured through the bond.

The magic was wild and strong, a beast of its own that would not be tamed. I let it go, nearly overwhelmed with the power, but I couldn't hold on to my cushion and I plunged into the top layer of fluffy white snow.

Kovis just stared.

I wasn't so much panicked as pissed that I'd fallen deep into the snow again. I recreated my Air cushion, found solid ground beneath me, and pushed myself up, then floated forward, even with Kovis again.

"Snow Princess," Kovis snorted, then rolled again. "You've got a snow crown."

I ignored him and redoubled my Air beneath me, then added my other hand to steady myself against this power's staggering strength. After a deep breath, I again envisioned ice flying across the expanse of The Canyon, forming a bridge. I gritted my teeth and closed my eyes—it took all my strength to direct it.

Wow... Kovis murmured.

My arms shook the longer I held it. I would do this. We had to rescue Alfreda and Kennan. We had to stop Father. I repeated the words over and over as power swelled through me and a thick sheet of ice shot up from the depths of the gulf. More and more. I was a conduit, a pathway of release. My arms shook. I had to hold on. I screamed as ice arced toward the far side of the canyon. Every muscle in my body throbbed, but still I held on. Just barely. And then I roared as the power overwhelmed me and I became one with the magic.

My eyes shot open as I felt myself lift off, the Ice magic sending me soaring as it caught me in its raw power. Up and up, higher and higher and higher I flew. Panic surged through me. I had to get free of it. It was hard to breathe. *Kovis!*

Think hot thoughts of me, came his jumbled reply.

Was he joking? *Kovis, I need you!*

That's right, you want me. You know you do. It was a purr.

He was still out of it, but he was right. I had to want something else. I turned my thoughts to my family and *longing* to see them again.

My pace slowed. The Canyon looked small from where I was. A heartbeat later, gravity took hold and I let out a shriek as I started to fall. My heart raced, and I gulped in air, but rational thought quickly asserted itself. I pushed back my panic and constructed an Air cushion then used it to bob and weave to slow myself as I descended.

I surveyed The Canyon and inhaled sharply. The sky around me was no longer tinged turquoise, although a swath of violet still rippled to my right and pale shamrock to my left. I'd desired to build an ice bridge. Oh, I'd built one all right. One that spanned the entire width of what had been the turquoise band. Crystal clear ice stretched across the chasm, solid from one side to the other. I could only guess its thickness. Below it, turquoise light from the now-capped Ice magic, danced. I couldn't take my eyes off it the closer I came.

My breathing hadn't yet returned to normal by the time I returned to Kovis, who continued rolling on his air cushion near what had been the edge of The Canyon. He grinned.

I shook my head as I buttoned my cape. "Let's go, Kovis." I was exhausted from the experience, but the sooner we crossed this gulf, the sooner we'd get to Dream.

"Anything you wish, Ali dearest. I'm yours. Oh yes, all yours." Kovis drew out the words then executed a forward roll as he moved to follow.

With my ice bridge spanning a good distance in width, I didn't have to worry about him falling off the side, that was for sure. I just hoped the effects of this power glut wore off once we distanced ourselves from The Canyon. I'd never seen him drunk, but I imagined it would be much the same. Small mercy, if he ever did, he'd be a funny drunk. As it was, he was beginning to grate on my nerves. Food and sex, that did indeed seem to be the extent of how he viewed the world in this heartbeat.

We crossed The Canyon without further incident, thank the gods. I didn't look back. I wanted to get as far away from it as we could as quickly as we could. Selfish as it was, I wanted the Kovis I knew, the man I'd fallen in love with, back.

The sun peaked and then continued its circuit through the sky as we flew on. By the time its rays grew long, my Dreambeam was back to normal and didn't remember a thing. He furrowed his brow as I told the tale. His eyes grew wide with disbelief when I got to the part where I'd seen the result of my work.

You could have been killed! All that power. You were lucky. Ali, promise me you'll never do something like that again.

I had no desire to experience anything close to that again, but the concern in his tone had me agreeing in a heartbeat. I just hoped we didn't encounter something else in our quest that would force me to go back on my word.

I was never more glad to set down and make camp than I was that night. I was physically spent and mentally exhausted. Kovis on the other hand, oozed with energy. I wasn't surprised. He spotted and killed a snow hare, started a fire, and constructed a crude shelter in no time, all the while encouraging me to rest.

I'd fallen asleep against the trunk of a tree by the time he roused me for dinner.

"We should reach the sea tomorrow," he said as he handed me a hot bit of hare.

I looked into his eyes, searching for any sign of jest. There was none. I let his words wash over me like the sweet music of a lullaby. The sea. The last obstacle before Sonmel Island.

My shoulders sagged. Knowledge that it was up to Kovis and me to save Alfreda and Kennan as well as stop Father had spurred us on. But at every juncture, we'd run into some obstacle. Only our determination had kept us going.

The rigor of it all felt similar to my preparation for The Ninety-Eight. Had all this been the gods' version of training for what was to come?

My stomach clenched. Were we ready?

Chapter Twenty-Six

Our destination was Sonmel Island. Stories told of it being haunted.

The knowledge did nothing to calm me. Four suns before, we'd reached the coast to find that the surface of the water was indeed strong enough to support our winds, so we'd been playing hopscotch between the various islands just off the coast since.

My stomach quivered as we at last approached Sonmel Island. The sun cast long shadows as we approached and with the orange rays dancing against the still-white snow, it looked innocent, uninhabited even.

My breathing labored. Should we be worried at the seeming tranquility? Did it mask some great evil waiting to unleash itself on us?

I exhaled when I found Kovis's thoughts were occupied, not with worry, but with the peak that rose in the distance. Taller by far than anything near it, it had to be Atrop, Porta's reciprocal peak.

My chest lightened. Was it really somehow a doorway between Dream and Wake? Did that fairy tale really divulge such a thing? Would I soon see my family again? I hardly dared to hope.

Is that…? I pointed, and he returned a smile.

I think so. Have faith, Ali. We'll rescue them.

So much rested on this. I clenched my jaw; perhaps it would give my resolve the boost of confidence it needed.

The mountain was too far off to make tonight, so we ventured inland to find shelter. We found a copse of snow-dusted evergreens that stood near a stream whose water still ran despite the temperatures, so we set down and took to preparing our campsite and finding dinner.

Kovis set the wards and hunted. I cleared the ground of snow, started the fire, and built a primitive shelter. Though we'd done these tasks every night, with the possibilities the next sun brought, this might be the last time. I'd learned to tolerate the cold—I'd certainly never enjoy it—but I might miss this routine with him. Call me a sentimental fool.

The nearly full moon peeked out from behind a cloud as I nestled into Kovis's arms, around a warm fire for the night. If all went well, dare I think it, we might be home next sun. Butterflies alighted in my stomach. But howling in the distance cut short my glee.

We hadn't heard howling in ages. Just our luck, maybe this was why people said the island was haunted. I tensed as thoughts of mares attacking us sent a wave of panic through me. The feeling of being watched galloped on its heels, and I shuddered.

My wards will alert us if they come our way, Kovis reminded me. *They're probably just wolves.*

Little comfort that gave because my mind started running through the litany of monsters and evil creatures that fairy tale had spoken about as coming through Porta. Perhaps it really was a connection with Hades itself. Maybe tales of Sonmel being haunted weren't so far off.

Kovis nibbled at my ear then kissed my cheek, no doubt trying to distract me. But I couldn't break the hold the thoughts had on me. Despite his actions, he wasn't into what he suggested either. One peek through the bond told me as much. His thoughts were consumed with the what-ifs of stopping Father once we got to

Dream, mixed with insecurities about overcoming the darkness that our conversation of suns before had stirred up.

I rolled over and rested my forehead against his chest. I couldn't see his tattoo under the capes as we were, but I speculated it might be gray, or lacking confidence if I remembered its meaning.

We'll do this, all of it, together, Kovis.

I felt his chin bob on the top of my head, and his arm hugged me tighter.

And so it went all night. Exhaustion won out at some point, but I woke when it was still dark, my mind no quieter. Even focusing on the babbling of the river not far off couldn't get me back to sleep. Kovis was no better off as I discovered after a quick peek. I doubted he'd slept at all. Although I continued to feel eyes watching us.

I tried to push it all aside as the sky at last lightened. The time for action had at last come, and my stomach fluttered at the thought. An antsy feeling beset me as we crawled out of our warm cocoon. Kovis was equally ready to go, and we were on our way not long after.

Everything in Wake had its reciprocal in Dream. I assumed that meant Sonmel was identical to Lemnos geographically, and if that was the case, we would arrive at Porta around mid-sun. We'd have plenty of light to search for the door or whatever connected them.

Clouds appeared as we flew and grew thicker and darker the further we went. It seemed as if they tried to shroud some dark secret the island held. I swallowed. Maybe they did.

We'd been flying for some time when I spotted something moving on the ground below. With it being winter, we'd seen virtually no life. But the closer we got, I realized it was a herd of wild horses, grazing. Their coats varied from white to amber to rust to black. They paid us no mind, intent as they were on feeding.

I glanced over at Kovis to find his brow furrowed as he studied the creatures.

I followed his gaze and inhaled sharply when fire erupted from one of the horse's mouths. The snow melted, and it continued grazing.

Did… did it just…?

I think so. He sounded as amazed as me.

Several more of the horses repeated the spectacle as we passed.

I'd hate to get on their bad sides, I told him to which he laughed.

The skies grew ever darker the further we flew. At this rate it would be pitch black by the time we reached Atrop. The air felt thick. I'd experienced the feeling of air heavy with moisture just before a storm, but this was different. It felt like I flew in soup.

I feel it too. We're slowing.

I hadn't noticed our progress stalling, but he was right. I tried sending more Air magic to propel me forward, but it had no effect.

Our magic is fading, Kovis said.

Fading? But how?

You don't have magic in Dream, right?

True, but… Did the non-magic of Dream spill over into Wake? A mixture of hope, but also angst rose. How I hoped I'd been right about that tale, but I'd never once thought about not having magic available in this quest, at least within Wake.

We'll soon discover if your theory was correct about the source of your magic.

He hadn't forgotten. I chuckled. *And if I am?*

Kovis looked over and winked. *I can think of any number of ways to reward you for sticking to your story.* While it came out joking, I sensed uneasiness behind it—not concerning the source of my power, but the possibility he would have none.

He was the most powerful sorcerer in the empire and while Altairn sorcerers trained with daggers, swords, and other weapons for situations like this, we had none of those either. He would be facing whatever obstacles we encountered unprotected.

You okay?

He was thoughtful for a heartbeat. *I could tell you I'm great, fine even, but it would be a lie and would feed the darkness. So, I'll tell you the truth. I'm scared, Ali. We don't know what we're up against, and the thought of something happening to you and being unable to protect you scares me shitless.*

I almost wished he'd lied. Not really, but his brutal honesty destroyed the calm that him beside me always created. He'd always been strong and protected me. He'd given me confidence when I'd had none. I longed for that sense of security, even if it was false. But I'd get none.

Atrop rose tall before us when the last of our Air magic evaporated and we stepped from our cushions into snow that rose to our knees. Kovis tried his Ice and Water to no effect. Simulus was a non-starter for me without his magic to leverage, but with no creatures to make slumber and the thick snows, it was impossible to tell if my Somnus magic still worked.

"Shall we?" Kovis said, adjusting his cape as he sized up the peak.

Dark clouds filled the sky, obscuring the sun completely. It felt like night even though we hadn't flown that long and I pulled my cape more tightly around me.

We waded through drifts, some to our waist, others covering only our feet. Some places, bare rock stuck up, refusing to submit to winter. My feet started going numb. I focused on the ground and putting one foot in front of the other; it was all I could do.

Ali. Alarm laced the word.

I looked up to see huge, black wings flap as a great bird launched off the side of the peak not far ahead, heading straight for us. It's screech proved deafening and my breathing labored. I clutched my cape as a second, identical bird mimicked in the blink of an eye.

Out in the open, there was no place to hide.

The first bird neared and realized it wasn't completely avian. Its head and torso were that of a naked woman, with breasts that rose and fell with each beat of its enormous black, feathered wings. Long white hair flowed in the wind, and its shins were covered in scales. It turned sharp talons toward us while still a ways off and flexed them, as if assured one of us would be its next meal.

Kovis, they're harpies! They guard the underworld! What are they doing here?

Its partner screeched and soared beside it.

"Dive! Roll!" Kovis yelled when the pair were nearly on top of us.

We'd practiced the move more times than I could count, and my body responded without hesitation. A sharp claw passed a finger's breadth from my cheek as I tucked. I rolled in the snow and came back up to standing near Kovis.

Harpies had been spotted only a handful of times in Dream since I'd been born, and they always created a stir. They were wind spirits that some called Dyeus's hounds because he used them to do his dirty work. Or so they said.

The harpies screeched, undoubtedly upset that we'd avoided them. They circled and approached, talons first, for a second pass.

We ducked and rolled again.

Kovis, we can't keep this up.

Do you have any better ideas?

More screeches, their intensity and pitch rose with another failed attempt. Their breasts, overlarge by my standard, undulated wildly as the harpies banked and soared overhead. I wished they'd knock themselves out with the things.

Knock themselves out. Wait. I bit my lip and prayed my power really did come from someplace other than The Canyon. Our lives depended on it.

We need to get them to land or at least touch the ground. I'll try to put them to sleep.

He didn't question, other than to ask, *Is there enough sand?*

I don't know, but this is an island. I have to believe there is. You have any better idea?

We dove and rolled a third time as they came closer than they had yet. But as they passed, my mouth fell open because I sensed the familiar feel of magic. They were wind spirits. It had to be the power of their winds coursing through them that I sensed.

Hope blossomed. My Simulus magic still worked.

I'd only ever pulled power from sorcerers, but what said that was my limit? I could do this.

How do you plan to get them to land? Kovis asked, unaware of my discovery.

Trust me.

I'd have to take them one at a time.

We dove the fourth time, but as I rolled, I latched on to the one above me and pushed it down with the force of its own winds. It shrieked as it beat its wings wildly but plummeted to the ground. Its wings whipped up snow, but I forced the harpy down until its overlarge bosom fondled bare ground.

Go to sleep. Go to sleep.

"Look out!" Kovis yelled, diving into the deep snow.

I rolled toward the harpy, which now lay still, wings outstretched, face planted in a snow drift. I had no sympathy for it.

I forced the other harpy down to the ground using its winds against it on its next pass. A heartbeat later, it, too, submitted to slumber as I assaulted it with Somnus magic.

I panted, on all fours in a drift when Kovis plucked me up and pulled me into a bear hug. *You did it, Ali. You did it.*

My feet dangled as he buried his face in the crook of my neck.

You did it, he murmured again, seemingly to reassure both of us of the truth of it.

Kovis... can you put me down? It was hard to breathe with him holding me so tightly.

He smiled, relief flooding his beautiful eyes, as my feet touched down. "That was amazing. You're incredible, Ali."

I bowed. "Why thank you. I try."

"Being a harpy is the tits," he said, looking over the downed pair.

I burst out laughing and cackled until my sides hurt. When I finally recovered, I said, "Looks like you owe me a reward for sticking to my story about my powers." My powers really did stem from a place beyond The Canyon. I'd sensed it all along but there was no denying it any longer.

Kovis laughed. "There is *nothing* I would enjoy more. Somehow I think we'll both enjoy it." He wagged his brows.

I snickered. Yes, food and sex. "Well, come on, oh great rewarder. We're not in Dream yet."

We both surveyed the slumbering harpies, black wings sprawled wide, before turning. They'd be out a good long time.

The triumph should have filled me with confidence but my mind focused on what else might lie in wait. I suspected Kovis felt much the same, for his face was tense as he twined his fingers through mine and squeezed my hand as we started off.

• • •

Chapter Twenty-Seven

According to the fairy tale, vile creatures had slithered and crept out of a door in Atrop, introducing evil into the world. And it was well known that harpies guarded the doors to the underworld, the home of evil. Unless the pair had been given a holiday for good behavior, we couldn't be far, and I told Kovis as much.

My breathing labored. We'd soon see what waited for us.

"But we don't want to head to the underworld," Kovis objected, his voice rising.

"I'm going on gut, but I feel like Atrop might be a conduit to more than one place, like maybe there's more than one door."

He cocked his head. "Why?"

Because not everyone goes to Hades. Some go to Tartarus, others to Asphodel, still others to Elysium. Why not to Dream realm, too? Like I said, it's a gut feeling. Trust me.

He rolled his eyes, but the corners of his mouth ticked upward. I'd told him the same thing in that confrontation with those harpies, and that had worked out okay.

I scanned the tall mountain. Now to find the right door, the one to Dream…

I studied the two massive chunks of fallen rock the bird women had been perched on as we approached—I'd seen the pair take flight. They supposedly guarded the doors to the underworld. Could it really be that simple? My stomach tensed. If there were multiple doors, how would we know which one to take?

Kovis reached over and took my hand, squeezing it. "One step at a time."

I bobbed my head.

We reached an area with crushed rock and pebbles under the blanket of snow and looked up, examining the mountainside for any hint of ingress. And found nothing.

"Let's just scale it," Kovis suggested.

But before we took one step, I heard what sounded like an animal lowing. We both looked up as a shaggy, hoofed beast with horns so heavy it couldn't look up, plodded out from somewhere inside the mountain. It slid at points as it sought footing in the crumbly ground.

It's a catoblepas! Don't move or look at its eyes!

I shuddered. Never in my life had I seen one, but I'd heard stories of the things turning people into stone with a look or breathing on them. Was this another of the creatures roaming this island? No wonder the island's reputation what it was.

We waited silently until the creature reached the base of the mountain and wandered away, never once paying us any mind. Thank the gods.

But it had exposed the mountain's secret.

There could be more, Kovis cautioned.

I'm sure of it. And probably worse.

We both took a deep breath before taking our first step.

"Come on," I said.

The door was easy to find after that. We hadn't seen it because a boulder had fallen in front of the opening, and while it was far enough away that it didn't block it, it hid it from eyes below.

We stood before the gaping hole and studied it, both silent. What lurked in the blackness beyond? Would we face more creatures looking for a quick meal the heartbeat we entered? Which way would we go? Up? Down? My stomach clenched. I checked the bond, and Kovis's thoughts mirrored mine.

It seems to fit the description you painted, Kovis said, as if rationalizing stepping forward to what could be our deaths.

We've come this far and we'll never save Kennan if we don't check it out, I added, more to push myself forward than reassure him.

At length I turned toward Kovis, and we searched each other's eyes for any signs of doubt. There were plenty, but necessity triumphed in the end.

"You ready?" Kovis asked.

I inhaled deeply. "As I'll ever be."

We stepped inside.

The rock was not what I was accustomed to, for colors ebbed and flowed, even swirled at points throughout a low-ceilinged chamber. They lit the space in blue, green, red, and purple. It was almost as if the lights of The Canyon had been captured.

"Where do we go from here," I wondered aloud. And just like that, stairs into the mountain appeared straight ahead, some going up, others down.

I swallowed hard. Kovis gave me a long look.

"I vote up," I said. Down seemed ill advised.

The stairs twisted and circled as they rose. The swirling in the walls ceased and was replaced by rough, rust-colored stone as we kept climbing. We'd both started panting by the time we reached a landing and the stairs became wider. Yet still we climbed.

A howl erupted above us as we scaled yet more steps. And it wasn't long before I spotted an ever-familiar purple glow coming toward us.

It's a mare, Kovis! Where could we hide?

As if the thought moved the mountain, the rock of the wall shifted and created a hollowed-out hideaway.

What did you do? Kovis's eyes were huge, but he didn't hesitate to pull me inside the shelter. The stench of the mares about made me gag, so I threw an elbow over my nose and waited. Kovis did the same.

I don't know. That's the second time the mountain has accommodated us, I said.

Accommodated you. It's like a thought can make it shift.

Shift like with dreams when I wove them... I murmured.

Kovis furrowed his brow.

I shifted and molded your thoughts as I wove your dreams. I changed your reality. Kovis, I think we've reached part of Dream. My stomach quivered with excitement.

You really think so? Hope filled his voice.

I do, but we'll soon find out. I peeked my head out several heartbeats later to see the backsides of at least eight mares ambling down the steps. Thankfully their stench dissipated with them. *Not yet. Let them get far away first.*

When we emerged from hiding, I lifted my foot to head up the next step, but Kovis held me back. "I want to try something. If this mountain changes to accommodate our thoughts, let's just have it get us to the destination and stop climbing."

I furrowed my brow. Could it do that? But a heartbeat later, the steps disappeared and two archways materialized before us.

"Kovis, you're brilliant." I reached up and kissed him.

"At that rate, I'll try to be brilliant more often."

Images of clouds against a dark sky filled both, like portraits in gilded frames, only with arched tops.

"Which do we choose?" Kovis asked.

While the pair resembled one another, there were subtle differences. We stepped forward and examined both. The one on the right was carved from two enormous ivory tusks. I shuddered to think the size of the animal that had forfeited them. Intricate carvings at the bottom of each depicted soldiers preparing for war— horses and wagons were being loaded with weapons and other supplies. At the top of each tusk, carvings of the gods doing the same, but with lightning and wind and waves, had been etched.

"Looks like conflict lays through that door, and lots of it," I reported.

"This one has teachers instructing pupils from scrolls," Kovis said.

I stepped over and examined it then ran a finger across. "It's made from lots of horns, all put together. Racka rams' horns from the looks." Racka were over-large, wooly sheep with unusual spiral-shaped horns. I found the seams that joined the pieces and counted seven on one side. Assuming every animal had two horns, all told, the complete arch had required that many sheep. I wasn't sure if I should feel sad at the sacrifice or happy that their contributions had been used in such a beautiful way.

"Which one do you think we should go through?" I asked.

Kovis drew a hand to his chest. "We've had enough conflict, we don't need more. I'd go through that one." He pointed to the rams' horn arch to the left.

"Despite sacrificing more animals to build it, that's what I was thinking too." I hesitated. "Of course, we know we're going to have to confront my father before peace can be had. With the mountain seeming to respond to our thoughts, do you suppose we need to choose the one with conflict?"

Kovis smiled. "Let's not over think this. We want peace in the end. I can only assume—"

A roar blasted through the archway on the right.

I looked at Kovis. "You're right, let's not over think this. Time to go." I stepped through the left archway.

And plummeted. I screamed as blackness swallowed me. Disorientation slammed into me. It was much like what I'd experienced when I'd plunged into the Dream canopy after going too high with Father during our Solstice dance.

"Kovis!" He didn't reply.

I was tumbling and realized my cape had vanished as an image flashed past—a girl played a flute and the notes sparkled in swirls that followed beside me.

I loosed a shriek as I continued to plunge and spin. A forest decorated in fall colors streamed past to replace the notes.

I flailed, continuing to scream, the weightless, falling sensation scaring me shitless.

I tumbled through a wishing tree loaded with pink and purple blossoms. Its willowy branches parted in my wake to make room for a vision of swirling clouds—lightning cracked and thunder roared.

"Kovis!" I couldn't hear him.

I'm falling through people's dreams! My mind had somehow pieced together the randomness and given me its best guess.

But it didn't matter what was happening because I couldn't locate Kovis, I still fell, and my stomach… I swallowed hard but couldn't keep… I retched as I zoomed past some weird, winged monkey-looking creature with blue horns floating on a rock. I retched again and again.

"Kovis!"

My eyes slammed shut, and I let out a wail as mind-numbing pain lanced my back. Then my chest started getting tight in my leathers. Something had gotten inside them, on my back, and was growing fast! I screeched. I couldn't get it off me. My arms and legs burned from the intensity of it. My leathers constricted like a snake squeezing ever tighter. Air. I needed air. The pressure was crushing my ribs, but I couldn't reach the buckles.

I whimpered when the pressure suddenly loosened then sucked in air and only then realized my leathers had split open in the back. Whatever grew still held me and had ripped right through them. I squawked, but it was cut short by stabbing pain.

I panicked and shrieked again. What was on me? I fought to reach back and get it off.

I continued falling and howled as the pain intensified. I'd knock it off; I had to. I threw a fist over my shoulder and hit whatever it was. Another jolt of pain wracked my back, but the thing didn't budge.

I had to pull it off. I threw my hand over my shoulder again, found the thing, and grabbed hold. I jerked as hard as I could and…

agony shot through me. My hand thrust forward and it came away with... I opened my tear-laden eyes just as I streamed past a river flowing with five colors of water. The image provided enough light to see that I held... I gasped. Black pin feathers.

I wept for the sheer joy of it. I would have wings again. Despite the excruciating pain and disorientation of still tumbling, I stared at the pin feathers through the changing light of the scenes I streamed past. Pin feathers.

At length, rational thought reasserted itself. "Kovis!" I had to find him.

More images flew past as I spun and tumbled, but they were a blur as I stretched out my immature wings that were still growing judging by the pain wracking my back. I didn't care. I would catch the winds with them again.

I was hurtling by two people rowing a boat on a misty lake when my flight feathers completed their expedited maturity and I caught myself, about seeing stars, but I slowed as I beat my new wings.

"Kovis!" I'd wondered before whether he would get wings. Had he or was he plummeting to some tragic end?

"Ali!"

I exhaled despite the desperation I heard in his cry. He'd fallen further judging by where his cry emanated from. He was, no doubt, still falling.

The pain in my back eased, and I tucked my wings and dove. "Kovis! Help me find you!"

"Ali!"

His voice was closer. I was gaining.

"Kovis!"

"Ali!"

Back and forth we called to each other until I spotted him. The new wings he'd sprouted flailed as he plummeted, back-first toward whatever it was we approached. Terror filled his eyes—they were bigger than I'd ever seen them.

"Ali!" Panic and desperation were all I heard as he caught sight of me.

Pull your wings in! I avoided them and their floppy, jerky movements as I soared below him.

I don't know how!

Then just relax them and trust that I'll catch you.

His flopping stilled in a heartbeat and all but his legs disappeared from sight as his wings blew upward in the rush of air.

I winced as I unfurled mine. My back was tender, but I caught the air then rose until the spot on our backs, where our wings connected with our bodies, touched. Contact yanked a yelp from Kovis. I swallowed a cry as I allowed the air to force us closer still, pressing down on my sore wings, until I bore his weight against my torso.

We glided this way for several heartbeats as the images ceased and the darkness eased and became charcoal, then slate. My gut told me the changes meant we were nearly at our destination and I needed to slow us.

This is going to hurt, I warned.

Kovis didn't reply. I speculated he braced.

I yipped and he barked as I forced my wings down. Again and again and again as the space became dim gray, then dusk.

I screamed, and Kovis bellowed as my feet touched down and I fell forward into rough gravel with his full weight atop me. He nearly pushed all the air from me, and I struggled to wiggle out from under him. But I finally did and sucked in blessed air, despite the rock at my face.

Were we in Dream or had we picked wrong?

Part III: Dream

Sweet and Low

By Baron Tennyson and Alfred Tennyson
Lincolnshire Wake Realm

• • •

Sweet and low, sweet and low,
Wind of the western sea,
Low, low, breathe and blow,
Wind of the western sea.
Over the rolling waters go;
Come form the dying moon, and blow;
Blow him again to me,
While my little one, while my pretty one sleeps.

Sleep and rest, sleep and rest,
Father will come to thee soon;
Rest, rest on mother's breast,
Father will come to thee soon.
Father will come to his babe in the nest;
Silver sails all out of the west;
Under the silver moon,
Sleep, my little one, sleep, my pretty one, sleep.

Chapter Twenty-Eight

I glanced about… and recognized the space. We'd landed in Porta's shadow and joy overwhelmed me. We'd made it to Dream realm.

"Are you okay?" I asked as Kovis remained silent.

"Shhh."

"What?" I whispered.

"I expected your father to be waiting for us, but I don't see any signs of him or those mares. We best stay alert."

Joy shriveled and I shivered despite the bright sunshine and mild temperatures. There wasn't a hint of snow in sight but with all the chaos, I'd forgotten about the threat Father posed.

Kovis yelped as he moved to get off me. "These are going to take time getting used to." He gritted out the words.

I looked down and realized I'd kept my blonde hair. And my body was definitely the human one I'd received based on my shortish perspective of the world. I'd become some combination of the two realms, but I suspected I hadn't regained immortality, not with human features.

Although my cape had gone missing, I'd kept my leathers and boots. Until this heartbeat, I hadn't even thought about the possibility of losing them. If this transition had claimed all our clothes like it had the first time… I exhaled. Perhaps it had claimed our capes as payment of a sort, but I wouldn't bother wondering further. I was just thankful it hadn't. I couldn't imagine being naked out here.

My wings seemed to have shrunken to match my new frame because I had no problem furling them. I brushed my bleeding palms together and bent over to stand, but my leathers rode up and struck my neck as I did. I glanced down. Of course they would. I felt air caress my exposed back. My wings had rent my leathers and now only the pauldrons covering my shoulders held the front loosely in place. Great, just great, but there was nothing to be done. I just hoped it didn't start to flop.

I dismissed the thought as I realized Kovis's thrum had ceased. We both knew it probably would, we'd discussed it, but I still sucked in a breath as I turned. Thoughts of loss fled as I got my first look at him and my mouth fell open.

He sat, legs outstretched, wings sprawled. He rubbed an elbow but my quiet drew his attention upward and he met my gaze.

Butterflies launched in my stomach. He'd been handsome with those blue and hazel eyes, chiseled features, and muscled chest. But his wings… they were *enormous*. And stretched out in abandon as they were, my mind brimmed with certain thoughts. What I'd love to do to him.

"What?" His furrowed brow shifted into an upturned mouth. Clearly our bond had endured the transition and he must have taken a peek.

I had to slow my racing thoughts.

No you don't, my love.

Warmth blossomed between my legs. *You're not helping.*

He scanned the area. *No one's around.*

Stop. Just stop.

Aw. You're no fun. He grinned. *Show me* your *wings, Ali.* It came out silky.

I felt my cheeks warm. I didn't know why. We'd seen each other naked plenty of times, but the idea of showing off *all of my wings* to him… was different. It was so much more intimate than nakedness. He didn't understand that.

I glanced over. His eyes had filled with longing.

Or perhaps he did understand. I'd said I wanted nothing between us.

I've never seen you with wings. They're such an integral part of who you were… are. I want to know all of you, Ali.

I'd willingly given them up for him, and he knew it. Emotions welled up, and I took a deep breath to keep tears from spilling over. I'd missed them but hadn't realized how much until the weight of my wings against my back made everything feel right again… and with Kovis here, it was perfect.

I looked down at the sapphire on my finger, resisting fidgeting, then scanned the area. I hadn't expected to see anyone, but still. I felt like I had when trying on ball gowns for Kovis at Madame Catherine's—I lifted my chin like she'd taught me and owned this. I wore significantly more clothes than I had then, but it didn't feel that way. I felt completely exposed, and I couldn't help not hugging myself as I slowly extended my wings, fully.

Put your arms down. I want to appreciate all of you, Kovis purred.

My breath hitched, but I did as he asked.

His eyes traveled up and down me, and he motioned with a finger for me to turn around. I heard his heart accelerate through our bond before I completed the full rotation.

I doubted it was possible, but you're even more beautiful with wings. I can't wait to see you bare with them, he murmured. *You've mentioned there are particularly sensitive spots on your back and wings. I want to know where each and every one of them are for I intend to pleasure you until you nearly lose your sanity.*

I yipped. I couldn't hold it in. I was sure my eyes bugged out, but his expression remained unchanged, and I whimpered. He twitched a wing, and I about lost what little control I still possessed. I needed to shift the conversation, or I surely would.

"Kovis, your wings are bigger than any I've seen before. Maybe it's your power translating into Dream that did it, but I've never seen wings the size of yours."

"It seems that's a good thing." He smirked. "Kennan loves to brag about 'other parts,' even though we're identical."

I burst out laughing. It came out louder than it should have, what with sexual tensions screaming for release. "What is it with males? It's the same here. Well, thou well-endowed one—"

"Imagine swooping in to your family's place. They'll take one look at me—"

I gasped and brought a hand over my mouth.

I had to steer this conversation elsewhere. I cleared my throat. "If you're ever to brag about your wings, you need to learn to use them first."

He frowned. "Fine."

I'd always had control of my wings, so I wasn't sure how to teach him. We'd have to give it our best. "Best for best."

He nodded then scanned the length of one wing. His flight feathers were scrunched and poking in assorted directions under the weight of bone and muscle.

"Stay seated. No point in making your back sorer while we try this. Bring your wing toward you and collapse it against your back."

He nodded. A pained expression crossed his face as his shoulder moved, mirroring what I assumed he attempted with his wing because scratching sounds rose as the feathers moved a fingerbreadth atop the gravel. After several heartbeats, he exhaled loudly. "Would you demonstrate how you do it?"

"You'd like that, wouldn't you?" I wagged my brows.

He chuckled. "I would."

So I slowly extended, then retracted my wings again, and again, and again as he studied the movements. I turned my back to him and was met with sounds of appreciation from Kovis. I rolled my eyes and repeated the motions.

• • •

"It looks like you contract your chest muscles and that causes this joint to bend." He indicated a location where the structure of his wing dipped before rising further down the appendage. He tried it for himself and his wing contracted by half. "Hey."

I clapped.

He furrowed his brow in concentration. "It feels like there's another joint right here." He pointed at the peak of the wing just before where the rest of the appendage sloped downward toward the longest flight feathers at the end. "They move together." He extended then contracted his wing a handbreadth. "So all I have to do is move this one and the rest of my wing should follow."

I giggled. "You're quite the scholar." He'd innovated with his magic, but I'd never seen him learn a completely new skill. Any I'd had to learn, he'd already mastered so it was fun watching him. I'd become the wizened teacher and he the student. How things changed.

He contracted his wing the rest of the way and it folded neatly into place against his back.

"You did it!"

Sweat beaded his brow, but he smiled then concentrated and pulled his other wing toward him and folded it similarly.

He blew out a breath. "They're bulky but not as heavy as I expected. My muscles are sore, but I can manage."

"Try it again."

He looked up into my eyes. "I knew I shouldn't have been so hard on you during training."

I snickered. "Turnabout is fair play."

He shook his head but got to work, grunting as he attempted to extend both wings simultaneously.

My mind wandered as he worked. He wouldn't fly this sun. Frustration flared for a heartbeat. We were so close to home. I longed to see my family and rescue Alfreda, but Kovis needed time. He'd been so patient with me while I was learning; I'd give him whatever time it took. I could do no other.

• • •

I itched to fly. I'd stay low, so I would be near if he needed me, but I *had* to fly. I informed him of my plan and barely waited for his response before launching.

The wind nuzzled my face and wings, and my spirit soared. I'd forgotten how free I felt when flying. I rose and swooped, banked and rolled in the balmy air, nothing compared. I scanned the distant horizon as I flew and oriented, and it wasn't long before I knew which way home was. Longing rose in me. But I needed to be patient.

To his credit, Kovis was a fast learner and strutted, wings furled, as the sun neared the horizon. I couldn't help but smile. He was so darn cute. And when he extended those great black, feathered pinions, he beamed. He could flex them without the feathers dragging on the ground, and it brought no end to his mirth. I'd peeked into our bond. He was focused on wowing my family. Such a male! Well, that and exploring new heights of intimacy with me. I chuckled. Definitely food and sex.

He'd been practicing on the gravel foothill of Porta where we landed, but we would need to find shelter overnight, for while the weather was balmy, a host of vile creatures roamed these lands in the dark, many of the ones we'd just missed and no doubt a host of others I had no desire to meet. And without his magic, we couldn't set wards let alone defend ourselves, at least not with Ice, Water, or Air; we had only Somnus between the two of us.

Clumps of tall, leafy trees rose up to meet the rocky base of the peak. Fallen boulders had crushed several but couldn't defeat their spirits for they grew up at odd angles from beneath. Unfortunately, none were large enough to provide the shelter I sought up off the ground. I'd flown near Porta and over the rocky valleys, hills, and a mountain or two not far off, so I knew this was typical of the terrain. It was foliage-covered, but rocky, desolate, and inhospitable and would prove a challenge.

The dream canopy, at least that's what I'd concluded we'd fallen through despite it being inside that mountain, had relieved us of our capes, so we had absolutely nothing to help our cause, not even flints to start a fire, let alone anything to kill prey we might venture upon. It left me feeling anxious.

"If you can bare to stop playing with your new toys," I said, "we need to find a place to make camp."

He drew a hand to his chest. "You wound me, madame. But alas, you are correct."

We descended, slid more like, in many parts but finally reached stable ground. Kovis stopped and picked up several rocks before the gravel surrendered to stubby grass as the terrain leveled out.

"We'll need to fashion spears as well as a blade if we are to eat."

My stomach grumbled at the thought, and my mouth was suddenly parched.

He handed me two of the stones and took to chipping the two he'd kept, one against the other as we walked. The sounds of his work, chattering birds, and chittering animals, while serene, did nothing to ease my angst.

He handed me his crafted rocks at some point, then left the animal path we'd been following with instructions to wait. He returned with two branches that were nearly two thumbs thick and nearly my height.

"Let's go this way," Kovis said some time later.

I cocked my head.

"We need water. You probably didn't realize it, but more and more animal trails are converging. Water can't be too far ahead."

My jaw dropped. I'd known he'd had to survive in wild conditions while fighting in his father's campaigns, but never had I imagined... "What else—"

Shhh. He nodded at a pair of trees ahead. Grunting of sorts emanated from beyond. We crept forward, clutching the pair of spears he'd crafted with the stones he'd chiseled. He was a regular outdoorsman.

We reached a good hiding spot with visibility to what it was that continued grunting. He knelt, I followed.

A pair of juvenile javelinas rooted in the bank of a modest creek. What had probably been pink snouts were caked with mud. Their activity had masked our presence.

Dinner, he said.

Music to my ears.

Go for the one closest. On my count.

I raised my spear and watched as his three fingers counted down. Three. Two. One. I drew it back and threw as hard as I could. While longer than the dagger I'd practiced with, it felt much the same.

I knew before it struck that my throw was solid. The animal squealed as my spear sank into its eye. Kovis's hit it squarely between the ribs, finding its heart. Its companion fled, and we emerged from hiding. Kovis made quick work of the animal, killing it before it suffered more.

We picked up drinking where the javelinas left off. It was clean water—they wouldn't have drunk if it smelled "off"—and while it was warm, I savored its wetness.

Thirst quenched, Kovis retrieved our weapons, skinned the animal, and extracted only the meat we would eat, leaving the rest for other animals so as not to attract other beasties overnight. That done, we headed back into the darkening trees. We'd get far away before we built our fire and cooked dinner.

We may have changed realms, but we stuck to our long-established routine as we located shelter. We found a shade tree that looked to be flexing its muscular branches a good ways above the ground. It would do. Then we prepared dinner and ate. The familiarity eased some of my angst.

"Sad," Kovis said as he bit into the tender meat.

"What's that?" I asked from beside him, sitting on the log I'd pulled up.

He looked up. "If we sleep up there, I won't be able to tease any of your special spots. How I miss my magic. We could have floated above it all"—he wagged his brows—"and had a little fun."

I snorted, sensing his true level of excitement through our bond. He was like a child, impatient to experience all that was new to him in this big world of possibilities. He'd never known any of this existed, and I would get to rediscover my own familiar world through his eyes. What would he notice that I took for granted? What would he want to try? What experiences would he fall in love with? My excitement grew the more I thought about it.

"You'll just have to be patient, my Dreambeam," I teased.

He yawned before long.

"Come on. Let's turn in," I said and stood, my leathers again cuffing my neck.

He rose, caught my arm, and turned me toward him. "Before we do, show me just one of your special spots… so I can dream of it." He rustled his furled wings, one against the other. He had no idea how seductive it was, and I lost it.

I reached up, pulled his face down to mine, then planted a claiming kiss on his lips.

He grinned beneath it.

It was all I could do to keep my voice even as I turned around. My stomach quivered as I said, "Do you see where my wing bends? Right inside."

He reached over. "Here?" He stroked ever so gently.

I moaned, and my legs wobbled.

"I'm going to love getting to know your spots." He nuzzled my neck and kissed my cheek, then mounted the tree.

I took several deep breaths before following him up.

Chapter Twenty-Nine

Ambien

Sleep refused to claim me, and I'd tossed and turned all sun. Frustration had finally forced me to rise, and I was none too happy about it.

At least I could find comfort in my drawing room as I stared at the backdrop of waves pounding the sandy shore outside—those waves seemed not much different than the undulations of my raging thoughts.

I leaned back in my leather chair and placed my black wings over the back, then propped my sandaled feet on the ebony desk. I sipped on a cup of chamomile tea in hopes of quieting my mind and returning to slumber.

"Why is Alissandra so committed to that human charge of hers?" I couldn't staunch a growl. I'd been pondering the nettling question since this whole fiasco began. My mind refused to wrap itself around what seemed to be the case, that she cared for a frail mortal more than me. I was her father. She owed her very life to me. Where was her filial piety?

Of late, angst had consumed me, dealing with her equally misguided sisters. They'd aligned with Alissandra and drawn my family into a war with sides drawn all because they'd deduced my plan to take Wake.

I'd initially decided to claim the realm because humans fascinated me—they had since I could remember, even when I'd granted them dreams—so I'd chosen to take them for my own. Many would call my reasons selfish, but what did it matter? I'd never had a nurturing relationship with them, more that of a scientist with study subjects. There were too many of them to have a significant relationship with any individual. Yet they enchanted me, nearly like a spell cast over me—they were weak with short lives, yet many found fulfillment... just like I'd felt way back when. But a sense of fulfillment and I had parted ways of late, and I missed that. Hades help me if anyone ever discovered my flaw. I'd look even weaker.

I understood that a sense of fulfillment stemmed from feeling valued—or at least that's what I'd deduced. I was a god. My value was innate. Humans had to earn their value; I did not. I was above all that. Or so I'd believed. But I'd begun to question.

Call it what you will, but I wanted that feeling of fulfillment, of meaning, back, and if controlling humans would grant me that, that is what I would do. It was clear Alissandra had found fulfillment by helping humans or her relationship with this one wouldn't have become intimate. And if she felt fulfilled, why couldn't I too? There was nothing wrong with wanting it. I didn't care what others thought.

But Alissandra disapproved, they all did, because they believed I would turn humans into catatonic beings. I had no such plans. Some called my designs ambitious. Perhaps, but I was a god. Go big or go home, it's what I'd always believed. I never did anything halfway. Why would I?

A knock at the door had me look up. "Enter!"

A servant bowed low.

"Rise."

"One of your soldiers is here with a report. May I show him in?"

I nodded and several heartbeats later Lethold, one of my commanders, appeared. His rumpled uniform and windswept hair told me he'd come in haste. After he genuflected, I motioned him forward as I put my feet on the floor and sat up. "Report."

"My liege, according to your description, our troops spotted Princess Alissandra at Porta Peak. Golden hair and black wings"—I hadn't mentioned wings, he must have assumed—"and she brought that human. You ordered that we inform you immediately if she was observed."

Alissandra had made it back *and* she had wings. I staunched my surprise and kept my expression neutral. "Yes, thank you, Lethold."

Alissandra had come home. They'd made incredible time.

"Will there be anything else?"

Anything else. I leaned back in my chair once more and steepled my fingers. Nearly a sennight before, reports had come to me that the pair had been spotted in Cochem Pass. They were being blamed for upsetting operations at the outpost.

How a human and… how two weak humans could exact that much damage was beyond me. I'd suspected someone wasn't willing to confess to what had really destroyed all of the explosives stored there, not to mention all the raw beetle eggs. I suspected incompetence, foremost. And right when we'd been about to launch an attack on the next gemstone mine. No matter, that situation was being dealt with—tongues had been straightened.

I'd burst out laughing when the next report arrived saying the pair had narrowly escaped, flying away across the depths of blizzard snows. Preposterous. Someone had been imbibing. But what else should I expect from humans? Afraid of taking responsibility. Weak is what they were. But I'd known that. Was I mad for wanting to control them? I wouldn't answer.

If those reports were true, which was highly doubtful, it meant they were heading for Sonmel Island. Their course had been nearly a straight line to the peak based upon earlier sightings. Perhaps those rebels were telling the truth, at least about them flying. No matter. What was done was done.

A smile blossomed across my face. My Alissandra had figured out the old stories and she'd come home. She'd found that door. Yes, that door. I'd known of its whereabouts for eons and been tempted many a time to venture through, but I'd always stopped myself, lest I became mortal. I shook my head. This whole business would have been so much easier if I could have just gone to Wake myself. Ah, well, in time.

Alissandra had found it. Call it pride, but I had hoped she'd see reason in time and it seemed she had.

I sat up. I didn't need to force anything. I was more curious to see what she'd do next. "Continue to watch them in secret. Keep me informed."

"It shall be done, my liege." Lethold bowed then turned and left.

I picked up my cup and took another sip. Alissandra had come home, and she'd brought her human. Good girl. What story she'd told the man to persuade him to risk coming to Dream, I looked forward to hearing. It must have been good. Either that or he'd convinced himself he truly loved her. Naïve fool. They deserved each other. What lengths would he go to to protect her? We'd soon find out.

I grinned. There was a reason Alissandra was my favorite daughter, and she'd just proven it. I had thought I'd lost the opportunity to use the prince with her escape, so I'd settled for having his brother at my command. But with their reappearance, I would again have the *crown* prince to help me.

I'd have both of them.

Chapter Thirty

Kovis sprawled face first on the ground, wings askew, below the branch we'd shared last night. He wobbled as he staggered up.

"I'm all right. I'm fine. Don't panic."

I grinned, not the least bit dismayed. He'd mentioned or in some way alluded to the size of his wings no less than five times already this sun. I'd warned him he wasn't high enough up for his enormous wings to catch sufficient air to fly before meeting the ground, but he'd ignored me. Typical male.

We cooked the rest of the meat Kovis had cut from the javelina and quenched our thirst in the stream before setting off. Undaunted by his first attempt at flight, Kovis practiced furling and unfurling his wings as we walked—each time we approached a pair of trees, he'd bring them close, then unfolded them again once we passed. The clumps of trees eventually surrendered to meadowlands, and Kovis took to seeing how fast he could unfurl them.

"I want to try flying," he said as the sun stretched toward its zenith.

"You think you're ready?"

"My muscles still pain me, but I've felt far worse in training."

Somehow I had no doubt based on what I'd endured.

We stopped in the middle of the meadow, and for the first time ever, I thought explicitly about how I moved my wings to create lift. "Stand aside, I need to show you."

Kovis wagged his brows. I frowned, then concentrated on the feel of launching. I extended my wings and moved them forward, then down. The motion felt awkward with no speed, and I second guessed myself. I closed my eyes and felt through the stroke again, a bit faster. Yes, forward, then down, that's what I did. I brought my wings up and repeated.

"You try it," I said after explaining it to him. "Slow at first. Get the feel of it."

Kovis stretched out his wings and did as I'd instructed.

"How's it feel?" I asked after he'd done it several times.

"Good." His eyes danced with excitement.

"Then do your downstroke faster."

He did and rose up on tiptoes as he caught the air. "Woohoo!"

Sweat beaded his brow as he practiced, but his face was alight with determination. His feet left the ground at points, and while he lacked grace with the landings, stumbling and nearly falling over several times, he grinned from ear to ear.

The sun had reached its peak when I said, "I think you're ready to try flying. I want you to crouch. When your wing bites into the air on a strong downstroke, jump. That will get you airborne. Then keep moving your wings, forward and down, like you practiced." I demonstrated several times.

"Moment of truth," he said and took a deep breath.

He crouched and brought his wings down hard, but with all the concentration, he forgot to jump. He laughed at himself then held up a hand. "Yep. Got it. I need to jump if I'm going to do this."

His next attempt had him jumping before he finished his downstroke and he fell hard on his behind. "I'm okay." He dusted himself off and stood.

His third try, he stepped out of his crouch too soon. And so it went over several more attempts.

He panted, sitting where his lack of coordination had left him after a twelfth failed try, wings pulled close. He shook his head. "You make it look so easy. I can't seem to get the timing right." He frowned.

I attempted to encourage him. "I've flown my whole life. You'll figure it out. I know you will." I sat down next to him and looked out across the meadow. A pair of birds flew over and alighted in a tree across the field.

"Show-offs," Kovis said and stuck out his tongue.

I snorted. Never in my life had I seen him do anything even remotely resembling that, not even in his dreams. So unprincely. "Your wings are *far* more impressive."

He grinned. "They are, aren't they?"

"Mm-hmm."

He leaned over and nuzzled my neck. "Show me another one of your special spots."

My mouth dropped open. "Ko-vis." I swatted him playfully.

He added kisses.

I wagged my brow. Time for him to experience what I'd felt when he'd stroked my special spot last sun. My arm moved in stealth, up and over until it was above the bend in his wing. I reached down and inside and stroked ever so lightly.

He sucked in a breath, then chuckled. "Oh, Ali, what you do to me."

I leaned over and kissed him, then said, "I believe your ego is sufficiently bolstered, oh great one. Time to try again."

"Yes, master," he replied with a wink.

"You can do this!"

He scrunched his face in concentration. He was just too cute. I could not wait for him to master this. We'd soar through the skies together. My heart sped.

He crouched, brought his wings down hard, then jumped. And rose on air.

"Flap!" I yelled when he hesitated.

He crashed face-first, and I rushed to him.

● ● ●

He moaned as he sat up. A trickle of red colored his forehead.

"You did it," I said as I wiped the blood with my thumb.

He chuckled. "I did, didn't I?"

"You just need to remember to keep stroking."

"I was so surprised I'd gotten the timing right that I..." He shook his head.

"Do it again."

So he did. And launched into the air. Downstroke. Downstroke. Again and again.

I launched and joined him. When I drew even, I looked over to see tears wetting his cheeks. *What's wrong?*

Stroke. Stroke. Stroke. *This was your life before you came... You gave this up, for me.*

I wanted to hug him, kiss him, touch him as we glided on the wind.

We flew over the meadow, over the tree the birds had landed in, over grasses and boulders and scrub.

Climb higher with me, I said, and he did. He was quiet for quite some time, and I left him to his thoughts as I savored the scenery rushing by below and the warmth of the sun on my wings. While I'd flown the sun before, I'd couldn't get enough.

He broke the silence a while later. *It's so beautiful up here. Our air cushions only got us so far, but they never gave us true freedom, not like this. I feel completely unfettered. Thank you, Ali, for teaching me to soar.*

I could have told him he'd done the same for me with The Ninety-Eight, or that he'd done the work that made this possible, but words seemed bulky, clunky. I chose to be still and just savor his words and appreciation.

We flew for some time before I showed him how to bank and dive. He caught on quickly, and soon we undulated above the field, laughing until our stomachs ached.

The sun had sunk halfway to the horizon when I asked, *Are you ready to meet Mema and my sisters?*

"Sure." But his smile seemed strained.

• • •

Chapter Thirty-One

We would make it home before the sun set. Excitement made me giddy, but I sensed angst through our bond.

Kovis met my gaze with an earnest expression as we flew. *Would you refresh my memory as to who all your sisters are? There's a lot of them.* His tone sounded strained, and I realized he was probably nervous about meeting them. Compared to his family, mine probably seemed like a small army.

Kovis, they're going to love you, so try to relax.

He forced a smile.

There are twelve of them. And then I have nine brothers, but you won't meet them tonight.

I heard him exhale through our bond. I just hoped he wouldn't feel completely overwhelmed. If I could help him know who they were, perhaps it would allay some of his concerns.

So first there's Velma. She's the oldest, I began.

The eldest. You've told me quite a bit about her. She sounds protective and spunky, he replied.

That's about right. You'll like her.

He chuckled. *Do you say that because there's one or two I won't like?*

I smiled. *No, you'll like them all. Then there's Wasila. She and Velma are roommates. Wasila is the second shortest of us girls... well, probably third shortest now, what with my changes, but she's playful and fun to be around.*

There's nothing wrong with being vertically challenged, Kovis countered.

I snorted. *Vertically challenged? Is that what you call it?*

He smiled. *So what is she like?*

Wasila likes to tease me about fostering romance among my charges. Sometimes I'd go on and on about how I was "helping" one or another of them "realize" what they felt for a particularly cute girl or boy. I was a great matchmaker if I do say so myself.

You never did that for me, did you?

I felt my cheeks warm.

Kovis laughed. *Keeping me for yourself, were you? Good thing you came, or I'd never have found true love.*

Anyway—I cleared my throat—*Wynnfrith is next oldest.*

Kovis interjected, *She was your roommate, and she likes plays.*

Yes, and she was *the shortest among us,* I interjected.

But alas, is no longer. Kovis chuckled.

He'd gotten lucky, I couldn't slap him, our wings forbade it. *Ailith is next. She's enthusiastic and creative. It seems like she can do almost anything that interests her.*

Isn't she the one your father also said he would make his favorite daughter? Kovis asked.

I frowned, and my stomach tensed. *Yes, I pray he hasn't.*

I didn't mean to make you worry. I'm just trying to piece together what you've shared with me.

I bobbed my head. *It's okay. So anyway, next is Bega. She's serious and likes tradition and safety.*

Don't we all like safety, at least to some extent? Kovis questioned.

Yes, but she avoids risk at nearly all cost and would never challenge authority. She, Eolande, and Eadu are all content being defenseless little princesses, having big, brave males protect them.

Kovis smiled. *You make it sound like that's a crime.*

It's just not my style. I could never stand to live that life, not enough excitement.

Kovis snorted. *So our little adventure would push them over the edge, you think?*

I grinned. *Just a little. Next is Beval. She's an artist, kind of like Kennan. Did I ever tell you about the Festival of Sandlings when she showed up in a fuchsia gown?*

Kovis shook his head.

She made the fabric, and then she made the dress. I shook my head. *That is impressive.*

After Beval is Deor. She's sharp and is quick to speak her mind.

Kovis added, *That mare imitated her with too much perfume, isn't that right?*

Leave it to Kovis to remember a beast imitating my sister. *Yes, that's right.* I shook my head.

Hey, just sorting them out, he defended.

Then there's Alfreda.

I know her. Well, I don't know her, but…

Yes. Then Eadu. She's analytical and less sensitive.

Like your brother Challis who figured out the math that sand people wouldn't procreate fast enough to handle so many humans' dream needs after a time.

I looked over at him. He really had been paying attention through all the stories I'd shared since we'd been in the wilderness. Gods knew we'd had plenty of time.

Of course, Ali dearest. If they're important to you, why would I not?

I grinned. *Forgive me, I didn't give you enough credit.*

Apology accepted.

Then there's Phina. She's the quiet one.

Only one in the whole bunch? Your family dinners must get—

Loud? Raucous? I chuckled. *You could say that. Farfelee's next. She's fun loving and lives for the moment.*

She's the one who always enthuses at seeing wildlife, Kovis added. *She's the reason you figured out you flew with mares and not your siblings.*

Yes! She is. Kovis, I'm so proud of you.

He smiled. *I try.*

Next to last is Amelia. She's a nurturer. She'll put everybody before herself, and she's very perceptive about people. I love that about her. She has this sense that I just don't.

And last but not least is Eolande, Kovis continued, *who you said was like Bega and Eadu, who prefer security over adventure. As well as sewing and the "maidenly arts," as you call them.*

I glanced over. *That's right.*

He grinned as if he'd passed some test.

Don't get me wrong, I love them. I'd just be bored.

I meant no offense. And I get it. With so many siblings, there have to be one or two you prefer over the others. You can't be equally close to all of them. At least I don't think I could. And from everything you've shared, I'd say you're closest to Velma, Alfreda, and Wynnfrith.

And you'd be right.

We continued on in silence for some time. Kovis digested what I'd told him like he studied for another test, at least it seemed so from what filled his thoughts when I checked a while later.

I caught the first glimpse of the sea off to the left soon after and then the outskirts of Sand City, one of the main populations and training areas of Lemnos, to the right sometime later. The city was just a short flight from home, so my siblings and I visited often. I'd definitely have to show Kovis City Center, its expansive central market area, sometime.

I let out a squeak as the white spires of home came into view. I couldn't help it. The palace of sand maidens was a sight to behold. I'd never expected to see it again.

Kovis's heartbeat had quickened. What was he thinking about this place that my heart overflowed with love for? With those I loved inside. I *had* to know. I popped into his head, looked through his eyes, and listened.

It's like a huge, white barrel rising from the bay, a good five stories. The setting sun makes the white stucco look pink and orange. One, two, three... nine cerulean-topped spires circle the upper floor, and archways add more decoration to that top level. He drew breath in sharply as we circled around the front. *Impressive. Water's gushing from spouts around the perimeter of two levels, back into the bay.* He chuckled. *And of course, an enormous pair of golden wings out front. And there's a veritable harbor at your doorstep. With people walking around. And flying!*

Turning to me, he said, *I don't know what I expected, but it wasn't this. You really lived here. Dream realm is real. Sand people live here. Lots and lots of them. And each one helps a human sleep and dream.* He shook his head. *For all you've talked about it, I don't know... it's still hard to believe. All this exists outside what we mere humans know. It's enormous.*

I wanted to laugh. But seeing my world through his eyes for the first time allowed me to glimpse the wonder of it, and I realized how much I'd taken for granted. My heart swelled all the more.

I returned to my own body and said, *I'm glad you like it.*

He could only bob his head as words abandoned him, grappling with the new reality.

Let's land on the third-level terrace, I suggested. *It's the grand entrance.*

What? Oh. Okay. Behind the wings statue?

Yes.

Never having executed a landing before, Kovis glided behind me, studying my movements as I prepared to do so. I spread my wings wide and tilted them up to catch the wind and slow myself. Then I pulled my legs forward and bent my knees, as if grabbing for the ground. I glided nearly to a stop and took a step, furling my wings in the process.

Kovis yipped right before his unfurled wing pushed me over from behind. He landed in a heap beside me with a grunt.

"Nice technique," I said.

He sat up smiling. "It wasn't graceful, but it got the job done."

"Halt!" The cry rose from above. A guard had an arrow trained on us from his position on the second level. Another guard joined him in a heartbeat, adding yet more weaponry.

I recognized the first guard as Wyke, but not the second. Wyke hadn't been around for that long when I'd left, but I hoped I could convince him of my identity. "Wyke, it's me, Princess Alissandra."

He pulled back in surprise that I would know his name but yelled, "Don't move!" Both the sentry's arrows remained nocked.

The ornate, oversize, white doors of the palace creaked open and Baldik, one of the hulking muscular sentries who had assisted me on that fateful trip to Father's just before I'd gone into hiding, stepped out along with another uniformed guard. Their thumbs twitched above the swords at their sides.

Still crumpled as we were from Kovis's spectacular landing, Baldik looked us over, but there was no recognition in his eyes.

"May we?" I asked, holding my hands up to show I was unarmed.

The pair of guards drew their swords and their wings tighter before Baldik nodded for us to rise.

Kovis shifted his wings beside me as I began. "Let me try this again. I'm Princess Alissandra. Baldik,"—he also drew back at my use of his name—"you tried to protect me at my father's palace several moons back. And when he… did what he did to me… you and Rowntree flew me back and brought me up to my bedroom, the one I share with Wynnfrith."

The male furrowed his brow. "I've no idea how you know that tale, but Princess Alissandra is dark complected, you expect me to believe you when your hair is golden? And she's much taller."

How would I convince him?

Pull your hair away from your face, Kovis suggested.

I held my hands up, palms out, then slowly drew them to my temples and placed them where they would cover my hair. "Come closer, Baldik."

The male shared a look with his fellow guard but stepped forward. His jaw tightened.

"Look closely. I have violet eyes. Pretend my hair is onyx."

The guard ruffled his wings but tilted his head as he studied my features.

"I've been gone for nine almost ten moons."

His eyebrows grew closer the longer he gazed, and then his eyes widened as recognition dawned. "It... it is you, Princess. What? How? What happened?"

Kovis exhaled beside me.

"Wallis, it's really her."

"Well, who is that?" Wallis asked, acknowledging Kovis for the first time.

"This is Prince Kovis Altairn... crown prince of the Altairn Empire... of Wake. It's a long story."

Both male's mouths dropped open for a heartbeat, but their training kicked in and they snapped them shut again.

"I think we best see them in, soldier," Baldik suggested.

"Yes, Sergeant." Turning to us, Wallis extended an open hand as Baldrik opened the hulking door. The pair ushered us through the high-ceilinged grand entrance and down a short but well-appointed hall. We stopped outside the dining room, whose carved wooden doors stood closed.

"Excuse us." We stepped aside as five white-gloved servers carried in three covered trays and two carafes.

Were they serving bublik and berries? It was hard to tell. It had been forever since I'd eaten the sweet pastry. They didn't have anything comparable in Wake, and I realized I'd missed it.

"They just sat down to breakfast. I dare say your return will improve their moods. Gods know they sure need it," Baldrik said, frowning.

Improve their moods. What did that mean? I looked to Kovis beside me. He was staring at the door, preparing himself, I realized judging by his heart rate through our bond, as we waited to be announced. Without turning, he reached over and took my hand and gave it a small squeeze.

Everything will be okay. We've come this far, he said.

What a man. He was reassuring me when he was under duress about what they'd think of him.

I winked. *Once this is over, we'll do something you like.* I had a few ideas I thought he'd consider.

The corner of his mouth turned up. *Is that a promise?*

I'd never jest about something like that.

He turned and raised a brow, just as the doors opened and servants exited, empty-handed.

Wallis held us back with an arm while Baldik entered. The sounds of clanking and rustlings filtered out to us.

After clearing his throat, he said, "Madam, ladies, you have unexpected guests."

"This can't wait until after we've finished breaking our fast?" Mema inquired. I clasp my hands together and drew them to my mouth, hearing her voice.

"I don't believe so, ma'am."

"Very well, then show them in." Frustration laced her words, and I furrowed my brow. She normally held her emotions in check.

Baldik stepped back, and Wallis motioned us forward. Butterflies launched in my stomach. And it wasn't because we hadn't eaten. I reached for Kovis's hand and drew him through the doorway with me.

The sun had abandoned the sky and dusky grays and the last hints of pink filled the floor-to-ceiling window behind where Mema sat at the head of the long table that ran the length of the high-ceilinged dining room. The crystal chandelier above watched over my sisters who lined either side in their prim dresses. I suddenly realized we hadn't taken time to clean ourselves up. I must look a fright, especially with my leathers in their current state of disrepair, but it was too late.

• • •

A steward stopped in the back, near one of the army of candles that illuminated the dimming room and relit one. No one paid him any mind. They'd all stopped eating and stared at us.

Mema scanned us, then sniffed. Judging by her frown, it wasn't a look of approval. Only my sisters' eyes moved, roamed over every fingerbreadth of us.

Until Wynnfrith gasped and drew a hand over her mouth. "Ali? Ali, is that really you?"

Every one of my sisters' heads ping-ponged between us and Wynnfrith, mouths agape. Mema furrowed her brow, searching for the truth.

"Wynnfrith…" I raised my arms, not knowing whether to run and hug her or stay firmly rooted.

Kovis compelled me to action, and I bolted for my former roommate. We enveloped each other in hugs, and a heartbeat later, Wasila, Phina, Amelia, all my sisters really, pushed away from the table squealing and engulfed me in hugs.

"You shrank! I'm not the shortest anymore." Wynnfrith beamed as she hugged me.

"And your hair. Wait until Clovis gets a look at you," Beval declared, referring to my youngest brother who arranged his hair in the most unorthodox of designs. It figured that as the artist among us, she would say something about it.

"I love it!" Ailith agreed, stroking my hair. She, too, had a creative streak, though it wasn't with paints, like Beval.

At length, I pulled myself away from them and looked to Mema, who stood at the head of the table, hands clasped, smiling. My sisters quieted and returned to their places. Neither Mema nor I said a word as I strode toward her.

Curiosity filled her eyes as she glanced over my shoulder at Kovis, and more butterflies launched in the pit of my stomach.

Chapter Thirty-Two

Mema looked down at my hand, at the sapphire adorning my finger, and again at Kovis who stood like a statue at the back of the room.

Hands at his sides, he hadn't moved since I'd dragged him through the door. His heart beat wildly, although you wouldn't know it to look at him.

"Please approach," Mema said.

Kovis's breathing hitched as he took a step.

Every eye was on him as he made his way past my sisters. Watching him, it felt like a very long path; I couldn't imagine what it was like for him.

When he reached us, he bowed low and held the posture until Mema smiled and said, "I appreciate you honoring me thusly, but you are not my subject, let alone one of Dream, rise."

His heart thundered through our bond as he said, "Pasithea. Wife of Hypnos, mother of Ambien. On behalf of all the citizens of Wake, thank you for your part in ensuring our sleep and dreams."

I stared at him. He'd figured out who Mema was. He understood the politics of our situation when I'd taken it for granted.

Mema nodded. "I presume it was you who bestowed this... medallion... on my granddaughter's finger?"

He never broke eye contact with her. "Yes. It was my mother's, Empress Onora Altairn. I'd always hoped my intended would wear it." He smiled at me. "And she is."

Murmurs broke from my sisters despite Mema's presence.

"Please do not take it as contempt on my part that I failed to ask permission for her hand in marriage. I would in no way dishonor you. I deemed it unwise to seek her father's permission."

Snickers erupted about the table, and a corner of Mema's mouth turned upward. "Please join us as we break our fast."

He'd done it. Kovis had won Mema over. My family faded from view as he reached over and took my hand, then looked into my eyes as he brought it to his lips. *I love you so much, Ali.*

And I love you, my Dreambeam.

Everyone shifted down a seat as servants scurried to set two additional places for us to Mema's right and left. All the while my sisters whispered and giggled amongst themselves at the goings on.

Let them talk. I had my Dreambeam.

Wasila leaned over and squeezed my arm as I sat down and drew my wings over the back of my chair—Kovis mimicked a heartbeat later. "I'm so happy for you, little sister." She beamed.

I patted her thigh. "Thank you. I missed you all."

How good it felt to be back. I scanned the table, thinking of how much my sisters meant to me. But my stomach clenched. Velma and Alfreda were both missing.

I dared not ask why until the meal ended though, for Mema would consider it in poor taste.

I hardly know how to act with her, she's a goddess, Kovis confessed.

I felt the same with Rasa.

He caught my eye. *Fair enough.*

I smiled.

A steward placed Mema's napkin across her lap once more, then did the same for me. She picked up her knife and fork and cut into her bublik then looked to Kovis before bringing it to her mouth. "As it seems we are to be related soon, please call me Thea."

Kovis coughed, but managed to reply, "Thank you. And please call me Kovis."

"Hyp is up at his cave. He'll be sorry he missed you. I do hope you'll be staying for some time." She almost hid her frown at Grandfather's absence, but I caught it. Yes, when he went to his cave up on the northern coast, he invariably fell asleep and she never knew when he might return. He was the god of sleep, and despite having quite a gift for it, it was just a good thing he no longer shepherded human sleep, or he'd be the only one getting any.

"We came for a reason beyond announcing our nuptials," Kovis replied as he cut a piece of bublik.

Mema nodded, her indication to continue.

"As you are aware, your son has plans for Wake."

Everyone stopped chewing and looked at Kovis. Would Mema halt the conversation?

"It is why I lost my granddaughter." Her tone was sad, and she reached over and patted my arm. She wasn't shutting this discussion down—it was so unlike her, but it told me just how deeply events had affected her.

Kovis continued. "Your loss was my gain as Ali goes, but it seems he has done something to Alfreda for he is controlling my brother through her."

Mema put her utensils down. "Both Alfreda and Velma have been missing for three moons. Alfreda disappeared first. We've searched and searched without result. Our efforts continue, but we've exhausted everything we know to try."

"No..." My whimper slipped out, and I threw a hand over my mouth. It was worse than I'd feared. Not only was Alfreda being coerced, but Father must have figured out Velma had sent me to Wake. Gods, what was he doing to her? The sergeant's comment about their sour mood made so much sense. I only wished it didn't. Several of my sisters sniffed, others wiped their eyes.

My conscience burned. I couldn't take it. "It's all my fault!"

Mema stiffened. "Now is not the time for fault finding, Alissandra. Velma knew the risks. And without you available to manipulate Kovis, I am surprised"—she shook her head—"but unsurprised that your father went after your sister." She sighed.

Kovis met her eyes. "Please do not take offense or consider me inappropriate—"

"This is not the time for proper decorum either. If what you have to say might contribute to bringing my granddaughters back, please speak your mind. It seems we share vested interests."

I furrowed my brow. Several of my sisters had too. Not time for proper decorum. Such words had never crossed her lips.

Mema continued, "You are commander of the armies of Wake if memory serves."

I glanced over quickly. She'd paid attention as I'd rambled on and on to my sisters about Kovis.

"I am." Kovis ruffled his wings and glanced my way.

"We have done everything we know, but with a different perspective, perhaps you will bring to light additional ideas," Mema suggested.

"Alfreda's as well as Velma's disappearances makes this a greater challenge than I had hoped. So if I may ask, what has been done thus far?" Kovis asked.

Mema took a deep breath. "Virtually all of the guards have been dispatched as well as my grandsons, to search for them in Ambien's usual haunts. They gained access to his palace while he was out and did an exhaustive search but turned up nothing. All of his siblings have been questioned but none knew what he was up to. We're also following him."

My sisters looked down at their plates. I could see the strain on their faces. It had definitely taken a toll on them.

Kovis continued, "Then we have three objectives, it seems. One, to locate Alfreda and Velma. But judging by the number of humans involved in rebel activities in Wake, he is controlling far more sand people than just them. And so our second objective is to free all of Dream's citizens. With any luck, he's keeping them together."

My mouth dropped open. I'd been so focused on my sister that I'd never given any thought to the others. Kovis was right. Father had to be coercing more sand people. What had he done to and with them?

Mema looked to be bracing as she asked, "When you say 'the number of humans,' how many are you referring to?"

She didn't know what Father had been up to in Wake. I sucked in a breath.

"Dozens at least, hundreds perhaps, maybe even thousands." Kovis sighed.

Yips sounded from my sisters, but Kovis plunged on. "Thirdly, and equally important, we need to find a way to stop Ambien from ever having designs on Wake or any other territory again. Ali's told me of his previous schemes, and while he is king of Dream, he needs to be stopped. I fear to think what chaos he might create for both our realms if he isn't."

Mema nodded. She'd never supported Father's campaigns but didn't have power to stop him, none of us did.

"Have there been any reports of other missing citizens?" Kovis asked.

"Not to my knowledge, but I will certainly check," Mema promised.

"Has anyone asked Selova if she might know where Velma and Alfreda are?" The words were out before I realized I'd spoken what had breezed through my mind.

Selova was the dream stitcher in our region of Dream—each province had one. She was a happy soul and the consummate sand-grandmother. But as a dream stitcher, she stitched dreams together, ensuring our charges slept through the entirety of the night. Might she know where the various connections she made were geographically?

Kovis smiled.

Mema tilted her head, considering. "No, Alissandra. I didn't even think of her, but it's definitely worth a try."

Heads bobbed around the table.

"If it's all the same to you, I'd like to go. I know her best," I said. I did. In addition to stitching dreams together, she also formed, or stitched baby sand beings, or sandlings, as the need arose. As I was the only one who seemed to need a regular sandling fix, I'd taken to calling on her every moon or so. She was easy to talk to, and we'd chat about anything as I walked between the cradles, cooing at the babes or picking one up and playing with him or her.

Wasila, Velma's roommate, raised her hand. "I'd like to go too. I'll at least feel like I'm doing something rather than sitting on my hands."

Deor, Alfreda's roommate, Ailith, Beval, and Amelia waved their hands at that.

Mema held up hers. "You can't all go. Poor Selova will feel overwhelmed. Wasila, you may go, if it's all right with Prince Kovis."

The other four sighed as Kovis nodded, then continued, "So we have two possibilities for finding them. What can we be doing to stop Ambien?"

"Has anyone told Dyeus?" I asked.

Kovis raised a brow. Had he been considering it too?

Mema frowned. "Your mother delivered a letter to him, but his ministry indicated that until we can find Alfreda and Velma, or I suppose any of these citizens as well, he won't do anything since we have no proof of what we allege." She cleared her throat. "I speculate his unwillingness also stems from bad blood between he and Hyp"—grandfather, or Hypnos—"And he certainly won't listen to me."

I huffed out a breath. Family politics could be so frustrating although I'd have been surprised if Dyeus easily agreed to help. On grandfather's account, the god still hadn't forgiven him for putting him to sleep at his wife's behest. She'd wanted to punish one of Dyeus's illegitimate sons for sacking a city she loved. When Dyeus woke, he was furious with Grandfather to the point that Grandfather fled and hid.

What's she mean Dyeus won't listen to her? Kovis asked.

His wife had an extramarital fling, and Mema was the result.

Kovis covered his surprise, but I could tell from his determined look that he wasn't done exploring this angle.

Bega, Eolande, and Eadu looked to be suffering, and I understood. Adventure and risk were the last things any of them sought, but it was time for action, not safety.

"We need someone to persuade Dyeus to get involved," Kovis said. "Who is close to him and has a good relationship?"

Deor, always sharp and quick to speak her mind, held up a hand then said, "Great Aunt Dite"— our term of endearment for Aphrodite, who wasn't technically our aunt but whatever —"from everything you've said, she's got her father wrapped around her little finger." She grinned. "Mema, I know you don't like to get the goddess involved in your personal affairs, but I think Prince Kovis is right. We need Dyeus's help to stop Father for good."

Kovis sent me a questioning look.

Mema is one of Dite's Graces.

Kovis bobbed his head. *That's right. I'd forgotten. She attends Dite with the other Graces—Splendor, Good Cheer, and Abundance. Your grandmother manages human's relaxation for the goddess.* Kovis smirked. *From everything you've told me about her, your grandmother seems a bit uptight though. How can she be responsible for relaxation… never mind. It doesn't matter.*

She takes her role very seriously. It was hard not to snicker because Kovis was right, Mema was uptight.

Kovis laughed through our bond, then feigned coughing to cover.

Mema leaned back stiffly and folded her hands in her lap.

Kovis looked to her, hope rising in his eyes. "Might it be possible?"

"It is, but as you know, as the goddess of love, she has many—" She raised her chin and sniffed. "—unusual proclivities. I worry what her price might be."

"Mema, we have no other options," I reasoned. "We need to at least ask her."

Mema gave me a long look. It seemed as if she weighed my being here, regaining a granddaughter she feared she'd never see again, against the future and considered what it might hold if Ambien wasn't stopped.

At length, she reached over and ran her hand across my jaw. "Very well, I will ask. I love my son, but I will not lose another loved one."

What would Dite say? What would she require in kind?

• • •

Chapter Thirty-Three

Would Selova be able to help us? How I *prayed* it was so, as the tan spires of the sprawling Palace of Sand rose from the horizon as we neared.

Unlike most of our homes, this castle was constructed entirely of sand. I'd always assumed that was because it was the nursery of crafted sand people, or sandlings as they were known. It made sense, at least to me.

It stood just across the bustling bay and was situated at the shore like the palace of sand maidens. But unlike ours, only the bay side was clear, stretching down to the beach. Selova's was surrounded by lush vegetation growing up on the other three sides.

Wasila flew to my left, Kovis to my right, and four guards surrounded us on all sides.

We'd retired shortly after breakfast to long looks from my sisters when I pulled Kovis into my old bedroom. Wynnfrith moved into Wasila's room to give us *privacy*—she'd said it with a wink and my face had warmed. Yes, I might be younger, but I certainly knew more in *that* domain than any of my sisters. Kovis had just laughed.

Yes, the difference between humans and sand beings could not have been more pronounced.

But it had been a long night of tossing and turning beside Kovis. It wasn't him, or the bed. My mind had dredged up horrific scenarios of what Father might be doing to my sisters—degrees worse than what my dreams had been so far—and I couldn't make it stop.

Of course, Kovis and I had been the only ones attempting sleep. Everyone, other than Mema, had been hard at work weaving dreams. It was odd to be back where night and sun activities were reversed.

Wasila lent me some of her smaller-sized clothes, and a servant had procured a limited wardrobe of Kovis-size clothes overnight. So we'd risen to a soft knock on the door just before the sun and eaten a light dinner of Sea Monk soup and meat pie with Wasila before leaving. We hoped to catch Selova before she retired.

My sister was not her usual joking, playful self. I couldn't decide if she didn't feel comfortable around Kovis, she was just tired, or if this "not knowing" was the culprit. Her sullen mood lifted for a time as Kovis attempted to launch, beating his wings and jumping—she actually had to cover her snickers.

Kovis had called me vertically challenged. Well, he was too, but in a different way. It took him five tries, and he looked ridiculous squatting just before jumping. He overcompensated as he beat his wings and nearly did a nosedive but corrected just in time. He was a good sport about it though and finally lifted off.

I knew the heartbeat Wasila got a look at his fully extended wings. She raised her brows and gave me a wink, drawing a grin from me.

Wasila noticed your wingspan, I told him. He beamed. Such a male.

We arrived not long after as the sun began its trek into the sky.

"Let's land on the beach," I yelled over the wind. I figured Kovis would have an easier time with sand than the hard surface out front of the castle.

• • •

Wasila, our guards, and I touched down and moved aside. Kovis spread his wings wide, tilted them up to catch the wind, brought his feet forward, and stepped. It would have been a perfect landing if he hadn't been several handbreadths off the ground yet. As it was, he beat his wings and peddled until his feet caught the sand at odd angles. Despite throwing his arms out to steady himself, he fell forward onto his hands and knees.

While our guards tried to hide their amusement, I caught one lift the corner of his mouth for a heartbeat. Another pretended to look elsewhere.

"That was only my second attempt at landing. I'll get it." He furled his wings, stood, and brushed himself off.

Wasila whispered, "He's too cute."

"What are you two whispering?"

"Wasila thinks you're doing well if that was just your second try," I lied.

"Well, thank you." Kovis bobbed his head and gazed up at the castle looming over us. "Shall we?"

We marched up the beach, our guardians again surrounding us after assuring themselves that there was no threat. We mounted the steps that curved up to the grand entrance and were met by Selova's guards.

Entrance proved significantly easier with Wasila and our guards with us. Selova's males recognized them and showed us to the door, which Sandrin, her steward, answered. He'd been in her employ for as long as I could remember and always looked handsome in his taupe livery with black accents. It coordinated well with his close-cropped, onyx hair, impeccably groomed wings, and gloves.

He welcomed us in but cocked his head when he saw me. I could tell I looked familiar to him, but he couldn't place me, for he looked back to Wasila and said, "Welcome to Selova's palace. I must say, it has been a long while since Princess Alissandra paid us a visit. I do hope she fares well."

Wasila looked between Sandrin and me, then said, "My sister is actually the reason for our visit. And in fact—"

"Hello, Sandrin." I waved.

He squinted as he studied my face, my hair, my flight leathers, then sized up my stature. I could almost see the wheels turning in his head. He drew back the heartbeat recognition dawned. "Why, Princess, is that really you? You've… changed." Propriety caught up with him and he blanched. "Forgive me, Princess."

I grinned.

Kovis smiled. Wasila's mood had again taken hold of her and she didn't respond.

"Please. Come in. Come in." Sandrin led us into the grand foyer that stretched up all four floors to the roof that let light in through the clear glass at the top, much as the central atrium in our palace. Selova had carried the theme of abundant foliage from outside into the space. A sequence of topiaries depicting the formation of sand beings being formed adorned the curved walls all the way up. Clearly, she loved what she did. I'd always thought her gardener must be a magician to maintain it all.

"Please wait here while I let Selova know she has some special visitors," Sandrin said.

I raised my hand. "Actually, could we come with you? I haven't seen the nursery in forever."

Sandrin smiled. "As you wish, Princess. Then, if you'll follow me."

Our guards remained in the foyer while Wasila, Kovis, and I mounted the sweeping staircase.

Kovis and I had never discussed children, but I speculated it wouldn't be long before we had that conversation, not after he saw all the adorable sandlings. At least I hoped he liked them as much as I did.

We stopped on the third-floor landing and the sound of weeping filtered out to us. Sandrin turned right and pushed open the nursery door. Crying grew in intensity, approaching wailing as I soaked in the sight of the three rows of cradles. Selova had been busy. I counted green or yellow tags on nineteen of them.

Kovis ruffled his wings and looked to me with big eyes.

I chuckled. Such a male. The most powerful warrior the Altairn Empire had ever known, overwhelmed by babes.

The three attendants had their hands full with other malcontents, so I plunged into the chaos. I quickly located the culprit. After checking diaper dryness, I scanned the chart. He'd been fed not long before. "You need a nap, young one."

I assumed my rocking stance and picked him up, feeling power well up at my feet from the sand structure. "Go to sleep. Go to sleep, little one," I whispered, then launched into a lullaby.

His eyes closed, and his wails ceased. Only his bottom lip quivered as the remnants of his tantrum ebbed.

I felt a hand rest on my shoulder and didn't need to look up to know it was Kovis.

Wasila had taken a seat in a rocker and forced a smile as I caught her eye.

I finished the second verse of the lullaby, gazing at this precious life in my arms. He was amazing in every way. Tiny fingers wrapped around mine. Tiny wings with tiny pin feathers. My heart filled, then overflowed with love.

"Don't you think you had an unfair advantage?" Kovis asked, a smile playing in his tone. "Using somnus on him."

I looked up. "He needed a nap."

"You're a natural."

"Do you want to hold him?"

Alarm filled his eyes. "No. No, I'm good."

I smiled. "He won't break."

Something akin to panic mounted Kovis's face.

"Alissandra, you've returned." I knew that voice even without turning.

I placed the sandling back in his cradle, leaving him to sweet slumber, and practically ran to Selova. I threw my arms around her, and she hugged me back. She gave the best hugs, the ones only a grandmother who'd spent her life around babes could. I inhaled her sand and sea scent—I loved it.

At length, I pulled back. She looked the same as always. Wrinkles—smile skids I called them—filled the corners of her eyes and mouth. She'd braided her long silver hair and let it flow over her black knit shawl. She'd added a white sheep scarf with sparkles over her shoulders—its horn and front hooves hung down on one side, gray tail and hind quarters on the other. She'd knitted it and many others, and always wore one, an animal of some kind. And of course, she wore fun leggings like always. They were red and pink horizontal stripes this sun.

"Sandrin told me you'd changed, but you're still a sight for sore eyes." She beamed as she rustled her wings, then ran her hand over my hair as if trying to understand how the transition had recreated me. "You must tell me all about it."

Kovis and Wasila joined us, and she looked Kovis up and down. "And you must tell me how you came to be in possession of these fine wings." Her eyes danced. I wondered if she looked for new ideas to try. Turning to Wasila she said, "Princess, it has been a very long time since I last saw you, but you're looking as radiant as ever."

Wasila leaned forward and hugged her. "Thank you, Selova. It's good to see you too."

"Let's adjourn someplace more comfortable to talk, shall we?" She headed out the doors, then up the stairs and turned left. We passed her workroom—she never allowed anyone in while she crafted sandlings, not even me—and stopped at the end of the hall. A moving sand sculpture greeted us—a sheep sitting on its behind held knitting needles that flew as it knit its own wool into a sock. A dancing sand hippocampus had greeted me the last time I'd been here.

Interesting. Kovis's comment held amusement, but also perhaps a hint of awe.

The sand of her door parted like a curtain, and we followed her inside, into her suites. Kovis looked around at the army of dream catchers adorning every sand wall—humans believed the things helped them dream when placed at the head of their beds. Wynnfrith, my roommate, had made one as a joke and put it on the wall above her bed. I'd never asked, but Selova had a funny sense of humor too. I could see her doing it for similar reasons.

"Please, have a seat," Selova invited. She headed to a dark wicker sectional with puffy white cushions. It had been situated before a large window that let in the cheery sun and permitted an expansive view of the bay. The seating arrangement filled the center of the spacious room atop a white-and-lime-patterned rug. A host of coordinating lime throw pillows made it even more inviting. Kovis sat down beside me. Wasila took the matching chair.

Selova clapped her hands. "Alissandra, it is *so* good to see you. But I dare say that's not why you've paid me a visit this sun."

I explained the situation regarding Alfreda and Velma going missing as succinctly as I could—she shook her head at parts and huffed at others. When I finished, I asked, "We were wondering if you know the geographic location of the sand person as well as the dreamer whose dreams you stitch together. If you do, we should be able to locate them."

She tilted her head. "You know, I've honestly never paid any attention. Location never seemed important to my work." I let my shoulders fall as she held up a bony finger. "However, I'd like to try."

I looked up with a flicker of hope that Wasila mirrored. Kovis put his hand on top of mine and squeezed.

"We can't use your human charge, can we, Alissandra?" She winked at Kovis. "So, Princess Wasila, would you do the honors?"

Wasila sat forward. "What do you need me to do?"

"You have a dream charge."

"Yes, Isabel. She's fourteen annums."

"Do you know where she is?"

"Let me find her." Wasila closed her eyes and several heartbeats later nodded.

"Put her to sleep if you would and get her to dream. I'll see if I can locate her when I connect that dream to the next."

• • •

Wasila remarked, "She'll get in trouble for wool gathering, but it's for a very good cause. Okay, I'm starting."

I bit my lip as I watched my sister. How I hoped this worked.

Selova yawned before closing her eyes to commence work. She covered her mouth. "Sorry, past my bedtime."

I hope she doesn't fall asleep on us, Kovis said.

Please, don't even say that.

Sometime later, Selova opened her eyes again while Wasila continued working Isabel's dreams.

"Well?" I asked.

Selova shook her head. "I couldn't tell where either were. Of course I knew where Wasila was, but I looked for indicators that would tell me where she was, as if I didn't already know, and found none. I couldn't tell where Isabel was either. But just because I couldn't doesn't mean I can't. I'll need to try a few things. I've had worse challenges than this in my time."

Selova had been selected from among the best and brightest when we all first learned how to help humans sleep and weave their dreams. She wasn't short of mind power, and that fact allayed some of my fears. That and I knew she could be tenacious.

"Have any other sand people gone missing?" she asked.

Kovis and I looked at each other and he said, *She's quick.*

"We don't know for sure, not yet," I said. "But we believe Father is somehow using sand people to force humans to do his will." I told her about Alfreda and Kennan and the times we'd run into rebels. "Every one of them had cloudy eyes. We believe it's the manifestation of Father somehow possessing them."

"Via their sand person," Selova clarified.

"Yes."

"If there were a number of sand people who... hmm... I wonder if that's why..." Selova brought a hand to her chin, considering.

"What?" I prompted.

"I've had a lighter workload of late. I wonder if whatever your father is doing is keeping dream connections from breaking."

"That's possible?" I asked. Father had never attempted anything like that between me and Kovis.

"So you wouldn't have as many to join," Kovis finished her thought.

Selova nodded.

"Each of the rebels are in what seems to be a dream state," Kovis added. "Kennan had fought his way out of what he described as one horrendously long nightmare when we saw him, like his dream state never ended. But based upon what he said as he dashed off, that connection might have been reestablished."

"I've never heard of a substance or spell that could accomplish such a thing, but your father is a crafty one. If he's formulated…" Selova shook her head.

Wasila had made Isabel wake and now rejoined the conversation. "Prince Kovis, if they're like your brother, once that connection is broken, they should have free will again, right?"

"It would seem so," he agreed.

"I pray it's so and they return to their homes." She bit her lip.

Kovis added, "Assuming several citizens have gone missing, we need to find them and your sisters as well as determine how to break that connection. Our list is growing."

Selova had continued thinking. "Prince Kovis, you said Kennan is Alfreda's charge. As I think about it, I haven't connected dreams for him in ages. It seems your theory, that he is again under control by another, may well have merit."

I frowned. Poor Kennan, he didn't deserve this.

"What is Velma's charge's name? And where was he when you last knew his whereabouts?" Selova asked.

"Her current charge is JT," Wasila replied. "He's a healer at the capital."

I furrowed my brow. I didn't think I knew that. Velma never talked about her charges. I'd never thought about why. Perhaps she wanted to protect them from Father. If so, I understood. I would have hidden everything about my charge too, based on what had happened between she and Father with the former Emperor Altairn.

The less anyone knew about them, the better. I did a quick roll call of my apprentice friends and acquaintances, but none bore the name JT. He must be in Sand City.

Selova clapped her hands, recognizing the name. "Oh, JT, yes. I connected dreams for him last night. That's good news."

My stomach quivered. Yes, good news, but how to find Velma through him?

Wasila looked hopeful.

Selova pondered further. "If I think through who I've stitched dreams for recently and determine whose missing, we should know who is affected. At least in this province. Perhaps you can see if you can locate each citizen and question them. Oh, but you said you believe the citizens have been taken. *And* this still won't locate either the human or the sand person. Well…"

Kovis held up a hand. "Selova, thank you for your efforts. Would you keep trying? Who knows what your insights might glean. Any information is better than nothing."

Selova rustled her wings and smiled as she rose. "It would be an honor. I'll keep trying and will let you know immediately if I discover their whereabouts. I'll also work to find a way to break that seemingly permanent dream state. They would at least wake up, and I should think that would prevent them being used."

We all stood, and I leaned over and gave Selova a hug. "Thank you."

"It is my pleasure, Princess Alissandra. I will do whatever I can to help you." She patted my cheek.

Wasila's hug extended longer than mine, and I heard her sniff as Selova held her tight. "We'll find them, Princess."

My sister bobbed her head against Selova's shoulder and wiped her eyes when she finally pulled back. "Thank you," she whispered.

Turning, Selova said, "Wickford." Another liveried steward appeared. "Please show them out and have the kitchen put on a large pot of coffee. Tell them to make it strong. I've got a long sun ahead."

I prayed it bore fruit, but my gut maintained a healthy skepticism.

• • • •

Chapter Thirty-Four

We made it back to the palace as the sun cast long shadows and learned Aunt Dite had accepted Mema's invitation to dinner next sun. While the news was encouraging, I was not at all settled.

We shared with everyone what Selova had said. I knew she would try her best, but we hadn't made any progress finding Alfreda and Velma, not really.

Wasila begged off further conversation and headed straight to bed. Perhaps having Wynnfrith to share her room with would make it not so lonely.

"You're rather quiet," Kovis commented. We'd headed to my bedroom, and Kovis sat beside me, stockinged feet, with wings thrown over the headboard. He'd stretched out his legs and crossed them at the ankle.

"I've been thinking," I said.

He gave me a long look.

"Dite is not really my aunt. We just call her that as an honorary title. But I do have three aunts, on my father's side of the family, Grandfather's sisters, that I've never told you about."

"Okay."

"Nona, Ches, and Ta. They live at the Palace of Time. Great Aunt Ches decides the length of every human life. Aunt Nona sets in motion a device to measure it when a human is born, and Aunt Ta ends it when it's over."

Kovis's eyes grew wide. "I'm familiar with them, but I never realized you were related to the Fates. You certainly have a colorful family."

"You've only met a few of my relatives."

Kovis grinned as he shook his head.

"Anyway, most people see them as reclusive crones as old as time itself."

"You mention them, why?"

"Father asked them to change your lifespan."

Kovis leaned forward.

"They wanted to get my side of the story before they acted, so I had to appear before them."

"Do I want to know what happened?"

"They decided not to change it."

Kovis exhaled. "At least I hope that's a good thing. I hope to live to a ripe old age… as humans go that is."

I smiled. "I think they might know where every human is located geographically."

Kovis's mouth dropped open. "Why didn't we go there first then?"

"Everyone, shall we say, holds a healthy respect for them… out of fear of what they can do to the humans they care about."

"You're talking about the Fates. I'd fear them, too."

"While I was there, I got to know them a little, and they're actually really nice."

Kovis's brow rose. "Hold on, everyone is afraid of them for good cause, but you're not?"

"It's hard to explain." I bit my lip. Was I crazy to think my aunts might help us? I'd gone the first time to answer their questions. But they'd wanted me to return with reading material. My face warmed at the thought. This time we'd be going to make a request of them, if we went. But what other choice did we have?

Kovis drew my hands together and held them. "Ali, I want to find them as much as you, but—"

"You don't understand. If anyone finds out, they'll try to stop us. I know they will."

"You're human now."

I pulled a hand away. "Kovis, I know this sounds crazy, but my gut tells me they'll see us as well as help." I prayed I sounded more convincing than I felt.

Kovis let out a long breath. "Ali, you know I love you, and I trust you. I just don't want anything to happen to you."

I forced a smile. "Nothing will. And I think we'll find my sisters."

Kovis closed his eyes and shook his head. "I can't believe I'm actually agreeing to this. When should we go?"

I drew a hand to the back of my neck. "We need to collect a few books to take with us first."

"Books? Like what kind of books?"

"Um..." My face warmed.

Kovis furrowed his brows.

"Don't ask me how, but I discovered they..." How to even say it. "They have unusual ways of... letting off pent-up passion." Yes, that's how Aunt Ches described it.

"Passion? What are you saying?" A corner of his mouth hitched upward.

"They're old and... it's just the three of them, and a few stewards and..."

Kovis's mouth dropped open. "No! Surely you don't mean..."

I scrunched my face and bobbed my head.

"How did you...?"

I buried my face in my hands. "Please don't ask."

"And that's the kind of reading material you plan to bring them?" His voice rose.

"They asked me to. The next time I came." I grimaced.

● ● ●

Kovis roared, and I couldn't hold back my merriment.

He held his middle and moaned in pain before he could stop laughing. At length he panted, "We best get to work locating these masterworks if that's the case." He cleared his throat. "And where do you propose we go to locate something of this nature?" He snorted. "Do you suppose your sisters…?"

I yipped, and my eyes bulged. "No! And not my brother's or Mema and Grandfather's place either." I'd be mortified if I was ever found looking for something like this. And I certainly couldn't ever tell anyone about my aunts. Ever.

Kovis grinned.

"I think we should go into Sand City. They have several book shops." Thank the gods I didn't look like my old self. With any luck, no one would recognize me. I'd wanted to show him City Center, but not with this objective.

"Then Sand City it is," he said, grinning.

———

We'd begged off breakfast and flown to City Center accompanied by two guards who I'd asked to dress in nondescript clothes, like my siblings and I always did when we went, so we blended in.

Kovis and I ate a bite at the Salty Seahorse as dusk settled in, then made our way to the first of a handful of book shops I knew of. It was just opening, and the bell clanged behind us as the door closed.

Kovis was bolder than me, and he smiled as he asked one of the proprietors where the books we sought were shelved.

My cheeks warmed as the male kept glancing between us, then at my ring. He winked at me and rustled his wings as he finally pointed to a shelf against the far wall. I felt his eyes boring into me until I ducked behind a tall bookshelf.

The apprentice or proprietor of each book shop we stopped in behaved similarly, and I was never so happy that we succeeded in our mission within a relatively short time. We'd found no less than ten books that fit our requirements—who would have thought books like these were so readily available.

I was exhausted and wanted to go home, to bed, once we finished, but Kovis's curiosity to experience the city won out, and rightly so. I'd always loved the warmth of City Center at night. Lights shining from the myriad of small shops lining either side of the streets, lavished their treasures on shoppers and revelers passing by. The effect was a warm and inviting atmosphere that always made me, and so many others, want to linger.

It definitely rubbed off on Kovis, who whistled as we walked, and not just any whistle but one resembling a rooster crowing as he carried the stack of books. I kept slapping his arm.

The farmers' market was brimming with activity this time of night, and the smells of cooking foods wafting about, oh be still my heart. Street musicians ambled between vendor's stalls, and we stopped to listen to several between our stops to taste samples. One place we paused had a green-and-white-striped, fabric awning and offered cheese and meat samples, which we gratefully accepted.

The owner of another stall, with an amber awning, beckoned us approach with her animated gestures and toothy grin. She promised an exotic array of fish—abtu, a sacred fish; samebito, an inky-black fish with emerald green eyes; isonade, a fish that glowed orange; and more—and she delivered. Kovis was enthralled with the diversity that he'd never conceived of and insisted we bring some back to the palace as a gift to Mema.

"What amazing fodder for my writing," he commented at one point.

I, for one, couldn't wait to see what stories he created from inspiration my home gave him.

A while later, my feet hurt and my energy sagged. It had been a very full sun, and I could no longer beat back my exhaustion.

So much was on the line.

• • •

Chapter Thirty-Five
Ambien

I needed to leash my temper, but Velma made it increasingly difficult.

I counted to ten, then to one hundred where I stood just inside the cave mouth. My eldest hadn't yet submitted to the lesson of being less, and she'd become increasingly obstinate, according to my soldiers.

Alfreda had again found her courage as a result and was following her sister's example. It was time to put a stop to this. And I had just the news to do it. When my soldier had first reported to me, I'd known his news would bear fruit at some point. And I was about to test that theory.

I returned my soldiers' salutes and stopped just before the archway so I could see Velma's expression when I told her—Alfreda would hear too.

As I expected, Velma leveled a cold stare at me from where she sat on her moss mattress. She looked feisty and in better health. Her stumps were healing. Good.

I locked eyes with her as I said, "I thought you both would enjoy knowing that Alissandra has returned to Dream."

Velma tried to hide her surprise but wasn't quick enough.

Alfreda gasped in the other room.

I grinned. "And she brought her human."

"No... oh no," Alfreda whimpered.

"All your work for naught, daughter." I shook my head. "And you've lost your wings as a result. Such a shame. You'll be less... for nothing..." I let my words linger.

Velma's mind whirled, I could see it in her eyes, but it just wasn't in her to back down. So like me. "What do you mean, she's returned?"

I chuckled. "I mean returned, as in come back. She's seen the error of her ways and has come to repent and beg my forgiveness."

"She said that?"

I smiled. "How much plainer must I be?"

Her breathing grew labored as I let the news settle.

"Abandon your little cause and join me. We can give humans better lives as they dream of only good things all their days."

Velma didn't reply.

Satisfied with the result of my statement, I ducked under the archway. Alfreda sat on her moss bed with a hand over her mouth, shaking her head. She looked up when I stopped a pace away and met my eyes with a blank expression.

"As for your charge—"

"No, please. Don't hurt him anymore. He can't help you anymore."

"Alfreda," Velma cautioned from the other room.

Alfreda pressed on, so committed to protecting the human. "His people found him." She looked up with venom in her eyes. "He was practically frozen. He'd collapsed in the snow. If it wasn't for those horses drawing their attention, he might well have perished. You shattered his mind with all your demands. He was delirious and kept mumbling, telling them about the gods punishing him, begging them to wake him, confessing his undying love for Ali. They think he's mad."

I kept my expression even. They'd found him. That was news to me… good news, really. They would revive him and make him fit again, ready to do my bidding.

"So you want me to break my hold on your connection with him?" I asked.

Those sand people I controlled had been doing my bidding with their charges in Wake for some time, but I'd seen the limitations of my earliest advances in that I could only control one human at a time—manually applying an adhesive to the human's thought thread wasn't a scalable answer. I'd had to resort to leveraging general dissent to mobilize humans in any great numbers, and I disliked being dependent on human whims—they weren't stable enough to build a new kingdom on, that was for sure. And so I'd sought for a better way, a way to control multiple humans simultaneously.

I'd tested my new methodology on Alissandra and her human first. I'd started with the basics, having her get him to move his arms and such. But my research had blossomed with Alfreda and her charge despite her protests. She could control virtually all her human's movements as well as his dreams, just like other sand people. But I could now simultaneously hold the thought threads of multiple humans at once, not just one, and have them all move as I instructed. I'd done it with three at once so far, and I didn't see why I couldn't add more. Time would tell.

"Please. He's sick and he can't go anywhere even if I tried to make him." Alfreda's tone was pleading.

She had a point. I could be reasonable. I had other subjects to continue experiments with. And appeasing her might make her, as well as her sister, less combative.

"Very well." I wouldn't tell her I had no intention of allowing this to be a permanent situation. No need to spoil my good will.

I closed my eyes and latched onto her mind. I easily located the connection we held with her charge—this one in addition to the permanent seed I'd planted in him earlier that she still knew nothing of.

With just a thought, I separated my connection with her. She clenched her fists and moaned.

"Let no one say I am unreasonable. Loose your charge's thought thread as you please."

"Thank you," she panted.

"Get some rest," I said in parting, ducking back under the arch.

But before I could instruct my soldiers to allow Alfreda ease, Velma snarled, "What specifically did Ali say when you spoke with her?"

"That's a private matter."

Argumentative, she rose. "I asked what Ali said. Specifically."

I frowned.

"You never talked to her, did you?"

"As I've told you, Alissandra has indeed returned."

"Perhaps, perhaps not. But she never begged your forgiveness. She'd never do that. You're lying to me."

I laughed. "Believe what you will. I have no time for this."

I gave my soldiers new instructions and strode out. Velma had seen through my ruse.

It was time to have that conversation with Alissandra. She would beg my forgiveness once she stood before me, I had no doubt.

I held back a growl. I'd thought for sure that when she'd reappeared in Dream that she had come to her senses and she would seek me out. I could conceive of no other plausible explanation for her risking the transition—she'd had no idea what it might do to her coming back, but she'd done it anyway. Inconceivable, foolhardy, and rash as well.

I shook my head and bit back a snarl. She'd been back three suns already and had been to see her sisters as well as Selova, but not me. Why was everyone else more important than her own father? It was time to put things straight.

Chapter Thirty-Six

Thanks to more horrific dreams, I woke as the sun cast its first rays through the window that stretched floor to ceiling to the left of my bed. Wynnfrith's bed stood on the opposing side.

Kovis roused shortly thereafter, hands nomadic as usual.

"I'm keen to read a few of those books." He wagged his brows, looking at the stack on the nightstand. "And try a few new things." He reached over and rubbed one of my special spots. His tattoo shown red across his muscled chest—he'd gotten to keep Kennan's artwork, but how I missed his thrum.

My stomach quivered with the touch. I longed to as well, but I stilled his hand. "Aunt Dite will be here for dinner soon. We need to get ready."

"You're no fun." He pecked my nose.

I took my time running a palm across his chest, fully enjoying the firmness of it. "You can read some before we head to my aunts. Maybe we'll even experiment." I winked.

That brought a smile to his face. "Are we going this sun?"

"I hope to. We'll know after dinner."

"I hope I don't think about… *their proclivities…* when I see them." He chuckled.

I snickered as he brought his forehead to mine.

"We'll find them." His tone was calm and filled with confidence.

"I know. I love you, my Dreambeam." My hand ran down his prickly, morning jaw.

"And I love you." He met my lips with a gentle kiss.

We lingered, but eventually I pushed myself up and out of bed. Dite awaited, and who knew what that might mean? I prayed it was less dramatic than what her reputation touted, she was the goddess of love after all. I'd seen her only a few times before, and Mema had hustled we maidens out every one of those times.

I hoped my fabled aunts proclivities proved far more provocative than Dite. We'd invited her here to help us stop Father. Wake's future depended on our success.

I'd endure whatever her price required.

———

Kovis donned a tailored, shadow-gray, casual shirt and black slacks that complemented his wings. He'd shaved, and one of our stewards had trimmed his hair and combed his wings. He smelled male in all the best ways and got my heart pumping.

I'd borrowed a pastel aqua-mint dress that extended to my knees, from Wasila. It gathered on one side of the bodice, had a boat neckline, and I loved how its fitted sleeves extended into flowing cuffs. It was pretty, but modest. Exactly what I'd intended. I felt feminine.

"Are you ready?" Kovis asked, nuzzling my neck after I finished brushing my hair and braiding some of my locks horizontally across the back of my head. I let the rest fall freely down my back. "You look beautiful."

I forced a smile. "I'm as ready as I'll ever be."

Kovis extended his elbow, and I placed my hand on his arm.

I counted every one of the one hundred and four steps between my bedroom and our dining room. I'd never done that before, but it helped calm me. Good thing because when we reached it, Aunt Dite was already there.

To say I sensed sexual tension in the air when I stepped through the doorway would have been an understatement. Aunt Dite radiated it. But her sensuality was more than her long dress—calling the two widths of black fabric that began as a straight across, low-cut neckline, and fell to the floor, a dress, was a stretch. Two handbreadths of her bronze skin shown where the laces holding the front and back together ran up and down her sides—she announced to everyone that she wore absolutely nothing underneath.

I instinctively looked for Velma to ground me, before remembering she was one of the reasons we had gathered. Judging by the wide and downcast eyes of my sisters, it seemed they also lacked an anchor in this storm.

The stewards had shortened the normally room-length table that accommodated my entire family, by half, in the large, high-ceilinged dining room. I could only assume the idea of shortening the table had been to make the occasion more intimate. I wasn't sure if that had been such a good idea.

My sisters had formed two groups and mingled to the left of it, but their eyes kept traveling to Dite. Unsurprisingly, several helped themselves to more cocktails as white-gloved stewards passed through their midst.

Mema held a forced smile as she conversed with the goddess who stood tall. But Dite was anything but stiff, not with the way she waved the hand she held her drink in. How was it even possible to feel that confident? She was a goddess, but still.

I wondered if Mema might accidently shatter the flute in her hand with the pressure her grip put it under. She'd dressed in a modest black dress whose collar hugged her throat.

Kovis exhaled heavily beside me. His heart had picked up pace.

As if sensing it, Dite ran a hand slowly through her long black locks and winked at Kovis, then took a sip of wine.

I cleared my throat, and Kovis startled.

It had been a few annums since I'd last seen her, but she still had an exotic look about her. Her face was perfectly symmetrical, her eyes ever changing, magical, and big, her eyebrows the perfect shape, her lips small and feminine. She had a beauty mark on her cheek that somehow added to her overall intrigue. But she lacked wings. Ha.

I rustled mine. I was shorter than her by far, but I had curves. Not as shapely as hers, but still. And I had gold hair, although Kovis had been attracted more to dark-haired women in the past. Would she seduce him? I bit my lip.

You're perfect to me, Ali. Kovis squeezed the hand I still rested on his arm.

But you—

She's a damn goddess, Ali, and the goddess of love at that. She oozes sex.

I snickered. *You think?*

I'm a bit overwhelmed by her.

I exhaled.

Wynnfrith came over. "Ali. Kovis. Come join us." She took my hand and led us over to those she'd gathered with—Ailith, Beval, Deor, Farfelee, and Wasila.

I positioned myself where I could keep an eye on Dite as Kovis and I grabbed wild-boar-wrapped sea serpent appetizers when a steward offered. I wasn't the only one watching her judging by my sisters' inattentiveness.

Mema ushered Dite to one group, thankfully not ours, and introduced her around. My *un*adventurous sisters Bega, Eolande, Eadu looked completely out of their element. So did Phina, as quiet as she was. But Amelia, ever the nurturer, grabbed her hand in a silent show of support.

Mema clearly understood how to play this game because these sisters were definitely a safe move. The goddess chatted as she looked around the circle, but polite as she was, her eyes still wandered over our group and hovered over Kovis's wings and behind.

Her assured smile, which told me she was calm and at peace with herself, never left her face, even when our eyes connected. Despite myself, I looked away and my stomach clenched.

Farfelee grimaced in a show of support. She'd seen.

Dite was the exact opposite of the wildlife Farfelee regularly oozed over, a predator more like if she didn't stop. I made sure she could see the sapphire on my finger.

A steward requested our attention and announced dinner's readiness not long after.

"As our honored guest, please sit at my right hand," Mema offered.

Dite batted her curled lashes and walked ever so slowly, seductively, to the proffered position.

Kovis and I were halfway down the table, headed for the opposite end, when the goddess asked, "Didn't you say Princess Alissandra was the one who suggested inviting me for this occasion?"

"She was. She and Prince Altairn." Mema gave nothing of her feelings away.

"I'd enjoy more conversation with them." Her tone became softer, silky.

My stomach knotted itself as Kovis and I took our places at Mema's left.

"Aunt Dite, thank you for coming," I said as a steward placed our first course, grilled salamander, before me. I put on my best smile, despite wanting to slap her. We needed her help.

"Thea, you told me Alissandra has quite the tale of love and loss to tell." She brought a hand up, rested her chin on the back of her wrist, then wrinkled up her nose as if I was the cutest little thing. "I just love stories like that."

I looked to Mema. No doubt she'd told Dite that to garner her interest. "I suppose you could call it that."

During the next two courses, I told the goddess about how I'd been privileged to be assigned Kovis as my dream charge, about my love for him growing as he grew—it proved more intimate than I'd wanted, but she'd seemed interested. She wiped tears from her eyes as I told her about my decision to leave my family and go to him when Father threatened me and Kovis.

She drew a hand to her chest. "Thea, you're so right. That is a such a touching tale." She oozed emotion. "It's so honest and authentic and more beautiful than anything I've heard in ages."

She was laying it on thick, but I didn't sense guile in her. No, she really was this crazy about love.

She continued, "Alissandra, you could have held back your feelings, but you didn't. You honor me by opening up and being so vulnerable with me." She drew in a breath. "You allowed me to see as you see. You are a rare gem if ever I've seen one." She sighed contentedly.

I was glad she liked my story, but would she help us? Kovis squeezed my hand under the table. I opened my mouth to ask her just that when Crewe, one of the stewards, interrupted.

"I hope you have been enjoying the meal so far, Goddess." He placed our main entrée before her, and she schooled her glazed expression into one more fitting for talk about the meal.

I liked the steward, I really did, but I wanted to strangle him. He'd shattered the mood into a million unrecognizable pieces.

"The cook knows you enjoy things that are out of the ordinary. This is fillet of scrofa. It is a venomous fish that he has taken great care to ensure is no longer harmful."

Dite lit up. "Why thank you."

As if taking his que, he continued, "It is prepared with a Salmoriglio sauce. Please enjoy."

I forced a smile as the steward placed my entrée before me. "So Aunt Dite—"

"Oh, this is lovely. Don't you think it's lovely?" Dite took another bite, savoring the flavor.

Mema managed, "It is flavorful."

Kovis ping-ponged looks between me and Dite.

My aunt finished her fish and, at length, wiped her mouth with her napkin. "I want to help you."

I wanted to exhale with relief, but I knew her cooperation would never come this easily. I braced instead.

"You need me to speak to Daddy about your father. Have him scold him or some such thing?"

"Scolding will never stop him, even if its Dyeus who does it. If my father isn't stopped for good—" I debated quickly before continuing, but selected my words carefully. "—the human affairs you love to encourage will be a thing of the past." My words were an ultimatum of sorts.

The goddess frowned.

Mema coughed. I didn't care. Aunt Dite had to do this for us.

"Then what are you proposing?" she asked.

Despite what Father had done, I still felt conflicted—he *was* my father. But Wake was at stake.

My stomach clenched. I'd known, despite not wanting to think of it, stopping Father would require physical restraint. I'd refused to think of any specific constraint, but I knew I would need to suggest one if we were to have a chance. I did a quick inventory and resisted all the options then took a deep breath. I needed to do this.

"We need Dyeus to bind him…"

Dite wagged her brows at that. I resisted the urge to fidget. Clearly, she had quite a different picture of *binding* than what I intended.

I pressed on. "Like he did Prometheus or something like that. Only that will prevent him from ever taking over another land."

Dite scrunched up her face as she tossed her locks over a shoulder. "Must your father's liver be eaten by a bird? It's so uncivilized."

I wanted to scream my horror, but I didn't. Despite what he'd done to me on more than one occasion, I needed Father bound, not tortured. "No. We just need him stopped." I waved a hand. "Perhaps what your father did to Atlas."

Mema looked frozen, but she didn't argue. It was her son I spoke of. I wondered if she'd known what I would propose.

Aunt Dite sat back and crossed her arms. "That is a tall order, I must say." She looked to be considering all she would need to do to accomplish such a feat. But as dessert was served, golden apple dumplings, a twinkle lit up her eyes.

An empty feeling filled the pit of my stomach as she turned her attention to Kovis. "Based upon all Alissandra has told me about you, I can tell you're a man who knows how to have fun and goes after what he wants."

She described anyone but Kovis. She was imposing her views of gods only knew who—her last paramour?—on him. I feared where this might lead.

Kovis cleared his throat and forced a smile. "Thank you?"

I peeked through our bond and heard only thoughts of loathing. It sure didn't show on his face.

Her tone turned silky as she added, "I go after what I want too."

Kovis sat up straight. "And what is that?"

She smiled.

Please no. Please no. Please no.

"I want..." She took to circling the air with her pointer finger before leveling it on him. "...you."

Mema coughed.

A utensil dropped further down the table.

Kovis wiped his mouth, leaned back, and grinned as he slowly placed his napkin beside his plate.

I went back to our bond to see what was swirling through his mind, but he'd blocked me. I frowned. What had his loathing thoughts meant?

Trust me, Ali. Three little words. It was all he sent before resealing our connection.

I'd told him to "trust me" twice on this trip. Somehow it didn't ease my angst.

● ● ●

"Prince Altairn, you fascinate me. I've had relations with many males in my time, god, human, some between, but never have I encountered a man who has been remade. I want you."

I felt as powerless as I did under Father's claws. Kovis and I were together. I wore his ring. Did that mean nothing?

Kovis's tone became deeper and richer as he said, "*If* I agree…" He paused, letting the words linger.

He couldn't be considering this. But he was.

"…will you promise…" Another pause.

He was bargaining with Dite. Had he forgotten his own words from earlier? She was a damn goddess.

"…to get your father's commitment to bind Ambien?" It came out a purr.

I was ready to roar.

Dite giggled then batted her lashes. "I can't promise he'll agree."

What? She wasn't giving any assurances. *Say no. Please say no*, I begged, despite knowing he still blocked me.

Kovis brought a hand to his chin. "Then it seems we have no deal." He rustled his wings.

I nearly yelled at him to stop encouraging her.

Dite tittered then ran her tongue across her upper lip. "I do love a challenge. Especially from a human."

Kovis just smiled at her, seemingly enjoying the game just as much.

I clutched the edge of the table. I was ready to dig my nails into his leg.

"Show me your wings," Dite said, mischief dancing in her eyes.

She'd accepted his decline? She hadn't been kidding. She wanted him. I stopped breathing.

Mema stared at her untouched dessert with horror-filled eyes.

Kovis never dropped his gaze as he pushed back ever so slowly and rose. It seemed as if he was asking her to look him over, thoroughly.

I wanted to trip him as he stepped around his chair, but I refrained.

• • • •

He spread his legs shoulder-width apart then placed his hands on his hips and paused, smiling at her. Then with one thrust, he unfurled his wings fully, completely. Every beautiful fingerbreadth of them. Every amazing feather. He put it all on display for everyone to see.

Yelps rose from my sisters. Mema brought a hand to her brow and closed her eyes.

I squirmed. *You're not a toy for her to play with!*

Dite's brows rose, along with the longing in her eyes as she ran her gaze across the breadth of them.

Kovis, stop. Please.

"The transition was generous with you. I trust it helped you… in other ways as well."

"You may never know." Kovis wagged his brows.

Still smiling, Dite said, "Perhaps I *can* persuade Daddy to *bind* Ambien."

"Where and when would you like your dessert?" Kovis asked in a smoky voice, rustling his wings.

Another yip from my sisters.

I wanted to cry. This couldn't be happening.

"That apple was a fitting prelude, but I'm ready for a real treat," Dite purred.

I'd never stood up to a goddess before, but I'd never forgive myself if I didn't do something. I sprang up, "Stop! Aunt Dite, you can't do this. He's my intended." I struggled to leash the growl that begged for release.

Mema looked like she'd suffered a heart attack.

Dite's gaze brushed me, and she scowled. "Dear child, that fact is precisely why I *will* do this."

Gasps rose throughout the room.

Trust me, Ali. It was all he said again as Dite left the room on his arm.

Oh gods, oh gods, oh gods. I knew him, he'd do about anything to save his brother, but would he sacrifice his very body, and in this way, to rescue him? The thought raged through my panic, but my gut knew the truth. He would.

I knew he wasn't telling me he no longer loved me… This wasn't about "us." I forced my mind to repeat the words, over and over and over again.

His darkness would be raging within him the whole time. He'd hate himself at the end. I kept rationalizing it, telling myself this and more despite knowing he'd still do it.

He and his siblings had endured far worse than this. I didn't know where he drew the line, but this wasn't it.

Chapter Thirty-Seven

Kovis

Every fiber of my being tingled as I walked with Dite on my arm. While part of it was from the goddess's presence, my body reacted viscerally to what I planned to do.

I'd barely tamped down my horror and revulsion as I seduced the female. After all I'd been through, sharing… intimacy with this sex-crazed goddess was the last thing I wanted. It felt like a betrayal of my love for Ali. Damn strategy, I was so anxious to save Kennan that when I'd spotted an opportunity to act, I'd seized it before reason could catch up. And one did not go back on their word, not to a goddess.

Ali had paved the way, and the goddess had behaved as I'd expected based upon the scandalous tales I'd heard of Dite's exploits. I just needed to satisfy her—the thought made my stomach sour.

I was scared shitless and felt like I had my first time. I loathed myself for offering my body in this way, but how else could I save my brother and my realm? I could see no other options. I could not fail. Damn my soul to Hades.

I blew out a breath, trying to calm my racing heart. Dite looked over and winked as we continued down the hall behind the steward.

It had about killed me to see Ali suffer. It was why I'd blocked our bond. I didn't want her to have to experience any more of this sordid thing than she had to. I'd come unhinged when she and Kennan had shared a kiss. How had I even considered doing this? I was showing myself to be the wretch I truly was. I would understand if Ali couldn't forgive me. She'd be right not to. I was betraying us.

We reached a guest bedroom that looked much like Ali's except without a large window. There was only one very large… oversize even… bed swathed in a purple covering that stood against the far wall. A wardrobe and dressing table with mirror were the balance of the room's furnishings.

The wooden door snit shut behind the steward as he left. We were completely alone, the goddess of love and me. My heart pounded. I prayed she didn't notice.

She turned, reached her hand up, and ran a finger down my jaw. "You have a strong jawline. I like that about a man."

I swallowed hard. I was sure she saw my throat bob.

She strode for the bed and sat down, then patted the space beside her. The fabric of her skirt fell away and exposed her bare thigh—the bow of the side laces hung down and begged me to loosen it.

My breath hitched, and I swallowed down my disgust. I could play her game. I could. I had to. Kennan and my realm were on the line.

I took three steps toward her, but she held up a hand. "I've changed my mind. I want to appreciate you first. Remove your shirt."

Despite my distaste, I had to make a convincing show of it or she'd never help. I took my time unbuttoning each and every fastener as slowly and seductively as I could. I ruffled my wings a few times for good measure. Sand people and their damn wings, good grief.

How I detested this, how could I do it to "us"? My mind grasped at straws. Ali had pretended I was Kennan when they'd kissed; what if I pretend Dite was Ali? It was the only way, so I forced my mind to imagine I was in this room with my beloved.

"Ummm..." The sound evoked my base male nature and sensations tingled in my groin as I slipped off one sleeve, then the other, and pulled it up and over my shoulders, letting it drop to the floor. I bore my chest to her. I'd soon be baring more. All. Butterflies launched in my stomach as reason fought fantasy. But I wrangled it down. I would make love to Ali.

"Red," she said, unaware of my struggle. "The transition let you keep it. Such a strong male. I love that your ink reveals passion."

"You know about our tattoos?" Her comment had caught me off guard. I'd expected her to dispense with conversation and head for the sheets.

"I know many things about humans. I get around." Her smile turned teasing.

She did? Was she saying she'd spent time in Wake? I didn't think the gods could, not without becoming mortal. Did she directly involve herself in human relationships? These and more questions swirled, but I forced my mind to refocus.

"Tell me about your tattoo." Her voice turned dulcet.

"My twin designed it," I began, forcing my voice to remain even. I told her of Kennan's love of art and about how he was under Ambien's control. I hadn't expected to, but I felt compelled to tell her how powerless I felt to free him.

She only hummed, then motioned for me to turn. Her request was much as I'd done with Ali to appreciate all of her in her shift at Madame Catherine's. I'd been enraptured by Ali in that garment and couldn't get enough of her. Was Dite feeling the same toward me? I forced myself to tamp down on my skin crawling.

I turned until she told me to stop. My back was toward her.

"Tell me about your scars," she said.

Another unexpected question. They, too, had survived the transition to Dream, much as Ali's bruises when she'd arrived in Wake. Why would Dite ask about them? I had no idea, so I answered truthfully. "I received them from my father." I recounted the punishments I'd endured after I'd stopped him from touching Rasa. My heart picked up speed throughout the telling. I'd become a master of burying the pain and hurt and had always leashed my bitterness. It was undoubtedly part of what had frozen my heart, but I'd never had any way to release it, not that wouldn't hurt those I loved.

I didn't know what came over me, but a presence, like a blanket, fell on me. I couldn't see it, but I felt its weight. It loosened my tongue like too much drink and compelled me to speak. But to her? A goddess? I couldn't. I wouldn't. My pain, my past, was a monster too awful to breathe life into, which was what speaking would do. I clenched my fist and fought it, but the feeling persisted, even intensified. I felt her eyes roam across my back—prey before the predator.

"What are you doing to me?" I ground out, realizing the only possible source. I drew a fist to my head.

"Tell me." Sultry, tantalizing. "Everything."

"You can't want that." I had joined with my pain. I was it and it was me. We were one, inseparable.

"Look at me." Delicious, luscious.

My breath hitched. She couldn't. She didn't. I couldn't.

"Turn and face me. Now." Venom had entered her tone.

How could I do this? My legs had turned to rubber under the struggle, but I forced myself to turn. Fists still clenched, I pulled my shoulders back and raised my chin.

"There's a good warrior, but your strong exterior can't hide you this time." There was no harshness now, only pleasantness, and it compelled me to listen. To do.

"I... I...," I stammered.

"Look into my eyes."

I drew my gaze up until our eyes met. My stomach twisted, and it was all I could do to stand firm as she seemingly looked into my very soul.

"Tell me." Her tone turned icy. It was a command, and my training kicked in.

I didn't hold back. I couldn't. Words flowed with abandon, emotion on their backs. All cares of what she might think of me fled. I cursed. I raged. I lashed out, even at her for doing this to me—making me confront my past, my pain, for giving me no choice. I poured it all out.

And fell to the floor in a pitiful, wretched, weeping heap.

My chest heaved. Exhaustion threatened to overwhelm me. It was too much. I curled up. That quickly, she'd broken me.

She waited several heartbeats before asking, "Is this living? Is there life here? You cling to it as if there is."

I couldn't look at her. I was a mess.

"Answer me."

I pulled my hands from my face. "No." I'd known it, but still…

"Is this what you want to feel every sun for the rest of your life?"

I breathed out a shaky breath. "No."

"Then what do you want to feel?"

"… alive." It came out a whisper.

"I didn't hear you."

"… to feel alive."

"Say it again."

"I want to feel alive."

"Again!"

I sat up. "I want to feel alive." My roar rippled about the room. Only after my words fell silent did I pour out more. "I want to feel again, like I do when Ali's near. I want to laugh with her. I want to hold her. I want to enjoy a sunset, marvel at the stars again, laugh with my siblings. I want to be passionate about… something, anything."

"Yes. That is living." She looked at me earnestly. "It's not forgiving or forgetting what was done to you. Living is pushing the poison out by embracing what you truly want. Fill yourself up so completely with life and what is good that the darkness has no room. Be so consumed with living that you have no time or desire to entertain these thoughts any longer. Embrace life. Suck every bit of passion from it."

My mind whirled and made simple what she'd said: Don't forgive or forget, but make it so insignificant in comparison that poisonous thoughts no longer controlled me. Could I do that?

"You don't mind if I call you Kovis, do you? It's what I'm more accustomed to." A corner of her mouth hitched up. "It's true. Alissandra is the granddaughter of my Grace, do you really think I wouldn't personally dabble in your relationship with her?"

She'd talked about me with Thea? Had she messed with me? Us? I opened my mouth, but she waved her hand.

"You cannot experience the plans I have for you until you overcome your pain. And you cannot overcome your pain until you face it. It is the prism through which you see life. It must change." As if administering a healing balm, she added, "You and Alissandra belong together. You have been made for each other, and I want to bless you, but you prevent me." She frowned but then schooled her face once more into the sultry seductive one I'd first met.

With her finger, she motioned for me to rise and approach. She wagged her brows then patted the covers beside her. She still wanted sex?

Confusion overwhelmed my mind. This made absolutely no sense. I thought she'd wanted me. But she wanted to bless Ali and me. So how could she possibly want… What god or goddess wanted to enjoy a human first before blessing them? She was insane.

My mind ceased to reason, and I clung to what I loved. This was Ali. She was Ali. I knew she wasn't, but I desperately embraced the notion, refusing to let it go. I couldn't cope any other way.

I wiped an arm across my eyes and struggled up, despite being emotionally and physically drained. I crossed the four remaining steps to her and sat gingerly beside her bare leg. And groaned. Sex with her?

Fondling Ali's breasts always excited me. Would she expect me to caress hers? Small mercy, my manhood didn't respond to the thought. But would it? She knew how weak I was as a man, and she was using it to her advantage. Damn me. I'd have no control the heartbeat I laid eyes on them. It was utterly unfair.

"Tell me about Dierna."

What? She startled me from my stormy thoughts. Dierna. She wanted to know about Dierna. No. No more. I gave her a long, pleading look. How did Dierna have anything to do with blessing Ali and me? "You already know."

She ran a caressing hand up and down my bare back. "Yes, I do, but I need to hear it from you."

I fought the urge to stiffen. I needed to be convincing. This was Ali. It was Ali caressing me. I took my time forcing myself to envision my love rubbing my back. Only Ali. Her hand felt reassuring, and I told her all the facts—I couldn't bear to endure the emotion of it, so I sequestered what was still so raw.

But when I finished, she asked, "And how did she make you *feel?*" She drew out the last word.

I was too tired to shout—that alone stayed my tongue. Had the facts not fully exposed my hurt? Was she going to force me to recount my deepest wounds? Ali would never do that to me. Couldn't I just show her my wings again? I knew the answer even before she replied.

"Not yet. While I must confess that I am seduced," her voice oozed sensuality as she ran a finger across the top of one, "we'll get to these magnificent wings of yours soon enough."

A shiver ran through me. Damn, Hades burn me.

I couldn't help myself. I bared my soul to her, fully and completely. I held nothing back. I'd felt used, betrayed, lied to. Dierna had utterly and completely broken my trust. Our relationship had been a lie, a charade. The pain was still so visceral, so real. The agony of it poured forth from my very soul. How was I to fill myself up so these feelings had no room inside me anymore?

"Tell me again what it means to live."

I took a deep breath and repeated what I'd spoken of my love for Ali, of the pleasures of life, of passion and wonder and dreaming. I needed to cling to the good things and refuse the old.

"You've held all this pain inside for far too long. No human is meant to endure so much." She ran a hand across my chest and hummed her pleasure, but I was so spent my groin had no reply. Good.

Dite kicked off her heels and moved over to one side of the bed, then rested her elbow on the pillow and patted the one beside.

She still wanted sex. How could I possibly perform—I had no desire for her. But we needed Dyeus's help. This was Ali. I'd be having sex with Ali. I'd repeat the mantra as long as I had to. I roused, kicked off my boots, and stretched out beside her, my head in my hand on the pillow opposite. Her hand found my chest in a heartbeat, and it roamed freely as I stared past her, gathering my strength.

Her hand circled lower and lower until she traced the top of my pants. "Dare to bare." It wasn't a question. She wasn't giving me the option to decline.

My eyes found hers, and I gave her a long look. She smiled sweetly.

"What most scares me about opening myself fully to Ali is…," she said.

I inhaled sharply. She somehow knew I'd held back.

She smiled sweetly.

It wasn't sex she'd wanted despite her reputation and I berated myself. This was the crux of it and what everything had been leading to, I knew it in my gut. But how could this be the pleasure she sought? I wasn't prepared to answer. At all.

Her look was fierce. "Ali gave up her immortality for you. Answer my challenge."

My mind slogged with the last threads of stamina. Ali had only ever been supportive and looked after my best interests, even when I didn't deserve it. She'd endured each and every time my insecurities put her to the test. Which was why I'd finally surrendered to her demand that I not battle my darkness alone but let her help me. So what was holding me back? I squirmed, but Dite's caress never wavered.

• • •

Fear of being hurt? She'd never hurt me, not intentionally. I knew that now. Fear of being vulnerable? Of her judging me and being found lacking? Fear of being exposed?

No, it was none of these. I had nothing to fear, not with Ali. She knew the mess I was. She saw past my insecurities and still loved me.

I could trust her completely. I let the thought flood my mind. Overwhelm me. Infuse itself into every fiber of my being. Only I stopped me. My mind. What I clung to. Ali loved me fully. I took in a breath as if for the first time and let serenity take root in me. *This* was living.

New energy filled me. Dite had accomplished what I'd been unable to. She'd been brutal, but her method had worked—I'd felt my pain, viscerally, and I'd pushed past it with the weapon she'd given me. I would not allow my past to drown out my future. Ali was everything to me.

Dite smiled and pulled her hand back, as if sensing my conclusion. "So what are you waiting for? Give yourself to her completely."

"You never wanted sex, did you?"

Pfft. "You delude yourself if you think you could handle me. Now go."

I grinned as I grabbed my shirt and boots and headed for the door. Relief washed over me, but I was utterly drained, and so when my wild, reckless side rose unbidden, I couldn't control it. I stopped and rustled my wings. "You sure?" I wagged my brows.

She just laughed. "You *are* seductive. I enjoyed the *intimacy* we shared," she drew out the word and ran her tongue across her lips, "but let's not destroy it with sex." She winked. "Ali is one very lucky lady."

I burst out laughing. "Thank you… for everything. Truly." It sounded weak, but it was all I had.

"Save your words. Go make Ali happy. That's how you can thank me."

⬤ ⬤ ⬤

I leaned against the door after it shut. I'd thought she was playing my game, but I'd been playing hers the whole time. She'd known about me and had seized the opportunity to rescue me from myself... for Ali. She'd wanted nothing for herself. Despite appearances, it had been a selfless act to come here, and I felt unworthy.

As if listening to my thoughts, Dite yelled through the door. "I'm addicted to love, what can I say. Now go enjoy intimacy with your beloved while I go talk to Daddy."

I grinned as I dressed, then made my way to find my love, and life, because for the first time, I knew I could do this.

• • •

Chapter Thirty-Eight

I'd gone out of my mind since Kovis left the dining room with Aunt Dite.

I'd tried the bond countless times to no avail. "Trust me," it was all he'd said. I trusted him. I wasn't so sure I trusted her. She was the love goddess for pity's sake. Seduction had blanketed the dining room. No good could come of this, but no one dared interrupt what was no doubt happening, not with Dite. I resisted the urge to hold myself.

Farfelee, Amelia, all my sisters along with Mema had tried to calm me. I didn't want to be calm. I wanted Kovis.

We'd retreated to the third floor sitting room. I paced, and they made efforts to stitch on their latest projects, but with the constant glances I felt, not much progress was being had. They'd given me hugs and all manner of support until Mema had gotten fed up and commanded we do something to occupy ourselves. Moping wouldn't speed things, she'd said.

Ali? Where are you?

I exhaled loudly. *Kovis? Are you okay? I'm upstairs in the sitting room with my sisters.*

My sisters converged on me in a heartbeat. Mema looked to be holding her breath where she remained seated, squeezing her needlework hoop.

"What is it?" Wynnfrith demanded.

"Kovis is done." It came out sounding weird. Done. Done. What did it mean? I shivered.

Mema looked to be summoning her courage as she rose. "I'll be seeing Aunt Dite out then."

In silence, we all watched her leave. I could only imagine how awkward that conversation would be, and I thanked… the other gods I wouldn't have to hear it.

Mema gave Kovis a long look as they passed each other at the door. He beamed.

I scrunched my face. My sisters' eyes grew large, several drew a hand to their mouths.

"She'll talk to Dyeus," he reported.

Mema closed her eyes in relief. At least I hoped it was that and not with grief at what Kovis had… sacrificed? Endured? Enjoyed? for the goddess's promise.

Kovis scanned the room and found me. Before I knew what was happening, he'd put his hands to my jaw and pressed a passionate kiss to my lips.

I love you so much, Ali dearest.

I tensed, then relaxed into the kiss. I didn't know what I'd expected, but it wasn't this.

Titters, oohs, and aahs erupted around us, but he didn't relent. I finally pulled away to find the room empty and the door shut.

"What happened?"

Kovis ran his hand across my jaw and stared into my eyes.

"What did she do to you?" This wasn't the man who'd gone with Dite. He hadn't stopped smiling.

I pushed him back, trying to break whatever trance she'd put him in.

He took my hand and led me over to a divan. "I don't know how to describe what happened," he began.

Oh gods… whatever it was, we'd face it together.

"She made me feel so many things."

I'm sure my eyes grew large. I didn't want to hear this. But I did. "Tell me everything."

He chuckled. "She said the same thing."

"What did she want you to tell her?"

"After she asked me to remove my shirt…"

Oh gods…

"She put some spell or something on me that forced me to cooperate."

Oh no… this wasn't happening.

"I felt as if I was inebriated."

I braced.

"Then she demanded I tell her everything… about my scars."

"Wait. What?"

"She forced me to tell her everything, including and especially how I felt about what happened."

"Why?"

"To heal me of my darkness. She made me tell her what happened with Dierna too."

Dite had rehashed his past? "Wait, I thought she wanted sex."

"So did I, to start."

"So you talked about your past and then she made you have sex with her? After all that?"

He chuckled. "No, she wasn't finished cleaning out all the darkness that festered."

Cleaning out his darkness? Kovis picked up my hand, then told me everything that happened. She'd been ruthless with him, yet he wasn't upset. And he hadn't shut down. How had she accomplished it? He never wanted to talk about the hurt. And I'd only ever known her reputation for seduction. This was anything but. But why was she interested in his darkness?

"And after all that"—he looked tired, but energized—"she forced me to realize I still held back—" He looked into my eyes. "—from giving every part of myself to you. She made me realize I hadn't yet fully trusted you… with my whole heart."

I drew a hand to my chest. Dite surprised me, but not that truth. Not really. Hope rose in my chest. "And?"

"Serenity. It's all I can think to call it. It overwhelmed me the heartbeat I surrendered. I am the luckiest man alive, to have you."

He leaned forward, but my lips reached his first. I couldn't get enough of him. The door wasn't locked, but I ignored that fact as I threw my arms around his neck and slid onto his lap. He was as hungry as I, for his eyes filled with longing.

"So this is where you had sex?" I asked.

He laughed. "No. This is where she told me I couldn't handle her and to go get intimate with you."

I snickered then pressed another kiss to his lips.

His shirt found the floor soon after, and my fingers danced across a spot at the base of his neck. He shivered but beamed. "Is that *the* spot?"

"What do you think?" Playfulness danced in my voice.

We explored the spot.

Kovis collapsed onto the floor, utterly spent when we were done, and I joined him.

"I missed your magic—no plants flying or water spouts—but your wings unfurling was a nice touch," he joked, despite his voice sounding sluggish.

I yawned my laugh.

We surrendered to sleep in each other's arms.

———

"Oh! Oh, excuse me." Nald, one of the stewards, woke me a while later. I recognized his voice even though the door had shut again by the time I roused enough to look. Warmth rose in my cheeks.

Kovis snorted. "It's not like we made it any secret what we were doing. No different than when my guards overhear us."

I remembered the grins on a few of his guards' faces when I'd left Kovis's suites, and the whole palace had known in quick order. My whole household would know before long. The warmth spread to my ears.

Kovis stretched and yawned. "Let them be jealous."

He joked at a thing like this. He didn't know Mema. Wait until she learned of our exploits.

"She's done it too." He grinned.

I scrunched my face. "I *really* didn't want to think about that."

"But you owe your life—"

"Stop! Just stop."

He kissed me and thankfully changed the subject. "I haven't felt this free, this light in… forever. I never thought it was possible. I never even hoped for what I'm feeling for you. You complete me."

I exhaled. I loved hearing his words. Somehow Aunt Dite had broken through to him as I'd never been able. Perhaps I'd been too hasty when I'd not trusted her. She'd returned my Dreambeam to me. How could I not?

"So it seems we have a visit to make to your aunts, books and all." He grinned, then put up a finger as his expression turned serious. "But first we must prepare."

"Prepare? We've got the books."

"I've no doubt your father knows we're here." My stomach clenched. "I may have lost my magical abilities, but I can still wield a sword. And you're not half bad with a dagger either, my love."

I cuffed his arm.

"If we're to fly to your aunts, we'll go prepared."

● ● ●

Chapter Thirty-Nine

My stomach tensed. What would we face flying to my aunts? Would they welcome us or send us away?

All was silent as we stepped out of the sitting room and made our way down the hall. Glancing over the third-floor railing, sun streamed through the clear, domed ceiling of the foliage-filled atrium, and the pair of pure white calandrias flew past, mirroring each other's flight and warbling.

From the silence, it appeared everyone had retired. Just as well. It would make our trip that much easier as I wouldn't have to overcome their objections.

I wrote a quick note telling everyone where we were going and not to come after us, leaving it on my pillow.

We changed into our newly repaired leathers—they'd been retrofitted to accommodate our new wings—put the books in a flight bag I found in my closet, then headed down the three flights of stairs to find a guard or two to accompany us. If Father might be after us, we'd take every possible precaution.

Wyke stopped us as we reached the armory hall at the back of the palace. "Princess Alissandra, Prince Altairn, can I help you?" He looked my leathers up and down, clearly not used to seeing a female in such gear.

I ignored his perusal. "We're headed to my aunts, the Fates."

His eyes went wide, but he didn't try to dissuade us. It wasn't his role. He knew the threat Father was, he'd been part of the search efforts to locate Velma and Alfreda.

Once over his initial surprise, he suggested, "If you don't mind, I think it best we bring Rowntree and Baldik with us as well."

"I agree."

"Let me go rouse them and ready myself," he said. The guard departed, and we walked into the armory to procure weapons of our own.

Rowntree and Baldik had been picked more than once because of their large builds, and I was glad they'd be joining us. I would have insisted on it if Wyke hadn't suggested it first.

Kovis scanned the walls lined with a host of swords and pikes and daggers and all manner of weapon. He strode to a rack of daggers that rose like a tree at the end of the long bench stretching down the middle of the room. "They're well equipped. It's good to see."

He extracted several knives, one at a time, feeling its weight and balance before settling on four and handing the first to me. "How's it feel?"

I tested all four and found them to be equally comfortable.

"Take all of them," Kovis said.

I set about adding them to my leathers while Kovis headed for the swords. By the time Wyke returned with the others, Kovis had a sword holstered on each hip and two daggers secreted away in his leathers.

The guards sent questioning looks at Kovis while they grabbed their own arms.

"Prince Altairn is commander of Wake's armies," I said by way of explanation.

The three nodded then refocused on their own preparations. We launched as the sun was halfway to its peak. If everything went well, we'd reach my aunts as the sun hit its zenith, maybe a bit after.

Kovis smiled at me as we leveled out. *My best takeoff yet.*

I grinned back. *You're really getting the hang of wings.*

Too bad I won't get to keep them, he added.

My heart panged. I'd given no thought to what would happen after we found and freed my sisters and stopped Father. Our mission had consumed me. And my other sisters… I'd just gotten them back. I couldn't think about losing them again.

Let's figure it out once we succeed, Kovis suggested.

I nodded.

Fluffy clouds joined us as we crossed the bay and grew progressively darker and lower as we flew over Selova's palace. I hoped she'd figure out a way to somehow disconnect whatever Father had done to keep humans in a dream state. How many sand people had Father sequestered or worse? It seemed they were the root of the rebels.

We were a ways out yet from the Palace of Time, emerging from a particularly dense cloud when Wyke, who flew to my left, whistled in alarm before flying upward. Rowntree and Baldik, in front and to my left, respectively, dove.

Two uniformed guards shot from the clouds above, four rose from below.

Mares! I shouted through the bond. *Can you see them?* I prayed he wasn't fighting blind like in Wake.

I can! Kovis already had both swords out and brought one crashing down on one of the enemy who approached from below. The thing shifted shape, becoming a turtle with spikes on its shell as Kovis's blade connected. Its new weight compelled it toward the ground, but it shifted in the blink of an eye and became a giant hawk with long talons.

I barely dodged the sword of another mare, this from above. I wasn't used to fighting without footing, and I hoped my aim was true as I released a dagger at where I anticipated its eye would be as it leveled with me. I connected. The mare clutched at my knife, but blood was already pouring from the wound as it fell away.

That's one.

I got one too, Kovis reported from beside me. *Look out! Above you!*

I moved sideways, barely avoiding the falling mare as it succumbed to Rowntree's blade.

Just the ones from below left, I said.

But I'd spoken too soon for the mare that had become an oversize hawk swooped down from above. The dark clouds had hidden its rise.

Kovis! Above you!

The thing extended its talons toward one of his wings but Kovis wasn't yet nimble enough to avoid it.

I sent a dagger at its eye and another at the claw that was a mere handbreadth from his wing. Blood sprayed as its foot fell away. It shrieked as it tumbled, but my second blade had missed.

Baldik's sword met it before it finished shifting into a dragon.

Two to go! Wait, where's Wyke? I couldn't see him anywhere, but another mare in the form of a guard drew my attention below.

Rowntree dove and slashed. Black feathers filled the air as he relieved the thing of flight feathers on one of its wings. It began shifting into who knew what. I threw my last dagger.

It would shift no more. It tumbled away, one wing flapping inelegantly.

The last mare beat a hasty retreat.

Where's Wyke?

As if on command, the guard leveled out beside Kovis.

I sighed. He was okay.

Kovis took a look at him, and before I could think, hurled a sword. End over end it flew. The guard hadn't seen it coming, and the blade opened a gash at the back of his neck. It must have cut deeply because his wings went limp and gravity claimed him.

What did you do? I screamed through the bond.

Wyke's wing was damaged. That was an imposter. That last mare shifted to look like him.

I drew a hand to my chest.

Is Wyke okay?

He glided down, Kovis said. *I couldn't watch him the whole way.*

We need to find him.

Not with the possibility of more mares. We keep going and come back this way once we're done. In the meantime, we hope he finds help.

It sounded cold, but I knew Kovis knew best in this situation. He'd been in war, no different than what we were.

One look at Rowntree and Baldik, and I knew they held the same view. They didn't look back as they flew on, protecting either side of us.

Father definitely knew we'd arrived. I only wondered what else he'd try.

You okay? Kovis asked.

Yeah, I replied, shaking off the attack. I adjusted the pack of books, making sure they were still safe against my chest, and we continued on.

A thirty-story edifice came into view against the backdrop of dark clouds. A multitude of ornate spires jutted from irregular, wart-like protrusions bulging from its sides. Nothing had changed.

Rowntree and Baldik, along with Kovis, all stiffened as we touched down in the shadowy courtyard near the massive tree in the middle, but only silence greeted us. To his credit, Kovis executed a near perfect landing. The three scanned the area, but I knew they wouldn't find any threats. My aunts had a reputation, and only the deranged would trespass.

We approached the massive wooden door and stopped before its stone frame. There was no handle so, with my encouragement, Rowntree put a shoulder to it. Unused hinges moaned but gave us entrance.

Our guards both held up a hand while they surveyed the dark interior, then motioned us forward after they decided it was safe.

• • •

I headed for the stairway I'd used the last time. It seemed no one else had paid my aunts a visit, judging by the dust that layered over our footprints from before. At least I assumed they were ours. There were certainly no fresh ones.

Kovis gave me a long look as I mounted the first step.

Trust me, I told him and smiled.

He frowned. He'd told me to trust him when it came to Dite. He mounted the step beside me.

We reached a landing, then the next flight of stairs that clutched the rounded walls. Up and up we climbed. Around and around. I stopped counting.

You ought to feel right at home with all these stairs, I told him. I remembered how I'd panted the first few times I'd climbed to the sixth floor where the royal suites were.

Kovis's heart was beating faster than usual, right along with mine, with the exertion. *There're only six floors at home.*

Step. Step. Step. It became monotonous, so I turned my thoughts to my aunts. I couldn't wait to see them again. The thought struck me, and I remembered how terrified I'd been to see the hall the first time. And here I'd thought nothing had changed with this place. No, everything had changed, at least for me. And I'd changed too. I was a force in this conflict. The realization filled me with joy. I'd never made a difference. But I would, right along with Kovis.

The books shifted as if reminding me of their… suggestive presence. I'd have snickered if I weren't panting so hard. It was my first time back, and I'd procured what they'd asked of me. I hoped they enjoyed them—I felt my cheeks heat beyond what our exertion produced at that thought.

Our guards slowed but kept moving ahead of us. I doubted they'd have breath to defend us if something attacked. But I doubted anything would—we were safer here than outside with Father's mares.

How many more flights? Kovis puffed.

Too many. Don't think about it. Just keep moving.

● ● ●

At long last, we reached the top, and we and our guards bent over to catch our breath.

Once sufficiently recovered, we headed down a dimly lit hallway to the left and stopped when we reached a pair of black-robed stewards, one on either side of a set of open doors from which artificial light and a cacophony of low mechanical noises emanated.

Kovis gave me a long look, all three of them did. And for good reason.

I had no guarantee despite bringing the books, I only hoped my aunts would welcome us.

Chapter Forty

Kovis wrinkled his brow at hearing the sounds.

I had the same reaction the first time. Just wait, it's incredible.

He tilted his head, clearly unconvinced.

I moved ahead of our guards, and the pair of stewards at the doors looked us up and down just like before. But unlike before, the one on the right smiled and said, "Princess Alissandra, so good to see you."

He recognized me? But I looked so different. "I'm sorry, I don't know your name."

"It's Jansha, Princess. That's Rinion."

"It's very good to meet you both," I answered.

Rinion raised a brow and gave us an evil eye. "Don't touch anything." Absolutely nothing had changed with him.

"You two will remain here," Jansha said to our guards.

Baldik opened his mouth to object, but I held up a hand. "It's okay. We'll be fine."

"But their… reputations."

I smiled. "I am aware. I don't want to risk your lives unnecessarily."

"It's my duty—"

Rinion scowled. "You don't listen very well. Perhaps—"

"No, it's okay. They'll stay here."

Rowntree returned a shake of his head to his partner's questioning look.

Baldik huffed but surrendered. "Yell if you need us."

"We will, I promise."

"One more thing before you enter. You will remove your weapons," Rinion growled.

Kovis and I looked between the males. They weren't kidding. I had no weapons left to surrender, but Kovis finally unbuckled his swords and handed them to Baldik, then added one dagger.

"That's all of it," he assured.

Rinion still scowled as if he considered possessing such implements to be vile.

I rolled my eyes.

"Princess, Prince. Come." Jansha turned, and without looking back, strode into the chamber, his black robes swishing behind his onyx wings. We followed.

Sun streamed through large windows in the far wall, but with the ancient shelves that stretched floor to ceiling, much of the light was thwarted. Torch light augmented the dim.

The smell of incense again greeted me along with the low sounds of the various timepieces that ensured every mortal got each and every heartbeat of life Aunt Ches allotted them.

What? Kovis questioned with wonder.

Timepieces. Ours are here, somewhere.

Kovis gave me a long look.

We followed Jansha between the ancient rows. Tan-robed attendants still flitted about, ensuring my aunts edicts were adhered to.

A ways in, nearly on the opposite side of the room, I saw that my aunts Nona, Ches, and Ta still sat on a dais, hunched in rocking chairs, conversing. Their stringy, white hair still fell over their plain gray robes with overlong sleeves.

The steward stopped, then bowed low. Kovis and I followed.

"Alissandra, rise child."

Don't rise yet, I coached Kovis as I rose along with Jansha. Despite my familiarity with my aunts, I knew they hid their true selves except when in private. We would show deference to them as if strangers until otherwise instructed.

"Who did you bring with you?" Aunt Ches asked.

I knew they knew Kovis. I'd divulged his most intimate secrets to them, but I'd play their game.

"This is Prince Kovis Altairn of Wake."

Aunts Nona and Ta steepled their fingers, elbows on the arms of their chairs, before nodding.

"A human in Dream, how curious," Ches said.

"Rise child," Aunt Ta commanded.

Kovis stood.

I hoped they'd take both Kovis and me into their hideaway so we could talk and he could see and experience all I had. I hoped.

"What are your intentions with the princess?" Aunt Nona asked. Not how did you come to be here, not tell us your tale.

Kovis's thoughts whirled in our bond, but he held himself and answered simply. "My intention is to make her my bride, make passionate love to her until she is senseless, and add more work for you with young. I'm happy to give more detail if it would please you."

I'm sure my eyes grew. *Wait! What? Stop!*

Ches let the corner of her mouth rise just a hint.

I'm merely speaking to what they most enjoy, Kovis added.

Yes, but...

I hope she asks for details, he added.

I wanted to slap him but refrained.

"Forthright, then we shall understand each other plainly," Aunt Ta said. "So it seems you are *finally* here to give us what was promised."

I inhaled sharply. Were they upset because I hadn't returned in a moon with their reading material? I hadn't been able to. Surely they understood that.

I opened my mouth, but Aunt Ches held up a hand. "Commitments were made… and broken."

Strictly speaking, she was right. I couldn't argue.

Unease blossomed and grew as all three of my aunts folded their hands in their laps and fell silent. Their quiet had unnerved me the last time, but I'd thought we'd gotten past that.

Panic rose as my mind wrestled with what, oh what, I could offer that might satisfy them.

The silence persisted, and Aunt Ta looked beyond us then gave a nod. I turned and saw an attendant bob her head, then reach out and halt a rolling metal ball in a timekeeping device. I inhaled sharply. Kovis did too.

Did she…?

I'd seen her do it before, but it still felt like a rock thudded in the pit of my stomach.

Yes, she just ended a human life.

I heard Kovis's heart accelerate and his thoughts with it—my aunts had a lot of power and we could not disappoint them, not without consequence.

"With your permission," he interrupted several heartbeats later.

Ta nodded.

"Perhaps you would fancy similar material… from Wake… on a regular basis."

Kovis! What are you doing? How am I going to do that?

We made it here, we'll find a way.

Nona smiled briefly then schooled her features and looked to her sisters, who shared glances as I'd seen them do before, communicating with some unspoken language, much as I pictured Kovis and Kennan doing when they were young.

It felt like an eternity, but each of the trio eventually nodded.

"Material from a different realm… intrigues us, greatly," Nona said in a low, but sultry tone.

• • •

"The habits and practices of humans might just be the thing to spice up our existence," Aunt Ches added in a hushed whisper.

Spice up their existence. I wanted to cover my ears.

"Very well," Ta declared. "Then it is agreed. Come."

She stood up, along with her sisters, and motioned us forward with an open palm, toward the right of the dais.

Kovis gave me a long look and took my hand.

Aunt Nona disappeared through the circular door that swirled in a host of colors. Kovis gripped my hand tighter as I stepped through and dragged him behind.

He exhaled heavily as we stepped into the room. As with everything else, nothing had changed. An expansive floor-to-ceiling window still filled virtually the entire far wall with the clear, blue sea. I still wouldn't probe concerning how that view was possible with the castle situated in the midst of dark clouds.

A huge crackling fireplace stood to the left, before which three sofas had been arranged with a short, wood table in the middle. Colorful rugs were scattered about. Every appointment was simple and lacked ostentation.

And as before, our hostesses all shed their pale garb in favor of vibrant colors. Ches donned a fuchsia robe with violet sunflowers. A steward helped Ta into a royal-blue, velvet tunic. And Nona slipped into a canary yellow robe with images of gears woven in—she buckled a belt made of discs and wheels about her waist, then picked up another mechanism and gave it a spin. Aunt Ta gave her a long look, and she chuckled as she silenced the thing.

Butterflies rose in my stomach. She spun *one of those* sex toys. I still couldn't get used to their explicitness.

Kovis just stood there, trying to take it all in.

I smiled. I understood. I was so glad they'd let him in alongside me.

"Please, have a seat," Nona invited, sitting to the right of the fireplace and drawing her legs up under herself. She leaned back and fingered the mechanism.

Kovis and I sat on the other side of the grouping, while Ta and Ches took the remaining side before the fire.

Ancel, the steward who had served me the first time, stopped behind us, his hands behind his back. "Would you care for something to eat or drink?"

We'd set out after a light dinner, and I was getting hungry I realized, so without hesitation I replied, "Those fairy dust pancakes were amazing. Could I please have some more with bubblefruit syrup and dragon horn tea?"

Ancel nodded then asked, "Sir?"

"I'll have what the lady is having," Kovis replied. *I have no idea what I just ordered.*

I smiled. *Trust me.*

Aunt Ches made it three orders of the pancakes and my other aunts just ordered drinks, a dragon fruit cocktail and a passion fruit sour.

Ancel retreated, and I took charge without a word, removing the pack and placing it on the table. I pulled it open and extracted the first book, *A Tumble in the Clouds*. I pushed down my embarrassment as I opened it and showed them the picture on the inside of the cover.

Kovis tried to hide a smirk. He'd figured them out to a tee as we'd searched for these books.

"Let's see it here," Aunt Nona requested. I passed it to her, and after a heartbeat she bobbed her head then passed it to Ches.

"Will these types of books suffice?" Kovis asked.

"Let's see the rest," Nona requested.

Beyond Positions, *Sweet or Spicy: Why Choose?*, *Hippoi Hoppoi*, and the others made their way around the trio.

"These types of books will fulfill your obligation," Ta asserted.

"Most definitely," Ches added, wagging her brows.

Nona sucked on a finger, moving it in and out of her mouth.

Ta furrowed her brow at her sister. "Must you?"

Nona just giggled.

Kovis grinned. He was as bad as she was. *What?* he tried to sound innocent.

Don't give me that.

What? I like her style. Is that wrong?

I just cleared my throat. Answer enough.

"You have come for reasons beyond fulfilling your obligation. You need something from us, don't you?" Ta asked.

The jovial mood flattened in the blink of an eye. Her sisters folded their hands in their laps once more.

I sucked in a breath. They were masters at keeping me off balance. It's what they'd done the last time too. Just as I'd relax, they'd shift things. They were forces, there could be no doubt.

Our food arrived before I could reply, giving me time to arrange my thoughts. Somehow my pancakes, while still amazing, tasted less so, along with my tea. Kovis was impressed with his meal nonetheless and spared no compliment in telling them so.

I wiped my mouth with my napkin, set it on the table, and looked to Aunt Ta. "We need your help, you are correct." I explained the situation as succinctly and compellingly as I could—we feared for Velma and Alfreda and needed to locate them, the bottom line.

Aunt Nona bit a fingernail, Ta and Ches both drew a hand to their chest.

"So what do you think? Can you help us?" I asked with some degree of uncertainty. I'd prayed they knew where my sisters were. I didn't want to think about what we'd do if they didn't.

They sat quietly, brows furrowed.

I bit my lip.

Kovis squeezed my hand.

At length, the trio began ricocheting looks, but still no one spoke.

I always hated this about them. Their silent debates amongst themselves held no tells. It unnerved me.

Aunt Ches cleared her throat while looking at Nona. Ta frowned at both of them. What did it mean?

Still not one word.

• • •

I wanted to scream.

"Your request implies a great deal," Aunt Ta at last replied.

I squeezed Kovis's hand but held my tongue.

"It implies firstly, that *immortals* have time devices." She gave me a long look, as if asking why I'd be crazy enough to believe that.

I nodded slowly. "I considered that, but I hoped that if you didn't control those, that you at least influenced all beings, not just humans."

"You give us much credit," Ches intoned.

"Secondly, it implies a time device is connected to the being in question geographically," Ta continued.

I held my tongue. I'd had little basis in fact, but it's what I'd hoped. There'd been an accident, with that one human the last time I was here. It had ended his life. They'd known immediately. I knew it was a stretch, but surely they knew where each subject was, no?

Ta went on. "Thirdly, it implies we would easily give up the information you seek. Or was there something more you offer?"

I pulled my head back. Wouldn't they? But I thought… Oh gods. I'd been naïve to think… No doubt they'd repurposed some human's device for me when I escaped to Wake. Aunt Ches would have set the number of my suns. My thinking had been way off. I was but a mere mortal with no right to make such a request. But Velma and Alfreda…

"I'm… I'm sorry. I assumed far too much. I apologize. I should never have—" I swallowed hard. Had I completely botched this?

Aunt Ta held up a hand. "Alissandra, I said your request implies a great deal. I spoke true. I did not indicate how we might respond."

I inhaled deeply and let it out slowly. I needed to calm down.

She continued, "The last time you came before us, we complemented you. Do you remember what for?"

My mind didn't have to work to remember. I'd treasured the praise. "I do. Aunt Ches, you said you thought that I'm passionate about humans and making their lives more pleasing and you wished more sand people were like me."

"Yes, high praise indeed," Ta added. "Has anything changed?"

• • •

Changed? I shook my head, unsure where they were heading with this.

"There you are incorrect." Ta held up a finger and looked to Ches.

My stomach tensed. They thought my feelings toward humans had changed? How?

Ches continued, "I've not had to set the number of suns for a human gone to Wake as you did, in eons."

She *had* numbered my suns. But wait. What? Others had gone to Wake from Dream? I sucked in a breath.

Kovis squeezed my hand.

"Alissandra, you willingly gave up your family as well as immortality for your charge," Ta continued.

"Of course. I couldn't have left Kovis to Father's devices." I resisted the urge to fidget. So what was she getting at?

"Granted, you had more than a casual interest in him." Aunt Nona snickered. "I quite enjoyed hearing the intimate details."

Ches cleared her throat.

Kovis's breath hitched. *What did you tell them about me?*

Later.

Nona quieted after sticking out her lower lip.

"Those weren't just idle words," Ta resumed. "But you don't see it. You were so committed to your charge that you put aside self-interest for his sake. How many others would do the same?"

"Umm... I've never thought about it."

Ta smiled. She let my comment linger.

"Is that bad?" I asked when the silence became uncomfortable.

Kovis pulled my arm and turned me toward him. "If I may translate, your aunt is saying no one else would have done what you did for me."

I felt like a fish out of water, opening and closing my mouth.

I scanned my aunts. Every one of them smiled warmly.

"But I..."

Kovis shook his head. "Accept their praise, Ali. Who knows what situation I'd be in this sun if not for you." His hands found my cheeks, and he slowly leaned in and planted a kiss on my lips. "Thank you."

"Again," Nona demanded, clapping.

So he did while she rose and strode to her workbench.

When Kovis finally pulled back, Aunt Nona reseated herself and held her hand out to me. A trinket lay in her palm. I prayed it wasn't a sex toy as I picked it up.

"I—we—want you to have this," Nona said.

"What is it?" I asked, opening the metal case that fit in my palm. Two toothed wheels circled the inside as if of their own accord.

"A little something for when you most need it." That's all she said as she closed my hand over it.

"After seeing what you did, we agreed that if we ever were favored to see you again, we wanted to give you that," Ches said.

Favored to see me again? Favored? My breath hitched. "I don't know what to say. Thank you so much." I drew a hand to my chest.

My aunts were honoring me. I had no words. They'd given me this trinket because they believed I'd done something extraordinary. I guessed maybe I had. Maybe. But honoring me? The Fates? I'd no idea what the piece did, but I'd treasure it the rest of my mortal suns.

"So we still have this matter of locating your sisters." Ta refocused our attention.

I nodded.

"As it happens, we do have time apparatuses for immortals," Ta said. "It is a false notion that immortals cannot die. They do, just not from the expiration of suns set for them, for Ches never numbers their suns. But an immortal or two has been known to expire from peril."

She gave Kovis and me a stern look. "As with our other secrets, you must promise not to breathe a word of it to anyone."

"I promise," we both said without hesitation.

Hope rose in me. My sisters would both have a device. But could we tell where they were from it?

Chapter Forty-One

Aunt Ta and her sisters rose and, with the help of a steward, shed their brightly-colored vestments in favor of their drab gray attire then headed for the swirling door without a word.

Kovis glanced at me, silently asking if we should follow. I nodded then fell into line behind them, back into the grand hall.

I clutched my new keepsake. No matter where I was, it would always connect me with my aunts. They'd given it to me because *they* believed I'd changed, that I'd done something extraordinary. My heart pitter-pattered.

As we emerged, a tan-robed attendant scurried over. "I apologize for interrupting Moirei, but we are having difficulties with a device."

"Who is it, Adeia?" Ches inquired.

"Fabia of Vaduz, village of Croft," she replied.

We'd been through the insorcelled village not long before. I wondered if we'd met the female. And what was happening to the woman if they were "having problems" with her device?

"It is not yet her time," Ches replied. "She has another dozen annums to what I allotted."

"Which floor?" Nona asked.

"The twentieth," Adeia replied.

The twentieth floor. I'd given no thought to what was on all those floors we'd climbed past. More devices? This place was enormous. My aunts had a formidable task to manage it all. All those humans. And immortals. And who knew what other creatures, perhaps. I shook my head.

That's a lot, Kovis whispered.

"I'm on it," Nona replied and headed off with the attendant.

Aunt Ches motioned us onward, back toward the door we'd entered the hall through and into the towering shelves. The first set we came upon, to the right, was filled with candles burning brightly. An assistant hurriedly rolled a ladder to the left and scurried up. She replaced a guttering candle in the nick of time. I exhaled at how close it had been to going out.

To our left we came upon shelves in which devices with a metal ball rolled down a zigzagging track to move the hands on a timepiece. These seemed more reliable and not subject to a too strong breeze. In the next set of shelves, more attendants added water to contraptions that dripped liquid to measure time.

We reached the entrance where Jansha and Rinion smiled, then bowed low. I wanted to comment on Rinion's change in disposition, but I bit my tongue. Kovis chuckled through the bond.

After the pair of stewards stood tall once more, Baldik, who had been waiting for us, strode forward and held out Kovis's weapons to him. Rowntree stopped beside his fellow.

"We're not yet ready to leave," I said.

Baldik gave a slow nod, although it was clear from his strained expression, he was none too happy about it.

"We'll be upstairs," Ta indicated to her stewards. Then turning to us, she said, "Come along."

We'd climbed thirty floors already, how much further would we go?

As we mounted the first set of stairs, Ches said, "In the beginning, there weren't so many floors, only three. But over time, the palace has grown to accommodate new life."

"Wow, they must be some builders," I said, scanning the ascending stairs.

"No," Ches corrected. "It grows."

"The palace grows?" I couldn't hide my surprise.

"It does. It's alive in a manner of speaking. It derives its life principally from me and my sisters but some from the life it stewards, as well. I don't pretend to understand it. Nona tried to explain it once, and I've never asked again." Ches chuckled.

I gave her a knowing smile as we started up the next flight.

"It's quite jarring when it adds a new floor," she added, rustling her wings.

Kovis laughed out loud. "I bet that's an understatement."

Ches smiled warmly. "Fair enough. Rumbling and jolting, we have to take great care that none of it snuffs out the life we steward."

My eyes were wide. I couldn't imagine a building moving with me in it. I'd be scared out of my mind.

She went on. "As I understand it, the Ancient One himself set it in motion before the gods appeared. He placed us here after creating us, but before breathing life into another being."

I'd suspected my aunts were older than time itself, now I knew. And as for the palace, I shook my head, unable to comprehend. The council building in Wake changed to display all the affinities through magic. But this was something entirely other. A living place. Unbelievable. I'd lived in Dream practically my whole life and I'd never known.

We reached the fourth landing since beginning our climb and Aunt Ta turned right. We'd reached the top. There were no more stairs to climb. There were thirty-five floors... for now.

We entered a space unlike the other. Shelves upon shelves upon shelves populated it, but these didn't stretch to the ceiling. They stopped waist high, allowing light from the windows and ceiling to shine and illumine the gold that gilded the shelves. It was beautiful. A place of the gods.

Kovis tensed beside me.

If they'd brought us here to find Velma's and Alfreda's devices…

My breath hitched with the thought. I doubted my timepiece was still here, but it had been? I was a child of gods, but I had no notions of being one any longer.

The several tan-robed attendants scattered about the space looked bored. They ambled between the shelves, wings slumped, with no task to occupy their hands.

"We rotate our attendants around every now and again, so they don't have to endure the monotony of immortals. Animals and other creatures are favored amongst the attendants. They keep them hopping. Us too." Aunt Ta chuckled as we started between the shelves.

Name plaques lined the shelf edges. I furrowed my brow.

What's wrong? Kovis asked.

I don't recognize any of the names.

"This is Ares's section," Aunt Ches indicated, breezing her hand through the air to the right. "The devices of all of the god of war's immortal children, legitimate or of love, are here, lest you wonder why some of the names don't look familiar.

"And this is Nike's section to our left. She definitely lives up to her name as goddess of victory." She cleared her throat. "Seems she's had a different sort of 'victory' or two from time to time." She laughed. I snickered. Kovis tried and failed to keep a straight face.

On the top of each shelf sat a circular bowl carved from a chunk of rough-hewn rock. The primitive vessels seemed out of place and at odds with the finery of the rest of the space. Perhaps the roughness of them was because the Ancient One had crafted each god from the ground itself. I'd no idea, but my theory would have to do absent confirmation or dismissal.

I peeked over the top of one vessel and saw that the rock had been hewn out and made smooth, and water swirled around and around inside—I couldn't determine what stirred it. Mine had no doubt been like this. I swallowed. What had happened to it the heartbeat I'd become human?

I pushed the thought away as Aunt Ta turned left and we entered my family's section, or so she said. I pulled a hand to my chest when I spotted Iris, Mother's name, on a nameplate we passed. I found "Dion" on another—my great-grandfather. Mema's, then Grandfather's name, then Father's. I tried to calm my racing thoughts. Could they just stop Fathers device? No. No. Not that. I backpedaled even as the thought formed fully.

As if overhearing my inner turmoil, Ta looked over at me. "You know not what would ensue if you changed time itself for one, no matter their deeds. You argued the same on behalf of your beloved, did you not?" She glanced at Kovis whose eyes had gone wide.

I hadn't seen it that way at the time. Kovis was good. But she was right, best not to change things no matter the nature of the being.

My breath hitched as we stopped. The top of the next shelf held vessels labeled in order of our births: Velma, Wasila, Challis, and so on. It felt so intimate to see every one of these basins. They controlled the very lives of my siblings.

I scanned the length of the shelf and my stomach tightened. Twenty-three vessels, or there would have been had there not been an empty spot down a ways.

"There you are." Aunt Nona's exclamation emanated from behind, and we all turned. She was furling her wings just inside the door. She'd made it back quickly, especially for one so ancient.

She straightened her hair and then her gray shawl and strode toward us, then shook her head when she reached us. "Defective calican. One of our recent shipments had parts not up to spec, but she should be all set for the rest of her time."

I'd no idea what a calican was, but it definitely sounded important.

"Does that happen often?" Kovis asked.

"Oh every now and then," she replied.

"What do they do to keep life going if the part fails completely?" I asked.

"An attendant keeps the device going manually, doing their best not to speed it up."

Aunt Ches interjected, "I tolerate a bit of additional time added to a life, but never less, especially not with humans who possess such a keen awareness of it and orient so much around it."

Kovis bobbed his head.

"Alissandra," Ta said, recapturing our attention. "Your request for help was to locate your two sisters. It implied that a time device is somehow geographically connected to the being in question."

Nona started bouncing on the balls of her feet.

"There's no way you could have known whether it does or doesn't. You were hoping, I think." She raised an eyebrow at me.

"Yes, I was."

Nona couldn't control herself any longer. "You're very smart to think that." She puffed up her chest. "Because it can. I make all those connections when I install a new device. It's a simple hookup actually."

I sucked in a breath. Was she really saying what I thought she was? Hope filled me as she went on to explain how she did it, but it all sounded foreign to me. Kovis just smiled and nodded. So did I, while my heart pounded.

Nona approached Velma's vessel. "So then, let's have a look-see."

She frowned as she looked in. "Wipe, please," Nona commanded a nearby attendant. The female returned with a square of fabric in a heartbeat, and Nona reached inside.

"This won't hurt her, will it?" I squeaked.

"No, child," Aunt Ches reassured.

I peered over the edge as she wiped a round disc in the center.

"That's better. So where are you, Princess Velma?" Nona talked to herself as she scrutinized the disc. Hums and harrumphs flowed from her as she studied it further. "Oh, there you are, you tricky little princess." She smiled and looked up.

Part IV: Night Terror

Try, Try Again

By Thomas H. Palmer
Kelso, Scotland Wake Realm

'Tis a lesson you should heed,
If at first you don't succeed,
Try, try again;
Then your courage should appear,
For if you will persevere,
You will conquer, never fear
Try, try again;

Once or twice, though you should fail,
If you would at last prevail,
Try, try again;
If we strive, 'tis no disgrace
Though we do not win the race;
What should you do in the case?
Try, try again

If you find your task is hard,
Time will bring you your reward,
Try, try again
All that other folks can do,
Why, with patience, should not you?
Only keep this rule in view:
Try, try again.

Chapter Forty-Two

The sun was halfway back to the horizon as Kovis, Baldik, and I flew north along the coast.

We'd dispatched Rowntree to rouse the rest of the family, let them know where Nona had said Velma and Alfreda were located, and ask them to meet us there. He would also get word to Dyeus and beg him to please, please, please come to the location specified in our note. I prayed Dite had spoken with him as well as gotten a favorable response. So much depended on it.

We didn't care which order he did the tasks, as long as they were done as quickly as possible. We planned to get a feel for the area Nona specified while we waited for the others.

Nona had tracked Velma to a sea cave just north of the mushroom caves that my siblings and I loved so much. She'd also examined Alfreda's vessel and found the same. Small mercy, at least they were together.

Father had no doubt held them there the whole time, which explained why no one had been able to find them in his usual haunts.

I loved spending time at the mushroom caves, but it wasn't a place to stay for moons. What had he put them through? And in what condition would we find them?

We're coming, sisters!

My aunts had bid us Godspeed after hasty farewells and a promise that I would not fail in my pledge, Kovis's really, to provide them reading material, no matter where I ended up. I thought it was their way of keeping in contact more than anything, and I was glad for it. I put a hand over the pocket in my leathers where I'd stowed their keepsake. A part of them would go with me wherever I went. The thought made me smile despite the situation.

The weather had not improved. The dark clouds of earlier seemed to have darkened further, and we kept hitting patches of rain. Even the water below was rough and peppered with whitecaps. I hoped it wasn't foretelling some doom awaiting us.

Nothing would be simple; so much could go wrong. I stopped myself and pushed the thoughts aside. I would stay positive. We'd rescue them, Dyeus would bind Father, and then we'd take my sisters home—and we'd all try to forget this whole nightmare.

For his part, Kovis was being silently supportive. His mind flowed with thoughts of Kennan and hopes for a positive outcome. So much rested on our success.

I hadn't appreciated the dark clouds until the white cliffs marking our destination came into focus—at least this looked to be the place Aunt Nona had described. Hopefully the darkness hid us from any mare soldiers that guarded Father's stronghold.

We touched down near the trees on the windswept cliff above the sandy beach and surveyed the area. Baldik drew his sword and crouched low, then scurried over to the edge of the cliff. Without a word, Kovis drew his blades and handed me his last dagger before we followed.

On our bellies, we peered over the edge. Rain had washed away much of the beach's tells, but I could still make out the divots of large feet. I glanced over at Kovis, and he nodded. We were so close.

◦ ◦ ◦

"Out for a stroll on this stormy day?" The growl came from behind us, and we whirled around and scrambled to our feet, raising our weapons as we did.

Six mare soldiers stood in a line, weapons trained on us, blocking any escape. Who knew where they'd been hiding. Perhaps they'd assumed the form of snakes—*getting back to their true selves*, my mind added.

Their leader, a hulking brute in a uniform, stood just forward of the other five and scanned us up and down. This would be a challenge but not insurmountable. Their first mistake, they hadn't just taken us. They'd had surprise on their side but squandered it. They'd decided to size us up first.

Just how much sand was this cliff made of, I wondered.

Ready? Kovis asked.

Ready. Then turning my attention to our foe, I thought, *Go to sleep. Go to sleep.*

Nothing happened. Our enemies didn't so much as bat an eyelash, let alone yawn. There had to be sand in the ground. Or were mares immune to my powers?

I tried again and again without result.

It didn't work, I reported. I'd never mastered the sword, but I'd do anything for my sisters.

The leader rushed Kovis and chaos erupted. Baldik was on two more mares in the blink of an eye, felling the runt of our enemies in a heartbeat—runt being relative.

I held a ready position, dagger poised, rather than charging ahead. Comparatively, I was small and certainly posed no threat. I hoped they'd ignore me.

Kovis's blade found their leader's stomach in short order, then extracted his sword in one smooth motion, stepping forward and engaging two more foe. Baldik raced for me but didn't reach me before the last enemy feinted to the right, bringing his blade whistling past my ear a hair's breadth away.

He'd made me flat footed, and I couldn't recover before he grabbed my left arm, knocked my dagger away as he spun me around, and pulled me against himself. He pinned my arms and wings and brought his blade to my neck… but not near enough. And that was all I needed.

I'd learned how to escape holds by slamming my heel down on an instep, so I gave it everything I had. But this mare had no reaction other than to pick me up, squeezing me tighter, making it hard to breathe as well as impossible to use the ground for leverage. Not to mention crushing my wings. I froze as the blade now kissed my neck.

Kovis!

Baldik's eyes bore into the brute from where he'd skidded to a stop. Kovis slowly stepped over the corpse of the last mare he slew and drifted over. He held up a hand as he walked, blade still raised. "Let her go."

The landscape was eerily quiet, only the clouds moved, drifting by, completely oblivious. Waves thundering against the sheer, white cliffs in regular rhythm were the only sound far below.

Five mare corpses lay sprawled at odd angles. It was just the four of us, three of which engaged in a staring contest. My captor pulled the blade closer as Kovis neared, and I felt a trickle of warmth run down the front of my neck.

"You will come with me or I will finish this one. Drop your weapons and move."

Go with him. We'll stall until the others get here. Wherever he's taking us, we'll probably find Velma and Alfreda, I suggested.

Kovis frowned as the mare nodded toward the cliff, but he and Baldik did as commanded and left their weapons behind before taking flight. My wings ached at the mistreatment, and I still struggled to breathe trapped against the brute's chest.

A heartbeat later, the mare launched from the cliff with me against his chest.

I let out a grunt at the force of impact, despite it being a sandy beach, as my captor regained his balance. He clearly had no prior experience juggling a passenger at sword point.

• • •

I looked about. A fissure ran up the face of the cliff not far away and footprints led toward it.

"In there," the mare commanded.

Baldik led the way, Kovis followed, and I with my captor brought up the rear as we entered the narrow-mouthed cavern. My captor pulled his wings close as we squeezed through the narrow entrance. As much as I hated to, I shrank back into his chest. It was that or lose skin. My wings felt numb.

"Bate, what's this?" another mare soldier asked just inside as my captor set me down. Air. Sweet air. I sucked it in and ruffled feeling back into my wings as I looked around. Blue crystals lined the wet cave walls and cast a glow that offered only dim light. Where were my sisters?

"Commander Lethold, we found them spying on the cliff. When we surrounded them, they engaged. The rest of my patrol is lost, sir."

The commander frowned. "These three bested five of my troops?"

"They did, sir."

Lethold gave Kovis and Baldik a long look, seemingly trying to understand how that could be. He ignored me. Clearly, he perceived me as no threat.

"Who are you? And why were you spying?" He directed his question to Kovis.

"Why are you holed up way out in the middle of nowhere?" Kovis replied.

"That's not an answer."

"Very well. We were taking in the sites," Kovis replied.

The commander stepped forward and struck Kovis across the face, making him reel back and sprawl across the rough rock floor.

I yipped.

Kovis rubbed his jaw as the brute strode to where he'd landed and kicked his side, it was no nudge. Kovis balled up, clutching his middle.

Are you okay? I moved to Kovis and squatted.

"That's what we do to those who don't cooperate." Turning to Bate, he said, "Take them back. If they found us, no doubt more will follow."

Bate saluted. Then fingering the top of his sheathed sword, he narrowed his eyes and growled, "On your feet."

Kovis grunted as I helped him up and grimaced as he put a hand to his side. Baldik extended his hand.

"I'm fine," Kovis said, declining the guard's help.

We passed two more guards and approached another standing at attention beside a figure sitting on the floor. My heart sped as our eyes connected.

"Velma!" I raced forward and fell to my knees onto the bed of moss she sat on. "Is that really you?"

"Velma, who is it?" Alfreda. My heart sped. It was her voice from the other side of the wall.

Velma looked me over, and I her, in the light of several torches that reflected off the white stone of the low ceiling. I sucked in a breath then drew my hands over my mouth. "Your wings... Oh, Velma. I never..." Tears found my cheeks in a heartbeat.

"Ali?" Despite my changed appearance recognition dawned, and she reached over and fingered my hair.

"Ali? It's Ali?" Alfreda shrieked. "Let me go," she protested to someone.

"You will remain here. Sit down," a gruff voice echoed through the space.

"Yes, it's me, Alfreda. We finally found you," I called out, then leaned forward and enveloped Velma in a hug. I bumped a bandage on her back, and she sucked in air.

"Oh, sister, it's good to see you, but you shouldn't have come." Her voice wavered as she clung to me. I let her hold me until she took a deep breath and let it out slowly.

I sat back, and we both wiped our cheeks but smiled. How I missed her, but her wings...

Kovis shifted, reminding me of his presence, and I looked up. "Velma, I'd like you to meet Kovis."

Kovis nodded. "Princess Velma, Ali has told me much about you. I'm pleased to make your acquaintance."

"The pleasure is mine," Velma replied. Despite her wings, her raven hair being in disarray, and dirt marring her dress in spots, she managed a warm smile. "Ali's told me much about you too. I'm glad to finally meet you. I just wish it were under different circumstances."

"All right, enough," Bate interrupted. Then pointing at Kovis and Baldik, he said, "You two, into the other room."

"Prince Kovis!" Alfreda exclaimed the heartbeat he disappeared around the wall. She'd seen enough of his and his brother's dreams to know who he was.

"You're my brother's sand maiden?" I overheard him ask, wonder filling his voice. "It's very good to meet you."

I smiled.

The guard next to us snapped to attention before I could hear more. They all did, and I understood why as familiar footsteps approached.

Velma whispered, "Give me your ring for safekeeping."

She'd noticed. And she was right, the less Father knew, the better… for all of us. I quickly slipped it off and handed it to her.

"My liege." The greeting echoed from several soldiers, followed by bows, as Father stopped before us. My stomach clenched. Had he been on his way and just arrived? Was this just unfortunate timing on our part?

"Rise." He held his chin high, his chest thrust out, and flared his nostrils with a great exhale. He was pissed.

My hands turned clammy despite Velma placing a hand on my arm. This was not how I'd pictured our next meeting. Truthfully, I hadn't pictured one.

"I see we've caught the hare. Bring Alfreda and the others here," he commanded. "It's time she is dealt with."

He sounded like he had a cold. It was a random thought, no doubt my mind's way of attempting to cope with my fear. His soldiers, like obedient mice, scurried to do his will, and Alfreda appeared around the corner.

If I weren't afraid of what was about to happen, I would have jumped up and kissed her. As it was, I sent her a smile as the guard beside us compelled Velma and me to our feet. Alfreda reciprocated the greeting from beside Kovis once we complied.

Baldik stood on the other side of another guard that had apparently been the source of the correcting growl.

Bate and several other soldiers filed in as Father took another step, his black robe hissing against the floor. With the weight he'd put on, along with his large wings, he was imposing in the limited space.

He smiled, but it didn't reach his eyes. "The prodigal daughter has returned. Or has she? You've been back in Dream for nearly a sennight and you haven't sought me out. You disappoint me. Is that what a favorite daughter would do?" He frowned.

Shit. Not that I'd expected him to, but he wouldn't have uttered that moniker if he still considered me such. Dread filled me.

"What did I tell you about falling into disfavor?" He raised an eyebrow.

I swallowed hard. How could I forget? "That it would be 'unfortunate.'"

"That is correct. And why do you suppose that is?"

He was surprisingly restrained. It almost seemed like he was regurgitating something he'd thought through numerous times and was only now acting on. How much did he loathe me?

Kovis shifted.

I bit my lip but finally managed, "Because you will punish me?"

"Correct again. Yes, I've overlooked your slights of the past, but this is the last time. You fled to Wake in hopes of preventing me from taking it. You held the crazy notion that you loved your charge more than me and had to save him." He shook his head, thankfully ignoring Kovis. "I hold your sister largely responsible for filling your head with such nonsense, but it was a cowardly thing to do. That said, how can I, in all good conscience, continue calling you my favorite daughter?"

His eyes pierced me, waiting for an answer.

I wouldn't respond.

Before I'd fled Dream, I'd come to realize he had been manipulating me, making me feel important by calling me his favorite, preying on my belief that it meant he loved me when all he was doing was preparing to use me for his purposes when it suited him.

Velma looked down.

So he would punish me. Sweat ran down my back.

Breathe, Ali, breathe, Kovis encouraged. *We'll make it through whatever he tries, together.*

Father snarled. "It would be well within my rights as your sovereign to end your miserable mortal existence." He let that thought linger. "But because I am generous, I'm going to extend leniency."

I wasn't sure I wanted his mercy. Would he take my wings instead? I'd just gotten them back!

"The root of the issue is that you believe you love another"—he looked at Kovis—"more than me."

He'd been hung up on me loving Kovis. He'd come unhinged over it. My breathing labored.

Father went on. "Now what would serve to properly punish you?" He tapped a finger on his lips as if to ponder. He wasn't pondering. He already knew what he planned to do; he just enjoyed being dramatic and hearing himself bloviate. After several heartbeats, he shook his head. "No. No. I think taking your wings would not serve my ends. You have adjusted to their lack in Wake. I must punish you differently."

I'd keep my wings, but…

"I'm going to punish you in three ways."

Oh gods, here it came.

"Endure these and I will consider your punishment satisfied and commensurate with the wrong I've suffered at your hands."

The wrong *he'd* suffered? He was delusional. What was going on in that head of his? Evil. Only evil. How had I not seen it before?

"So let's begin."

• • •

Chapter Forty-Three

"One thing I have learned about you, Alissandra," Father said, brushing his robe, "is that you care for others more than yourself. Therefore, the first punishment will be for one you love *more than me* to be punished on your behalf."

I sucked in a breath. He wouldn't.

In a heartbeat, a guard beside Father transformed back into its base form, a smelly, feral, purple-haired beast and lunged at Kovis. It had him on the ground in the blink of an eye.

"No!" I brought my arms down sharply.

Alfreda shrieked and ran to me, clinging to my arm before I could race for Kovis. I couldn't support her, not now. I moved out of her grip, and she drew her arms around herself.

The soldier beside Baldik tackled him as he moved to intervene.

Velma gripped my other arm. I tried to shake her off, but she held firm. "He'll hurt him worse if you go to him," she whispered.

No, she was wrong! She'd never known love like I had. I had to save him. I struggled again, but still she held firm as the mare bit into Kovis's shoulder and tossed him about. Despite his struggling, he succumbed to sleep quicker than I could blink, his body going limp.

Kovis! Only silence replied.

I heard his heart accelerate through the bond. This couldn't be happening. If the terror was too horrific, he would have a heart attack and could even die! Father had wanted to eliminate him, and he was trying.

Velma still held my arm firm, firm in her beliefs, but I would help Kovis. But how?

The mare transformed into the shadowy form of Kovis's father, the late emperor, and rose. I'd seen the man in Kovis's memories enough times to know. The figure bent over and grabbed my Dreambeam's neck in a death grip.

Kovis had been attacked by a mare while we were in the wilderness, but I'd had magic then. I'd wrenched Ice from him and frozen the foe, then shattered it into a million pieces with my winds. But I had no magic. What could I do?

I tried to calm down despite Alfreda whimpering beside me. No one moved, transfixed by the scene.

And then I knew. Velma would help despite her restraint, by steadying me.

I willed myself into Kovis's mind while keeping my expression neutral and staring at the scene like everyone else. I had a good idea what I'd find when I arrived in his head, and I wasn't wrong. The late emperor was choking him while kicking him in the stomach. I just caught a glimpse of a green robe fluttering out of the room.

"You've interrupted us for the last time," the emperor roared in Kovis's mind.

"Kovis! Listen to me!" I called, then conjured an image of him fondling my breasts, his eyes filled with passion and desire.

Another kick, this one missing Kovis's stomach and hitting his groin. Kovis cried out. His heart pounded faster than I'd ever heard it.

"Look, Kovis! Do you remember?" I tried to beat back my panic that was rising and added more explicit exploration of my ladies.

Fondling one, then the other. So soft. So supple. He leaned forward and suckled them.

The late emperor raised a knee to follow up on his last kick, but it turned to mist before reaching him.

I sighed contentedly through the bond. *That feels so good, my love.* I said it in a seductive tone and showed him squeezing my flesh again, his mouth never parting from my pebbled tip. Suck, lick. *Yes. That's it, my love.*

When strangling and kicking ceased to work, the mare pulled back and threw an uppercut, but as it reached Kovis's face, its hand faded into mist.

It was working. It was working. I redoubled my efforts and created the image of Kovis taking his time, savoring every inch of me, kissing all the way to where my navel should have been, and below to the curly wisps of hair. *Mmm, oh, Kovis...* I moaned.

His heart, while still beating rapidly, slowed. I hoped it was from the images I'd been showing him and not the mare. And when he roused, I knew.

I opened my eyes—Kovis's eyes—and looked at the scene: so many beings stared at me, transfixed by the sight of me on the ground.

Through my eyes, looking from the other side of the room, Father frowned as Velma still held me back. Did they know what I'd done?

I let a small smile breach my face.

The stench as the purple beast materialized again about overpowered our senses, but we took a breath through our mouth. Kovis's arm throbbed where the thing had sunk its teeth.

I willed myself to return to my own head as the beast shifted back into its soldier form. "He bested me, my liege. I couldn't hold him."

With a growl, Father tossed his head, indicating for it to resume its position behind him. How I abhorred those abominations.

• • •

"On your feet," the soldier beside Kovis commanded, and he struggled up, holding his arm. A trickle of blood oozed from beneath his hand as he schooled his expression and locked eyes with me.

Damn. And just when it was getting good. But his words came out uneven. He knew how close we'd come.

I exhaled—it looked like Kovis's leathers had taken the brunt of that beast's maw. Velma released my arm with a squeeze.

The soldier didn't permit Baldik to rise, but kept him facedown, against the cave floor.

Father drew his lips into a flat line and looked at me with a furrowed brow. Clearly, he'd hoped for a different outcome. He'd never admit defeat, so I wasn't surprised when he dispensed with comment and just plunged in. "For your next punishment..."

One punishment down, but two to go.

We'll do this together, Ali. We'll make it.

"I believe we need a few more involved who you love more than me," Father's tone was condescending, "just so they can see how much pain you can cause them... like you've caused me. Perhaps they'll reconsider blindly loving you." He nodded, and the soldier beside Kovis stepped toward us and grabbed Alfreda by her forearm. She yipped, and despite resisting, the brute was stronger and dragged her before him.

"Have a little dignity, child," he reprimanded her.

Alfreda bit her lip as she held herself. She was a dirty mess—dress thoroughly rumpled, hair stringy and tangled, feet bare. Her eyes looked vacant until she turned her head and refocused on me. She'd endured too much. What else would he do to her in my name?

"I love you," I mouthed to her. A corner of her mouth hitched up.

"I'm calling this punishment a family affair. Alfreda, retrieve your charge's thought thread."

A family affair? I pulled my elbows into my sides. No. No. No.

"Now," he added with a growl when she didn't comply immediately.

Her breath hitched, and she looked to me with apology in her eyes. There was no fight left in her. Father had utterly crushed her spirit. Would he crush mine before he was done? I had no doubt he'd try.

She closed her eyes and did as commanded.

"Very good. Now, hand it to me." He grinned when she did. "It seems one of my daughters knows how to obey. Hopefully this punishment will improve your obedience, Alissandra."

Alfreda's shoulders slumped.

"Come here," Father said to me.

The soldier beside Velma and me wrenched her grip from my arm and marched me between him and my sister, then stepped away.

"You and I are going to hold this thread and you are going to inflict pain on your beloved's brother until he shrieks."

What? For what purpose? Never. *Kovis!*

"No!" Alfreda shouted. "You can't! You brute!" She clawed at the mare-soldier until he restrained her.

Father's eyes found Alfreda in a heartbeat. "Need I remind you that I am your sovereign?"

Alfreda continued struggling, but Father returned his focus to me. "Let's begin. Hold the thread with me."

Velma closed her eyes and bowed her head.

Kovis, I can't.

He'd already closed his eyes and thoughts of Rasa's abuse swirled in his mind. While he hadn't been forced to participate, he'd felt just as powerless.

"Do you need help to comply?" Father's words dripped acid.

"I can't," I replied.

He smiled. "Ah, but you must. You have no choice. This is part of your punishment for what you've done to me. Sometimes we get hurt for no reason. We're just in the wrong place at the right time."

I shook my head and felt him place his claws on my mind.

I fled to Kovis's mind. Perhaps the bond would buffer some of the pain.

"You cannot experience the plans I have for you until you overcome your pain. And you cannot overcome your pain until you face it. It is the prism you see life through. It must change." Kovis had shifted his thoughts and replayed a memory of what Dite had told him. He was forcing his mind to focus on this rather than the evil of the late emperor.

I felt discomfort as Father stroked my mind, making my body twitch. I would cope. I had to.

"You and Alissandra belong together. You have been made for each other. And I want to bless you." Kovis's memory went on. Dite wanted to bless us.

I filled my mind with that hope too and blocked out Father's next stroke.

"Tell me again what it means to live," Dite had asked. Kovis relived the deep breath he'd taken, then spoke of how much he loved me, of the pleasures of life, of passion and wonder and dreaming.

I filled my mind with these thoughts and of how much I loved Kovis, of how lucky I was to get to know him like no other sand person knew their charge, to experience what it means to love and allow myself to be fully loved, warts and all, in return. To be vulnerable and unafraid. To help him become all he was meant to be.

Father's claws dug deeper, and I focused all the harder on what was good. Kovis was my refuge and shelter.

And you are mine, my love.

While I'd been consuming my focus with all that was good, he'd been listening in and had joined in my narrative.

We both grimaced on Father's next pass, but Kovis chuckled.

What?

How about we pick up where we were when we were so rudely interrupted?

I laughed into the bond. *There's nothing I would enjoy more.*

Kovis brought to mind the image of his hands exploring my ladies more explicitly. Fondling one, then the other. So soft. So supple. He leaned forward and suckled them. I sighed contentedly through the bond.

● ● ●

How's that feel, *my love?* he purred and showed me his hands squeezing my flesh again, his mouth never parting from my pebbled tip. Suck, lick. Yes.

That's so good. Mmmm. I could barely think until Father's next pass left us both panting. But the pain fueled our passions hotter than they'd ever been. Father could do anything to me, but he would fail as long as Kovis was by my side.

And sex would be incredible. Kovis's hands continued their migration southward and my core burned ever hotter with desire.

And when Father scraped his claws slowly in his deepest pass— more excruciating than *ever* before, the thrall overwhelmed me and my body climaxed.

Blackness nibbled at the edges of awareness and sounds welled up from deep within, unbidden, and I surrendered, shouting my release, equal parts agony and rapture. My knees gave way, and I again met the floor as I channeled the torment. Climax had never felt so intense, so exhilarating… so unthinkably extraordinary. I didn't care that everyone heard. They had no idea what made my body spasm and tremble.

In my delirium, somewhere between the cold, hard cave and a warmth outside myself, I pondered. What was it about pain and pleasure? They seemed so at odds, yet they could be harmonized. Pleasure could bring pain, just as pain could yield pleasure. But together, they were… indescribable.

When I at last opened my eyes, I was looking at Kovis across the room.

How are you doing, Ali dearest? Worry marred his face.

I've been better.

I'll always be here for you.

My head pounded, but it was a small price to pay for what I'd thwarted. Yet it had been close. Had I not had Kovis, I would never have survived, I knew it with certainty. Father had been crueler than anything he'd dished out before. I'd dodged an arrow, but he wasn't done. Could I endure? Doubt nibbled at my throbbing mind, and my stomach felt like a stone.

• • •

Father cleared his throat, and I turned my head to find him looking down at me. "You have endured." He seemed conflicted, even as he said it. "I dared take this no further lest I cause irreparable damage, for that would ruin your last punishment. No, you need to be fully aware for that."

Tears streamed down Alfreda's face. I couldn't tell if they were for the pain I endured or from dread of what was to come. Or from being so thoroughly broken that she'd never be able to stop.

Velma looked equally spent.

Father had meant what he'd said about that punishment being a family affair. He'd dragged Alfreda and Kennan into it, and Velma and Kovis right along with us.

Father commanded Alfreda back beside Velma, then the solider at her side to control her.

He looked at me, standing again before him, and said, "And so, your third punishment."

• • •

Chapter Forty-Four

He was going to push me until I broke, like he had Alfreda. Like he was trying to do with Velma. These first two punishments had been horrific. What could he possibly do to top them?

"Velma is learning the error of her ways in encouraging your flight to Wake, but you are equally at fault. You followed her council and fled out of love for her as well as this mortal. Unfortunately in life, we can't have everything. So for your final punishment, I call you to choose between them."

What? "No… no, you can't be serious!" Panic rose.

Alfreda shrieked, and the soldier beside moved to restrain her.

Velma and Kovis exchanged a look but otherwise stood motionless. Had they expected it would come to this?

"Oh, but I am." He spoke slowly, as if I was a child being reasoned with. "It seems I can't have your love, nor theirs." He nodded to my sisters. "I don't get what I want, so neither shall you."

"But you caused the rift between us," I argued, despite knowing it was futile.

He raised a brow. "I beg to differ with you."

"I acted to protect my charge!"

"Who you loved more than me," he boomed. He bobbed his head, and two of his minions hauled Velma and Kovis behind me. I whirled around to face them as his minions forced them to kneel, remaining with a hand on each.

No, no, no, no. This couldn't be happening. He'd meant to break me. He'd succeed if he forced me to choose. Gods no! Where were my brothers? Where was Dyeus? Only he could stop this madness.

"Alissandra, you will do this."

A soldier stepped forward and extended a shiny dagger. I fisted my hands. He could never force me to take it.

Without turning my head, I eyed the space, noting where each soldier was, the number of their weapons, how many blocked our exit, where Baldik renewed his struggling, spurred on by what had just unfolded, a soldier astride him.

One blade against so many.

My power hadn't worked against the mares before, but I had to try. I focused my mind on the soldiers blocking our escape. *Go to sleep. Go to sleep.*

But as before, nothing happened. Mares were immune.

Father chuckled. He'd no doubt sensed my attempt. "Neither calculations nor powers will do you any good, Alissandra. There is no escape. You must choose."

The soldier renewed his offer, extending the blade closer.

"I won't."

I couldn't imagine choosing, couldn't imagine a world without either of them.

Father chuckled. "Then I guess I shall choose for you… but you will still carry out the deed."

No. No. No. I knew how that would end.

"Be done with this and your punishment will be satisfied," he reminded in a singsong tone.

• • •

"Ali," Velma said.

"No, don't say anything." I feared what she'd say and didn't want to hear it.

"Ali," Velma persisted.

"No!" I waved my arms, as if it would silence her.

"You *must* save Wake. You two are the only ones who can." Resolve filled her voice, and her eyes turned fierce.

I wagged my head from side to side, unwilling to listen.

"Make your choice, or I will," Father commanded.

The soldier pushed the blade toward me.

I couldn't choose. I wouldn't.

The chaos and demands faded and silence blanketed my mind. There was one other choice, beyond what Father offered. As soon as the notion surfaced, I knew it was the one I must take. I would take. It was of my own making, and while Kovis would be devastated, it was the only way to save them both. Peace and calm filled my mind. I'd wanted to build a happily ever after with my Dreambeam, but it wasn't meant to be. And I was okay with that as long as Velma and Kovis were safe. My mind returned to the cave.

I took the dagger and studied it. It was a fine weapon. I'd trained with blades in Wake, and this one equaled the best I'd handled. Its blade had been polished to a high sheen, and it tossed about the light from the few torches. Its carved handle, oak I guessed, was too large for my small hands. Its weight was greater than any I'd felt before, but it wouldn't matter. I would make my stand.

"And if you take your own life, I will still choose between them."

Father's promise shattered the peace, and I sucked in a breath. How had he known?

"Ali, let me do this. For you. For Wake." Velma rushed on before I could stop her. "My life has been forfeit since I took a stand against him."

Father growled.

Alfreda sobbed uncontrollably.

Kovis didn't move, didn't breathe.

Say something, I pleaded with him.

That would be utterly unfair to you.

He didn't beg me to spare his life, didn't plead in any way or even remind me he loved me. He simply looked into my eyes, absolute trust and love shining there, as if telling me whatever my decision, he would support it.

Taking my own life wouldn't save them. Taking one of theirs wouldn't save me. My soul would die either way. My brothers hadn't arrived. Dyeus tarried—if he was even coming—and all the other gods remained utterly silent.

"Choose."

Tears streamed from my eyes, clouding my vision. Velma and Kovis both looked at me, eyes clear. How could I choose? Yet I would be forced to, and the horror of what I was about to do, like a monster with a putrid, gaping maw, closed in on me to swallow me whole.

For Wake, for Kovis, for both our realms…

I took the longest, most barbarous step I'd taken in all my suns, all my annums, and stopped before Velma.

She dipped her head.

Alfreda cried out, then fell to the ground in a heap.

Velma's life in exchange for Wake's salvation, despite there being no guarantee. But her life would not be taken in vain. We would overcome whatever evil Father threw at us, and we would overcome him, no matter the cost to us. Only for that promise, my unspoken vow to her, could I suffer her loss.

The knife felt so heavy in my treacherous hand as I raised it. My heart raced. She didn't look at me, as if making this as easy on me as she could. Her black eyes were steady, not a tear in sight, as she stared ahead—resolved.

"Stop," Father commanded.

I turned around in a heartbeat. Did Father mean to just get me to this point of decision, but not intend to suffer Velma's loss? It would be beyond cruel, but I could imagine him doing such. Hope rose in me.

He strode from behind me, around Baldik who still squirmed on the ground, and stopped behind Velma. "I want you to look at me when you drive that into her heart, and picture it as what you did to me."

Hope shattered, along with my soul.

"Continue," he commanded.

"You can do this, Ali," Velma said. "Save Wake."

My hand shook as I brought the blade up again. "I love you so much, Velma."

"I know, and I love you, Alissandra. Now be brave." She closed her eyes.

Alfreda wailed.

Kovis remained still as a statue.

Father stepped behind Velma, wanting to ensure I didn't forget him.

I gripped her shoulder, and with a wail of my own, I drove the dagger into her heart. I would never in all my suns forget the vibrations from her bones crunching against the blade as it found its mark. Blood. Her blood. Innocent blood. So much of it. Warm. Its tang smelled of death and flowed onto my hand. "Traitor," it screamed. And something inside me shattered into a million tiny pieces that could never be repaired.

Velma's eyes shot open, but she staunched the cry that begged for freedom—she wouldn't give Father the satisfaction—before bringing her hands up to clutch the hilt, then collapsing onto her side.

"No! No!" Alfreda screamed at the top of her lungs. She landed on her knees beside Velma, pulled her onto her lap, and rocked back and forth with her in her arms. "Don't go, please don't go," she begged.

Kovis enveloped me as my knees hit the hard ground, and I broke in his arms.

"I didn't think you had it in you," Father said.

I shut him out. Her blood coated my hand, marked me, branded me, burned me. I didn't care what the bastard had to say. He was not my father. I refused to see him as that any longer. No, he was just a tyrant, a narcissistic tyrant who would be stopped.

Despite my anger, the river of tears flowed, unabated. Kovis hugged me tighter, more fiercely, never saying a word—no meaningless platitudes, no words of comfort, for there were none. They didn't exist, not for this.

I couldn't even end my life to find relief, for that would make Velma's sacrifice a farce. There was no way out. And never would be for what I'd done.

I pulled free of Kovis's embrace and turned. Alfreda still rocked Velma, her hands bloody around the dagger that stuck from her chest. But her eyes stared vacantly.

A whole new round of sobs welled up in me then spilled over. I wanted to collapse onto her, hug her, bring her back, but that damn blade needed to go first. Like Father, it was an abomination that had no place anywhere near her.

"Alfreda," I sobbed. "Stop."

My sibling's look was vacant as well when our eyes connected. I said nothing more as I reached for the handle. The knife had been too big, too heavy, too everything, yet it had still taken her life. No, I corrected, I had taken her life. And I would live with that guilt every one of my remaining mortal suns.

I set my jaw and gripped the handle, then tore it out and flung it with what little strength remained. I didn't care where it flew or who was injured, those I loved surrounded me and would never be hurt by it.

Blood flowed from the wound as a cry rose up, just before the blade clattered to the floor. It echoed about the cold, hard space,

* * *

mirroring my empty chest. Red pooled above her heart, and I fell forward, unleashing more tears. Alfreda sandwiched me, sandwiched us, with a hug. We'd all been broken. I retreated far from here, into myself.

How long we stayed that way, I'd no idea, but Kovis gently shook my shoulder, bringing me back. Alfreda gasped and covered her nose as we sat up, joining me in staring at the reeking purple bodies of hairy mare soldiers strewn around the space. At Baldik who stood, holding his captor captive at knifepoint. At Father who frowned not far away, arms crossed, wings furled tightly—his attire was the complete opposite of the two white robed males he stood between, each of whom held a golden sword to his throat.

But that's not what caught my attention. No, it was the muscled, older-looking male with a white beard and hair pulled back in a topknot that captured my focus, standing where Father had stood as he'd passed judgment on me. A white tunic with gold trim flowed to the floor, stopping just above this male's leather sandals.

He'd come. Dyeus had come. Too late for Velma, too late for my shattered heart, but not too late to give meaning to our sacrifices.

His blue eyes were filled with sorrow as he gazed at me, at our heap. He drew a hand to his chest and spoke. "Princesses, my daughter made an impassioned plea on your behalf. I'm only sorry I could not get here sooner, that I could not spare you from this."

He turned smoldering eyes on Father. "Ambien, lust for power has blinded you, warped your mind, and consumed you, above all other, even and especially your family. It started as but a kernel, but you nurtured it, fed it, encouraged it to grow. And now, what you so carefully cultivated, has devoured you, wholly and completely, and has become your master." He went on to iterate all Father's deeds, most of which I knew about, a few I didn't, but wasn't surprised.

At length, Dyeus pulled a golden rope from his robe. I looked toward Father. His jaw was tight, but his eyes… only I would have seen the barely veiled humor that danced in them.

He alone would find this amusing.

"It has been requested that I bind you so that henceforth you will have no power to impose your will on others. And so it shall be." Turning to Father's captors he said, "Bring him here."

In a heartbeat, Father vanished.

A collective gasp rose, and I pivoted my head this way and that. What unknown power did he possess?

A thunderbolt struck the wall behind where Father had stood, just above a mare corpse. And another purple-haired beast materialized. Blood flowed from its unmoving side, the killing blow piercing its heart.

Alfreda shrieked. Kovis grabbed me, again enfolding me in his arms.

A mare. A mare. A mare had done this!

It hadn't been Father at all!

It's how he had arrived so quickly after us. It's why he'd sounded like he had a cold. It was why it seemed like Father regurgitated something practiced, because no doubt this mare and Father had. It's why he'd found Dyeus's condemnation humorous, because he planned to trick him. And he almost had.

Father was at the heart of this, I had no doubt. His mares were highly trained. No mare-soldier would ever execute a plan of this magnitude outside his sanction. He was a monster and had had his soldiers do his dirty work. He'd escaped punishment. Fury rose in me. He would pay.

Dyeus lowered his arm, his thunderbolt retracting back inside his wrist, and shook his head, grief written on his features. "It shifted into a gnat and attempted a quick getaway."

He knelt down and gazed at Velma, then put a hand to her neck as if… no, Velma was well and truly gone. He closed her still-staring eyes.

What if… wait, could he…?

"Dyeus."

"Yes, princess."

"Could you bring her back?"

He forced a smile but shook his head. "Only the Ancient One gives life."

My shoulders slumped. But my brain dwelt on "gives life." Gives life. Gives life.

Hope rose in me. We had to try.

I explained my hasty plan.

Baldik bid us Godspeed, saying he'd deal with the remaining captive as Kovis, despite his own wound, picked Velma's body up. We took hasty steps, following Dyeus out of the cave, to his waiting chariot.

The four horses pawed the ground and bobbed their heads as we appeared. The chariot was surprisingly roomy inside, far bigger than I had anticipated from first glance.

I spread Velma's bandaged stumps as Kovis lay her down on the soft, red cushioned seat that extended down the left side, behind where Dyeus stood. Dyeus's two males secured Velma then took their positions, one on either side of the god.

Heart in my throat with hope, I sat down on the right seat, between Kovis, who held his arm, and Alfreda. I put a hand on Kovis's thigh and clutched one of Alfreda's hands. This had to work. It had to.

Dyeus picked up the reins and commanded, "Hold on."

We lurched skyward.

Chapter Forty-Five

Alfreda stared at our sister's still form, crimson leaching across the entirety of the front of Velma's dress.

Alfreda was utterly expressionless, limp, and unmoving, holding herself, her wings as tight as she could make them. Gooseflesh pebbled her arms, but I doubted it was all from the wind that whipped her long onyx hair about. I was no better.

I stared too. Velma had lost lots of blood. No, it didn't matter. I refused to let myself wonder "if." I slammed the door on doubts. I gave them no space, not when it came to my sister.

I forced my attention instead to the other questions that raged in my mind. Could my shattered heart be remade *when* Velma was restored? Could I ever forget the feeling of her bones protesting, then giving way against the blade as I drove it into her? Could I ever forgive myself?

Kovis nudged me with his shoulder. *This… was not your fault.*

I met his gaze. How long had it taken him to work up the courage to say that? After all he'd been through growing up. After how he'd held himself responsible for what had happened to his sister. Was this Dite's work manifesting?

But I couldn't consider that right now. Couldn't manage even a speck of light in my darkness. Not when it had been *my* hand driving that dagger into Velma's heart. Everything… was my fault.

Thankfully, it wasn't long before the illuminated spires of the sprawling Palace of Sand rose before us as darkness replaced dusk. Dyeus circled around to the bay side and set down on the beach.

The god made his apologies—things would be easier if he weren't there to distract folks from what was critical—but he asked that we let him know the outcome and indicated that his stewards would search out Father.

Kovis picked up Velma's body, and we fought the sand to race up the beach then mounted the steps that curved up to the grand entrance. Selova's guards again met us, but unlike before, one look and they moved aside, even threw open the doors.

We breathed heavily as we stopped in the grand atrium. Candles outlined the four floors of the space, between the topiaries, and reflected against the clear glass at the top. Darkness loomed beyond. It might have been an amazing sight if not for our situation and had the stars been out, but clouds still hung heavy.

Sandrin, Selova's steward, met us several heartbeats later and stepped quickly when I explained what we needed. It appeared he'd just roused from sleep judging by his hair—it was the first time I'd ever seen it in disarray.

He dispensed with formality and headed up the first flight of stairs, a silent invitation to follow.

We stopped on the fourth-floor landing and turned left. Sandrin stopped us outside Selova's workroom door.

"She'll be along promptly," he informed.

How word had gotten to her so quickly, I didn't know, but as promised, she joined us in no time, looking equally unkempt, her long hair uncombed. She might not have tarried with her outfit, but she still sported a unique scarf over her black knit shawl—it was a starfish. Seafoam and white horizontal stripes decorated her leggings.

Her eyes roamed over us, stopping on Velma's still, wingless, and bloody body, then turned wide eyes on me.

I explained, "How this happened can wait for later. What we need is for you to bring her back to us. You give life to the sandlings you create; I'm asking you to do the same for Velma. Please…" That last word came out a prayer.

Selova took a steadying breath, then stepped closer to Kovis, still holding Velma. She looked her over, assessing.

"A dagger to her heart…" I bit out, blinking back tears.

"And her wings?"

"My father cleaved them," Alfreda snarled.

Selova followed her growl, looked her up and down, understanding there was far more to this story, then returned to Velma. "I've never attempted giving life to a being other than my creations. I don't know." Her lips opened and closed like a fish. "There could be complications…"

"I understand, Selova, but we don't care. We need you to try." Kovis and Alfreda bobbed their heads in confirmation.

I willed her to agree, to at least try.

Selova nodded once. "Very well, then bring her inside."

We all moved to follow as she turned, but she stopped and held up a hand. "Only the prince, and only to bring her where I can treat her."

She'd never allowed me inside her sanctum, and it seemed this time would be no different. Alfreda and I took a step back as Sandrin opened the door for his mistress, and Selova and Kovis stepped through. I tunneled into Kovis's mind in a heartbeat and her workroom appeared.

Before us, two wooden tables commanded my attention. On the far one, a mound of sand the length of my forearm looked as though hands had begun to be fashioned. The table closest was empty, and Selova directed Kovis to lay Velma on it.

I scanned the rest of the space while Kovis strode forward. All manner of shelves, cluttered with bottles and jars, occupied the sand wall to the far left and wrapped around to the doorway they'd just walked through. Vats of sand stood at the ready against the far right wall, alongside a large basin of water and another of a dark liquid I didn't know.

Something on the full, but orderly counter beyond the tables flickered and drew my attention. At first I thought it was a glowing yellow flame, but the color danced, changing to orange. I watched, mesmerized as it shifted again to red, then purple, then blue, cyan, then green, and back to yellow. The same colors as the Lights in Wake! Was it a coincidence? Was this the source of life that Selova gave to her creations?

"Do not breathe a word of what you have seen in this room to anyone," Selova commanded once Kovis had laid Velma down.

"You have my word," he promised.

"Then if you'll excuse me, I have much work to do." She motioned him to the door as she rolled up her sleeves, approaching Velma's form.

He returned to us in the hall, and I returned to my own head.

We'd done everything we could; now it was up to Selova. How I prayed this worked. It had to.

Sandrin approached, then stopped before us. "Perhaps you would appreciate a more comfortable place to wait and something to eat?" He'd taken time to assemble himself more thoroughly, and his attire as well as his wings and hair were again impeccable.

"Thank you," Kovis said, rubbing his arm absently. I wondered if his wound still bled.

We followed as the steward headed toward the end of the hall, back to Selova's rooms. A tumbling fish that pretended to sing—yes, a "starfish." Selova certainly had a wry sense of humor—now greeted us in the moving sand sculpture just outside her door. She'd again coordinated her attire with her creation, or the other way around.

The sand of the door parted like a curtain, and we followed him inside. Sandrin turned and asked, "Would you care to freshen up?"

He was right, we were a complete mess, Alfreda worst of all. What she'd been through… I couldn't fathom. "How long…?" I asked.

"She'll be at it for quite some time. You certainly have time for baths," the steward assured.

We had time, and this might give us all something to occupy ourselves. "Yes. Please. And thank you," I replied.

Sandrin forced a smile. "I wish I could do more, but I'll have them draw water for you."

Only darkness shown through the large window I wandered over to. I knew it overlooked the bay, but without the light of the moon, I couldn't even see the waves, only the darkened foliage directly outside, which bobbed on the breeze.

The window became a mirror, and I looked at myself, really looked at myself for the first time in… since when? My hair was dirty and tangled, my face smudged, my leathers dark with Velma's blood. But it wasn't that which captured my focus. It was my eyes. They looked droopy, old, worn. They used to be vibrant… before all this began, when only hope and optimism filled me. Yes, I'd changed.

I ran a hand over where I'd pocketed the piece my aunts had given me. In the chaos, I'd forgotten all about it. They'd said to use it when most in need. Might it have saved Velma if I'd remembered? Had my aunts known what we'd face? Had they intended I use it? I sighed. If I'd botched that… I'd only know their intentions if I asked. I didn't think I could face them if they had. Guilt seared my heart.

I finally looked back up at myself in the reflection. I was thinner than I'd been, no doubt due to the time we'd wandered about in the wilderness. We'd subsisted, survived. It had to have left a mark. But my gut told me the change I saw in my eyes had begun before that. It had probably begun when I'd shed the cloak of naivete that had protected me from the truth about Father, for eons. Any remaining good I'd ascribed to Father had been ripped to shreds, utterly destroyed, this sun.

I felt old, weary.

Amazing how some of the most significant changes in life could transpire so quickly, relatively, upending what I'd foolishly believed to be lasting. One annum in my four hundred odd annums. A speck. Yet not. Not the impact.

I let the thought linger as I refocused on the blackness outside, an abyss of sorts. When I'd gone to Wake, I thought I'd be facing the future without my family, but now that we'd found a way back, I'd allowed myself to believe we could figure a way out to see them more, especially after what I'd promised my aunts. But after all this… I might well let the abyss swallow me up.

Alfreda's gone to bathe, Kovis said as he wrapped his arms around my wings and shoulders and drew me against himself. He rested his chin on the top of my head. *Those are some very dark thoughts.*

I feel… drained of life.

He didn't say another word, only started humming a lullaby I'd sung to him as a child, "Little Man." My mind filled in the words, as I'd modified the song for him:

> Little man, you're cryin', I know why you're blue,
> Someone took your big, black horse away,
> Better go to sleep now,
> Little man, you've had a busy day . . .
>
> Kennan took your cookies, tell you what we'll do,
> I will get you new ones right away,
> Better go to sleep now,
> Little man, you've had a busy day . . .

Alfreda cleared her throat behind us before we got to the next verse. "I'm finished. I got it pretty dirty, so they're drawing a new bath." She wore a clean, white robe and slippers, and continued drying her hair with the towel. Her olive skin against that whiteness, that purity, made the bruises on her face scream all the louder of what she'd endured.

I slipped out of Kovis's embrace, and while I didn't want to soil Alfreda's new cleanness, love drew me to her. I held her gaze as I strode to her then wrapped my arms around her. She didn't whimper, didn't cry, just stood there, like a board, and let me hold her. I'd expected her to cry, but perhaps she had no more tears left to shed. I certainly felt that way. Or perhaps it was brokenness numbing her now that the trouble was behind her. I wouldn't ponder it further, at least for now.

"Your bath is ready," Sandrin announced, so I finally stepped away.

Alfreda sat down on the dark wicker sectional, pulled her legs beneath her, and drew one of the lime green throw pillows into her embrace. Her eyes drifted to that dark window, where she gazed into the abyss. She didn't respond when I told her I'd be back in a bit, just continued staring into the darkness.

Kovis didn't try to reassure me that she would be fine in time; he didn't say anything as he took my hand and followed the steward into Selova's private bath.

The room was tastefully appointed with an oval tub from which inviting steam rose. A chamber pot graced the far corner, and a long counter with a washbasin ran the length of the wall to the right. Exhaustion overwhelmed me, and I paid no mind to any other of the room's accouterments. I felt as limp as I had when Kovis began my training regimen, what seemed ages ago.

He must have sensed it through the bond because once the steward left us, Kovis put his arms on my shoulders and looked into my eyes. "Let me help you."

• • •

I only nodded and stood there as he gently removed my boots, then unbuckled my leathers and removed first the top, then the bottom. Then he pulled off my braies. Excitement had made my stomach do flips back then at the vulnerability of being naked before him. Melancholy was all that filled me as he helped me into the hot water.

"Lay back," he said after removing his boots, blood-covered leathers, and the top of his braies—blood caked the top of his arm around where the mare's teeth had breached his leathers but it looked like his wound had stopped bleeding.

His tattoo shown brown, heaviness, as he knelt beside the tub. With no magic in Dream, he picked up the soap, worked up a lather, then slowly began cleansing me of the dirt, the blood, and its tang, but perhaps more. Perhaps with his tenderness, he began washing away a small bit of the horror and trauma of this sun.

He picked up with the next verse of the lullaby he'd begun as he worked:

> You've been playin' soldier, the battle has been won,
> The enemy is out of sight,
> Come along there, soldier, put away your sword,
> The war is over for tonight . . .

> Time to stop your schemin', time your day was through,
> Can't you hear the trumpet softly say?
> Time you should be dreamin',
> Little man, you've had a busy day . . .

He began the lullaby over again as he started on my wings. So gentle, never seductive, just steady, thorough. They'd be cleaner than they'd been in forever.

* * *

The water had cooled by the time he finished, and a chill shook me as he helped me stand, then wrapped me in a large, fluffy towel, and lifted me out of the tub.

He didn't ask if I felt any better, just let me be as I dried off and slipped into another white robe that had been left for me, then fished in the pocket of my leathers and handed me my aunt's medallion. I held it tightly as their words echoed in my mind—use it when you most need it. Regardless of the situation, just having it—having a part of them—with me provided a small measure of comfort.

Kovis emerged from the bathroom only long enough to request more hot water and plant a soft kiss on my lips. He assured me he wouldn't be long.

I placed the piece in the robe's pocket and rubbed it as I wandered about the room examining the dream catchers that Selova decorated the space with. A tree had been woven into the circle of the one I stood before. Beads adorned the threads that hung long beneath it, representing roots. Another had three circles joined at two common points to make a ball from which beads and feathers hung. I stopped before several others, but the theme was the same—mortals believed they helped them dream. How I wished I could summon a new reality with such a simple trinket. If only.

After distracting myself for as long as I could, I retreated back to the couch, sat down, and drew my feet up under me. Alfreda hadn't moved and still stared vacantly into the darkness—Kennan wouldn't be getting any sleep this night. JT, Velma's charge, wouldn't either—I feared what would happen to him, whoever and wherever in Veritas he was.

How was Selova doing? I'd danced around this worry, successfully beating it from my mind until now, but it refused to be silenced anymore. I joined my sister in staring out the window.

And so began my wait in earnest.

. . .

Kovis found me—wrapped in a white robe of his own—and sat down beside me. Despite his comfort, the night was unbearably long not knowing anything about Velma's condition. My only consolation was that if Selova had failed, she surely would have come to tell us. Perhaps no news was good news. At some point, Sandrin offered us something to eat, but I declined. I had no appetite. He had no news yet.

The sky was just pinking when I overheard the steward open the door. "This way," he said.

Chapter Forty-Six

I turned.

Wynnfrith cried out, "Alfreda." She rushed to embrace my sister, who still stared blankly out the window. Deor, Farfelee, Ailith, Beval, all my sisters and Mema were close on her heels. Through it all, Alfreda had no reaction. She submitted to the hugs but didn't smile or in any other way acknowledge them, just sat there.

They hugged me too, and a few even embraced Kovis, but a hush fell over them at seeing Alfreda so.

Sandrin and another steward brought more chairs in, and I scooted over on the couch. Wasila's eyes were red and puffy, but she stifled tears as she sat in a chair opposite me. Mema sat at the end, beside me on my right, Kovis on my left. Amelia, ever the nurturer, squeezed between Kovis and Alfreda, picked up her sister's hand, and began stroking it.

All my sisters kept sneaking glances at Alfreda, not wanting to be improper, but worried all the same.

Mema broke the tension as she said, "Sandrin dispatched one of Selova's guards to our home. The male didn't say what had happened, just that you were here and that we should come. We stopped by your brothers' palace on our way, but asked them to stay away lest we overwhelm our hostess. When we arrived, Sandrin explained what he knew of the situation." She leaned forward and looked down the sofa, assessing Alfreda, who still stared, past Deor, out the pinking window.

Mema ran a jerky hand over her skirts then asked, "So what happened?"

She was unglued. Never in my life had I seen her shake, but this had done it. My sisters bit a lip, twisted their hair, rubbed their hands on their skirts, as to be expected. But Mema's hand shook. She was our rock. I wanted to tell her to stop, to take a deep breath, to stiffen her neck like always and keep it together, but she was being as vulnerable as she'd ever allowed herself to be before us. It told me she couldn't help it.

I reached over and squeezed her hand as I summoned my courage. Despite my efforts at composure, I didn't get far. The tale was too fresh. I tried to talk through tears that rose, but soon choked on them.

Kovis squeezed my knee, an offer to take over the telling, and I nodded. Farfelee handed me a tissue as Kovis picked up. Wasila shrieked and began sobbing when he told about us arriving to find Velma's wings cleaved.

Deor lost her composure as he shared what we knew about Alfreda—Deor and Alfreda had been roommates for eons, and while Deor clearly didn't know how to cope with Alfreda in her current state, they shared a close relationship.

Kovis told about my first punishment—sicking a mare on him— to gasps and looks of disbelief. He recounted my second punishment and swelled with pride at how I'd refused to allow Father to hurt Kennan, but rage filled his eyes when he spoke of the agony I'd endured as a result. As he reached the third punishment, he choked up. Only after a lengthy pause did he manage to finally get out every sordid detail.

I picked up there, telling about Dyeus finally arriving and my idea of coming here.

Shock, disbelief, disgust, dread, rage, the whole range of emotions played on my sisters' faces throughout. Mema squeezed my hand hard at points. Did she hold herself responsible for Father's conduct? I prayed not.

How was Selova doing? I bit my lip as the thought reasserted itself. There'd been no word despite repeated inquiries and all distractions had now expired.

I took to pacing along with Deor and Wynnfrith. Mema didn't reprimand, she just sat quietly, Bega, Eolande and Eadu taking turns giving her hugs and she they. Through it all, Alfreda never moved, and Amelia never stopped stroking her hand.

The sky was bright when Selova finally made an appearance. Her shoulders slumped, and dark circles filled the space below her eyes as she shuffled toward us. Much of her long silver hair had come loose from its confines and fell randomly on her black knit shawl. She wore no scarf.

We held our collective breaths.

She stopped behind me and forced a weary smile as she looked down at me into my eyes. "As I mentioned, I've never tried what you asked me to, giving life to a being other than my creations, but she responded."

My breath hitched, and I squeezed Kovis's leg. Did she mean what I prayed she did?

"She is alive once more."

A collective exhale, then shrieks of joy from all my sisters, leaping up, hugging, and rejoicing. Mema closed her eyes, leaned forward, and brought a hand to her chest.

Selova smiled, truly smiled, but raised a hand. "I warned that there could be complications."

The room became deathly silent in a heartbeat.

"I repaired her heart, but her wings… I could only make them anew. They took several hundred annums to gain their former size and will again. They are those of a newborn. I'm sorry." Selova frowned.

Translated, Velma wouldn't be flying for a very long time. Selova couldn't apologize for that. Her standards were entirely too high.

I leapt up on the white cushion and wrapped my arms around her. "It doesn't matter, you've given her back to us." Tears streamed from my eyes. "Thank you so much."

At that she drew her arms about me. "I tried so hard. I really did."

"I know. Thank you."

"Can we see her?" Deor asked, silencing everyone.

"She's resting comfortably but is not yet awake. I suppose one or two of you could go see her. She needs much rest."

Mema stood. "Alissandra should go, and Alfreda if you're feeling up to it."

Alfreda didn't move, didn't so much as acknowledge the offer.

I sighed. "Wasila, come with me."

"We brought you these, Ali," Wynnfrith said, holding up a simple dress and undergarments, all neatly folded, along with a pair of shoes.

Eolande stepped toward Kovis and handed him a stack of his own—my brothers had to have donated them. Phina, ever the quiet one, placed another stack on the end table beside Alfreda, looking her over as she did. I could nearly hear her willing her sister's recovery. Everyone watched but said not a word.

I'd change after I saw Velma. While Selova had promised she rested, I had to see for myself before I could truly believe.

Sandrin appeared to take us to Velma.

"Come rest yourself, Selova," Mema invited as we headed out the shifting door.

We followed the steward back down the hall, past Selova's workroom, past the stairs we'd ascended and beyond until he stopped before one of several doors along either side of the passage. Fifth on the right. I'd remember that.

I squeezed Wasila's hand as the male slid the door open then touched a finger to his lips. We tiptoed into a lavishly appointed room. Pretty, lined, pastel pink curtains had been drawn across the large window to the left of a set of doors—they no doubt led out to a balcony. Velma slept on her side amongst a myriad of pillows on the ginormous bed to my left. A sitting area, equally lovely with its white furnishings, lay beyond.

I drew a hand to my mouth as I studied the steady rise and fall of her chest. She really was alive. Selova had done it. Wasila swiped at her eyes. They'd cleaned her up, not a speck of dirt in sight, and Velma's black locks were clean and ordered. They'd put her in a white robe like mine. The only giveaway that she'd been through the trauma was a large white bandage on her chest that peaked out—where I'd stabbed her. My breathing hitched.

I had to see her wings. I walked on silent feet around to the other side of the bed and spotted them peaking out from under the covers. Selova had been right, they were the wings of an infant. But they replaced those ugly, infected stumps she'd had—it looked like Selova had removed those entirely and started over. They were kind of cute actually. More bandages surrounded their base. But no, Velma would not be flying anytime soon. My heart hurt for her. It was one thing to not have wings in Wake, but here…

I hadn't sought torture for Father when I'd asked Dite to have him bound, but now… I hoped Dyeus caught Father soon and repaid his "gifts" in full and more. Wasila looked equally angry.

Sandrin motioned us to come, and we retreated back into the hall. "She will probably sleep for the sun and will need to rest for a sennight, at least."

Wasila and I both nodded. Velma could take as much time as she needed. She was well and truly restored to us. Selova was a genius.

We made our way back to the others and shared our news to smiles and rejoicing. Selova, bless her heart, had stayed until we returned. She tried to hide a yawn as Wasila and I hugged her thoroughly. "Stay as long as you like," she said, smiling kindly as she left to get some rest.

Selova had saved Velma and I would never cease my gratitude toward her for it, but I didn't know how I'd live with myself after what I'd done to my sister.

• • •

Chapter Forty-Seven

Father's nefarious deeds had impacted far more than Kovis and I and every one of us was spent.

My siblings had been up all night weaving dreams when the news arrived. Their work had been made more difficult without Selova available to stitch the dreams they wove together—their charges kept waking and they had had to keep putting them back to sleep. Every sand person in our province would have experienced the same. Humans in Wakc's reciprocal province would not be in good spirits this sun.

Sandrin showed us all to other guest rooms. Amelia offered to room with Alfreda and care for her—we'd all sent her appreciative looks, especially Deor who, although being Alfreda's roommate, looked unsure how to attempt the feat. We all understood. None of us knew how to truly bring her back.

Kovis and I ended up two doors down from Velma. The space was appointed similarly to hers, but in shades of blue. Kovis drew the curtains, plunging us into semi-darkness. We shed our robes and climbed into bed. I couldn't help but see the analogy to our nakedness—we'd been stripped bare of so much this sun. I always slept in Kovis's arms, but now their sturdiness, their firm, muscled tone surrounding me, felt like my only anchor.

Kovis kissed the top of my head. "I love you."

I shifted my wings against his bare chest, allowing his words to settle over me. "And I love you." I kissed his arm beneath my head.

———

Images of events plagued my sleep, and I woke several times, feeling no better rested. I finally gave up and rose. Kovis joined me not long after, and we rang for service. I threw open the curtains to chase away the darkness—another analogy not lost on me—and let the sun fully envelop the space as well as enjoy the view of the bay.

A maid I'd not seen before, dressed in the same tan livery as Sandrin, answered our summons with a small knock on the door shortly thereafter. She followed Kovis over to where I reclined on the white cushioned sofa in the sitting area.

Before I could make a request for coffee, tea or anything that would wake me up, she dug in her pocket and pulled out… my ring. The diamonds surrounding that teardrop sapphire sparkled. I'd forgotten all about it with everything that had happened—as if I needed confirmation of how upside down my world had become. I'd given it to Velma to hold for safekeeping the heartbeat we heard Father's footsteps entering the cave.

"They found this in your sister's clothes. Sandrin thought he remembered seeing you wear it."

The girl handed it to Kovis, and while I ordered coffee for both of us, I watched him out of the corner of my eye—he held the ring up and moved it about in the light, but his pensive expression told me more was going on with him. Once the girl left, he strode over to me but didn't sit.

I looked up and met his eyes.

"Do you remember the night I proposed to you?"

I nodded. I'd never forget the honesty we'd shared. We'd been completely vulnerable before each other as we made those pledges to each other. I still held it as my goal, for us, for always.

Without another word, he reached over his shoulder and undid the button securing his robe above his wings, then untied the sash and let it fall to the floor. He unfurled his wings fully and took a knee before me and said, "Princess Alissandra of Lemnos, you saved me from myself and my darkness. Brick by brick, stone by stone, you tore down that fortress I built around my heart and helped me love again." He paused, letting the words he'd spoken that night sink in to my situation.

He continued, "I've been thinking a lot about what Dite said, to fill up my life with what is good to the point that there's no room for darkness. I'm trying, and it's working. I feel like I'm truly digging my way out. But I fear the evil you experienced could do the same to you, and I don't want you to have to endure what I have. My dearest Ali, my love, my life, could we focus on what is good together, so that darkness has no place for either of us?" He held the ring out to me.

My Dreambeam, my love. It felt like the first ray of light in the darkness that was settling over my soul. I'd been so consumed by my overturned world that I hadn't thought how it must compare to what he'd experienced. I'd been hoping to help thaw his frozen heart without truly understanding—no, that wasn't the right word. Understanding was in your head, not your heart. I hadn't *felt* deeply, like in my bones felt, what he had. I hadn't experienced what had caused his frigidity. Perhaps it had been a mercy.

"Is this how you felt?"

He nodded.

I took a deep breath, a heavy breath, and let it out slowly. "I can't imagine enduring this by myself. It's a wonder you're sane at all."

He let a corner of his mouth hitch up.

. . .

"Thank you for being here for me." I reached behind me and unbuttoned the fastener securing my robe, then opened the sash and slipped out of it. I unfurled my wings fully and slid onto his leg as I had that night and extended my finger.

Kovis slid the ring on and sealed it with a kiss, like that night.

This was pure. This was vulnerable at its best.

He brushed my lips with his own, then kissed me gently. It wasn't one of claiming, but of deep understanding that I truly wasn't alone no matter what had happened.

"You may not be ready, so tell me if not, but if we are going to fill up our lives with what is good so there's no room for the bad"—he stared into my eyes—"may I make love to you? Because I can think of nothing that is more 'good.'" There was no hunger or lust in him, just sincerity and love.

Sex had been the farthest thing from my mind.

Intimacy, my love, sex is only a part.

Intimacy. I yearned for it. I yearned for that seed of goodness, of purity, that frigidity could not coexist with. It might help me feel again. "Help me."

And so he did. I furled one wing, and with kisses and gentle caresses, he laid me back on that couch, then took his time pleasuring every measure of me—my hair, my neck, my jaw. My ladies, he treasured with his hands, his touch so light, so gentle, then his tongue, licking; his lips, suckling. My core began to warm—he was thawing the frost I'd let settle on me. He showed me love along my wing and all the way down my middle, stopping at the hair which he ran his fingers through, stroking, pleasuring.

He pulled back and resituated himself by my feet and began working this new form of magic on my toes—he licked and sucked each and every one. My feet he caressed, never tickling, but cherishing. My calves he worked with equal care, my knees, then my thighs—he worked the outside first and made his way around and up, at last reaching my center. My core burned in anticipation. This was good. Every heartbeat of his care warmed and restored life in me.

Intimacy, Ali. I treasure all of you.

He paused, and our eyes met. *Tell me to stop if you're not ready.*

But I was ready. He'd been right, intimacy included sex but was so much more. It was appreciating, cherishing, showing me exactly what I meant to him. And it was life.

"Please." I spread my legs.

Still neither passion nor hunger filled his eyes, but earnestness and love. And so, as he'd been, he kissed, caressed, and loved every part of me, thoroughly and completely, until that heat that had been rising in my core exploded into bliss that overwhelmed me.

Only as the heat dissipated did I realize I'd doubted if I would ever feel again. Certainly not like this. Kovis was right, this was definitely good. I could fill myself up with this kind of good. We both could. And we could both breathe life into the other, because we deeply felt what the other had endured. And we would never be alone.

I looked at my ring that sparkled in the morning light. It had become a symbol of more than just our love. It was now a reminder to fill up life with all that was good, to overflowing.

I ran my hand down Kovis's stubbly jaw. "Thank you."

• • • •

Chapter Forty-Eight

Two suns later and Velma finally woke, much to everyone's relief.

She cried for joy when she discovered she'd been brought back. The gift of life restored had filled her with gratitude, and she overflowed with thanks at every opportunity. She confessed that she'd allowed bitterness at Father to suck the life from her over the annums, and it seemed she intended to make up for lost time. She was filling herself up with life too.

Velma's condition was enough for Mema to command all but Alfreda, Amelia, me, and Kovis back home so as not to overstay our welcome. So we hugged and kissed everyone goodbye despite some of my sisters resisting, but Mema would hear nothing of it. She insisted the rest of us would be back home before they knew it.

I now occupied my time between the nursery, sitting with Velma, and attempting to engage Alfreda in conversation. Even Velma hadn't been able to reach her despite having endured the horrors of that cave together. No one wanted to say it, but we all feared whether we'd ever reach her. She'd shut herself off, and no one knew how to breach that wall.

Three suns later, the five of us reclined in the sitting area of Velma's room. Velma convalesced in bed propped against an army of pillows. She'd taken short walks to the nursery and about the palace, but she tired easily and still needed rest.

Alfreda hadn't said another word, even though Amelia never ceased comforting her. I'm sure worry lined my face as it did the rest of us when we glanced at her. I wondered how Kennan faired. He certainly wasn't getting any sleep. He'd already been through so much. How much more could he take with Alfreda unresponsive? Or had he already reached a point of no return.

The sun was just setting when Selova knocked. She beamed as if she was a cat that had just finished off a tasty mouse. She'd donned a purple scarf in the likeness of a seahorse, and her leggings echoed the color scheme in stripes—I wondered if she'd changed the sand sculpture to coordinate.

"As you know, I've been trying to work through how to break that seemingly permanent dream state, and I believe I've figured it out." She seated herself on the edge of the bed.

All of us, except Alfreda, sat up, anxious to hear her remedy.

"The only problem is, my fix will require each sand person be present for me to administer it." She shook her head, the light fading from her eyes.

Selova hadn't asked, and we hadn't disclosed how we'd found my sisters, but from her statement she was inquiring now. So I offered, "If you can give us a list of some or all of those you haven't stitched dreams together for in some time, we can find them the same way we found Velma and Alfreda." I wasn't about to divulge our source, not even to Selova. Some things would always need to remain confidential to protect my aunts and their reputations.

Selova brightened and didn't probe further. "I can easily do that."

The rest of Dream's citizens hadn't been with my sisters in that cave. Wherever they were, I hoped Father had kept them together. I fingered the token in my pocket. I hoped my aunts were willing to again lend aid.

We'll need to bring your aunts more reading material, Kovis said, a small smile appearing.

My face flushed.

"Are you feeling unwell, Ali?" Selova asked, worry lining her brow.

"Oh… oh, no. Just feeling a little warm," I replied, making Kovis choke down a laugh.

Selova took a deep breath before changing topics. "Word about your guards, Rowntree and Wyke, just reached us."

I sat up. In all the chaos, I hadn't remembered them, and I felt guilty for it.

She went on. "Rowntree was found not far from your brothers' palace."

"Found. What do you mean? Is he okay? And Wyke?"

Selova shook her head, and my stomach clenched. "Rowntree is dead. They said it looked as though some wild beast mauled him. Wyke is on the mend."

Rowntree was dead. Dead. The words clanged in my head. He'd been loyal to the end, I had no doubt.

It explained why my brothers hadn't come to the cave. They hadn't known. The male had gone to Dyeus first and hadn't gotten to alert my family. That was no wild beast that killed him; it was a mare, I was certain. So much destruction.

———

A sennight later, Kovis, my sisters, and I sat in the sitting area of Velma's room. Thanks to my aunts, we'd discovered the location of the rest of our province's citizens, and Selova had flown to them along with a retinue of guards to affect her treatment.

I dared let a sliver of hope rise in me. If she succeeded, Father's hold on the rebels of our Wake province would shatter and their treachery would be a thing of the past.

Before she left, Selova had sent word to her counterparts in the other provinces, but according to Sandrin, none had yet replied. Things were looking up, although I would be cautious in my optimism until Father had been captured and bound.

And so a mood of optimism abounded as I held Kovis's hand, seated on the couch, Alfreda beside me. Velma and Amelia occupied the chairs bookending the chaise. Velma had been quieter than usual, and I wondered what occupied her thoughts.

"While you were gone, I did some thinking," Velma said, her face turning serious. My stomach clenched. When she looked this way, she had something big to share.

Kovis squeezed my hand as if to remind me to breathe.

"Father doesn't know I'm alive, but if he ever finds out, he will come after me and finish me for good." Matter-of-fact and to the point, like always.

I didn't disagree. But what was she suggesting?

"I want to go to Wake with you, Ali."

"But what about your charge?" I asked.

"JT is a healer at the capital. I'll go to him like you did, Ali. I'll build a life as you have and be blessed to have you near."

The conviction in her voice told me she'd decided and there would be no changing her mind. She'd give up immortality as I had, but I couldn't pretend to be disappointed. I'd have my big sister again.

"I will go too." Everyone looked to Alfreda, eyes wide. They were the first words she'd spoken in suns. Her shoulders still slumped, but her eyes no longer looked vacant. "I will go to Kennan. I will be his comfort and he mine."

I chanced a smile. If coming with us meant getting Alfreda back, I'd welcome it.

"How… how will you go?" Amelia asked.

"I believe Selova can assist us. I will explain how I accomplished it with Ali, I have no doubt she can do the same."

She'd really thought this through. I'd begun mourning losing my family once more when our work here was complete—when

Father was bound—but it seemed I wouldn't be losing them after all. What would it be like to have both Velma and Alfreda in Wake with me? I couldn't hold in a smile. Kovis mirrored my reaction—family was important to both of us. Only Amelia looked sad.

———

And so, when Selova returned two suns later, sharing news of her guards breaking through Father's mare soldiers with limited resistance and her remedy breaking the bond that held so many captive, Velma began explaining to and practicing with her concerning how to send us to Wake.

With our plan in place, I was encouraged that Alfreda had shed her malaise and joined us, seemingly again committed to living. She wasn't effusive by any means, but she engaged in conversation and began ministering to Kennan once more.

Alfreda made so much progress that Amelia decided she was no longer needed and headed home after securing our promise that we would say goodbye to everyone before leaving.

But despite all the good happening, two things continued weighing on me—Father still had not been captured and Selova hadn't yet heard back from any of her fellow dream stitchers. She wasn't concerned, but I couldn't shake my worry.

———

Three suns later, we flew back to the palace of sand maidens. Kovis carried Velma and our guards were vigilant and overly protective the whole way. I knew we would stay for only this sun, so I had mixed feelings as we returned.

After hearing our plans from Amelia, Mema had called a family dinner and all my sisters, brothers, and even Grandfather showed up. Throughout the meal, my brothers kept peppering Kovis and me with questions about Wake and what it was like to actually live there.

I shared my biggest surprises, and Kovis told tales of riding Alshain across open plains and of wielding his magic. He got them all laughing when he told tales of me learning to use mine—hitting Kennan in the side of the head as just one.

With each tale, excitement blossomed in Velma's eyes. She was ready to embrace this new adventure. Alfreda looked to be at peace.

When the end of the meal arrived, my sisters hugged me tight and shed more than a few tears. My brothers said their goodbyes with checked expressions, but most had silver-lined eyes—such males.

While sadness dogged both Grandfather and Mema, they shared their dream that we might see each other again—we'd done it once after all and I shared their hope. If Kovis and I could figure out how to fulfill our promise to my aunts, we'd see it happen.

So parting, while sad, didn't fill me with the same emptiness that it had that first time. I'd have two sisters with me to experience it all. And I'd once again see the family-of-sorts that I'd started in Wake—Haylan, Hulda, all my friends. I was looking forward to deepening my relationship with them as I revealed everything about me and my past.

I giggled to myself, thinking about Hulda's sure-to-be-exaggerated expressions when I told them. I felt blessed to have people I considered family in both places. And of course I had my Dreambeam.

So Kovis—again carrying Velma—Alfreda, and I, surrounded by a dozen guards, headed back to Selova's.

———

All was in readiness when we arrived back at the palace of sand. Selova had practiced with Velma for several suns and felt certain she could send us to Wake.

So we soon stood in a circle in Selova's rooms, anticipation making my stomach feel like butterflies fluttered with abandon. Velma and Alfreda looked anxious. Kovis did his best to look unconcerned, probably for their sakes, but his heart beat a bit faster than usual.

"Let's hold hands," I suggested. My sisters forced smiles but seemed to appreciate the grounding.

"Are you each ready?" Selova asked, looking around the circle.

Alfreda nodded, eyes big. Velma's face held resolve as she brought her head down. I squeezed Kovis's hand as I bobbed mine.

"Here's to a new and bright future," Kovis said, ruffling his wings.

"Very well," Selova said. Then she closed her eyes and breathed over us.

Chapter Forty-Nine

I bounced on the soft ground, no not ground, on the bed as the world came into focus—Kovis's bedroom. I stared at the white ceiling and the empire's symbol, the swooping altairn, emblazoned on the inset. An army of pillows stood at attention just above my head.

Kovis's landing pushed me upward a heartbeat later, but we settled, rolled over, and looked each other over. Kovis had lost his wings. So had I, judging by the lack of weight on my back. Despite having known I'd probably lose them again, their loss sent a wave of sadness through me.

I had my sisters, I reminded myself. Yes, my sisters, the medallion from my aunts, and my ring—the sapphire and diamonds on my finger sparkled in the morning light. At least the transition hadn't taken this symbol of Kovis and his love from me, from us.

Kovis grinned. "That was a much less painful arrival this time, but what's this fetish with our clothes?"

I laughed. Indeed. The transition had left us naked once more, but at least neither of us would have to endure the embarrassment I had my first arrival.

I rose to sitting, expecting to see my sisters sprawled on the floor, but no.

"Kovis, where'd they go?" My voice rose. Had they made it? They had to have. I'd consider nothing less. The transition had to have split us up. That's what this was. It had to be.

Thoughts of all I'd endured when I'd first come sent my heart racing. They were here, we just had to find them. And quick.

"Alfreda might have landed in Kennan's rooms," Kovis suggested, clearly not considering what my mind had. "At least if the transition followed the same logic as with you."

I couldn't argue, it was a place to start looking.

"My wings…," Kovis said, frowning as we bolted from bed. "And just when I was really starting to enjoy them, every handbreadth of them."

I laughed, relieving some of my angst. "Such a male."

"What?"

"You know what."

He grinned. "What can I say? You'd be disappointed any other way."

We reached his closet and threw on the first clothes we both found—for Kovis that was a gray shirt, and black slacks. I found one of my green healer's robes and slipped it on. No shoes, slippers would have to do.

"Ready?" Kovis asked.

My hair was a wreck, but no one would care. We headed out the bedroom and crossed the sitting area. Kovis had just reached for the door handle when I squeaked.

"What is it?" Kovis asked, turning.

"Your thrum is back! Kovis, your magic…"

He paused, and I could see him inventorying his powers—ice chilled the air, water misted a nearby plant, then air brushed through my hair, making it flutter.

I tasted his powers too, just a little, and found their eager response to me. "Mine are back too. I wonder what powers Velma and Alfreda will get?"

"Speaking of them…" Kovis pulled open his door.

"My… my prince," Allard stammered. The guard was unable to hide his surprise at our appearance.

"You're back, my prince," Cedric added. They both were clearly trying to puzzle out how they hadn't known of our presence.

No one stood guard across the hall at Kennan's door.

"Where are his guards?" Kovis asked.

"Shouts came from inside his room just now. They went to investigate," Allard explained.

Alfreda, I said, exhaling.

"Cedric, call for Jathan. Kennan's going to need him," Kovis commanded, clearly remembering how my coming had caused him a massive nosebleed and splitting headache.

"Yes, my prince." The guard bowed and dashed off.

I crossed the hall and grabbed the handle. Kovis followed. We had to save Alfreda from what I'd endured.

"Wait, my prince. It's not safe," Allard cried.

"Unless I miss my guess," Kovis started, "it's Ali's sister who has caused the disturbance. She's no danger, trust me."

The guard furrowed his brow but didn't question. "Then let me at least go before you. In case, my prince." He drew his sword from its holster.

Kovis invited him to lead the way with an open palm.

Nothing had changed. Books, paintings, easels, and musical instruments cluttered nearly every surface. Well, he'd moved a few paintings around, but the overall look was the same.

The layout of the suite was a mirror of Kovis's rooms, and we rushed past the desk and sitting area toward the commotion—through the bedroom's double doors. I followed Allard, and to my horror, a guard I'd never seen before held a blonde-haired woman at sword point. Alfreda trembled where she lay on the floor in a pile of sand, eyes wide, trying to shield her sand-covered, naked self.

I'd forgotten about the sand I'd landed on. I hadn't landed on sand this time, neither had Kovis for that matter. Was it the manifestation of a sand person being born anew? Selova's creations must start life similarly. I pushed my errant conjecturing aside.

"Alfreda!" I cried, drawing the guard's attention.

Kennan lay in bed, but his eyes shot open at hearing my voice—dark circles beneath them told me he hadn't gotten much sleep. He opened his mouth and roared, fisting his hand until his knuckles turned white.

"Stay back," the unknown guard warned.

"She's my sister," I insisted.

Kennan moaned. Blood flowed from his nose, beneath his hand, onto his sculpted chest. He squeezed his tea-steeped brown eyes tightly, his brow furrowed in pain. His tattoo—a flaming, arrow-pierced altairn—glowed red.

"Markett, call Jathan," the unnamed man commanded of another guard who had been standing behind one of the doors so I hadn't seen him.

"On my way," Markett replied.

"He's already been called," I informed, bringing him up short.

"Put your sword away," Kovis ordered.

"But, my prince…"

"What's your name, soldier?" Kovis asked.

"Canter, my prince."

"How long have you been serving Prince Kennan?" Kovis inquired.

"For a moon, sir. He added me to his personal guard after he was returned, Markett too."

I looked back at my sister. Like me, Alfreda had gotten smaller in the transition and no longer sported her beautiful black wings. But her face was the same as it had always been—almond-shaped eyes, and full eyebrows—blonde now—to match her thick waves with a tight but small chin and long nose.

Her eyes went wide, and she yipped then froze, her mouth half open where she lay.

Kennan moaned again.

"Alfreda!" I pushed past the guards and fell to the floor beside her. I tried to lift her head, but she was completely stiff like I'd been for a short time when my bond with Kovis had locked into place.

"Get her a blanket," Kovis ordered.

Alfreda convulsed, and I pulled her into my arms.

"Ali," she whispered.

"It's all right. We're here," I soothed.

She pulled her hands to her head and cried out at the same time as Kennan. Gods, help her, help them. I knew that pain, excruciating didn't begin to describe it.

Master Lorica appeared in the doorway, Cedric following.

"My prince, Ali," the master exclaimed at seeing us. She bowed to Kovis who asked her to rise. "I didn't realize you'd returned. Jathan just took ill, violently so. He's unable to attend Prince Kennan. How can I help?"

Kennan and Alfreda moaned in unison, and Lorica glanced between the pair. "This is what Jathan…" She shook her head, not finishing her sentence, and began barking orders to prop Kennan up.

Allard returned with a blanket, and I helped cover Alfreda, then stroked her back in an attempt to comfort.

Several heartbeats passed before my brain kicked in and I wondered aloud, "If she touches him, will the pain ease?" Master Lorica looked to me, and I said, "She needs to touch him."

It was only a theory, but if I'd gotten to touch Kovis when I'd first landed, might both of our pain have stopped?

Allard looked to Kovis and then the healer for confirmation, but Lorica nodded, so he scooped her up and laid her beside Kennan atop the fluffy covers. Kennan now held a bloody rag to his nose, but his eyes travelled over her. He knew she was my sister; I was betting he remembered me telling him she was his sand maiden. His lack of protest told me he did.

Kennan reached over and gently took one of Alfreda's sandy hands in his. She looked at their clasped hands, then up into his eyes, and smiled. They both did. She actually smiled. I hadn't seen her smile since before… in a long time.

Kennan's shoulders relaxed. He drew his free hand to his head and took a deep breath. "The pain… it's gone. Just like that."

"We need to find Velma," Kovis reminded. Then turning to the healer, he asked, "You said Jathan exhibited the same symptoms as my brother?"

"That's correct, my prince."

"What is Jathan's middle name?" I interjected.

Lorica gave me a questioning look but replied, "Thaddeus, why?"

I nodded at Kovis. Jathan Thaddeus or JT for short. I'd never guessed.

"We'll be back in a while," I promised Alfreda, who barely spared me a glance before returning her gaze to Kennan. They'd been through so, so much, but they'd experienced it together. Would they be able to help each other heal? I prayed so.

Lorica had things well in hand, so Kovis and I left Kennan and Alfreda in her care. We headed down the hall, then spiraled down all six flights of stairs, took a right at the bottom, and strode past the kitchens and dining hall.

Swete, a fellow apprentice, let out a cry at seeing me, raced around the circular desk that marked the beginning of the healers' suites, and threw her arms around me.

• • • •

"When did you get back?" She stepped back and only then realized her slight. Her petite face blanched, and she fell into a bow.

"Rise, please," Kovis said, unfazed.

"We got back not long ago. I'll catch you up later, but can you tell me where Jathan is?"

"He's not feeling well." She bit her lip.

"I know. Master Lorica told us. But where is he?"

She pointed to one of the treatment rooms. Myla, another of my apprentice friends, exited the room wearing a concerned expression and carrying bloody bandages. She lit up when she spotted me but excused herself immediately to attend to her duties.

There was no easy way to explain, so I just asked, "Did you happen to find a maiden wearing nothing at all around?"

Swete gave me a long look. "No, and why…?"

"Maybe she's in his rooms," I suggested to Kovis. Turning to my friend again, I said, "Thanks" and waved. We turned and headed to the stairs leading to the healers' private quarters up on the third floor of the wing.

It was quiet as we strode down the hall—everyone was working downstairs or sleeping after a night shift. Jathan's chambers were at the end. I'd never been in his rooms, but Haylan had pointed them out when I'd first become an apprentice. I glanced at my old door as we passed. My nameplate still adorned it despite my lengthy absence. Was it their way of hoping I'd eventually return? So much had changed since I'd first slept here.

No guards stood outside the chief healer's room, and it took Kovis only a heartbeat to freeze the lock. I gave him a long look when he punched it, shattering it into several pieces.

"You prefer to wait for someone to come unlock it?"

I rolled my eyes and shook my head as Kovis pushed the door open.

"Velma," I called, and Kovis echoed.

"Ali?" Her voice sounded faint, strained, but I heard her and exhaled.

We rushed through the living space. A sofa stood before a fireplace with a desk to one side. Stacks of books and papers had been arranged neatly around the perimeter of its top. Shelves and shelves overflowing with books adorned two walls, floor to ceiling.

"Ali?"

Velma's voice emanated from one of two doors. We passed the one to a bathroom and entered the other. A modest double bed filled most of the space, a navy quilt overtop, bookended by two nightstands. An ample dark wood wardrobe stood to the right against one wall.

"Velma," I fell to the floor and hugged her despite her being covered in fine sand.

She'd also changed in the transition. Like Alfreda and me, she sported golden locks. The wings Selova had crafted for her hadn't made the crossover, but she'd kept her facial features, including a distinctive mole on her upper lip. I still didn't understand why the transition kept some features and banished others—not that it mattered.

Velma clutched her head, eyes squeezed tight, and moaned. We had to get her to Jathan.

"Where's Alfreda?" she ground out the heartbeat the pain eased enough to talk.

"She's fine. She's with Kennan. And we need to get you to Jathan."

Velma gave me a long look but finally nodded. The next heartbeat she groaned.

Kovis rummaged through Jathan's wardrobe and found a blanket, then brought it over and covered her with it.

I grinned. "So Jathan is your charge."

"Yes, why?" Another spasm rocked her body.

I ground my teeth, commiserating with her until it ended, then continued. "What happened to Jathan?" she repeated, panting.

"Do you remember telling me that my connection with Kovis would break when I came?"

"Yes," she managed.

"Well, you were right. And when it does, you and your charge are in extreme pain. You need to touch him to make it stop."

"Take me to him. My legs don't work." Despite the pain, her eyes held intensity.

"I know. They're as strong as an infant's. You'll need to exercise and build them up. I had the same problem."

"Are you ready?" Kovis asked.

"Yes." It was all she could get out as another wave of pain struck.

Kovis waited for it to ebb then bent down and picked her up as gently as possible. I adjusted her blanket so she was covered completely and we hurried downstairs.

I wanted to try and distract her from the agony, so as we walked, I chattered. "You've always woven Jathan's dreams, did you know he's treated me upon occasion?"

She panted after breathing through the next onslaught. "No."

"There was a time when I nearly died." Her eyes grew large. "Jathan figured out how to cure me by having Kovis send me his magic through our bond. Speaking of which, did your body freeze, like you couldn't move?"

"Yes. What was that? It wore off, but it was frightening while it lasted."

The next spasm struck, and Kovis's eyes grew wide and we hurried. I waited until it ended to continue chattering.

"I'm guessing you now share a bond with Jathan. Like Kovis and I do. And Alfreda and Kennan do. I'll tell you more about the bond later, but you never saw me in any of Jathan's memories?"

"Not that I remember. Although I must say I had no idea what you looked like, so perhaps I did, but I didn't recognize you."

We arrived back at the healers' suites and headed to where Swete had indicated Master Gavin treated Jathan, ignoring exclamations and surprised looks at our presence.

I pushed open the treatment room door to find Master Gavin and Haylan at Jathan's side. Tension filled the room, concern etched in the eyes of the healers as they studied their master.

Chapter Fifty

"She needs to touch Jathan," Kovis declared, stepping toward the table with Velma in his arms. His tone left no room for argument.

I was glad he was here; they would have questioned me, but his position silenced any resistance they might offer. His sudden command surprised them, but I sensed it also sent a measure of relief that someone might have some clue as to how to treat their master.

Haylan's eyes grew wide at seeing us. We'd been gone for moons and now appeared out of nowhere. While she smiled at me, I could see her mind buzzing.

Jathan and Velma panted, breathing through the next burst of blinding pain.

"My prince." Master Gavin's brow furrowed, also shocked to see us, but he didn't argue, just motioned Haylan to help slide the chief healer over to make room for another on a table meant for one.

Grains of sand fell to the floor as Kovis set her down gently. Velma leaned forward and met Jathan's eyes. For his part, he studied her every movement, clearly unsure what to make of her. But as the next wave began, Velma thrust her hand from beneath the blanket and grabbed the healer's. The wave died as suddenly as it began and they both exhaled.

We all did.

Jathan tilted his head and raised an eyebrow before bringing a hand to his head, as if assessing his own condition. His eyes roamed over her, up and down, not with lust, but searching for answers.

"How did she…? How did you know…?" Gavin struggled to speak and finally abandoned the effort.

Kovis opened his mouth to respond, but I held up a hand, cutting him off. The gesture was met with a gasp from Myla. Gavin jerked his head back, but Haylan grinned as she spotted my ring.

I'd promised myself several moons before that once we got back to Veritas, I would trust my friends with my whole story. At the time it had been as a counter to Kovis's dark moods, but he'd grown so much since then that it now seemed unnecessary. I shook my head. No, I needed to do this for me. I needed to trust that my friends could handle my background, no matter how odd, and still accept me, and while I hadn't foreseen a situation like this to do so, it had presented itself.

"This is my sister Velma," I began. "Another of my sisters is upstairs with Kennan. We all just arrived… from Dream realm."

Kovis laughed at the four's expressions of disbelief, probably seeing it as vindication for his own reaction when I'd first told him.

I told them the whole story—well, I omitted the part about wings, but everything else—and explained why I'd returned with my sisters.

Hands found chests as I began. And throughout, I couldn't help but continually look to Haylan to see how she was taking my reveals. Her brows rose a good many times, and she gave me incredulous looks, but never once did she frown. Heads nodded as I concluded.

Jathan stared at his and Velma's joined hands. His eyes sparkled with curiosity and wonder as he brought them up and looked into her eyes. His voice was filled with awe as he said, "We've been bonded. The same as Prince Kovis and Ali."

She gave him a small smile, and in that heartbeat, I realized she and he were a lot alike. Jathan had experimented many times, saving me with Kovis's magic, case in point. Velma had experimented and sent me to Wake. They were both smart and shared a curiosity that few held.

"Prince Kennan and Alfreda have also been bonded," I added.

Jathan's eyes lit up even more at that. "I've studied bonds."

Kovis chuckled. "More will 'soon be known about them' it seems."

Jathan laughed then told about Kovis's first experience with the bond, and how he'd only been able to answer repeatedly, that 'little was known about them' to Kovis's insistent questioning.

I'd never thought of Velma as a romantic type, but as we talked, she rubbed Jathan's hand with her thumb and her cheeks pinked. Jathan flushed as well. Before I'd come, she'd suggested I kiss Kovis to initiate contact. Had she held out on me? Had she thought similar thoughts about Jathan? The little minx.

I clasped my hands and drew them to my chest. They were so incredibly cute. Who knew how their relationship might grow, but it would be fun to watch.

I hated to interrupt, but I looked to Master Gavin and said, "When I first came, Master Lorica had to work on my magical channels. You may need to take a look at Velma's." I still didn't fully understand how they worked, but if it meant the difference between her having magic and not, I'd ask him to examine them.

"Is it okay to let go?" Jathan asked. He glanced at Velma, concern written on his face.

I couldn't wait to see his reaction when he learned what they'd need to do to dream. I chuckled to myself, then pushed back the thought and cleared my throat. "I'm no expert, but in my very limited experience, as long as you've touched, you should be okay... for this sun. Experiment and see how much you need each other." I gave Velma a wink.

She and Jathan again pinked as did Master Gavin. Kovis, Haylan, and Myla grinned.

• • •

"Well then," Gavin said, clearing his throat. "Let's get Velma into an examining room of her own."

Kovis excused himself to seek out his sister, and I stayed to oversee Velma's care. It wasn't long before Alfreda was brought down to the healers' suites for further attention at Master Lorica's direction.

But once Velma and Alfreda were settled in treatment rooms and Jathan returned to his private rooms to convalesce, Haylan and Hulda ambushed me in the hall, making an Ali pasty of me.

"Ali! Haylan told me the short version, but I want to hear *everything*, especially about that not-so-little rock on your finger." Hulda winked and clapped, her red locks flapping behind her. "I *knew* there was something going on that you weren't telling us."

"I knew you'd say when you were ready," Haylan remarked.

I chuckled.

"Our shifts just ended. Let's go talk upstairs," Haylan suggested.

And so we headed up to the Common Room and sat on our preferred couch, the one with a view overlooking Veritas. I retold my tale, adding details about our wilderness wanderings that hadn't been relevant downstairs.

Hulda examined my ring—giggling with glee then oohing and aahing at her father's artistry—and insisted on hearing all about how Kovis and my relationship had grown and blossomed. She begged for intimate details, but thank the gods Haylan was there to rein her in. It seemed she and Cedric had gotten more serious as well—I couldn't wait to hear Kovis's reaction to that, not after all that had transpired between the two of them on the road to the competition.

"So you're a princess in Dream," Hulda said as I ended. Both she and Haylan still grappled with there being a Dream realm and having sand people who shepherded their dreams, but they didn't act as if I'd sprouted two heads.

"That's right."

"Then you'll have fun with Empress Rasa." Hulda wagged her brows. "Second woman in command, nipping at her heels."

Haylan swatted her.

Rasa. The thought made my stomach feel like I'd eaten a stone. Would she chew me up and spit me out again? How would she react to Kovis and my engagement? I supposed that was one thing he would address with her. Only time would tell how my relationship with her would go, but Kovis would coach me.

Rasa aside, my sisters had always accepted me, warts and all, and as Haylan and Hulda listened to my stories with eagerness and accepted all I had to say—accepted me—I felt a kinship I'd only ever felt with my family. These women had always been eager to accept me, I realized. It had been me, in my fear of being rejected, who had been the impediment to something closer. I couldn't wait for them to get to know Velma and Alfreda. It felt like I had four close sisters here.

For their part, they told me all that had happened after we'd disappeared from The Ninety-Eight—about the fear that had settled on everyone, about rumors that insorcelled citizens had kidnapped the crown prince and the champion and were holding us hostage until Empress Rasa recanted her statements about dissolving the competition. They told about the empress dispatching search parties, about how the council members had reacted, especially Lord Beecham who had apparently barely suppressed a smug grin, and about the journey back to the capital.

I was so glad the rebels were a thing of the past thanks to Selova and her fellow dream stitchers. At least I assumed they were. Between them and the council, they'd made Kovis's and my life a living hell. I was ready to start a quiet, boring life enjoying my husband—that sure sounded good—and my sisters.

Once all of our telling was done, we sat in silence. I drank in their acceptance and love.

"Winter solstice is two suns away," Haylan said, breaking the quiet. "And now that you're engaged, you'll probably be expected to spend it with your intended." She wagged her eyebrows. "Since I am unattached and your sisters won't yet be mobile, I'd be happy to spend it with them if you'd like."

"Thank you so much. That would be amazing." I didn't deserve her. I hadn't realized the solstice was so near, nor had I thought about what my obligations would be as intended to the crown prince. Yes, what would they entail? No doubt Rasa would be a part.

• • •

Chapter Fifty-One

Anxiety to hear how Kovis's conversation with Rasa had gone filled me as I reached Kovis's rooms—I told myself I should start referring to them as "our" rooms. It had been a long sun, a busy sun, and I hoped beyond hope that Rasa had warmed to my relationship with her brother.

Bryce and Ulric bobbed their heads in greeting as I reached the door. They hadn't been on duty last night, but clearly they'd been told Kovis and I had returned because no surprise registered on their faces.

"Welcome home, mi'lady," Bryce said.

"It's good to see you again," Ulric added. "Prince Kovis has already returned for the sun."

"Enjoy your evening," Bryce said as I walked through the door, and he closed it behind me.

Kovis rose from the couch that was nestled before the crackling fire, swooped in, and planted a kiss on my lips. He followed up with a sensual hug, running his hands up and down my arms.

His tattoo was yellow—optimism, confidence, if I remembered correctly—as it peaked out from where the two top buttons of his fine, white shirt hung open. A shadow, a sun's worth of growth, accented his chiseled jaw. His eyes—I'd still lose myself in those pools of blue and hazel one of these suns—were filled with love and acceptance. He smelled like fresh air after rain, mixed with a hint of evergreen, male in every way.

"Mmm. I like how this evening is beginning," I said, returning the kiss. I wished I'd had a chance to bathe and change. I still wore my green healer's robe from this morning.

I'll love you no matter what, he said.

So I did smell ripe.

Kovis laughed. "You smell fine." He took my hand and led me over to the dining table. Memories of the first time I'd eaten at this table woke. It had been awkward and uncomfortable and had started everything between us… less than an annum ago. I shook my head. It hardly seemed possible.

He stopped at the head of the table and pulled out the chair. "Ali dearest." He wagged his eyebrows. A mischievous look lit up his face. What was he up to?

Two place settings—a white plate, navy trim, with the Altairn emblem in gold in the middle, and a host of utensils on either side— had been set. No sooner had Kovis pushed in my chair than a knock came at the door.

"Come in," he called, still smiling.

Four liveried servants entered, bearing trays of wonderfully aromatic dishes.

One of the ladies halted the entourage and said, "For your dining pleasure we have roast mutton in a cream unchun glaze, sautéed mushrooms, green root terekle, and for dessert we have fresh whastaberry compote. Please enjoy." Each server removed the silver top off their tray as she introduced it, then placed it before us.

I grinned. It smelled amazing, but more, it's what he'd ordered for us that first meal we'd shared together, the meal he'd later confessed he'd never planned to have with me, but had been overcome and unable to help himself.

A steward poured white wine in our glasses, while another woman winked at me, then sprinkled red cut-out hearts across our places. My heart grew, and I drew my hands to my chest.

"Thank you all," Kovis said to them before they let themselves out.

Once they'd left, Kovis took my hand in his and stroked my ring with his thumb. "We've come a long way, and I wanted our first night back to be memorable."

"I love you so much, my Dreambeam." The words flowed naturally from my heart.

"And I love you." He leaned over and kissed me, then raised his glass. "To us and a long and happy future."

"To us and a long, happy, and very boring future," I replied, earning a chuckle.

"Yes, very boring," he agreed. We clinked our glasses then dug into the sumptuous meal.

"So, I take it things went well with your sister?" I asked, trying to push down my angst.

He looked into my eyes. "She's coming around now that she knows we're engaged."

"Is that any different than where she's been concerning me?"

He smiled and shook his head. "Not really. She'll get there though. I know she will. She wants to see me happy, and since you are the one who does that for me..."

"So I still have a lioness to tame," I replied.

"She's not that bad."

"Easy for you to say."

"Let's not worry about my sister tonight," Kovis said as he picked up a serving fork and filled my plate with the amazing fare.

● ● ●

I didn't want to think about the empress either, not when Kovis had taken pains to make this a special evening. So I pushed my worries aside, and we laughed and joked and exchanged mundane conversation about what had occupied our suns—I could get very used to this.

We'd just finished our meal when another knock came. Was he up to more mischief?

Apparently not, judging from the puzzled look that rose on his face. "Enter!"

It was Allard. He strode to a stop, hands behind his back, and bowed.

"Rise," Kovis said.

"I hope I'm not interrupting anything. I'm not on duty tonight, so I hoped this might be a good time to return what is yours." Allard pulled out a smallish box and a royal blue bag.

I knew exactly what they were, and my breath hitched. In all the chaos, how had he managed to think about…

"I took the liberty of keeping these safe for you." He handed them to me then stepped back again.

Kovis beamed as I set them down and opened the box, already knowing what I'd find. A gold clasp, with complimenting gold chain, to fasten my robes. Each clasp was a swooping altairn with a sapphire inlaid in its breast. They were as beautiful as the night Rasa had awarded them to me as her champion.

I returned them to the box and set it aside. The family of every competitor who made it to the final round of The Ninety-Eight never needed to work again. I'd wondered what the winner received, but with all that had happened, I'd never had the chance to find out. I held the bag and grinned, it was a substantial sum judging by its weight.

"What will you do with it?" Kovis asked.

I loosened the string at the top and turned it over. We had different currency in Dream, but I knew a lot of money when I saw it. Gold coins—crowns, one side bearing the image of Rasa, the other, an Altairn—spilled out. It was more than I'd seen in one place, and they were all mine.

I looked to Allard. "Thank you for keeping these for me."

"It was my pleasure, mi'lady. Now, I'll not intrude any longer." The guard smiled warmly, then turned and left.

I'd never been poor, and I certainly didn't consider myself money hungry, but having all this gold… I ran my fingers through it, to which Kovis laughed.

My thoughts returned to Kovis's question. What would I do with it? Mema had directed most of my choices. This was an opportunity to have some fun. But even as I thought it, I knew I wouldn't be satisfied spending it all on trivial things, especially when I considered its origin. I'd fought hard during the competition, at points barely making it out alive. I'd been fortunate. I'd won, others had forfeited their lives. This money was an opportunity to make a difference somehow.

"I don't know," I finally said. "But I think I'd like to help some people."

"Would that fill up your life with good?"

I hadn't thought about it that way, but I supposed it would. "Yes, I think helping people would be very rewarding."

He grinned. "While we're on that topic, I have a few ideas of what we might do to fill up our lives with what is *very good.*" It came out a purr. "Starting with helping you bathe." Hunger had filled his eyes, and the part of his tattoo that peeked above his open shirt had turned red. It matched the red hearts the server had sprinkled on the table.

I laughed. "Will there be magic involved?"

"Most definitely."

"Then show me your wizardry once more." I giggled as his thrum intensified.

• • •

377

And so he bathed me, and we pleasured each other for as long as we could stay awake. Then he enfolded me in his arms. While I loved my wings, there was definitely something to be said for feeling his skin against my bare back as he drew me against himself. Yes, he was my home.

Chapter Fifty-Two

Kovis was gone when I woke the next morning, and judging by the coldness of the sheets, he'd left early. No doubt Rasa already had him busy, especially with Kennan sidelined. Yes, Kennan. I hadn't been able to assess his frame of mind last sun with the chaos that had erupted from Alfreda's coming. I wondered how he really fared.

Memories of him finding us in the wilderness filled my mind. He'd been in a very dark place—confession over what he'd done to me had spilled from his lips, including the fact that he'd lied out of cowardice. It still rankled.

While the confession had been heartfelt, every word had stemmed from him wanting to ease his own guilt. I didn't doubt that if he could make me whole again, he would. But that wasn't possible. He couldn't undo time—some things in life you didn't get a second chance at, and he needed to understand that.

But despite all that baggage between us, I needed to make a friendship with Kennan work for Kovis's sake, especially now that we were engaged. Kovis needed his family, just as I needed mine, and I refused to be a wedge between them. Kennan wasn't evil. He'd panicked in the name of protecting his brother when I'd been uncooperative. I didn't yet know what might form the foundation of our friendship, but I knew friends didn't have to see eye to eye on everything, and this would be one of those things.

And so I dressed in a day dress and sandals that someone had brought up to our rooms, ate a light breakfast then wandered across the hall, bidding good morning to the four guards.

"He's in good spirits," Markett remarked, smiling as he opened the door to Kennan's rooms.

"Is that unusual?"

He schooled his expression. "I'm afraid he hasn't been that way of late, since they returned with him." Clearly uncomfortable with the conversation, he bobbed his head, encouraging me to enter so he could close the door.

I wouldn't press him. I'd see for myself.

I crossed the cluttered living space and knocked on Kennan's bedroom door. "It's me, Ali," I said.

"Come in." Kennan smiled and motioned me forward from where he sat in bed, covers pulled to his waist. His eyes still had dark patches beneath them, but they seemed a bit lighter, or perhaps that was wishful thinking. "It's good to see you. Come sit." He patted the covers. The part of his tattoo that peeked out from his pajamas was yellow—friendship among other meanings.

"How are you feeling?" I asked.

"Better now that Alfreda's here. Last night, I slept for the first time in many suns. We talked until they insisted on taking her downstairs to treat her channels."

"She's trying to cope with all that's happened too. You're not alone."

Kennan forced a smile that didn't meet his eyes. "I thought I was being possessed again just before she appeared." He swallowed hard. Something of a ghost flashed across those tea-steeped brown eyes. "It certainly felt that way. But the pain that followed"—he touched the sides of his head—"I thought my head was being cleaved in two. I've never experienced anything so painful. I didn't know what more I could endure." Despair was written over his face.

"Who found you and how?"

He shook his head. "Rasa got word of what happened with you and Kovis and sent three search parties from the guards that accompanied you to the competition. She had no idea I was even out there. One of the search parties found me. It's all a blur. I didn't know what was nightmare and what was real. It all blended together. I just remember that I was sleeping, nearly frozen to death under Alshain and Onyx when they found me."

I inhaled quickly. "You found Alshain?"

He nodded. "Yes, Alshain and Fiona. I found them in Croft in some farmer's barn and brought them with me."

I shook my head. What were the odds. When Kovis heard that Alshain… I couldn't think about it or I'd be crying, so I refocused on what Kennan was saying.

"I felt an unspeakable urgency to save you two, and after I thawed, I fought the guards the rest of the way back, but they refused to release me. They didn't understand. They ended up putting me in chains." A dark sound rumbled in his chest.

"Oh, Kennan."

"It's why I'm still on 'bed rest.' They thought I was demented. My guards became my wardens." He frowned. "My situation aside, I feel sorry for Rasa."

My stomach clenched. As much as the empress and I had yet to see eye to eye concerning Kovis, I couldn't help but feel sympathy for her. One brother missing and probably feared dead after all the time we'd been gone. The other missing, then found but judged insane because of all he'd endured, and not knowing if he'd ever recover. No one had come out unscathed.

"How is she bearing up?"

A pained expression ghosted across Kennan's face. "Rasa's Rasa. She holds a stiff upper lip… especially when she's hurting."

No doubt Rasa abhorred sympathy, so I would temper my reaction when I saw her, but she'd been through a lot too. She needed space and understanding, just like everyone else.

"Despite my confinement, I've still been busy." Kennan's eyes brightened for a heartbeat, as if he was still pushing back the demons. "I fired those guards and had them punished."

I gave him a long look. He didn't need to elaborate on which guards. I pushed the image of Creepy, as I'd nicknamed him, from my mind but couldn't stop gooseflesh from rising. Kennan had promised to get rid of them, but... "Is that why—"

"I have new guards. It is." He finished my sentence. "With them viewing me as demented, it was a struggle"—his expression told me there was a story there, but I didn't press—"but I finally convinced them to let me act. I think they saw it as humoring me. I personally selected each and every one of my new guards based on their record of personal integrity and defending those in need. They have to be able to fight too, of course—" A corner of his mouth turned up for a heartbeat before falling away. "—but they are of much better conscience."

"Oh, Kennan, that's wonderful." I didn't know what else to say. His clenched jaw told me only sheer determination had accomplished the feat.

He held up a finger. "I also tried to resign my position, but Rasa refused to accept, not with everything else going on. I think it's her way of refusing to accept that I'm whacked."

He'd done it. He'd done what he'd said he would despite his mental state.

He pressed his lips together as he looked at my ring. "It seems we'll soon be family."

I braced. He was a bit unbalanced. He'd planned to woo and marry me. Father claimed it's what had kept him sane.

He seemed to be considering his next words. "When?" He hid his feelings as he lifted my hand and studied my ring.

"We haven't set a date."

"No, when did he propose?"

I inhaled. This Kennan was different than the one I'd come to know, and my stomach clenched. It seemed his trials had taught him a thing or two, and he no longer cared about politics or correctness. He had a boldness about him he'd never had before.

I hadn't been courageous enough to confront Kennan about that kiss. I'd hidden from it, and it had caused no end of troubles. It was an awkward question, but I wouldn't hide behind it.

"At The Ninety-Eight. He proposed the night I was crowned champion."

He nodded, and I saw a whirlwind of emotions stir in his eyes. "I didn't see it the night I found you two."

"It was dark, perhaps—"

"It was my mother's," he interrupted, not allowing me to speculate further. "I think she would be pleased to call you daughter."

But what did *he* think about it? I tried to keep my knee from bouncing. Perhaps I should have just let it go, but I needed to know. "My father claimed your feelings for me were the only thing that kept you sane as you searched for us. He's lied about a lot of things, but was that a lie too?"

Kennan locked eyes with me and stared me down. "It seems I misunderstood that kiss." No mincing words.

I sucked in a breath. I'd asked for it. His misunderstanding had been my fault, and I needed to woman up. I could do this. I exhaled slowly. "Kennan, I apologize. I kissed you when I was desperate to regain Kovis's affections. I imagined you were him, and it was wrong of me."

I struggled to stay still as I spoke the truth. What would it do to him in his fragile condition?

Kennan let my words linger and the silence grew uncomfortable. "I see."

I rubbed my hands up and down my legs.

He forced a bitter laugh. "The gods allowed your father to possess me—" He shook his head. "—and the whole time let me think you were my salvation. I believed that once I'd atoned for my wrongdoings, somehow… I thought they'd bless me. I was naive.

The gods have *never* blessed me. They took away my mother, left a monster for a father, and cursed Rasa, Kovis, and me."

It felt like he punched me in the gut, seeing me as equal to the other pain he'd endured.

He continued, "So why I thought this might be different, I'll never know. Clearly I'm a sucker and they know to exploit my weakness."

This was not the time to debate with him. There was a fire burning in his belly that would not soon be extinguished, and I had no idea how to help.

He schooled his features and pasted on a smile. "I wish you and Kovis every happiness, sister."

"Thank… thank you." The words felt sour on my tongue.

"What, disappointed with my response? Excuse me if I'm not jumping for joy, or would you prefer I pretend?"

My hands were sweating, and it was all I could do to slowly rise and take several jerky steps back toward the door.

"Oh, Ali, don't let me scare you away. The gods share equal blame, maybe more."

I turned. "I should let you rest."

"Rest, more rest. Yes, just what I need." He forced a laugh.

I beat a hasty retreat.

I couldn't spend time with him, not when he was like this. My presence just stirred up anger. But clearly someone needed to. Could Alfreda get through to him? Could they heal together? I prayed it to be so.

Tears welled up as I reached his door, but I fought them long enough to cross the hall. That conversation had been brutal, and I couldn't stand up against all that hurt. I let my tears flow once the door closed behind me.

Chapter Fifty-Three

It would be just Rasa, Kovis, and me presiding over winter solstice festivities, and my stomach kept doing flips as I waited in our rooms.

I hadn't yet seen the empress since we'd returned, and while Kovis had said she'd received his announcement of our betrothal as he'd expected, I feared to experience her real sentiments.

Winter solstice events would unfold at the theater that ran behind the artist district. We would make our way up to the mezzanine that opened to the outdoors, and Rasa would say a few words. I'd be standing beside Kovis in an official but silent capacity. I'd done similar things in Dream, and it didn't bother me in the slightest. Being with Rasa, that was a wholly different matter.

Everyone had promised me that I'd feel giddy on winter solstice with the glut of magic that overflowed from The Canyon—it supposedly made every sorcerer behave as if inebriated. I'd been looking forward to experiencing it even before crossing The Canyon with Kovis—the thought of his giddy behavior as it overwhelmed him made me smile. Since then, I'd been even more curious at the solstice. Would it affect him as it had? What if Rasa succumbed to it too? I couldn't hold in a giggle. Rasa acting inebriated? *This*, I *had* to see. I couldn't fathom most of the capital behaving thusly.

When would I feel it? I had only Air magic so I wasn't sure how I might feel but I welcomed it taking the edge off tonight. I took several calming breaths, and as I did my ring sparkled in the firelight. I studied its facets—it was indeed beautiful, just like my Dreambeam.

Aw, stop, you're making me blush.

I laughed back through our bond.

Just need to put on my socks and shoes.

Take your time.

I'd visited Velma and Alfreda down in the healers' suites earlier then returned to our rooms, bathed, and dressed. This night promised to be enchanting, and I'd donned a long, flowing gown whose fabric glowed like The Canyon. Yes, it actually glowed. I'd never seen anything like it. Even Deor, my artistic sister, had yet to come up with anything so stunning. The full skirt that mimicked the colors of Wake's powers brushed the ground with every step, and the sleeveless top hugged all my modest curves like a glowing corset. I'd wear a coordinating cape, in more shimmering material, to fend off the chilly night air. Haylan had helped me put my hair up in an elegant, braided bun and given me a squeeze to allay some of my worries.

Rasa's not going to eat you, Ali. She's only human with Terra and Wood affinities—she was a healer if you remember. A healer, as in someone who tries to care for and nurture.

That is true, but the way she carries herself—

Kovis strode from the closet over to where I watched the Lights growing brighter and brighter, shimmering in their full glory through the fancy, glass doors leading to the balcony. He enfolded me in his arms before I could finish my sentence.

"I'm yours and you're mine, Ali. Never forget that. And I'll be there with you. Besides, I think I've nearly won her over." He grinned then pushed my nose playfully before adding a kiss.

I forced a smile and willed my stomach to still. He was right. We belonged to each other, and nothing would come between us.

Kovis stepped back, and I ran my eyes over his gold coronet. Five gold, swooping altairns adorned the abbreviated crown, equidistant, a sapphire set in each of their breasts. It coordinated perfectly with his navy, patterned tunic—gold trimmed the stand-up collar—and floor-length, sleeveless overcoat. It, too, had been accented with the Altairn emblem.

I couldn't help myself. My heart pitter-pattered. I would never get tired of seeing him all cleaned up.

He wagged his brows and extended his elbow. "Is that an offer for later?"

I grinned. "Definitely." I placed a hand on his arm. "Are you feeling The Canyon?"

"I'm beginning to, and I'm looking forward to fully experiencing it with you."

————

With the number of guards needed to protect the royal family, Kovis had agreed to meet Rasa at the theater at the appointed time. We and our retinue of six guards took a carriage to the river's edge then hopped a water taxi to the artist district.

Hoots and hollers and all manner of merrymaking emanated from both banks of the river as our captain steered us through the tangle of watercraft. Between that and starting to feel the magic that wafted through the air, I forgot about Rasa and let myself soak in the night.

I knew when we drew close to the artist district because an Ice mage on shore magicked a spray of ice crystals in The Canyon's colors, and with the help of an Air sorcerer, they undulated like a curtain above the river bank, just like the Lights. Onlookers cheered and a few ventured close enough to stand in the rippling ice—they were rewarded with frozen hair. One woman whose husband looked a bit tipsy, grabbed his arm before he tumbled into the water.

* * *

A Water mage conjured a fountain further along. With the Lights shining brightly as they were, the water glistened, catching the array of colors as the mage made the liquid bend and twist into animals and a host of shapes.

I'd never seen a Terra sorcerer work crystals, but as we approached, a woman was fashioning a larger-than-life size altairn, wings and talons outstretched for landing, out of a huge chunk of lapis. She used only her mind and gentle touches to carve the sculpture—had this been how Hulda's father fashioned the stones of my ring? I, along with passersby, watched with wide eyes as the bird came to life. A child squealed as a large piece fell away. It would be beautiful when she was done.

We had nearly reached our destination when I spotted small flames dancing, as if on invisible cords in the air, above the crowds, no doubt the work of Fire mages. Every cord led toward the theater that loomed over the galleries dotting the bank before it. We disembarked and followed the crowds. Several ladies oohed when they saw my dress, and I smiled back.

We were nearly to Rasa. The thought made my stomach jump. Kovis squeezed my hand on his arm. I gazed up to see the corner of the theater building, a portion of which had been peeled back and opened to the elements this night.

I spotted the empress in a sparkling, black gown that flowed into a short train, crown atop her immaculately dressed hair, holding a drink, near the railing of the mezzanine.

Our guards parted the crowds, and we strode through the open square. We reached the doors and two more guards opened them for us. A quick walk through the lobby had us climbing one then another flight of stairs. I swallowed as we emerged onto the terrace and Rasa turned.

My hand slipped from Kovis's arm as I bowed, low, and held it.

"Sister," Kovis said.

"Rise, please, Ali," she said.

Her tone was even, and I couldn't judge anything by it. But three little words. She'd included a "please" and used my name, her champion. Was The Canyon's influence helping me?

I braced.

She looked my dress over then nodded before speaking. "You're, no doubt, the most stunning lady here this night."

Was that a good thing? I forced my limbs still.

"And rightly so, for I understand congratulations are in order… sister." She handed off her drink, then smiled as she stepped forward, opening her arms.

My knees nearly buckled. She'd called me sister.

I stepped into her embrace.

I'd expected it to be stiff but found the opposite to be true. She hugged me with a fierceness I could never have imagined her possessing, and I relaxed in her arms, hugging her back with equal intensity. Sister. I would have another sister, but I would be her only one.

I spotted silver lining her eyes when she stepped back. I'm sure mine betrayed me equally because the corner of her mouth hitched up for a heartbeat.

"I think I'm going to enjoy having a sister," she added. Her voice wavered.

I could only nod as I brought a hand to my mouth. Rasa sought the closeness of a sister. With me.

Everyone on the mezzanine had fallen silent. Only the noise of revelers drifted up as Kovis stepped forward and wrapped an arm around my waist.

Told you she'd come around.

Did… did you know?

Only that she'd softened toward you, toward us.

One of Rasa's stewards stopped beside her and cleared his throat. "I apologize for interrupting, but it is time, Empress."

Rasa's gaze lingered on me for a heartbeat longer, but she said nothing more before turning toward the railing and her duties. The same steward lined us up beside her, a step or two back, but it barely registered as she schooled her features and began speaking to the citizens in a voice I was so familiar with, the voice of her role.

Only when Kovis nudged me did my attention return to hear Rasa say, "And so, it is with great pleasure that I present to you the crown's champion and Prince Kovis's intended, Princess Alissandra." She was smiling, actually smiling as she turned.

She'd called me "princess." I doubted many caught it. I was not yet a princess of the Altairn empire, but she'd recognized my nobility all the same.

I told her everything, Kovis said.

My heart soared as we stepped forward to a roar—Rasa knew and accepted me for me. As if mirroring my joy, the Lights glowed ever brighter, and I felt the magic as it washed over us. I couldn't hold in a giggle.

Kovis turned me toward him then planted a long, sensuous kiss on my lips—it had to be The Canyon responsible. He would never do something so scandalous in public on any other occasion. Whistles and hoots rose in response.

They're envious, he purred, deepening the kiss.

I burst out laughing before we turned toward our admirers and began waving. I couldn't stop smiling, and my face started to hurt, but I wouldn't cease. Only Kovis's proposal eclipsed the happiness I felt in this heartbeat. This was truly what it meant to fill my life, our lives, up with all that was good so there was room left for nothing else.

• • •

Chapter Fifty-Four
Ambien

The sun had set and a full moon favored us on this longest night of the annum. While they'd held the Solstice Ball at Mother and Father's palace earlier, it was not in my best interest to attend, not with Dyeus after me—damn nosey god—so I'd spent the sun here at my brother Beto's palace.

It's where I'd come as soon as word reached me that Dyeus had struck Morfran, my commander, down. I'd known our plan might result in his death, we both had, but he'd never once balked, never questioned as we rehearsed countless times until he could impersonate me precisely, tells and all. I'd miss his loyalty.

Beto had, of course, invited me in without comment or judgment as I'd expected he would. And he'd diverted Dyeus's sentinels since. Nothing like a reputation for having mares and other dark creatures about to keep even those do-gooders clear of here.

I took another sip of the aperol spritz I'd been nursing, sandaled feet propped on the table that stood in the middle of the courtyard. The stars were bright this night, and as I gazed at them, I wondered what the future held.

Selova had thwarted me, breaking that permanent bond I'd formed between dream weavers and their human charges. She'd gone so far as to find and release the citizens we'd captured and were using in our province, sending them home. I couldn't help but growl. Thank the gods my soldiers had intercepted her messengers to the other provinces or my plans might have been in shambles. I needed those human rebels at my command if I hoped to claim Wake. I'd deal with her if she caused me more trouble, but for now, she needed to keep stitching dreams together so my plans could come to fruition.

Alfreda had been weak, but she'd at least been moldable. The new type of connection we'd forged with her charge would work to allow me to control many more humans at the same time. I just needed to finish testing it, then roll it out once my troops captured several dream weavers and brought them here.

I shook my head. It would be so much easier if I had access to all of those humans to plant a seed of loyalty in their minds like I had Alfreda's charge, but no matter. I'd make do with what I had available.

I chuckled. Yes, things were looking up, for they would never anticipate my next move. They could try to thwart me, but they would never succeed. I would conquer Wake and then Dream and when I did, they wouldn't just value me, they'd worship the very ground I walked on.

The epic conclusion of The Sand Maiden series awaits in Twinkle, Twinkle. Get it at https://lrwlee.com/products/paperback-of-twinkle-twinkle-autographed.

* * *

You can make a huge difference by Leaving a Review

Did you, your sand man, or sand maiden enjoy this book? Share your thoughts in a quick review on Amazon at:
https://tinyurl.com/BuyGoodNight
It can be as short as a sentence! Make a difference.

––––––––

FaceBook Fan Group

Did you have an emotional roller-coaster ride reading this book? Do you need others to talk to about it?
Join The Sand Maiden FaceBook group at
https://www.facebook.com/groups/LRWLeeStreetTeam
All the feels and fanning you can handle!

––––––––

Stay Informed!

There are more books in The Sand Maiden trilogy.
To instantly receive notice when L. R. W. Lee releases the next one or has news about other upcoming events, sign up at
https://lrwlee.com/never-miss-out/

Other Books by L. R. W. Lee

Be sure to check out L. R. W. Lee's award-winning, seven book, coming-of-age, epic fantasy series

Andy Smithson

Download the first ebook free from Amazon now at
https://tinyurl.com/BoDFBook1

Video games can't train you to fight dragons!

800+ five-star reviews. Experience it for yourself!

Gamer Andy Smithson is whisked away to the magical land of Oomaldee, where fire-breathing dragons, giants, and deadly curses lurk around every corner.

Trading his controller for a sword of legend, Andy embarks upon an epic quest to break a centuries-old curse oppressing the land. It isn't chance that plunges him into the adventure though, for he soon discovers his ancestors are behind the curse.

Blast of the Dragon's Fury is a coming-of-age, epic fantasy adventure featuring fast-paced action, sword fights, laugh-out-loud humor, with a few life lessons thrown in. It's perfect for fans of Eragon, Fablehaven, Percy Jackson, Magemother, and Aster Wood!

Get it now at https://tinyurl.com/BoDFBook1

Connect with L. R. W. Lee

BookBub has a New Release Alert. Not only can you check out my latest deals, but you can also get an email when I release my next book, by following me here:
https://www.bookbub.com/profile/l-r-w-lee

http://www.LRWLee.com
https://www.facebook.com/lrwlee
https://www.instagram.com/lrwlee/
https://www.pinterest.com/lindarwlee/
https://www.twitter.com/lrwlee
https://www.goodreads.com/author/show/7047233.L_R_W_Lee

———————

Acknowledgements

This is always my most favorite section to write of any book because writing a book is a team sport. LOL. I mean that. If not for the input of the following folks, this book would not be what it is.

The first person I want to thank (who shall remain a nameless mystery, but you know who you are) is someone who loves literature and from that love graciously agreed to read the roughest draft of *Good Night* and give comments on the content. And when I say *roughest draft*, I mean exactly that. I'd barfed up the words on the page (lovely thought) but had done absolutely NO editing, so it was a labor of love to wade through several parts, but she did. The comments she came back with brought the draft up a whole level. For your comments I thank you, but more importantly, I appreciate you. Thank you for infusing yourself into this work <3.

* * *

I also want to thank my beta readers: Kirstyanne Ross, Lauren Hassan, Rachael Rousseau, Solaris Duvaniel, and Shannon Childress. Thanks to your comments and feedback, you helped make this book even better, and for that I am grateful, because you make every reader's experience all that much better. <3 So much love.

The other group of very special ladies that I want to thank is my merry mayhem makers (aka Street Team moderators): Claire Manuel, Courtney Belaire, Georgina Gallacher, Kiersten Burke, Samantha Zeman, and our newest Cabiria Aquarius. Ladies, you make the journey as an author so fun, but it's about way more than books. This group is about sharing life. Between hyperventilating walruses, sparkly nails, and book recommendations, sharing your journeys has been rewarding as well as humbling: crying along with one of you when your brother was diagnosed with cancer, mourning the loss of a brother to suicide, celebrating when one of you got engaged then bought your first home, cheering one of you on when your hubby went through the rigors of training to make chief, seeing one of you triumph in your battle with weight then enjoy a much deserved vacation, rooting one of you on when you interviewed for a new job, celebrating one of you getting your braces off, and more. This group is truly what it means to embrace life, both its highs and lows. Thank you for allowing me to walk through it with you. I am truly honored.